"A masterful thriller is created by a masterful writer, and James R. Hannibal is at the top of my list. I devoured every page with the lights on!"

DiAnn Mills, DiAnnMills.com, author of *Airborne*

"James Hannibal once again displays his dazzling prose and ability to keep even the more experienced readers guessing. In *The Paris Betrayal*, Hannibal sets his hook deep and early, then drags you through a riveting, edge-of-your-seat story. Another gripping, high-octane book from one of the best thriller writers in the business."

Simon Gervais, former RCMP counterterrorism officer and bestselling author of *Hunt Them Down*

"Riveting and action-packed! *The Paris Betrayal* is everything you want in a thriller—suspense, intrigue, and white-knuckle action. Hannibal has a knack for keeping you guessing in a plot that moves at a breakneck speed. This is one you don't want to miss!"

Ronie Kendig, bestselling author of The Tox Files

THE
PARIS
BETRAYAL

THE
PARIS
BETRAYAL

JAMES R. HANNIBAL

Revell
a division of Baker Publishing Group
Grand Rapids, Michigan

© 2021 by James R. Hannibal

Published by Revell
a division of Baker Publishing Group
PO Box 6287, Grand Rapids, MI 49516-6287
www.revellbooks.com

Printed in the United States of America

Library of Congress Cataloging-in-Publication Data
Names: Hannibal, James R., author.
Title: The Paris betrayal / James R. Hannibal.
Description: Grand Rapids, Michigan : Revell, a division of Baker
    Publishing Group, [2021]
Identifiers: LCCN 2020042207 | ISBN 9780800738501 (paperback) | ISBN
    9780800740054 (casebound)
Subjects: GSAFD: Christian fiction. | Spy stories.
Classification: LCC PS3608.A71576 P37 2021 | DDC 813/.6—dc23
LC record available at https://lccn.loc.gov/2020042207

21 22 23 24 25 26 27   7 6 5 4 3 2 1

1

From a rooftop perch, Ben Calix watched the courier leave the Tiber and cross the piazza. He traced his scope from the man's temple down to his forearm. No cuff secured his wrist to the steel briefcase. Foolish. Ben's team had been tracking that case since Morocco. This morning, they'd claim their treasure.

"Micro, Saber has eyes on."

"I hate that call sign."

Ben frowned in Dylan's direction, his young Welsh hacker-slash-technician, out of sight and grumbling in the ancient sewer beneath Rome's Piazza del Popolo. Smelly, but warmer than Ben's post. The night's frost still whitened the stone lip of the roof. He shivered, returning his eye to the scope. "Now is not the time, Micro."

"Right. Sorry. Micro copies your eyes-on call. I'm flipping the switch. The system is hot."

The day's first tourists filtered out onto the streets—the early risers and the overzealous fathers dragging bleary-eyed kids. In this city, even in the dead of winter, an operative could always count on a crowd. Rome—the true neutral ground of

7

the espionage world. The Swiss claim neutrality, but everyone knows they have an underlying conscience. Rome does not.

The Italians maintain a true *laissez-faire* approach. Americans, Russians, Iranians—everyone does their own thing with impunity. Bullets must fly in the open streets for the Italian cops to take an interest.

Ben dialed in the scope's rangefinder. "Nightingale, he's twenty meters out. You're on."

Giselle Laurent, a platinum blonde for this op and sporting faux fur, tipped her oversize sunglasses down the bridge of her nose. "I see him. Poor little man." She set off from her post at the piazza's sphynx fountain on a course to intercept.

"See," Dylan said, jamming up the comms. "That's what I'm talking about. The Company gave you Saber, like you're the tip of the spear or something. Miss Tall, Questionably Blonde, and Gorgeous gets Nightingale. And what do I get? *Micro*. What are they implying?"

"They're implying you're short. Shut up. She's almost there." Ben wiggled a black box in his fingers, as if the kid could see it. "The thing you gave me. Do I need to point it like a TV remote?"

"A TV remote? Nice, Grandpa."

"I'm barely thirty."

"You're making my point. It's not a TV remote or a gun. No need to point it at anything. The antenna is omnidirectional."

"Uh. Sure. The antenna." Ben turned the box over and found a black rubber nub buried in a hole in the top. He grabbed it with his teeth and pulled. "Got it."

Down in the piazza, Giselle hit her target full on with a cappuccino. Ben winced at her squeal, piercing despite the comm link's static. She bellowed at the target in French about fur coats and coffee stains, poking him in the chest. He backed away, expertly steered into a lamppost with a false utility box Dylan had placed there the night before. Trapped, the courier set his case down to fend off the crazy fur lady.

In the middle of her tirade, Giselle spoke the trigger word. "Mink."

Ben pressed the switch.

By the time the courier reached for his case again, Dylan's contraption had swapped it with a duplicate—same make and weight, thanks to Giselle's photos and Dylan's calculations. A moment later, Ben heard the buzz of a motorbike in his earpiece—Dylan tearing away through the sewers with the prize. "Micro has the package. Contents look good. I'm off."

Ben didn't envy the courier, poked and swatted by Giselle before breakfast and destined for a pre-lunch beating once the buyer opened a case full of blank papers and empty steel tubes. But he'd brought the beating on himself with his sins. Ben and Giselle wouldn't interfere. They'd need to watch the buyer to see what he did next, now that they'd messed with his world.

With the real case in hand and the buyer under surveillance, the Company would finally get a trace on the organization behind the destruction in Munich, St. Petersburg, and Tokyo. Each strike built upon the ferocity and death toll of the last until Rotterdam, when the bomber had botched his job and killed only himself.

Rotterdam was the break the Company needed. An undetonated fragment proved the attacks involved a new type of explosive—CRTX, five times as powerful as C4 and previously considered impossible to make. With the bomb compound identified, the Company field operatives went into overdrive searching for leads. Ben found the big one. An Algerian contact in his home base of Paris hinted at an order of rare chemicals heading to a bomb maker. Ben put a hasty mission together, pulling in Giselle and the Company's top tinker—Dylan. The Algerian's info led them to the case, and the case led them here.

"Micro," Ben said, laying his scope in its case. "That's a job well done. Enjoy the flight home. Nightingale, keep tabs on the target. I'll—"

A shadow darkened Ben's perch. Strong arms flipped him over and slammed him down, breaking roof tiles.

A brute stood over him—bald, Arab, packing a SIG. "Enjoying the show, Mr. Calix?"

"Massir?" The Algerian—the criminal from Paris whose rumor about an order of bomb-making chemicals led Ben to the case. Ben feigned relief and exasperation and rolled onto his shoulder, hiding his hand in his coat pocket. "Did you follow me?"

He didn't give Massir a chance to answer. In a snap motion, Ben reversed his body and used the momentum to scissor the Algerian's legs from beneath him. The SIG flew from Massir's hand. Scrambling over the tiles, Ben pinned him down, one knee on an arm and the other across his chest. His left hand brushed Massir's side, leaving behind a gift.

Massir swung a knife.

Ben jerked his face back and caught the man's wrist. He clamped a hand over the fingers, trapping the blade. "Bad idea." A strike to the elbow bent Massir's arm, and with both hands, Ben pressed the knife down until the tip found Massir's Adam's apple. "When we met in Paris, I used an alias. How do you know my real name?"

"Jupiter has been watching you. He is pleased."

Screams hit Ben's ears—two versions of the same scream, one live and one over the comm link. Giselle.

"Saber, this is Micro." The echoing howl of a motorbike in a sewer pipe nearly drowned out Dylan's voice. "Something's wrong."

"No kidding."

"Should I go back?"

"And do what?" Ben knocked Massir out with a right cross. "You never carry a gun." He launched himself over the ledge and rode the fire escape down until it clanked against its stop, leaving him dangling five feet above the pavement. He dropped to the ground in a crouch. "Go, Dylan. Get out of here."

Ben rose and turned. The crowd before him scattered, some running for their lives.

Fifty meters away, a red-haired man the size of a small house held Giselle by the neck, dragging her backward toward a runabout bobbing against the Tiber River docks.

Ben charged.

Giselle's attacker raised a SIG like Massir's to her neck. "Stay back. I'll kill her."

Without slowing, Ben drew a Glock and leveled it. "Not a chance."

2

With a speed Ben could never match, Giselle's hand flashed up to her attacker's wrist. The gun spat as she pushed it away. A single round sparked off an ancient paver, eliciting new screams and gasps from the onlookers brave enough to have hung around. Giselle elbowed him in the ribs and spun. "Now!"

Two quick trigger pulls sent the redhead reeling off the dock. His skull glanced off the hull of a runabout, and he sank like a stone. Ben advanced, keeping his weapon trained on the cold froth that remained.

Whistles blew. Shouts reached his ears from a hundred meters away. He tucked the Glock away. "Giselle?"

"I'm fine. We need to go. Contingency Alpha?"

"Yeah. See you soon."

Giselle ran west across the bridge. Ben headed east through the piazza and into the maze of gardens and monuments comprising Villa Borghese. He scanned the walkways and trails.

The courier was gone.

Too many eyes witnessed the shooting. Bullets had flown in the streets. Ben had crossed the Italian cops' only line, and now they'd come looking. He'd have to lose himself for a while—no time to search for the courier. Fortunately, he'd created another option to salvage the mission.

Pick up the trash, boys. The gravelly voice of Colonel Hale, the Company schoolmaster, still rang in Ben's ears on every field op.

Field ops are like hockey. One miss doesn't mean the play is over. When your team takes a shot and the puck glances off the post, trap the rebound and slap it home. Pick up the trash. The heart of field ops is flexibility. Missions go wrong. Deal with it. Regroup and try another angle.

Ben slipped between a pair of sculpted hollies to let a cop run by. He'd trapped this mission's puck by placing a tracker on Massir during the rooftop scuffle. He'd lost one quarry but picked up another—one who knew way more than he should.

The smartphone in Ben's pocket buzzed. He checked the screen. Massir had reached the limits of the tracker's range, deeper into the park gardens. Ben broke into a jog, fallen leaves crunching under his Oxfords. A tracker allowed him to split his attention—evade the cops while following his quarry. But this one had a severely limited range.

Trackers with full satellite connectivity never got much smaller than a smartwatch—good for planting on gofers and delivery boys, but not real players with the training to spot them. For alert adversaries, Ben preferred a lighter touch. He'd placed a thumbnail-sized patch known as an *echo* on Massir's coat. Nothing fancy. Just two layers of electromagnetic insulation to passively reflect a short-range signal from Ben's phone—caveman tech by Dylan's standards. "The oldies still have their place in the field," Ben had told him when the Welshman scoffed at the echo earlier that morning. "Like my dad used to say when building cabinets. For some jobs, a hand tool serves better than an electric, as long as you don't mind hard work."

He slowed, checking behind him for cops. His gray canvas

trousers and a wool coat helped him blend into most crowds, but they didn't fit the image of a man out for a jog. On the upside, the run pulled Massir's blip into a comfortable range, continuing south along one of the park's gravel paths.

The park's tree-covered path gave way to a set of worn stone switchbacks descending to a sidewalk and a busy street. A light snow fell, making the cobblestone walk slippery. Ben pulled his coat tight and ventured off the curb into the chaos, dodging a scooter and offering a congenial wave in answer to the angry shouts of a taxi driver. On the other side, he joined the flow of pedestrians passing between the gate towers of an ancient wall. His target had crossed into the old city. Ben checked his watch, cognizant of the fact that while he pursued his quarry, the Italian cops were pursuing him.

Go far fast. Then go farther faster. Ben heard Colonel Hale in his head again.

In the mathematics of escape, time and distance have an exponential relationship. Move two or three hundred meters away from the crime scene in the first three minutes, while confusion reigns. In the next five, as hair and clothing descriptions are gathered and police radio nets go active, you need to be on a train or bus, putting kilometers between yourself and the scene.

Ben needed to talk to Massir, but hanging around in the city put him at risk of capture or exposure, and by extension, his whole team.

The echo, two streets ahead, shifted west. Ben did the same. He turned one street short and paralleled its course, quickening his steps. If he could move ahead and find a crossing alley, he could intercept.

Mistake.

No alley appeared. In a sector of Rome known for narrow passages and hidden courtyards, Ben had picked the one block without a single cross-through. Ahead, a cop wearing the black coat and wheel cap of the old city *polizia* looked his way, talking into his radio. By now, they'd recovered the sniper scope and broken tiles on the rooftop. They'd have questions Ben didn't feel like answering. He averted his eyes and made an abrupt turn through the open doors of a basilica.

The blip kept going, moving out ahead of him on a street Ben couldn't reach. He'd lost the courier, and it looked like he might lose Massir too.

3

Ben hurried down the marble colonnade beside the pews. A crack of light appeared at the far end—a door opening. He broke into a run and squeezed through, nodding to the entering priest. *"Grazie, Padre."*

Confusion creased the priest's brow. *"Eh . . . Prego?"*

Steps led down to a small piazza where pigeons fluttered Ben's way. He jogged to a stop in a courtyard and checked his phone. Massir stopped too. But where? The blip covered the square's opposite half. At close range, the echo reflected a signal too large for precision.

The locals coming out to snap pictures of the rare snowfall strengthened the numbers of the usual tourist crowd. Ben spotted a familiar jacket on a man facing away from him. The bald head, partially hidden beneath a new winter cap, turned left and right as if looking for a contact.

He closed in. Fifteen meters. Ten. Five. The Glock came out of its holster, held low.

The target wheeled around and stretched out a hand to a woman near Ben. "There you are. I thought I'd lost you."

"Sorry," she said. "I stopped to get a picture."

The two embraced. The man kissed her on the cheek. Wrong guy.

Ben altered course and hid the Glock under his coat, coming to rest against a rounded wall in the courtyard's northwest corner. The echo's signal return surrounded him. It made no sense. Massir had to be right on top of him.

Right on top.

He turned to glance up at the rounded wall—red plaster, marred and broken, so much older than everything around it. He chuckled at himself. Coming upon it from the rear quarter, Ben hadn't recognized the famous circular structure. The Pantheon. The upper level's hidden corridor might be a great place for a meet. Massir had to be inside.

Three-story bronze doors led to a marble rotunda surrounded by angelic statues. A shaft of gray, littered with falling snow, shone through the open oculus at the dome's peak. The tourists entering with Ben gaped up at the iconic hole, once a natural spotlight for the emperor. Ben's gaze went straight to a set of wooden steps between the inner and outer walls, guarded by a velvet rope. He unclipped it and walked through as if he worked there. No one challenged him.

Red ropes always have a reason. The upper passage, created using an early version of concrete, had started to crumble since the last time Ben worked a job in Rome. He crawled through an obstacle course of scaffolding filling the tight space, built as much to hold the place together as to support the restoration. He reached an arch looking out across the interior, locked an arm over the scaffolding, and hung sideways in the planks and pipes, listening. Whispered voices hovered above the crowd, caught in the strange acoustics of the dome. One male—Massir. One female.

"Who are you," Massir asked. "Where's Hagen?"

"Jupiter sends his regards."

"What is that? What are you doing?"

Ben saw them through a sister arch across the rotunda. The stray light from the oculus caught the Algerian's face, but the woman remained in shadow. She pointed at Ben and vanished.

Massir stared back at him with a question in his eyes. After a moment, light dawned on his features and he patted his coat. He ripped off the echo and showed it to Ben with a defiant grin. Then he tossed it into the crowd and backed into the darkness.

Ben clambered over the scaffolding, making a racket, until he reached a stretch of new concrete and raced toward Massir's position. Two-thirds of the way around, he found an exterior window with a ladder. He took a gamble.

The three-tiered roof behind the Pantheon offered short hops to the street below, where Ben spotted his quarry pushing his way through tourists crowding an alley. He ran along the lowest rooftop until it curved away, and leaped into the crowd. Two men softened his landing. He patted them both on the back, planting his hands to push himself to his feet. "Thank you, gentlemen."

They shouted at his back in a language he didn't know. Hungarian, maybe.

All Massir's shoving had cleared a serviceable path. Ben timed his move to match a side passage marked *Privato*. He caught up, hooked an arm around the man's waist, and spun him through the opening like a dance partner.

Massir drew his gun. Ben smacked it against the wall, crushing his knuckles, and wrenched the weapon from his grasp. He jabbed it into his ribs. "Walk."

The private passage ran deep into the buildings beside the Pantheon to a small quad bounded by tall apartments. Rugs and clothing hung from the windows. Ben stopped Massir short of the light and shoved him against the bricks. He lifted the Algerian's chin with the SIG's barrel. "Who are you working for?"

"Your mother."

"That's original." He tensed his finger on the trigger. "What is this? A SIG P2022? Bold choice. Don't prefer it, myself. I could never get used to a weapon with a heavy first trigger pull. The question of when that very first bullet will leave the chamber is always a giant guessing game." He added pressure and made sure Massir could feel it. "How did you know my name? Who is Jupiter?"

"I—" Massir clutched the arm braced against his chest.

"Don't even think about it. I *will* end you."

But Massir's eyes lost their focus. A gray blister developed on his face.

Ben released him and backed away, keeping the weapon trained. More blisters appeared. Dark tendrils radiated from each one. He watched the lines weave like snakes through Massir's veins. They reached his eyes. Blood trickled from his tear ducts.

"What is this? What's happening to you?"

The fear in Massir's eyes told Ben he wanted to answer. Unintelligible gurgles erupted from his throat. He clawed the air, sliding down the bricks until he hit the cobblestones, convulsed, and went still.

4

"How? Why?" Ben raised his hands toward his temples and noticed he still held the SIG. He tossed the gun into Massir's lap and examined his own fingers, as if he might see lice wriggling under his nails. Ben knew this disease. Every Company operative had been trained on the big ones in their bioterrorism course. Massir's symptoms were atypical, but close enough.

The Black Death.

The plague, yersinia pestis, is the most frequently weaponized disease in history. Spies and kings have used it for centuries. Thanks to the bacteria's persistent, never-say-die nature and the misguided efforts of bush-league terror organizations around the globe, the plague has long outlived the history books. Fortunately, these days, the early appearance of symptoms and the slow spread through the body make it a feeble foe.

"But you," Ben said under his breath, no longer addressing Massir but the thing eating his dead body. "You moved so fast."

He tried to remember the transmission methods, aside from the traditional rats and fleas. Bubonic or pneumonic—injection or respiratory mist. "Please have a needle mark. Please don't be airborne." He bent as close as he dared and checked the arms and neck, but the boils and blackened skin left no chance of finding a needle prick.

Ben checked himself. No scratches. No blood. Did he feel feverish? Maybe. His pulse was up. His eyes returned to the body and he gritted his teeth. If a dog so much as licked Massir's face, this thing would spin out of control.

A race through his recent memory brought Ben to a homeless man, begging in the street ten meters or so past the passage entrance. He found the guy still at his post, the best hope in the immediate area.

The precious bottle lay poorly hidden beneath a blanket, an obvious bulge. A handful of coins, scattered on the pavers, distracted the beggar and compensated him for his loss.

"Ladro! Ridameelo!" came the rasping cry as Ben took off with his whisky. *Thief! Give it back!*

No one gave either of them more than a passing glance. Ben needed one more item, always in plentiful supply on the streets of Rome. An obliging young local three paces in front of him lit a cigarette. Ben altered course, bounced a shoulder off the alley wall, and ripped it right from the kid's mouth.

The smoker and a friend, young enough to be dumb and brave, gave chase, shouting a hybrid stream of Italian and English. Apparently acting like a jerk automatically made Ben an American.

In this case, they weren't wrong.

Ben reached the body and turned, firing his Glock into the bricks above his head. "Back off!"

The young men skidded to a halt, hands raised. Others peered into the passage from the street.

Ben fired again. "Beat it! All of you! *Vai via!*"

They left him in peace—for now. Wasting no time with pouring, he smashed the bottle on the bricks above the slumped Massir. He gave the whisky only a moment to soak into his clothes, then kneeled beside him. "I'm sorry, friend. I suspect this is not the burial you wanted, but I can't take any chances." He let the cigarette fall. The whisky willingly ignited. "What did you get us both into?"

Ben stood to watch the flames spread around the SIG in Massir's lap. The cartridges inside would soon kick off, non-lethal but loud enough to keep any responders at bay until the bacteria burned away.

Would the fire get it all? Maybe not. Ben knew of one potential carrier about to walk away from the scene.

A chill swept through him. Unconsciously, he pressed the barrel of his Glock up under his own chin. Held it there for a long moment and inched close enough to the flames to smell the burning flesh.

The thing moved fast. Ben saw it. And right now, he felt nothing. Maybe he'd gotten lucky. He holstered the gun and forced his way through the gathering crowd.

5

Get far fast. Then get farther faster. Time and distance. An exponential relationship. Less than fourteen minutes after burning the body in the old city, Ben emerged from the EUR Palasport Metro station, nine kilometers south.

Known as the Euro Quarter and planned by Mussolini in the 1930s, Rome's Esposizione Universale Roma looked like the Epcot of fascism. Broad streets, dystopian megastructures, and the lightest foot traffic in the entire city made it Ben's first choice for a contingency rendezvous.

Ben grabbed an outdoor table at Geco Ristorante, which gave him a nice view of the quarter's central obelisk and the approaching roads, and ordered some focaccia and a sparkling water.

Giselle appeared on the sidewalk beyond the obelisk just as Ben dipped his second bite of focaccia in the olive oil at the edge of his plate. He held up an open palm when she took the chair across from him. "Stay back, but don't make a scene."

"What is it?" She rested her elbows on the table and leaned close in blatant defiance of his request. The fur and the platinum hair were gone, replaced with a red wool overcoat and a darker honey blonde. "Are we social distancing again?"

"Just . . . don't touch me. Something happened in the old city."

"I assume you are referring to the burning body near the Pantheon."

He let his eyes give him away, not bothering to hide the guilt.

"So, it *was* you." She gave him a playful gasp. "Ben, I have seen you get violent in the heat of battle, but lighting a man on fire?" Her gaze drifted up to the stocking cap he'd stolen on the train. "Nice hat, by the way. Green is your color." She reached for a slice of focaccia.

"Don't!" He reached to push her hand away, then thought better of it and pulled back. The outburst brought a look of concern from the waiter. Ben gave him a fleeting smile and lowered his voice. "I had to burn him—the body, I mean. There's a bug. I may have been exposed."

Unconcerned, Giselle lifted the bread from the plate and touched it to her bottom lip. "What kind of bug, *mon chéri*?"

"I thought we agreed not to use that term in public."

"Like anyone can hear. The comm net is off, yes? Dylan is long gone." She took a bite, talking as she chewed. "What bug, Ben?"

"The symptoms looked like the plague. Black boils near the lymph nodes, a sign of the bubonic form. But he also lost the ability to speak, which hints at pneumonic, and that could be airborne."

She put the back of her hand to his cheek.

"You shouldn't do that."

"Quiet, please." She checked his forehead next. "Nothing. No temperature. Your color is good."

"My heart rate is up."

"Isn't it always when I am with you?" Her lips curled into a smile and she stole some more focaccia, dipping it into the olive oil.

"Giselle . . ."

"You're fine. Relax." She took a bite, pointing the remainder his way. "What about this morning? What happened at the briefcase switch?"

"You tell me."

"Ambushed by a Dutchman in the square. And you?"

"Accosted by an Algerian on the rooftop. Massir. The guy whose info led us to the case."

"And this Algerian, he was your burning man?"

"I planted a tracker during the fight. I'd have held on to him, but I let him go when I heard you scream. Giselle—"

Another couple claimed a table not far away, loudly calling the waiter over. Ben watched them.

Giselle touched his arm. "They are no threat, Ben. Go on."

"Massir . . . uh . . ." Ben finally tore his gaze from the couple and met Giselle's eyes. "He knew my name. Not the alias I used the first time I found him. My real name. He called me Calix."

She laughed. "Don't be absurd."

"I'm serious."

"You misunderstood.

"No. I didn't. He said someone called Jupiter has been watching me, and he's pleased."

She made a face, flicking her hand. "I guess that's better than displeased."

"Don't joke. I heard the same name later." He told her about the chase to the Pantheon and the woman who met with Massir. "I think the Hagen he mentioned was your Dutchman."

"Probably. What about the woman? Could you describe her voice to the Company analysts?"

Ben shook his head. "Her whisper masked any tone or accent. But she has to be the one who hit him with the weaponized bug. The symptoms came on so fast."

The idea gave him hope. If the woman infected Massir, then she'd probably used a needle. A virus requiring injection left Ben in the clear.

Ben had been drinking the water straight from the bottle. The waiter pointed at his glass. *"Posso prenderlo, signore?"* *May I take that, sir?*

"*Sì. Grazie.* And another bottle for the lady."

Giselle waited for him to walk out of earshot. "All this tells us is another team was guarding the courier, yes? We were blown."

"We were blown from the start." Ben clenched a fist. "Massir gave me the intel. That means the case is suspect at best. Our bomb maker may not exist. This whole thing could be a setup."

"For what purpose? For the Algerian to give you Jupiter's praise and then die?" She laughed.

He didn't.

They ate in silence for a while, until Ben pushed his plate away. "I'm not going straight back. I need to see Tess."

Giselle coughed on her sparkling water. "You *don't* need to see Tess. You're fine."

"I need to get checked out."

"By the pretty doctor?"

"I trust her, more than I trust the other medics. And if I can catch her in Belgium, it'll only add a few hours to my trip—a day at most."

"She'd better not keep you a full day." Giselle set her bottle down with enough firmness to make Ben worry it might crack. She pursed her lips and sat back, crossing her arms. "Fine. I am taking a detour as well."

"For what?"

"It's personal. You know the rule."

She meant their rule—Giselle and Ben's—not some section of the Company regs. When their less-than-professional entanglement began a few weeks earlier, they'd agreed to keep their past lives separate from their present. Hidden. Unspoken. It was better that way.

"I'll meet you day after tomorrow," she said, scooting back her chair and dabbing her lips with her napkin.

"Where?" Prudence demanded they avoid each other's residences.

"Remember that cottage I showed you in Chaville?"

"You bought it?"

"Cash. The Company is no wiser."

A lot of cash. Ben had seen the asking price when they walked through together. He lowered his chin. "Not your go fund, right?"

"I wouldn't dare. Our go funds are Company money. I told you I had some personal savings." She gave him that mischievous smile. "And now I have a personal safe house. Meet me there. You'll know I'm home when you see the Peugeot."

"Giselle, I—"

"Till then." She stood and leaned in to kiss him.

Ben drew back, but Giselle caught the back of his head with her usual speed and strength. How often he forgot her capabilities.

She kissed him on the lips—a longer goodbye kiss than usual. "That is for you to remember when you see Tess."

"You really shouldn't have done that. What if I'm infected?"

"Then Tess will know, and you will find me at my little safe house, and we will go through this together."

She straightened and buttoned her coat, and Ben caught her fingers before she turned to go. He'd never spoken the words, but with that touch, he said *I love you*.

Neither had to say it out loud, especially not Giselle. Her disregard for the danger of infection—that kiss—said it all.

6

Emil Jupiter sipped his evening espresso and studied the holographic screen hovering above his porch table. A distant huff and snarl stole his attention for only a moment. By the sound of it, somewhere out in the dark mountainous acreage of his personal retreat, one of his projects had found its supper.

More than a dozen windows divided the holographic screen into stock tickers, news reports, video feeds, and the like. Jupiter frowned at a decrypted message rolling across the top and flicked it away into oblivion with a swipe of his hand. He turned his attention to a video in the lower corner and moved it to the center. A courier crossed a square, carrying a briefcase, viewed from a distance. A woman in fur and sunglasses spilled her coffee. A determined fighter changed the vector of his opponent's knife, letting the blade's sweep come within a centimeter of trimming the deep brown hair spitting out from under his wool cap.

Jupiter paused the playback when the camera zoomed in on the fighter. "Ah. Mr. Calix." He spread his fingers, and flashing

28

holographic dots spread like foam, adding dimension to the flat image. He turned the fighter's face left and right, like an uncle holding his nephew's chin, and studied the hazel eyes. "Confident. Assured in purpose. I'm told you're a patriot, a true believer. We'll see."

The face of the unseen opponent, the one wielding the knife, must have looked quite different. Jupiter imagined Massir wearing an expression of surprise and dismay. Pitiful. His job had been to control Calix while Hagen dealt with the woman, and he'd failed.

Massir was loyal, if not adequately skilled, and Jupiter regretted his death. But someone needed to die in Rome to pull the first card from the Director's precarious house. What had his old friend Hale used to say? *Pick up the trash.* A hockey term. When an operative misses the goal, trap the rebounding puck and shoot again.

Jupiter had salvaged the operation by sacrificing a player. Now Hagen needed to follow up.

A knock on a porch pillar interrupted his analysis. His executive assistant waited for an acknowledgment and then spoke. "Our Dutch friend is here to see you, sir. He brought the guest you requested."

Speak of the devil.

Jupiter pressed the hologram down into the tabletop and stood. "Thank you, Terrance. Bring them through."

Hagen stepped out of the palatial house with professional bearing. He had walked the paths of Jupiter's private reserve before.

The courier had not. He had likely never heard of Jupiter Global before Hagen had dragged him out of Rome earlier that day. Shells and subsidiaries kept the main corporation well-insulated. The young man bore the look of a mouse entering a lion's den. Not far from the truth.

Jupiter spread his hands. "Hagen. Thank you for coming.

Did you enjoy your swim in the Tiber?" He saw a flash of fear in Hagen's eyes. Good. So, he still had a brain.

The Dutchman lowered his gaze. "Cold."

"Not as cold as the morgue I'll stick you in if you come up empty-handed again. I sent you to extract the woman. Instead, you brought me this"—Jupiter looked the courier up and down—"loose end."

The courier turned a shade whiter.

Jupiter polished off his coffee and poured a tumbler of seltzer water to clear his palette. "Relax. I'm joking." He walked behind the two men. "Mostly."

Neither turned, and both kept their eyes level. Like all his employees, Jupiter had taught Hagen never to look down at him, despite his less-than-average stature. The courier wisely followed Hagen's lead.

"Oh, cheer up, children. The operation went as smooth as I expected. The Company, and thus the rest of the world's key intelligence forces, will remain distracted, looking for bomb makers."

This seemed to strike a nerve. Hagen had run point in Tokyo and Munich. "The CRTX explosives did well for us." He pronounced the acronym as *cortex*. "The markets moved as we predicted. Your investments—"

"How many times must I tell you?" Jupiter smashed his tumbler on the pavement, making the courier yelp in surprise. "This is not about money!" He kept walking, returning to the front of the two men. Inhale. Exhale. Pulse rate descending. He unclenched his fists one finger at a time. How could he make them understand?

Jupiter glanced through his home's open wall at a picture of a young couple in Hong Kong. The antique frame was the only wood in the grand interior veranda of marble, aluminum, and glass. The couple looked out of place, a Greek American and his pregnant wife among a throng of Chinese protestors, as if the crowd might envelop them at any time. Pure chaos. No control.

Stepping carefully around the broken glass, Jupiter raised a hand. "Who likes hunting?" He pointed at Hagen and the courier one at a time. "You? You?"

They both just stared at him.

"Terrance, get the cart."

The assistant pulled up with his cart moments later. The courier moved to get in, but Hagen caught his arm.

Jupiter chuckled. "The cart is not for us. It's for Terrance. The three of us will walk." He reached into the small cargo box at the back and drew out a short-barrel rifle with a four-round magazine. "Here, have a gun."

They strolled along a flagstone path winding its way through lush grass, while Terrance rolled silently behind. Jupiter shouldered his rifle and glanced at the courier. "Forgive my outburst earlier. But all of this." He waved his hand over the green expanse. "Our work. It *is* personal. What I'm trying to accomplish for the world is a mammoth task, made harder by rejection from those who should have embraced me. Many years ago, I was one of them—part of their club. But when I brought my mentor an ultimate solution to all his labors, he turned his back. He has no stomach for true sacrifice."

By the pallor of the courier's skin, Jupiter could tell the man dared not ask the identity of his mentor. And Jupiter did not offer it.

The green lawn faded into the sage of a natural range. The path became gravel, sloping upward toward a rocky outcropping. Jupiter paused to track a Spanish partridge and fired. The gun made no more noise than a sharp *click*. The bird dropped from the sky. Terrance set off overland in the cart.

"Silent rifles," Jupiter said, answering the question in the courier's eyes. "Piston-launched subsonic rounds. Two technologies, each more than a decade old, finally combined into one ideal package. A subsidiary of ours is close to a conversion for pistols." He shifted his gaze to Hagen. "Where was I?"

31

"True sacrifice, sir."

"Right. No stomach at all. I showed him the route to a prosperous, unified world. Complete control over every outcome. And he fired me—had me followed, hounded, wire-tapped." Jupiter fired again. Another bird fell. Terrance chased after it, disappearing behind a knoll.

"To escape my oppressor, I had to die. I had to fall into darkness and reemerge an entirely new creature. We keep in touch, now and again. But I am safe from him here. Safe to follow the route he should have taken. Understand?"

The courier nodded.

He didn't understand. Jupiter could tell. Too bad. He brought the rifle up once more. A small antelope buckled. Terrance reappeared with the cart, but Jupiter waved him off. "Leave that one for my beauties. Just dig out the round. We wouldn't want them to ingest it."

Terrance offered a thumbs-up.

The path spiraled into an aluminum and concrete platform built into the rock outcropping. A valley spread out below, with the remnants of its former roads and half-built homes still visible in the fading sunlight. Jupiter had bulldozed the few houses left standing after the developer went bankrupt. But he'd kept a small playground near the center. Call it art. Call it a trophy. A forlorn playground in the wild represented the failure of a world system with far too many uncontrolled variables.

At the platform, he kneeled on a cushioned bench and positioned his rifle barrel on a sandbag draped over the rail. He waved the other two over to kneel beside him. "I've built an empire, all without his help or his resources—much to the contrary. And look at the results." Jupiter tapped the courier's scope, indicating he should use it, and looked through his own to show him where to aim.

Down on the playground, a tiger walked free, softly padding

through the gravel between the swing set and the merry-go-round.

"Do you see him?"

For the first time, the courier spoke. "Y-yes, sir."

"You are looking at a myth, a legend—a Maltese Tiger." The big cat stretched, and portions of its slate-gray flank glinted blue. "The name refers to its color, not its origin. They're native to Southern China, hunted near to extinction for use in worthless medicines. But my people found two, and I've built a new family—a streak, as they're called. Something like a pride." He took his eye away from the scope and bent closer to the young man. "I have enough now that I could release some into the wild, but the world would only squander my gift. So, I maintain control. Occasionally, I must trim our population."

The courier bit his lip, tracking the animal but not firing.

Jupiter touched his shoulder. "Go ahead, son. Pull the trigger. Every man should experience the thrill of taking down a majestic creature before his death."

Click.

The tiger fell. A growing blotch of red stained his blue-gray coat.

"Well done, young man. How'd that feel?"

The kid backed away from the bench, letting his rifle hang from his right hand. "Amazing."

"I'm glad." Jupiter lifted his rifle and fired one round straight into the young man's chest. The courier dropped, stammering, to the aluminum grate platform.

Hagen's features remained placid.

Jupiter appreciated his calm. "They'll be looking for him, wasting time and resources. No sense in leaving him running around to be captured."

"Yes, sir."

Did Jupiter detect a touch of exasperation in his operative's tone? "You think my former employer treats his people any different? I gave this man a fair chance."

No answer.

Jupiter nudged the body with his toe. An arm jerked. Probably a postmortem response. "I told him I planned to kill him. Twice. And I placed a weapon in his hands." He racked back the bolt of his rifle and showed Hagen the empty chamber. "And I left myself only one round. The Director is never so just with his victims. He never plays on a level field." He went quiet and looked out at the tiger, at the red stain on the beautiful blue. A necessary sacrifice. Many more were coming.

"You have another mission for me, sir? The woman?"

"No. She's taken care of. Right now, the Director is learning that one of his agents has not checked in—disappeared—another failure from the Rome fiasco. Forget the woman. I want the man who shot you. His name is Ben Calix. We already have a city. Paris. Find him there and bring him to me."

"So, this is a retrieval-only job."

"Don't sound so disappointed." Jupiter turned to go, but sensed a question forming on Hagen's lips and tried to head it off. "I know the task seems daunting. How do you find a ghost like Calix in a city as large as Paris? But trust me, within hours, he'll be forced from hiding. Be ready to move in and take him."

"Why not just kill Calix? Let me drop another of the Director's soldiers and be done with it."

Jupiter pursed his lips and let out a sharp breath through his nose. "Because I don't *want* to kill him. What do I always say about death?"

The Dutchman had to think far too long before he managed to regurgitate the answer—or part of it. "Death is a tool."

"*Not a goal.* 'Death is a tool, not a goal.' That is the complete saying. Why do I impart my wisdom to you if you can only remember half a phrase?"

Hagen kept silent.

34

Jupiter frowned. "We do not fight on a conventional battle-field where the side which wreaks the bloodiest havoc on the other wins. Espionage is not a war of attrition but a war of control. Consider chess. The endgame is not to kill the king, but to own him. Control, not death. And in our far more complicated game, controlling a knight or even a pawn moves us toward that goal."

At the phrase *controlling a knight*, Hagen's eyes gained a smidgeon of clarity. "So, you want to turn Calix."

Jupiter ignored the *why didn't you just say so* tone in the operative's voice. "It's a little more complicated than that. As in chess, were I to take the whole board—and I will come close, I assure you—I still could not kill the Director. But I don't have to kill him to gain victory. Our intelligence tells me Calix is special to him. By simply creating the illusion that Calix may be a traitor, I will hurt my old boss. By proving it—by making it so—I will destroy him."

The smidgeon of clarity in Hagen's eyes faded.

Jupiter shook his head. Cretin. Why did he bother trying? "You don't need to understand. Just get it done. I'll take care of the rest. Right now, I need to be . . . away from you. I'll walk back to the house alone. Terrance will pick you and the body up when he returns with the tiger. Tell him to have it incinerated." He took a step and paused, catching himself since he now had grave concerns about the man's intelligence. "I mean have the body incinerated, Hagen. Not the tiger."

7

Ben watched the freight barges on the Meuse River as his train crossed into Belgium. He tried to convince himself he'd done the right thing, but a question kept pounding at him—had he taken too many risks?

With the last-minute change to the plan, driven by his need to see Tess and get checked out, he'd been stuck with an aisle seat. As he took his gaze from the river, the elderly woman in the window seat next to him caught his eye and gave him a quick smile. She wanted to chat. He did not. He didn't want to breathe.

For nine hours—the flight from Rome, the train from Stuttgart—Ben had been afraid to exhale. He'd purchased all new clothes and ditched the old ones by sealing them in a trash bag and depositing them in an unattended janitor cart at the airport. He wore cotton gloves and kept a scarf up around his nose and mouth most of the time. Once, his behavior might have seemed odd, but not now in the post-pandemic world.

Was he doing the right thing? Or had America's enemies made him a modern-day Typhoid Mary, carrying a destructive disease across Europe and into the Company's strongholds?

"Pardon, monsieur." Ben's elderly seatmate needed the restroom.

He stepped into the aisle to give her space and cringed when she touched his armrest.

So many risks. Ben needed answers. He needed Tess.

The dark of night outside gave way to the deeper dark of a tunnel and then the blue-gray light of Platform 3 at Brussels South Station. Drawing his arms in to avoid brushing any shoulders, Ben merged with the crowd and made for the exit.

The Brussels night crowd had yet to flood the streets—that strange city quiet when the restaurants are closing but the clubs are not yet open. Ben preferred this hour, even when not on the job. He checked a map on his phone and continued straight down Hollandstraat. With any luck, Tess had reached the med station ahead of him.

A thumping drew Ben's eyes skyward. A chopper lifted off from the pad at the top of South Tower, the city's tallest building. He wouldn't find the med station up there. Ben didn't belong to the caste of spies who merited executive operating suites or the Company's light and agile FLUTR medevac vertical lift aircraft—so named for their butterfly-like appearance when the four stealthy ducted rotors tilted into position for cruise.

The Company maintained covert medical outposts all over the globe, always in one of two locales—top floor or ground floor. Nothing in between. No one wanted operatives bleeding out while sharing an elevator with a bewildered businesswoman or a soccer dad and his kids. The Company reserved the shiny top floor stations served by FLUTR medevac craft for top brass and high-value assets like Dylan. Run-of-the-mill field operatives like Ben got garage utility closets and abandoned laundromats—and they walked, drove, or crawled to these places on their own.

"Nine six six five . . ." Ben repeated the grid coordinates, checking the map one last time before pocketing the phone and making a right down an empty one-way street. In Rome, while escaping the old city and the burning body, he'd sent out an encrypted data burst requesting med support, adding a special request for Ambrosia, Tess's code name. As expected, he received a set of coordinates in the self-deleting response. He hoped he'd got them right.

Ben came to a garage door covered in graffiti—the delivery entrance for a bodega—and chuckled beneath the scarf still covering his mouth. "This looks about right." He bent and gave the handle a tug. The door rolled up with ease, and the wash of the streetlamps spilled in around him, giving definition to shapes in the dark.

"Hello?"

Wireframe shelving. A box of molded fruit. A rusted freezer. Ben used his smartphone light to illuminate the rest. A rat scurried away from the beam.

"Anyone home?"

A metal door opened at the back, and a woman stood in the frame, shorter than Giselle despite her spiked heels. "You planning to come inside or stand out there caterwauling all night?"

Nothing said come hither like a Georgia accent, especially when combined with a crooked smile like hers. "Hey, Tess."

"Hey yourself, honey." She backed up, pulling the door wide. "Get in here. I don't have all night."

She waited for him to pass and then flipped on the halogens overhead. Stainless steel, glistening clean, dominated the room—counters, two sinks, and an exam table. Tess tied on a surgical mask and pointed at the latter. "Sit and strip."

"Giselle warned me you'd say that. I'm supposed to remind you I'm spoken for."

"Hilarious. Why is your shirt still on?"

As the halogens warmed up, Ben got a better view of the outfit beneath Tess's lab coat. Her sleek, emerald-green dress said Studio 54 more than Mayo Clinic. The lack of a bio suit gave him hope. He'd added a high-level hazard code to his request for support. If Tess had bypassed her protection protocols, she knew something Ben didn't. He removed his jacket and pulled his shirt over his head. "Hot date later?"

"I have a friend in the city." She pushed her hand into a latex glove. "And yes, we're meeting up tonight, so don't get any blood on my dress."

"I'm not bleeding."

Tess wiggled a syringe with a needle as thick as a ten-penny nail. "Not yet."

A monitor with two handles hung from the ceiling by a combination of joints and telescoping arms. Tess set the syringe beside her patient and pulled the screen in front of his chest, lining up a set of laser crosshairs.

Ben harbored a closet aversion to crosshairs. "What is that?"

"Microwave imager."

"Is it dangerous?"

"Yes. Don't move."

The machine hummed, building energy. Tess left it in place and pulled up a stool. "Tell me about the victim. Describe the symptoms."

He did, emphasizing the speed of the black tendrils creeping through Massir's veins.

Tess checked his skin, nose, and eyes, and interrupted with the occasional question. "And he went from healthy to dead in how many minutes?"

"Five. Seven max, based on the chase between the Pantheon and the alley where I cornered him." Ben started to relax.

She threatened him with the syringe. "I said don't move. So, you're assuming the female operative your victim met is the one who dosed him?"

"Should I suspect otherwise?"

"No. I think that's valid. And the lack of any other cases cropping up in Rome is encouraging." The machine's hum reached a crescendo. Tess grabbed both handles. "Here goes nothing."

39

Ben tried to look down at the crosshairs with just his eyeballs, keeping his head still. "Wait. I think I moved."

"Yeah, you did, honey. But it's probably fine."

"Probably?"

She pulled the trigger, and the hum ended with a *snap*.

He could swear he felt a burst of heat pass through his torso.

Tess studied her screen for a few heartbeats, then nodded. "We're good. Turn around."

Ben raised his legs and spun them to the table's other side. The humming rose to another crescendo. The machine gave another snap. A second burst of heat passed through his body. He started to ask about it, but the coolness of an alcohol swab at the small of his back refocused his attention.

"Bend over," she said, gently pressing him forward until his elbows rested on his knees. "This is going to hurt." Without further warning, she stabbed him.

Tess had never had much of a bedside manner—probably the reason she'd wound up in intelligence, pulling a government paycheck, instead of the private medical sector.

After several moments of excruciating sliding and tugging, she yanked the needle out again.

Ben felt the sting of a clotting agent pressed against the wound, followed by a bandage and a slap to make sure it stuck. "Ouch, Tess. Not so rough. I swear, you're worse now than you were four years ago in Grozny."

She slapped the patch again. "Don't be a baby." When he reached for his shirt, she slapped his hand too. "Leave it off, I'm not done. And for your information, I must be improving. The Director's bringing me home to DC."

He spun around again, watching her return to the counter with a test tube of pinkish fluid. "Back to the ranch. Really? To treat the big brass?"

"Mm-hmm." Tess seemed to be only half listening. Using an eyedropper, she placed a few drops of the fluid into the four clear sections of a centrifuge card. "It's all champagne and caviar from here out." She closed the centrifuge door and started the rotation, bobbling her head. "And maybe the occasional Shake Shack burger."

Ben couldn't picture Tess with the brass. She didn't fit the corporate image. "Think it'll change you? Make you jaded?"

"Why would I get jaded?"

"You know. Seeing how the DC crowd does business. The politics. The compromises."

This captured her full attention. She glanced over her shoulder, a touch of anger in her eyes above the surgical mask. "I'll be working with the Director. He's not like that. And if he is, all this—everything we do—is a waste of time."

"Right. Of course. But what about the hoarding of intel, keeping teams in the dark. You walked in here with total confidence, even after I sent you a hazard warning. Did the top brass know about this bioweapon? For that matter, did they suspect a trap and send us in there unprepared?"

The centrifuge whirred to a stop, and Tess lifted the card. She slid it into an electron microscope with a little more force than seemed necessary and studied the screen. "Do you know how the Company began, Calix?"

He'd heard the story—never written down, always passed from the senior class to the incoming class at the schoolhouse. "Thirty years ago. Conceived by an aide to the president. Formed by an ad hoc intelligence subcommittee under a charter with an 'any means necessary' clause."

"And to run it, they chose that same presidential aide, incredibly young for such an important position—the Director." Tess turned a couple of dials next to the keyboard, then inclined her head as if looking at the result sideways. "Faith like that speaks of a man of unimpeachable character."

"And you think the Director is still unimpeachable? After all this time?"

"If not, the Company would be notorious or gone, or both. He'd be living on an island somewhere, counting his money." Tess turned and rested her hips against the counter, pulling down her mask. "Good news, honey. You're going to live."

Relief washed over Ben. "No plague in my system?"

"Oh, it's there."

"What?"

She held up a *don't worry* hand. "The fluid sample I took shows inviable spores. Dead. Your body never activated its defenses." She walked to a refrigerated cabinet at the counter's end and drew out a vial of liquid and a new syringe. "The plague's saving grace is its combination of quick symptoms and slow progression, but this version moves fast. Super-fast. And dies fast too. Whoever engineered it—"

"Created a weapon for assassination, not mass murder."

"Looks that way." She dribbled alcohol onto a patch of gauze and dabbed at his right arm above the bicep. "Even so, I'm going to give you a shot of antibiotics, just in case."

Ben looked away. He'd always hated needles, even needles hidden in a rapid-injection CO_2 syringe. "Tess, how do you know the Director isn't . . ." He hesitated.

"Rich? Corrupt? Hoarding the ill-gotten spoils of a thousand covert campaigns or sending us into the field without necessary purpose?" She jabbed him with the injector, causing a pinch and an ice-cold hiss. "Faith."

8

Ben climbed the stairs from the metro station at Saint Germain and turned north on Rue Bonaparte under the late morning sun. Its rays did nothing to ease the winter cold, and he altered his route to his flat in the 16th arrondissement to take him past a favorite café.

In the ten months of Ben's posting there, Paris had stolen his heart. He loved his country, certainly, but his American roots had thinned. His parents had him late in life and passed while he was still muddling around in his six years at Rice University, deciding what he wanted to be when he grew up. He knew he didn't want to be a cabinetmaker, so he'd sold the family business, the last tie binding him to his hometown, and moved on. No siblings. No connections. The Company sought out people like him. They'd recruited him—rescued him—during his first year as a commodities trader.

Life at the schoolhouse ended nine months later with his death. Drug overdose. Tragic. His professors at Rice would have never guessed. The Company resurrected him in London as Ben Calix, and he'd never looked back.

43

With a fresh cup of tea to warm his hands, Ben crossed the river at *Pont Neuf*—New Bridge, the city's oldest—and made a casual glance at the street vendor stalls at the north end. A bad sketch of Elvis Presley hung prominently in the third stall from the east. The drop signal.

Already?

Ben wanted his bed, nothing more. No new missions or assignments. He hadn't slept well on the cot at the back of Tess's medical station, and he'd used the sleepless hours and her encryption equipment to file his after-action report. Maybe the signal meant the Company had more questions. The mission hadn't exactly gone as planned. He'd fill out some digital forms, leave the file at the drop point an hour later, and pass out for a couple of days.

A couple of loops around the Louvre served as a hasty check for tails and a chance to finish his tea. After tossing the cup in a bin, he pressed west into the Tuileries Garden parks and reached into his inside pocket for his phone.

The old-school HUMINT signal methods never went away—a potted plant in a window or an Elvis picture hanging in a street market. But the drops themselves have all gone digital. Near-field communication, the same technology that enables consumers to tap-and-pay with a smartphone, enables spies to download large encrypted files simply by walking past a lamppost.

The Tuileries Garden had such a lamppost, planted with several others in a miniature forest like fixtures in a fairy tale. The fifth lamppost from the east had a digital dropbox hidden in its rusty iron base.

Children in mittens and stocking caps played hide-and-seek among the trees, their laughter visible as mists in the cold. As Ben palmed his phone and drew it from his pocket, a boy charged his way. *"Faites attention,"* he said to the child, spinning and lifting his arm to keep clear.

"Désolé!" the boy replied without looking back.

Their mini ballet had brought him too close to the lamppost. He hadn't made the phone ready to receive. Ben slowed his steps to an awkward gait, punched the phone's power button to activate the receiver and ping the digital drop box, and felt a haptic kick.

File received. But not with the subtlest choreography.

Ben would have to modify his route home to make sure no one had been watching.

Spies live every day as if their contacts have been compromised, because one day they will be, even when that contact is a lamppost half a klick from the Louvre. The best defense is a surveillance detection route or SDR—walking in pointless, meandering circles for blocks on end or randomly swapping from a northbound train to its southbound counterpart. Any stranger matching such antics is up to no good.

Ben had run a hasty SDR before picking up his file by circling the Louvre. For the post-pickup SDR he took his time. He hopped on the metro at Pyramides, rode the same line in two directions, then walked a meandering route into the labyrinth of old buildings west of Les Invalides. He picked a dead-end alley with no vehicle access, rested his back against the limestone blocks of an old apartment building, and flipped his hand over to check the phone.

The motion brought the screen to life. A little blue box shifted into view.

1 new file: 256 mb

Big file. A new mission? If the Company sent him out again, he'd miss his chance to see Giselle outside of a professional context—or at all, if they didn't put her on the team. Ben glanced up at the narrow strip of gray sky visible between the buildings. "Thanks, Boss."

A numbing flash of electricity coursed up his arm. Ben dropped his phone and watched it fall, sparking and popping, to the cobblestones. The screen had gone black. He bent to recover it. "What on—"

A bullet ricocheted off the wall where his head had been an instant before.

Sniper.

Instincts kicked in. Ben stayed low and ran. A second round hit the wall. A third. Flecks of centuries-old limestone grazed his cheeks and neck.

Thought fragments flashed through his mind.

Kids playing tag.

The boy.

The lamppost.

Elvis.

Corrupted file.

Burning phone.

Another round clipped the corner as Ben reached Rue des Archives and turned, breaking the sniper's sightline. He kept running.

His pickup had been substandard, sure, but not bad enough to send him into a sniper's crosshairs. He'd done his penance with a long SDR, checking for tails. How could this happen?

He vaulted a stone barrier, landed in a half-controlled tumble on the river walk ten feet below, and sprinted west. None of this made sense, but one crystal-clear thought overshadowed the rest. Ben was blown.

9

Bleach erases. Fire destroys.

Another of Colonel Hale's pearls of Company wisdom hung before Ben's vision. *Erase biological signatures. Destroy equipment. Slash and burn. Leave nothing for the enemy.*

Ben removed his coat to change his profile as he passed under the bridge and came out the other side at a walk. The sniper had shot him from above. A high perch inside a building made post-ambush pursuit a near impossibility. Ben had breathing space, but not much, and he'd have to work fast.

Like Hale said, slash and burn.

Every Company field operative installed a cleaning kit at home base—incendiary cords in the drywall, electromagnets in the computer desk, bags of bleach with explosive squibs in key DNA collectors like the bathroom and bed area. Standard procedure, but Ben had brought the skill and attention to detail of a childhood spent in a cabinetmaker's workshop to the task. He'd crafted a seamless and invisible system with a trigger linked to a panic function on his phone.

Except the enemy had killed his phone.

He'd need to activate the kit manually. Stopping by the flat on his way out of town might prove deadly, but recovering his go-bag and erasing his life here were both worth the risk.

The sniper had given Ben no chance to go for his weapon. He refused to be caught unprepared twice in the same day. Entering his building's stairwell, he drew the third-generation Glock 42 from his waistband holster and hid it under the coat folded over his arm.

A blue-haired girl came down the steps, holding a dachshund close to her chest. "Haven't seen you in a while, Jacob." Her Slovakian heritage colored her English, which—as she had told Ben when they first met—she spoke better than French. The girl, Clara Razny, knew him by his local cover name Jacob Roy, a wool salesman from Montreal.

Ben didn't have time for this. "Winter sales route. Lots of stops. Big time of year for wool." He tried to squeeze past.

She didn't let him, tilting her head and shoulders to block. Ice-blue eyes looked up into his. "We could get something later, if you like. No need to cook if you're worn out." The dachshund lifted its head from her forearm, eyes pleading for the extra evening company.

"Not tonight, Clara. Maybe another time."

She always asked. He always declined. After this it wouldn't matter.

"Yes." Clara set the dog down at the base of the steps. "Another time."

He almost laughed. She'd never see him again.

At the landing four flights up, the entrance to his floor stood ajar. He nudged it open with a foot, standing to the side. The door let out an awful *creak*. Ben winced, then leaned to the side to take a peek. Movement. A woman and child walked toward the exit at the hall's opposite end. He waited until they were clear.

His flat remained locked. Maybe the sniper had acted alone. Maybe whatever agency had taken a shot at him only knew about the lamppost.

Unlikely.

How had they defeated his SDR? How had the sniper gotten into place so fast?

Ben put an ear to the door. He heard a rustle, almost imperceptible, but enough to confirm his fears of a lurking intruder. He laid his coat to the side, let out a long breath, and silently turned his key.

Here we go.

With a stiff bump from his shoulder, the door flew open. He let the Glock lead the charge over the threshold. A flash of black drew his eyes left. Gun? No. A baton. Sparks crackled, burning into the back of his hand. His arm went numb to the shoulder, but still he managed to cling to his weapon.

A gloved hand seized Ben's shirt and spun him ninety degrees, bringing him nose to nose with the Dutchman he'd faced in Rome—Hagen, according to the whispered conversation he'd overheard at the Pantheon.

"You," Ben grunted. He tried to raise the Glock. His arm wouldn't budge. "I thought I killed you.

Hagen only smiled. He held Ben at arm's length and raised the baton, ready to shove the electric prongs into his chest. "Someone wants to talk to you. Alive. I'm not sure you'll make it."

Feeling was coming back—a million stabbing needles—but not enough to give him control. Ben took a swing with his left and connected with the baton. It flew across the room. He grabbed his opponent's leather jacket and jerked him close, head-butting the bridge of his nose, then shoved him away. Hagen fell against the doorframe, bleeding.

Ben tried to transfer his gun to his good hand, but fumbled the exchange. The Glock bounced on the carpet. Hagen bull-rushed him.

They hit the floor next to the bed with Hagen's head caught under Ben's left arm. He tried to cinch the choke, but Hagen wriggled free and straddled him, raining punches. With only one and a half arms, Ben mounted a feeble defense. He caught a left across the chin and let out a pained grunt.

Every spy stashes weapons and other key items around the house in hidden compartments known as slicks, *because you never know when a crazy Dutchman might sneak in and try to kill you. And because, when you're bored on a weekend or locked down for months during a pandemic, what else are you going to do?*

Ben bucked and rolled, inching backward on his shoulder blades toward the midpoint of his bed frame, and sacrificed his defense to reach under the mattress for salvation. He found a KA-BAR knife secured in the stuffing, yanked it free, and stabbed at Hagen's side.

The knife sank into yielding but impenetrable material. Body armor, probably the same vest that saved Hagen in Rome. Hagen grinned, blood staining his teeth from a split lip. "Sorry, friend."

They fought for control. In the flurry of movement, Ben slashed his opponent's shoulder. Hagen let out a cry and pulled back—enough for Ben to push him off. He slashed back and forth, making space to gather his legs and press up to his feet. Hagen might want to take him alive, but Ben had no obligation to reciprocate the effort.

Apparently Hagen hadn't committed to the idea either. He drew a SIG and aimed.

Ben sliced his forearm with the blade and the gun fell. He kicked it under the bed. "Who sent you? Who do you work for? Jupiter?"

"What do you know of Jupiter?"

"Not enough, it seems." Ben had backed Hagen past a standing mirror. He punched the glass, shattering it, and ripped a strip of duct tape with three scalpels off the backing. "Who is he?" He threw the first, burying it deep into Hagen's thigh. The second one landed next to it.

Hagen let out an angry growl. "He's someone who'll be disappointed when I hand him your head instead of walking you through the door. But he'll have to get over it."

"And the shooter? It couldn't have been you." Ben threatened him with the third scalpel. "How did he know where I'd go?"

Hagen charged.

Ben chucked the last scalpel, and Hagen raised a hand to defend himself. The blade went straight through. He howled.

The Glock lay across the room. Ben took advantage of the pain distracting Hagen and clutched the round hilt of his KA-BAR like a bare-knuckle boxer gripping a roll of quarters. He dodged a wild punch and landed a left hook, following with a slash at Hagen's bicep.

The blade cut through the leather and found flesh. Ben gave Hagen a right to the gut, then locked a hand behind his head and tried to pull his neck to the knife. Hagen wedged in an arm, holding back. They turned as they grappled for control. Ben cast a glance at the gun, almost in reach.

Hagen had other plans.

The Dutchman kicked the inside of Ben's knee, and both stumbled across the small flat into the bathroom, far away from the Glock. The impact of Ben's lower spine against the porcelain sink robbed him of any control. He dropped the knife. Hagen pushed a bloodied palm heel up under his chin, with the scalpel still sticking through his hand. With a burst of power, he smashed the back of Ben's head against the cabinet mirror. A pill bottle and a toothbrush fell into the sink amid shards of glass.

A gray fog invaded Ben's vision, threatening to end the fight. He felt a growing wetness at the crown of his head, and his breath came short and labored.

This guy was strong. How had Giselle bested him so easily in Rome?

"It does not have to be this way, my friend." Hagen shook his head, as if sorry for him. "I'm supposed to take you quietly. Relax, let me inject you with a sleep agent, and you'll wake up in our medical facility. Jupiter's physicians will treat your wounds."

"Why?" Ben said, wheezing against the pressure on his neck and fighting to keep both of Hagen's hands busy so he couldn't go for the promised syringe. "What does he want with me? Information? Torture?"

"I don't really care. My job is to bring you in alive, but if you're a vegetable, that's on you, not me." Long fingers found Ben's carotid arteries and squeezed. "There's a narrow space between coma and death when cutting off the blood flow to the brain. I'm not that precise. Good night, Calix."

Bleach washes.

Fire purges.

The gray fog closed over his vision, and Ben's duty to activate the cleaning kit became his final focus. He did not intend to be taken and tortured. With his final ounce of consciousness, he'd destroy the flat, protecting the Company. His kit had two manual switches—one near the front door to be activated during escape, the other in the bathroom as either a backup or a suicide switch. With the last of his fading consciousness, Ben abandoned all resistance, tore the scalpel from Hagen's hand, and jammed the blade into the bathroom socket.

The fake socket caved in, and the scalpel stuck into the rubber switch behind it.

A series of pops rippled through the walls and ceiling.

Hagen loosened his grip, looking up.

Ben rolled free, coughing, and yanked the vinyl shower curtain down over his own head.

10

A heavy mist of bleach and acetone filled the bathroom. Under the vinyl curtain, Ben dropped to his knees. Free of Hagen's grip, he had time for three wheezing breaths before the fumes creeped under the edges to find him. A patch of his face burned. He must've been cut in the fight. Outside his makeshift shield, Hagen gagged and groaned. The dresser rattled. He'd fled into the main room. Ben had to press his advantage before his attacker recovered, and before the second, deadly phase of the cleaning kit kicked in.

Two more packets of bleach had exploded over the bed and in the kitchen, leaving no safe space in the flat. Ben stumbled from the bathroom, fighting the urge to breathe, and found Hagen growling and trying to wipe his eyes with the sweatshirt under his jacket. Hagen heard Ben coming and took a swing. Ben sidestepped the punch, lining up a shot through his blurred vision, and landed a hook that toppled his opponent. He stomped on the two scalpels still buried in the man's thighs, forcing a scream that would only pull in more choking gas.

His lungs begged for air, and his mental clock kept ticking. The incendiaries were timed to ignite two minutes after the chemical packets blew, when the air had reached the right saturation of flammable vapor. He couldn't hang around to play with Hagen any longer.

Ben recovered his Glock and Hagen's cattle prod from the carpet and kicked through the drywall beside the door, bending to work a hidden backpack free from the resulting hole. The hall outside seemed strangely quiet after the tumult of the fight. He gently closed the door, picked up his folded coat, and pulled it on over his bleach-stained shirt. To cover the throbbing wound on the back of his head, he used a stocking cap from his go-bag. Then he shouldered his pack and feigned the calm of a man heading out for a walk.

He made it halfway to the stairwell door before it opened. Clara came walking through.

She had the dog with her. She always carried that dog. Ben could never remember its name. "Clara?" He glanced behind him. Only seconds to go now. "Your floor is one down."

"Yes, I know. I want to talk. Earlier when I spoke of dinner—"

"We said we'd do it another time." He tried to steer her back toward the stairwell.

She jerked her arm free and stopped, poking him in the chest. "*You* said another time, Jacob. As always. You are busy, or tired, or packing, or unpacking. I'm not proposing marriage. Just dinner. Two neighbors, foreigners in this city sitting down for a meal."

"Either way, I'm spoken for."

"Really?" She made an indignant side-to-side motion with her head, flopping her blue strands back and forth. "I've never seen this woman. Is she real or imaginary?"

Ben had lost count of the seconds, but the two minutes had to be almost up. "I have to go." He kept walking. "*We* have to go."

Thankfully, she followed, sniffing the air. "Why do you smell like bleach?"

"Calix!" Hagen burst out of the flat and staggered into the hall. He extended his SIG.

Ben stepped in front of Clara, drawing his Glock and firing at the same time. He never saw if his shots hit the mark.

A blast rocked the building. The fireball enveloped Hagen. Cracks ran up and down the hallway plaster, and dust fell from the ceiling. The cleaning kit's incendiary cord had finally lit the fumes.

The explosion buried Clara's scream. Before it settled, Ben had her moving toward the stairwell. "Like I said. We have to go."

By the time the two reached the street, police sirens wailed in the city—three, maybe four blocks away and closing. Pedestrians shouted, running into the traffic to get away from the building. Ben pointed north, up the river. "Go that way. There's a clinic on Rue de la Tour. Get checked out."

He walked south, glancing up at the smoke rising from the building. Everything he owned, everything but the clothes on his back, destroyed.

"Who was that man, Jacob?" Clara walked beside him with the dachshund on his leash, stubby legs racing to keep up. "Why did he call you Calix?"

"I told you to go to the clinic."

"You shot him."

"You can't prove that's what killed him. Might've been the explosion. You need to go. It's not safe."

"Not until you tell me what's going on. The cuts? The swelling? My father was a mean drunk. My brother took the worst of it. I know a face that's taken a beating when I see one. You had a fist fight, shot that man, and then blew up your own flat."

He wheeled around on her, speaking through clenched teeth. "Go away."

His sudden turn seemed to catch two men off guard, half a block behind. A man in gray trousers and a brown jacket averted his gaze. A black man wearing a dark blue sweatshirt made the same movement, walking through the park across the street from the first. A good twenty meters separated the two, but they were clearly working together. Hagen had brought friends, and they'd seen the girl talking to Ben.

"Fine," he said. "Come with me."

He led her another block to the river and the walkway under the Passy Viaduct, in the Eiffel Tower's shadow.

Clara had almost as much trouble keeping pace as her dog. "You could slow down, you know."

"No we can't."

She stopped anyway—not from defiance, but because the dog had picked that moment to draw a line in the sand. He tugged at his leash, refusing to go on.

"Ugh. Otto! Come, boy. Otto, come here!"

"Pick up your dog, Clara."

"He's fine. He'll come. He's not usually like this." She patted her leg, switching to Slovak. *"Otto, ty tupý pes, ku mne! Ku mne!"*

Ben watched the bridge behind them. Mr. Brown Jacket and his friend Blue Sweatshirt knew they'd been made, and they were no longer trying to blend in. Both men power-walked their way, with Blue Jacket staying wide to flank.

If Ben ditched the girl now, maybe they'd forget her and follow. "I'm sorry, Clara. I have to go. Good luck."

"Good luck with what?"

He didn't stay to answer, he'd already turned and broken into a run.

Behind him, the dachshund barked. Clara let out a squeal.

11

Ben jogged to a stop. His gamble had failed. He turned to see Brown Jacket with an arm around Clara, holding her shoulder in an iron grip.

"Calix! Get back here."

"Yeah. Okay. The spys walk of shame.

Blue Sweatshirt continued strolling toward him—a sheep dog corralling the stray.

The dachshund never ceased its barking.

Pedestrians on the bridge paused to watch.

Brown Jacket flashed a badge. *"Capitaine Luis Duval, Sous-Direction Anti-Terroriste,"* he said and continued in French. "Nothing to see here."

The Anti-Terrorist Sub-Directorate. SDAT. A French counterterrorism cop. Strange. All the law enforcement databases listed Ben as Jacob Roy. This cop had called him Calix. And while Ben could believe SDAT might respond to an explosion in a flat, these two had been there when the explosion happened, already watching. Plus, Ben didn't like Duval's face. He couldn't leave Clara with these guys.

Duval returned the badge to his belt and shoved a hand in

his pocket. An angular form appeared in the fabric—a gun aimed at Clara's spleen.

Blue Sweatshirt had taken up a post at Ben's shoulder, walking a step behind him. "Nice and easy, Calix. This is over for you and your girlfriend. Don't make trouble."

There are no coincidences in the intelligence world. A virus doesn't just happen to start in a town that has a virology lab without a direct connection to that lab. The cousin of a known terrorist doesn't just happen to travel to a US city a week before a bomb goes off. And two French cops don't just happen to appear outside a spy's apartment building on the day his world goes haywire.

Don't make trouble.

Ben's flat was gone.

His stuff, gone—nearly everything he owned bleached and burned.

His head pounded from where it had hit the medicine cabinet.

His face still burned from where bleach and acetone had sunk into his abrasions.

And that dumb dog wouldn't stop barking.

Yeah, he thought. *I'm gonna make some trouble.*

Ben accelerated his gait, pushing his center of gravity forward like a boulder on a shallow hill. "Clara! Can't you shut that dog up?"

The shout, meant to off-balance Duval, worked. The stern look of total command on his face waned. Blue Sweatshirt lost the professional composure he'd maintained since taking up his post at Ben's shoulder. "Calix?" he blurted out. "What are you doing?"

Ben kept accelerating.

The dachshund took this as his cue to double down. He ramped up the intensity and the pitch, front legs bouncing off the ground with each piercing *yap*.

Blue Sweatshirt jogged to keep pace with Ben. "Calix, stop."

First confusion, then anger filled Duval's eyes. With Ben two meters away and not slowing, he pulled the gun out of hiding. He didn't have time to aim.

Ignoring the weapon, Ben slammed a heel in Duval's chest. He felt a rib crack. The gun hit the bridge. Ben snatched it up by the barrel—a Beretta Nano. He gave a tilt of his head and pushed out a lip. "Not bad."

Fingers grazed his shoulder, not yet catching hold.

Ben spun and smashed the Beretta's butt into the bridge of Blue Sweatshirt's nose. The man staggered back and dropped to a knee, blood spurting from his nostrils. A follow-up smash to the temple put him out cold.

"You wanted to come with me?" Ben grabbed Clara's hand. "Fine. Let's go."

A few steps in, once she had recovered some coordination, she planted her feet and yanked his arm right back. "Not without my dog."

"Leave him. He'll slow us down."

"No!"

Duval groaned and struggled to regain his feet. He still had some fight in him.

Clara pointed at the dachshund. "Otto comes with us. That is final."

The pedestrians had formed a circle around them, several filming with their phones.

Ben didn't have time for an argument. He tucked the gun away and went back for the dog. On the way, he gave Duval another kick to the ribs. "Stay down." He picked up the dog, and the two sprinted together across the footbridge into the busy streets south of the Eiffel Tower.

12

Get far fast. Then get farther faster.

The same rules that had applied to Ben's escape from the old city in Rome applied in Paris. With a dachshund named Otto clutched in his arms, and a blue-haired woman he hardly knew hanging on to the loose, bleach-spotted fabric of his sleeve, Ben ascended the steps to the above-ground platforms at Bir-Hakeim Metro Station. He had one driving thought on his mind.

He had to reach Giselle.

The reappearance of the dead Dutchman and the second mention of the mysterious Jupiter tied Ben's present very-bad day to the botched mission in Rome. He had to warn Giselle before whatever malady had brought his life crashing down infected her too.

He used cash to buy paper tickets for the turnstiles, unable to trust the Navigo transit card registered under Jacob Roy. Given the day's events, it had probably been burned before he first set foot in Paris late that morning.

The midday crowd left Ben and Clara standing in the aisles of the eastward train. When it lurched into motion, Ben grabbed the overhead bar, leaving Otto tucked under one arm like a football. The dachshund seemed happy there, but once the train settled, Ben pressed him into Clara's arms. "I think this is yours."

She scratched the dog's ears for a moment, then reached up to touch Ben's cheek.

"Don't." He caught her fingers and gently pressed them away. "Please." What had started as a cut left by a knuckle had grown into a knot, partially closing his right eye. He checked his reflection in the train window. The distortion didn't help, but even without it, he looked a fright.

The hand Ben had pressed away from his cheek now rested on his arm. "I'm making this harder for you, aren't I?" Clara said. "Whatever you're doing. I'm not helping. I'll get off at the next stop."

"You can't. They'll scoop you up."

"Who? Those policemen?"

"I don't know. The badge looked real, but I think they're working for someone else—someone bad. Do you believe me?"

The answer came back without pause or hesitation. "Yes."

How could she put her trust in him like that? So soon. So easily. He narrowed the eye he could still control. "Why?"

"You might have pushed me away these last six months, but I've seen you—the way you help old Madame Bisset when she comes home with her shopping, the way you pick up rubbish the teens leave in the stairwell." She smiled. "The way you lie about always having someplace to be, just to spare my feelings. You are a good man, Jacob—" Clara stopped and cocked her head. "I mean . . . Ben Calix?"

He nodded. "Yeah. Ben."

"So where are we going, *Ben*."

"We need to get you out of town, somewhere safe. And then we can figure out next steps. I know someone who can help."

"Your imaginary love?"

He nodded. "She's part of my world. And she's skilled. She'll know what to do."

Clara went silent as the train stopped at Dupleix and La Motte-Picquet–Grenelle stations in quick succession. She made no effort to get off at either. It seemed she meant what she'd said about trusting him. "And what happens if these dirty cops catch us?" she asked as the doors closed again.

"Hard to say. Torture, probably. Whoever's paying them will work me over for weeks to get at everything I know." The train set off again, diving from the aboveground tracks into a tunnel. "You, of course, don't know anything. They'll figure that out pretty quick. A smart interrogator might hurt you to make me talk—for a while, anyway. A few hours. A few days. Eventually they'll get bored with it and kill you."

An elderly man seated on a bench at Ben's knee tipped up the brim of his cap with his cane and stared at them both.

Ben frowned back at him. "*Une blague,*" he said in French. "A joke."

The old man didn't laugh. He didn't get the chance.

A screech of brakes brought the train to a halt and sent passengers bumping and stumbling into each other. Murmurs passed through the crowded car.

"What was that?" Clara asked.

"I don't know."

The conductor made an announcement a few seconds later. "*Mesdames et Messieurs,* the station ahead has asked us to hold here due to a problem with our track. We will update you with more details as they become available."

Ten minutes went by, and no more details came.

No coincidences.

"I don't like this," Ben said, leaning over the old gentleman to peer through the window. He saw nothing but the black tunnel wall.

Clara shrugged. "It happens . . . sometimes."

"Yeah. But why today?"

Before he finished the question, the train started up again.

The station lights appeared a few heartbeats later. Pedestrians gathered on the platform, impatient. Ben recognized two figures among them.

Looking harried and abused, one holding his ribs and the other holding a kerchief to his bleeding nose, Duval and Blue Sweatshirt strode up and down the platform on the wrong side of the yellow line, searching the incoming cars for their targets.

13

Passengers moved to the still-closed doors and patted the glass. Duval and his partner worked their way inward from the platform ends, peering into windows with cupped hands.

Clara leaned a shoulder into Ben's chest. "Why don't they let us off?"

Without answering, he pivoted his body to hide hers, so that only the dachshund separated them. He stared into her eyes and slid both hands behind her neck, thumbs tracing her jawline.

She swallowed. "Um . . . What are you doing?"

"Hiding your blue hair." He tucked the blue strands back and pulled the fur-lined hood of her coat up to cover her head. "There. Now we're not quite as conspicuous, are we? Can you hide Otto in your coat?"

The murmurs in the car grew louder. The patting on the glass became a pounding on the doors. A woman shouted in French at the security cameras. The conductor answered with an announcement. "Mesdames et Messieurs, the track problem mentioned earlier has engaged our train's safety measures and will not allow us to open the doors. We apologize for the inconvenience and again ask for your patience as we work to resolve this issue."

"Yeah, right." Ben gave Clara a skeptical look. "Time to go."

"How? The doors won't open."

"The side doors, sure. But every one of these trains has a fail-safe door at the back. Let's head for the rear car."

He let Clara take the lead. The trapped passengers were more likely to make way for a young woman with a dachshund poking out of her coat than a man with a swollen face.

Duval reached the end of their car, close enough for Ben to see his jaw tense with each breath. It looked like the broken ribs were taking their toll—and keeping his anger piqued. Ben saw a group of uniformed cops approaching. He touched Clara's elbow. "Wait."

"What is it? What do you see?"

"A distraction."

The two froze until the uniforms engaged Duval. By the looks of their angry gestures, the cops didn't know why they'd been called to the station. It seemed Duval had been acting on his own. He shouted back at them, looking away from the train.

Ben bent close to Clara's ear. "Go now. Walk fast."

They hurried through the cars joined by rubber gaskets and steel plates, until they reached the last. Ben flashed his Jacob Roy International Wool Merchant's Association card at a woman standing with her daughter at the rear door. "*Pardonnez-moi, madame,*" he said, continuing in French. "Metropolitan Transit Security. Please stand aside and remain on the train."

She didn't question his false authority. No one ever did.

The lever turned, and a sharp jerk broke the magnetic seal designed to deter passengers. Ben hopped out first, then took the dog so Clara could follow.

"How did you know we could get out that way?" she asked.

"Madrid and London." He helped her up onto a narrow walkway at the tunnel's edge and shoved Otto back into her hands. In answer to her questioning look, he pressed his lips together and gestured for her to keep going. "Madrid and London—the train bombings in the mid-2000s trapped many passengers. Today most trains have a fail-safe evacuation route. Tough magnetic seals give the illusion of a locked door to discourage jumpers, but the rear exit should always open."

Thirty meters from the train, a red ACCÈS DE MAINTENANCE sign pointed them to the way out—an alcove with a steel staircase leading up to an alarmed door. Ben pushed through and set it off, blinking in the winter sunlight. He turned north on the sidewalk, away from the station entrance. "Come on. I have to make a call."

Clara hurried after him. "You don't have a phone?"

"It died."

"Mine still works. You should've asked."

"I'm asking now. Can I borrow it?"

Shifting the dog into an awkward position, Clara dug into her purse. A moment later she held up the phone.

"Thanks." Without breaking his quick stride, he swept the device from her hand and chucked it sidearm across the street, skipping it into a sewer drain.

"Hey!"

He shot her a flat look. "Given everything you've experienced so far, are you really that surprised?"

"Yes. I am."

Ben sighed. "This is gonna be a long day."

His plan of hopping a B train to Montrouge looked less and less likely with each moment. Hagen had been in Rome, almost certainly driven by this Jupiter character and the organization rumored behind the attacks—Leviathan, according to the Dark Web whispers. But how did Duval fit in? Were he and his partner acting alone—two dirty cops—or had Leviathan infiltrated the *Police Nationale*'s higher echelons? The uniforms in the station looked angry and out of the loop, but Duval couldn't have stopped the train without support from his headquarters. From that moment on, for Ben and Clara, no more train stations.

Several blocks north of the station, Ben found what he needed—a boutique electronics store with the kind of cheap knockoff products most people avoid. "Stay out here," he told Clara before going in. "Keep an eye out for police and our two friends."

She set Otto down to let him stretch his legs. "So these cheap phones are better than mine?"

"I'll only be a few minutes."

The concept of a burner phone all but died in the United States and Europe in the early 2010s. Most current sellers require an ID, and most service providers require a credit card and address to connect the device. Only the most disreputable dealers still sell cash phones. Fortunately, Paris has more disreputable dealers than most cities.

Ben picked a Chinese knockoff of a Motorola Razr and handed it to the short man behind the counter. His name tag read YNOVIK—JE PEUX VOUS AIDER? French for *May I help you?*

Ynovik scanned the package. *"Cinquante euro."*

Ben drew a fifty halfway from his wallet, then paused. "How much to activate the phone for me?"

"Another twenty-five, but I need a name and address. It's the law. Seventy-five in total."

Ben pulled out a second bill and handed both over. "Here's a hundred. The name is Jean Tout-le-monde. The address Number Five, Avenue Anatole."

Jean Tout-le-monde. Jean Everyman. He might as well have said John Doe.

Ynovik considered the name and address, pupils drifting, then grinned. "So, Monsieur Tout-le-monde. You live beneath the Eiffel Tower?"

"It's a very expensive flat."

"Yes, it is." Ynovik snatched the bill away and held out his palm again. "That'll be another fifty."

Ben didn't hang around the store to make his call. He and

Clara found a small garden park, surrounded on three sides by a wedge-shaped block of homes and businesses. A wrought-iron fence, overgrown with ivy, offered a touch of cover from the street. He sat down on a bench and dialed the number. "I'll catch no end of grief for what I'm about to do. But we need an exit, and my boss needs to know what's happening. His people will take care of us."

Static buzzed on the line—no surprise with a Chinese knockoff—but Ben could hear it ringing. One. Two. Three. An automated voice answered. "If you know your party's extension, please dial it now." He punched in a nine-digit emergency code. "Thank you," the automated voice said. "One moment, please."

More ringing. One. Two.

Otto trotted over to him, whimpering. The dog met his eyes with a concerned gaze and then turned his head to watch the street. In the next instant, a cacophony of distant sirens grew loud enough to overcome the hum and bustle of the nearby traffic.

Clara looked toward the sound.

Ben tried to reassure her. "We set off an alarm when we used the maintenance exit, that's all. They'll blow right past us a few blocks south, closer to the station. Count on it."

Six rings. Seven.

The sirens grew louder, closer—at least three cars.

"Ben?"

"Hang on. I'm almost through."

Nine. Ten. A screeching tri-tone beep sounded in his ear. "We're sorry. The number you have dialed is no longer in service."

He closed the phone and stood, staring down at it. "This can't be right."

The incoming sirens grew to a deafening blare, accompanied by the chaotic flashing of blue and red lights. Police cars stopped nose to nose, blocking the park's wrought-iron gate.

"Ben Calix! *Ne bougez pas!*" A voice said through a loud-speaker, then repeated itself in English. "Don't move!"

14

Ben crushed the phone under his heel. "I'm really sorry about this."

"Sorry about what?"

He let the ferocity in his eyes give her his answer. With a rough hand, he spun her around and jerked her back against his chest, while Otto yipped and barked. The dog had trusted him before, but manhandling Clara clearly crossed a line. Ben ignored him. He drew the Beretta he'd stolen from Duval and pointed it at the police cars. "Leave me alone!"

A locked gate at the park's rear barred Ben's access to a cobblestone path—the start of a network of residential walkways leading deeper into the block of buildings. Most blocks south of the river had similar networks, and none were alike. Centuries of building and rebuilding had created mazes of paths. Some had street outlets. Not all.

The police showed no inclination to obey his previous command. They poured from their vehicles, taking cover behind the hoods and doors.

"Back!" he yelled and put one round each into the front tire of the closest two.

The men ducked. The Beretta's sharp reports earned him a startled cry from Clara.

She pounded his arm with a fist. "Let me go!" Either she had turned against him, as she should have long before, or she was playing along. He couldn't tell.

One policeman shouted into a radio, and a motorcycle sped in from behind a building, halting next to him—the on-scene commander by the look of things. He pointed east. The motorcycle shot away. The commander was positioning his men, raising the walls of Ben's cage. Good man.

A swift kick busted the park's back gate open. High limestone buildings on either side caused a funnel effect, masking Ben and Clara in shadow as he dragged her through.

The cops maneuvered to keep him in sight but stayed behind their vehicles.

"I said leave us alone!" He aimed the muzzle at Clara's head. "I'll kill her, I swear!"

One brave man made a rush for the front fence, and Ben let out a frustrated growl. He bounced two shots off an iron post, sending up sparks. The man dove for cover behind a bush.

"That's right. Stay back!"

Ben had fired four shots with Duval's gun, two in the tires and two to put hero-cop into the bush. He had three left—he hoped. He didn't know Duval's habits. Maybe he liked to carry a round chambered. Maybe not. Maybe he'd left the office that morning without a full clip. Ben had one more shot for sure. He'd need at least two.

The path curved, hiding them from the cops' sightline. Ben relaxed his hold. "Are you with me?"

"Yes," she said, pushing his arm away. But the anger in her eyes said otherwise. She punched him in the shoulder. "Don't you ever use me as a human shield again."

He made no promises. "Argue later."

Without gunfire to pin them down, the cops would be on

them in moments. The path ended at a T-intersection, with cobblestones leading right and downward steps leading left. "Steps," Ben said, pointing.

Clara scooped up her dog. "Why?"

"The motorcycle went east."

As if that were a reasonable answer, she nodded and followed. They jogged down into a low courtyard, then took a right and jogged up again. Another bend brought them within sight of an arched exit. Ben saw no cars in the two-lane street beyond. He never expected to.

If the motorcycle cop had followed standard procedure, he'd cleared the street of traffic and barricaded himself behind his bike. But to which side of the arch was he waiting? Ben couldn't afford to sneak up and look. He had only seconds, if that, before more cops arrived.

He increased his speed, pushing farther ahead of Clara and staring at a narrow patch of empty street visible through the arch. "Come on, buddy. Give me a sign."

The motorcycle cop did not oblige. No matter. A man in an apron stared out from a café window across the street, looking to Ben's left—just the signal he needed.

He twisted his torso as he ran through the arch, hitting the street with his weapon tracking, seeking the bike and its owner. In an instant, he locked on and pumped one round into the engine. The next two went skimming across the vinyl seat into the cop's upper right chest.

The Beretta's slide locked back. Ben let the weapon drop and kept running.

"You shot him!" Clara yelled, fighting to keep up. "That makes two today!"

"This one'll be fine. He had a vest."

"And the gun? You don't want to keep it?"

"No."

A chopper passed overhead. Ben took the dog, and with

Clara in tow, he ran two blocks farther east and cut through a hall of shops, slowing and looking left and right as he ran out into the light again at a well-traveled boulevard. "All right, kids. Where are you?"

Clara came puffing up behind him. "What kids?"

"Here comes one now."

Scooters took over Paris in 2019—not Vespas, but in-line skateboards with a post and handlebars—strewn about the city by four or five companies, including Uber. Rent a scooter with an app, ride it across the city, and leave it for the next person. Unhindered by traffic, rules, or any sense of civilized behavior, they've become the fastest way around Paris.

But you need a smartphone.

Ben had no smartphone. He did have a gun and a wad of cash, though.

Four scooters headed Ben's way, two in the bike lane and two on the sidewalk. He chose the Bounce brand. They had fatter tires and bigger weight limits.

The young man on the Bounce hit his brakes hard, skidding to a stop with his back wheel off the ground and his face six inches from Ben's Glock and a pair of fifty-euro bills.

"A hundred euros for your ride."

The kid nodded, took the bills, and ran.

Ben made room between his body and the handlebars and nodded at Clara. "Hop on. Once his phone breaks the Bluetooth connection, we'll only have a minute or two of run time."

The chopper had drifted into a slow outward spiral. If the crew ever had a visual on Ben and Clara, they seemed to have lost it. Maybe they wouldn't notice a couple joy-riding on a scooter—at least until someone reported the hijacking.

Ben drove north and east until the scooter died. Its speed took them outside the net of police, but that net would grow fast. He parked on the sidewalk and pulled Clara under an awning. "French cops don't react well to being shot at. I mean"—he bobbled his head—"no cops like it, but these guys have a rep. They'll bring in SWAT teams by the truckload and shoot me on sight without too much worry about who gets caught in the crossfire. We need a place to lie low."

"It is Sunday," Clara said, stroking Otto's ears. "Perhaps we should go to church."

"You're kidding, right? Too many people."

She leaned to look past him down a long lane and thrust her chin at an island in the river. "Not in that one."

Notre Dame. The cathedral had been under renovation for years, with years of work still to come.

"There are no workers on Sundays. I'm sure of it."

He had to give her credit for the idea, but it wouldn't work. Notre Dame was a national treasure standing empty in a city known for persistent squatters. To keep them out, the government had surrounded the renovations with a ten-foot wall of sheet metal, topped with concertina wire and bristling with cameras. "Too much security. We might as well break into the *Ecole Militaire*."

"You think so?"

He sensed a smile in her tone. She knew something he didn't.

Clara took his fingers—just his fingers—and led him toward the river. "You're not the only one in Paris with secrets."

15

Ben and Clara sat on the stepped foundation of Hôtel-Dieu, a giant seventh-century medical center on the Paris river island of Île de la Cité, waiting for the street bordering the construction zone to clear.

A cathedral-shaped shell of pipes and plywood covered two thirds of Notre Dame. Ben shook his head. "Between the lead poisoning of workers and the pandemic, I hear the restoration will drag on late into the decade."

Clara laughed. "She took more than a century to build. What are two or three extra years when you consider the endless backdrop of history?"

Giselle had said something similar before the team left for Morocco.

Ben missed her. Whenever the high stress of a mission threatened to drag him under, even before they started dating, Giselle's *c'est la vie* outlook brought balance. Now, after his failed attempt to contact the Company had brought the entire Paris police force down on his head, he needed some balance.

Ben rested his back against the hospital bricks and saw himself falling into her arms, hearing her whispered comfort. The world had gone off-kilter. Together they'd set it right again. As long as he reached her before Jupiter and Leviathan did.

Clara touched his arm. "You ready?"

Ben sat forward. "No."

The police were spreading an ever-widening net, checking all trains moving out of the city. Giselle might as well be a world away. He had to focus on the present. Ben made a slow nod at a panel in the steel construction wall—one Clara had shown him when they first arrived. "It doesn't look loose to me."

"The workers are not idiots. They pull it tight to keep up appearances."

"And the hazmat procedures?" The fire had vaporized the cathedral's lead roof. After a string of poisonings among the crews, the government mandated new gear and protocols.

"A show for the public. If the crews had to shower every time they wanted a smoke break or a coffee, they'd spend more time in lines than on the job." She tugged at his fingers. "Street's clear. Now's our chance."

The positioning of the security cameras gave credence to her claims. The closest two pointed away from each other, creating a blind spot. Ben ran ahead and pulled the panel's lower corner away for Clara. "How'd you know about this? Are you seeing one of the crewmen?" He cringed at the touch of jealousy in his voice. Where had that come from?

She scrunched her nose and gave him a mysterious smile before squeezing through. "Come inside and I'll tell you."

The loose panel let them into the yard, and Otto trotted ahead into the cathedral, dwarfed by the four-story Portal of the Last Judgement where the central doors had hung. Inside, scorch marks marred the open floor of the cathedral nave. The dachshund spun in a circle and wagged his tail. He seemed to know the place.

Ben turned in a slower circle behind him. "Unbelievable." So much had been stripped away—a throwback to the cathedral's medieval days. Two wings of the old hospital next door might fit end to end in the great emptiness.

Patches of sunlight filtered in through white tent coverings far above. Nearer, below the vault supports and buttresses, a metal net stretched across the nave. Scattered chunks of masonry lay in its grasp. The cracked face of a cherub stared down at Ben through the mesh. He shuddered and looked to Clara. "Haven't they recovered all the debris yet?"

"Those pieces likely fell in the night. The fire weakened the stone more than anyone guessed. Two years later, the church is still crumbling. Shoring it up is an endless task." She lifted a folding chair from a cart, popped it open, and patted the seat. "Come. Sit."

He obeyed, removing his backpack and gloves and setting them between his feet. Otto sniffed at the backpack. Ben shooed him away. "You still haven't told me how you knew about the panel."

"And you still haven't told me why the police showed up the moment you called your precious boss."

She had placed so much faith in him—undeserved despite his earlier confidence. But her faith had waned. He heard it in the question. A reckoning was coming. He delayed a little longer. "So, the panel. Do you work here?"

Clara pulled a first aid box from a plywood cabinet and brought it back, dragging a metal stool close to his chair. "Do I look like a construction worker?"

"Maybe."

She frowned.

He shrugged. Giselle had taught him the proper escape route for such moments. "Who am I to throw up arbitrary gender barriers?"

"Funny." Clara sat with the first aid box on her knees. She drew a miniature water bottle from her purse and poured some on a strip of gauze. "I'm an artist, thank you. I came to Paris to study."

"And that study includes breaking into cathedrals?"

"Take off that silly hat."

He narrowed his eyes. "What's silly about my hat?"

"The way you're using it to hide the gash on the back of your head. It bled through." She yanked the hat off for him and pulled his head down to dab at the wound.

"Ouch!"

"Don't be a baby."

"When did you first notice the blood?"

"On the train." She paused her work to add more water to the gauze.

"You didn't say anything."

"We were busy."

"The panel, Clara." He raised his head.

She grabbed both his temples and pulled him down again. "After the fire, I moved to Paris to sketch the restoration . . . and to avoid returning home to my father. I pitched the project as a master's study to my university in Bratislava. They bought it, and here I am with a full stipend."

"And this project included permission to enter the construction site?" He found it hard to engage in meaningful conversation while staring at his knees.

After a few last painful dabs, Clara lifted his head. "Not exactly. I tried to get permission, but the contractor denied the request. Then one day, while sketching the western façade, I saw two crewmen sneak out for a smoke break. Same thing the next day and the next. The following Sunday, when all the crews had the day off, I took a chance." She lifted a sketchbook from her bag and handed it over. "I've been sneaking in every Sunday since."

The detail in her work stunned Ben. He flipped the page to a sketch of the north gallery columns, shifting his gaze to the real columns and back. A perfect match in both appearance and emotion. The broken stone on the paper bore such texture and loneliness, he imagined he might feel the depth of the cracks and divots if he dared touch the page.

He flipped backward in the book through buttresses, angels, and gargoyles, until he reached sketches from before her arrival in Paris. The earlier work felt darker—a young man bruised and crying, an older man in grubby coveralls passed out at a mechanic's worktable. He wasn't sure she'd meant for him to see those, so he turned back to the column sketch before handing her the book. "These are incredible."

"They're okay."

Clara gave him the bloody gauze and first aid kit in trade and pointed over her shoulder. "The trash can is back there. On your way, you can return the kit and tell me why your call for help brought the *Police Nationale* down on top of us."

The gauze went into Ben's pocket, not the trash. He'd wiped his DNA trail by destroying the apartment. He didn't feel like starting a new one in the middle of Notre Dame.

He wandered up the nave to the altar, gazing at chipped masonwork angels and crumbling prophets. He struggled to find even one intact. "Duval—the man in the brown jacket who grabbed you on the bridge—I think he works for a terrorist group called Leviathan, but he carries a French anti-terrorism division badge."

"So he's a dirty cop." Clara appeared behind him in one of the patches of filtered light. "You said that before. But can a dirty cop command so many police and make them appear at our precise location even after we'd escaped him?"

"I don't know." It killed Ben to say those words. "I made the call. My agency's automated system picked up, and then the line went dead. Maybe the system sensed a local hack trying to break in."

He was reaching—finding excuses for the Company. And he knew it. The operative side of Ben's mind shouted about timing and traces. If Duval or Jupiter's people were trying to hack the call, why had the system waited ten rings before cutting him off? He buried the thought. "Cell tower triangulation."

"What?"

"A hack. Like I said. Leviathan intercepted my call. My agency cut the line, but too late. They'd already gotten a trace." He nodded, trying to convince himself as much as her. "If Leviathan's people infiltrated the *Police Nationale*, they'd have the local resources and the clout required to send in the troops."

The answer seemed to satisfy her.

He wished it had satisfied him. "And now the whole Paris police force is looking for us. They'll have all the exits from the city covered."

"So, we're trapped here."

"I didn't say that. We just need to wait until late tonight, that's all."

Clara stepped closer, lifting her chin. "You sound like you have a plan."

"Don't be fooled by my confidence. It's a spy thing. Fake bravado. I don't have a plan. I have a loosely formed idea that will probably get us both killed."

16

Luis Duval shoved a handkerchief into his sergeant's chest as the two reached the third floor of 36 Rue du Bastion, the *Police Nationale*'s headquarters for criminal investigation and anti-terror operations. "You're bleeding again, Renard. Go to the infirmary."

"But, *Capitaine*, I—"

"Now."

The sergeant tilted his head back with the kerchief to his nose and walked off, feeling his way along the hall's marble panels.

"And you can keep the kerchief, you understand? I don't want it back."

Renard waved.

How had Calix gotten the better of them both?

Foolish question. Duval knew how. The do-not-kill order. Calix had blown up a flat and killed a man—the act of a terrorist. Even with the witnesses and Renard watching, Duval could have justified shooting him. He needed to make a call.

On his way to the tiny windowless office he shared with Renard, he pointed at the section's intern. "I'm not to be disturbed. I don't care if the director general calls."

The young woman opened her mouth to respond.

Duval cut her off with a shake of his finger. "No interruptions." He slammed the door, and the impact's percussion passed through his broken ribs. He groaned and lowered himself into his chair. "Calix."

The secure line took ninety seconds to connect using the encryption app on Duval's smartphone. By strict police regulations, all employees left their personal devices in their lockers, but the rank of captain came with certain privileges—certain rules that no longer applied. Everyone knew this.

He heard a click and a change in the static.

A young voice answered in English. "Go ahead."

"This is Alpha Eight One, secure. I need to speak with your boss."

"Do you have an appointment?"

An appointment? *Imbécile.* Duval leaned forward to place his elbow on the desk, but the pain in his side made him rethink the move. He sat back again, speaking through clenched teeth. "Just put me through. It's urgent."

"One moment."

The line clicked.

"Hello?"

He recognized the American's voice, the touch of Manhattan Greek. He'd never gotten a name, only threats and money. "This is Duval. We need to ___"

"I know who you are. There is a reason we talk so rarely, Captain. The risk is too great."

"Your man Hagen. He's dead." Duval lifted a paper from his desk. "According to a preliminary report, Calix stabbed and shot him before dismembering him with an explosive."

The American laughed. "Not unexpected. Is that all?"

"No. I need clarification."

"You have thirty-five seconds. Go."

Duval checked the clock hanging above his desk. He'd

learned from past experience that when the American set a time limit, he meant it. The second hand passed the one. "Why the do-not-kill order? I can justify shooting Calix on sight. I've done it for you before with targets who've done less."

"I don't want him dead. Not yet. Call it a recruitment exercise." The second hand raced on, passing the three. "Calix is a favorite of my primary competitor. Think of him as the biggest prize on the carnival shelf. You are the ring I'm tossing at the peg to win him in this particular round. Got it?"

Not really. Duval let out a huff he instantly regretted. He needed to get his ribs looked at. "Your competitor is a fool. Calix isn't that good. A civilian spotted him in the park, flashing his gun. The anonymous tip brought half the force flooding in before I could reach the location. I almost lost him to a pack of patrolmen."

"An anonymous tip?"

"Yes." The second had passed the six. Ten more seconds. "Anonymous."

"So, to rephrase, you had a squadron of patrolmen at your disposal, and he escaped you again?"

Duval had walked right into that one. He flattened his tone. "Correct."

"Then perhaps you shouldn't criticize. Find Calix. Hold him alone in a soundproof interrogation room and notify me. I'll send someone to fetch him."

"What about the woman?"

"She's spent too much time with him. I don't want her talking to your people, lending credence to anything Calix tells them. I want him isolated—completely. When you take him down, make sure she doesn't survive." The second hand hit the seven. The line went dead.

17

Suspicions nagged Ben. He needed confirmation. "I'm going on an excursion."

Clara lay between the shelves of tagged stone fragments, snuggled under her coat with Otto. She pushed herself up on an elbow. "It's ten to eleven. You said we should wait until after midnight."

"I know what I said. Stay here." He checked the magazine of his Glock 42 and slid it into the holster inside his waistband.

She narrowed her eyes. "I thought you didn't like guns."

"What makes you say that?"

"Duval's gun. You threw it away. You said you didn't want it."

"My gun is a .380. So are all my spare rounds. Duval's was a Beretta nine-mil, which I emptied ticking off the French police. A gun with no bullets is just a burden." He covered the Glock with his sweatshirt. "You get some rest. There are egg white protein bars in my pack if you're hungry. I'll be gone two hours."

"And what if you do not come back in two hours?"

"I will."

During the hours of quiet, staring up at the cathedral's torched stones, Ben had tried to link all the day's events to the mysterious Jupiter. But every solution required leaps of logic he couldn't

83

afford. The answers, like lost sheep, wouldn't come home on their own. So, like any good shepherd, he set out to find them.

Notre Dame sat on an island in the Seine, known locally as Île de la Cité and to the rest of the world as the Island of Paris. He crossed to the city's south side using the Double Bridge, named in antiquity for its toll rather than its size. Restricted to foot traffic, with foliage at three of its four corners, the Double Bridge offered more cover than the island's other four. The late hour and the long manhunt had thinned the police presence. Cops patrolled the streets as pairs instead of troops.

More than once, waiting for a patrol to pass or turn their backs, the temptation to ditch Clara struck Ben. Justifications came at him in his own voice.

Traveling with a civilian and her dumb dog is insane—bad craft, and you know it.

You'll both be caught. What good will that do?

Leave now. It'll be a gift, not a betrayal.

He shook the arguments off. Until he learned more, he couldn't leave her. To walk away might mean handing her over to Leviathan, an organization that had murdered thousands in the last six months.

At a quarter to midnight, Ben's day came full circle. He cut across Rue Cler and ducked into the dead-end alley where the sniper's bullets had almost removed his head. He went straight to the spot where he'd dropped his phone, but it had vanished. Either the sniper or some passerby had taken it, as expected. But Ben hadn't risked this journey for the phone.

Voices. Two men.

He pressed his back against the alley wall, behind the dubious cover of a nineteenth-century rainspout, and turned his head as much to hide the moisture from his breath as to shrink his profile. Duval might be dirty, but not these men. Ben had no desire to hurt them. He willed them with all his might to move on.

The cops paused at the alley entrance. "How much longer must we continue this madness?" one asked, speaking French. "The night is cold. I'm starving. And this American imbecile and his woman could be in Calais by now, for all we know. They're gone."

"We're done when the lieutenant says we're done."

"Yeah, yeah. So you keep saying."

The wall across from Ben lit up. A flashlight beam panned to the alley's end and froze.

He held his breath. After too many heartbeats, the beam evaporated.

"Come on. I know an all-night bodega on the next block. I'll buy you a bag of macarons to still that rumbling belly."

The voices drifted off.

Ben released a great fog of breath and continued his work. He clicked on a penlight and searched the cobblestones.

A streak of char marked the spot where the sparking phone had fallen. He panned the light up the wall beside it to head level and found a pockmark—a hole, really. Limestone never held up well against high-velocity rounds. He shined the light inside, and his shoulders drooped.

Nothing. The sniper had cleaned up his own mess, digging his slugs from the wall.

The second and third holes confirmed it. No slugs. No answers. A wasted trip. Ben sighed and let himself fall back against the limestone to rest and prepare for the trip back through the police net.

Something glinted in the beam of his penlight.

Ben panned the light over the cobblestones and found the object again, in the crack between two blocks. He dropped to a crouch. Fingers wouldn't do the job, but the multi-tool he'd brought along worked nicely. Steel scraped against stone and grout as he worked the tool's needle-nose pliers into the crack. Carefully, he drew out a metal sliver—a curved piece of a dark alloy. He held it under the penlight. The sniper had not been so thorough after all. He'd left a bullet fragment behind.

The alloy looked familiar. Ben dropped the sliver into his fingers to measure the weight and rigidity. Tungsten carbide.

He sat back on his heels and lowered his head. A name fell from his lips. "Sensen."

18

A trio of policemen unknowingly pinned Ben down in the boxwoods of René Viviani Square, across the water from Notre Dame. The cops hadn't seen him, but they hung out on the Double Bridge, smoking and shooting the breeze at the dead center.

Often the best thing an operative can do is wait. Diversions and distractions are designed to draw attention. Gunshots and broken windows are great for pulling a sentry away from a gate or street corner, but in the long run, when you're trying to disappear, they only invite more trouble.

French cops and their smoke breaks.

The group hung around for another thirty minutes, so long Ben almost nodded off. When he finally got moving again, after more than two hours in the city, the cathedral island's streetlamps looked like warm windows in a cabin at the edge of a dark wood.

Ben checked the river on the way across. A thin coating of vapor hung over the surface, building fast. The cooling air trapped in the canal above the Seine had started its nightly winter magic. He and Clara needed to get moving, but as he quickened his steps, the hairs on the back of his neck stood up.

He heard heavy breathing. Or was it the scuff of his own soles against the cobblestones?

The river made sounds hard to trace. Ben put a hand near his gun and checked the steps to the water at the north. Silent—nothing but stone and moss. He relaxed.

The *crunch* of steel against the base of Ben's skull sent a shock wave through his body. He crumpled, groaning, blinking to banish the haze from his vision. Instinct kicked in. He felt the Glock's grip already in his palm, halfway out of the holster.

"Do it, Mr. Calix. Draw your weapon." A man, breathing heavy and wearing a familiar brown jacket, materialized from the blur in Ben's vision. He bent close to hold a compact revolver a foot from Ben's nose. "Give me a reason to shoot."

"I'd rather not, Monsieur Duval."

"It's *capitaine. Capitaine Duval.* Get to your feet. I'm tired and hurt. And I'm sick of this game."

Duval's gun arm hung a little low, a result of his broken ribs. Ben guessed he couldn't hold the revolver much higher than his navel without serious pain. "Is that your spare?" He grinned and answered his own question. "Must be. Your Beretta is probably in an evidence lockup by now. I bet it's embarrassing for an SDAT investigator to have his piece stolen, emptied in a standoff with patrolmen, and tossed into the street."

"I said, get up."

"Sure." Ben took his time. Nausea swept over him, threatening to knock him down again. He swallowed back his bile and straightened. "How'd you find me?"

"Our police forces are covering the roads and trains, leaving you only one route out of this district—the river. I've been patrolling the south bank. Tell me. Where is the girl?"

He must not have seen Ben leaving the cathedral earlier. He hadn't found Clara's hiding place.

"She ditched me."

"Smart girl. I'll find her for you. I'll take good care of her."

A surge of pain washed through Ben's head, sending another wave of nausea through his gut. It might have been concern for Clara. Then again, he'd taken two good knocks in the same day. He'd be lucky to get out of this without long-term damage.

Duval had him—wounded and covered. But the cop hadn't called in the troops. Not a good sign. "Who are you working for? Jupiter? Leviathan?"

Duval's eyes went vacant for a fraction of a second. He didn't seem to recognize those names.

Ben chuckled. "Do you even know who you're working for?"

"I work for a man who pays well and wants to speak with you. That is enough."

So, he didn't know. Another answer remained out of Ben's reach. "Sorry to disappoint your boss, but I won't be taken alive."

"I can't tell you how gratified I am to hear you say that."

"Don't be. Previous experience tells us your chances of winning this fight are slim." Ben's hand inched along his hip.

The cop saw. "Yes. Good." Duval slowly raised the revolver to level, clenching his jaw against the pain. "A gunfight is what I want, like something from your Old West movies. But before we see who's fastest, you should know something. The girl—"

A flash of gray appeared in the lamplight, crashing against Duval's temple. His eyes went wide and a rasp escaped his lips as he fell forward to his knees. Clara stood behind him, holding a chunk of stone from a cathedral statue.

"What did you do?" Ben asked.

She set the stone on the ground and lifted her hands away, leaving half of a scorched shepherd's face to stare up at the night sky. "I'll put it back. I swear."

"That's not what I meant."

Trailing blood, Duval rolled over and aimed his gun at Clara. Ben kicked it away, then fell to his knee, driving a punch down into the same spot Clara had hit with the rock.

The cop went still. Ben grabbed him by the ankles, dragging him toward the steps. "We have to move. Help me."

She stared at him.

"Now, Clara!"

She picked up the revolver and aimed at Duval.

"Don't you fire that thing." Ben spoke the words as a growl. "A gunshot'll bring every cop in Paris down on us. Plus, I'm not making you into a cop killer, dirty or not." He kept dragging Duval, around the stone rail and down the stairs. The man's head bounced on every other step.

Clara followed in a daze, holding the gun in both hands. "He . . . He was going to kill you."

"Story of my life."

She never helped him, only watched, as Ben laid Duval out flat on the river walk, under the bridge. He removed Duval's belt, flipped him over, and bound his hands, then flipped him again and went through his pockets. The wallet went in the river—after Ben confiscated the cash, of course. And he found two moon clips of .38 Special to feed the revolver.

Cautiously, he took the gun from Clara. "How about I hold on to this for you, hmm? This one came with extra bullets, so it's worth keeping." When she didn't respond, he touched her cheek. "Hey, you with me? Where's Otto?"

"In the cathedral. Asleep."

"Good. That's good. Why don't you go get him while I stay here and clean up this mess? Grab my go-bag too. We're leaving."

19

At the schoolhouse, Colonel Hale had opened Ben's Escape and Evasion course by extolling the virtues of fog. A man-made smokescreen is, by its very nature, also a signal. A Mark 18 smoke grenade obscures your activity on a battlefield, but it also declares your position to the enemy. Fog and mist are natural. Fog a gift from the Almighty.

The rivers running through the larger European cities make fog nightly, and in most, it grows densest in winter. Utilities and tunnels running under the water pull heat from the city. When the night air trapped between the channel walls grows cold, the warm spray at the surface creates a blanket of vapor, thickest in the wee hours. Even advanced thermal sensors struggle to penetrate its natural cover. Spies and the specialists who hunt them both have a name for this effect.

"We call it the smuggler's mist." Ben helped Clara up onto the deck of a houseboat, secured for the winter at a post not far from the place they'd left Duval. The vapor had grown so thick, he couldn't see the channel wall, less than ten meters away. "Surveillance guys hate it. Plays havoc with every form of optical sensor. Thermal, infrared—doesn't matter. Cops searching with their naked eyeballs alone don't stand a chance."

Stealing the houseboat's tiny skiff required no more effort than cutting a line with his KA-BAR and turning a crank. Together they lowered it to the water, and Ben loosened the tarp's stern end. He climbed in. "Give me the dog."

"Otto."

"Whatever."

"If you are going to steal a boat," she said, handing him the dachshund, "why not one with a motor? Won't it be faster?"

Otto paddled his legs in desperation until Ben had him safely on the skiff floor, nestled on a life preserver under the aft bench. "We need stealth, not speed." He held out a hand. "You next."

She clearly hadn't spent much time in small watercraft. The skiff appropriated her nervousness, wobbling so much as she stepped in that even Otto gave her a frustrated look. Ben steadied her all the way down to the bench. He didn't let go of her hand, long after she'd settled, studying her face. Her timing had been impeccable. How would Duval have finished his last statement if Clara hadn't slammed a priceless chunk of masonry into his temple? *Before we see who's fastest, you should know something. The girl—*

"Why are you looking at me like that?" Clara asked.

"It's nothing." He let go and looked away. "I mean . . . I'm not."

She lifted the KA-BAR from the houseboat deck, slapping the hilt into his palm. "Don't forget this."

"I won't."

When he opened his go-bag and dropped the knife in, Clara reached in after it. Going for the revolver? He flinched.

She drew out a protein bar, frowning at his response. "What's wrong? You don't want me to have this? You said to eat one if I got hungry."

"Right. Sure."

She set the wrapped bar on her knees and dove in again.

"Hey," Ben said.

"I need one for Otto too."

"The dog?"

"You want him to starve?"

The dachshund raised his head, releasing something between a mutter and growl, as if Ben was riding on the edge of his good graces.

Along with the second egg white bar, Clara drew out a thick roll wrapped in cellophane. "Forget egg whites. We should be feeding him steak. There must be thousands of euros in this roll."

"Ten thousand, to be exact." Ben closed the bag before she could start counting the rest. "Going on the run gets expensive. For instance—" He plucked the roll from her fingers, poked a hole in the center, and pulled out a 500-euro note the way he might pull a Kleenex from a box. He crumpled it into a ball and tossed it onto the houseboat deck before pushing away. They drifted noiselessly toward the faster current at the river's center. "That's to compensate our benefactor for the skiff."

"Won't the owner find the boat once we're done with it?"

"No. We'll have to sink her. We don't want the police figuring out where we put in."

The current checked the drift and held the skiff near the river's center. They picked up speed, maybe four knots. At that rate, they'd be out of the city in two hours. Ben hoped the smuggler's mist would hold that long.

Clara lifted a small case from her purse and shook out a couple of pills. "Take these."

He let her set them in his hand. They had no markings. "What are they?"

"Ibuprofen. Your head hurts, right?"

"Right."

"Then take the pills. Show a little faith, please."

Faith. Tess had mentioned faith. The day had shaken Ben's—in the Director and in Clara. But the pounding in his head drowned out his suspicions. "Yeah . . . okay."

He chased the pills with water from his go-bag, then settled in for the long haul. He sat on the bottom and pushed his feet toward the bow, resting his shoulders against the bench. "You, too," he said, tapping Clara's arm. "We'll cover up with the tarp before we reach the tower. The Champ de Mars and Quai Branly never sleep. The cops'll be watching the streets there for sure, maybe patrol the bridges too."

"If we're hiding under the tarp, how will you steer?"

"No need. The current near the river's center will lock us in." He laid a hand on a plastic paddle clipped to the interior hull. "The hard part will be getting to shore south of the city."

Clara squeezed in beside him and used a life vest as a cushion for her neck. Otto had claimed the other one as a bed. Ben let him keep it. He needed a little discomfort, anyway—to keep him awake. His eyes felt heavy. He pressed his body against the hull to give Clara some room. "What were you doing outside the cathedral?"

"What else? Looking for you."

"I told you I'd come back."

"Oh yes. I remember. You said you would come back in two hours. 'What if you do not?' I asked. And what did you say?" She deepened her voice, adding some Texan. "'I will, little lady.'"

"I didn't say 'little lady.'" He laid his head back, trying not to put pressure on the painful knots back there, and looked up through wisps of vapor at the void above—no stars, no discernible clouds. Just emptiness. "And I don't sound like that."

"Perhaps not, but you did say two hours. You were gone almost three. I was worried. I took a stone for protection and came looking." She pulled her coat tight about her. "I also thought you might have run away."

"If I wanted to ditch you, I would have done it this morning. And if I had, you'd be dead."

She snorted. "So would you."

"I had Duval handled."

"Mm-hmm." She mimicked him with the bad southern accent again. "I had it handled."

"Stop that."

An echo of voices interrupted the argument. Ben touched at her arm. "Here comes Quai Branly. Help me with the tarp."

She held it taut while he stuffed the corners under a bungee cord strapped to the stern gunwale. The two lay there, scrunched so close together that when Clara rolled her head toward him, her breath tickled his ear. "Are you sure this will work?"

"Gray boat, gray tarp. In this fog, we're invisible. Trust me."

"What do you think I've been doing all day?"

He felt the sting in her voice, despite the whisper's softness. She had trusted him—over and over. Why did he find it so hard to return the favor?

Some tragic secret had died on Duval's tongue when Clara knocked him out. Ben had seen it in his eyes—heard it in his voice. The dirty cop knew something about her. Maybe it had been the plans he had for her after killing Ben. Maybe he'd been a breath away from revealing her as a plant. She might be the reason the police had found them in the park and the reason Duval had found him at the bridge. Hale had warned his entire class.

The deadliest betrayals come from those closest to us, people. Watch your backs.

In a few short hours, had Ben let this woman get too close?

When he considered their relationship, she'd been close to him for months, even if he'd tried to push her away. How many times had she run into him in the stairwell? Were all their meetings chance? Were any of them?

Trust me. Ben's words. Maybe his error too.

The boat shifted sideways, tempting him to peel back the tarp, but the current soon corrected the drift. The river must

95

have split at the narrow island southwest of the Eiffel Tower. The voices faded. "We're clear," he said. "But keep the tarp in place."

Clara rolled onto her side. "What about river traffic?"

"No traffic at this hour—not in winter. We'll be safe all the way to Meudon. An hour and a half or so."

"In that case, I'm going to sleep. You should too." With no small amount of bumping and bustling, she unfolded the life vest. "Here. Lift your head. We can share it as a pillow. This aluminum shell cannot be healthy for those bumps on your head."

He let her slide a portion of the vest into place behind him. "Thanks. I'll stay awake, though. One of us has to."

"Suit yourself." She closed her eyes, leaving him alone with no sound but the steady *chirr* of Otto's nasally breathing.

Ben stared at the tarp's underside, a few inches above his head.

Trust me.

The thought came fuzzy this time. He had a hard time keeping it in focus. He had a hard time keeping any thought in focus. Important questions had occurred to him before the shift of the current passing the island had stolen his attention. He tried and failed to recapture them.

Ben closed his eyes and saw Duval. He saw the revolver extended, the cop's smirk, some vicious revelation forming on his lips. But a crashing rock had cut him short. Luck?

Show a little faith. He heard her voice this time, not his.

He saw Duval crumple—saw Clara behind him, frightened. No.

Had she looked frightened? Or had his memory filled a gap with an assumed detail. The light from the streetlamps and the growing fog had obscured his vision. Had he seen her face clearly enough to register fear? He lost his hold on the image.

His thoughts dissolved into black.

20

Ben woke to the sting of a finger flicking the end of his nose. He swatted the finger away, and the back of his hand grazed the underside of a tarp. Why was he lying beneath a tarp?

"Hey, wake up," Clara flicked his nose again. "We've stopped."

The tarp. The skiff. Ben's head felt ready to split. He groaned. Clara moved to flick his nose again.

He fended her off. "I'm awake."

"Really? You don't sound awake, especially not for a man who declared only hours ago that he refused to sleep."

A shock of fright-induced cortisol snapped him to full wakefulness. He rolled onto his side. "Hours?" The drift south to Meudon should have taken no more than ninety minutes. "How many hours?"

Clara showed him a watch, some Fitbit knockoff with a rectangular face and pink glowing numbers. "Too many, I think. It is a quarter to five."

"Why did you let me sleep?"

"Let you? You're the one in charge, remember? And I only woke up moments ago. Now get up and get us moving."

Clara's indignation raised her voice too far above a whisper

97

for Ben's comfort. "Quiet," he said, and pulled the tarp free from the bungee cord holding it in place. He rolled it back.

The skiff had come to rest in a tangle of willow branches bending low to reach the water. The fog remained as thick as ever, but black willows meant they'd reached St. Germain, a mile-long island near the 150-degree bend where the Seine snaked from south to north after leaving Paris. Meudon, their goal, might be a hundred meters away, or it might be a thousand, depending on what part of the island had trapped the boat. With zero visibility, they'd have to feel their way along the shore to find out.

Ben unclipped the plastic oar. "Sun'll be up in three hours. We have to keep moving." He poked at a willow branch. "Sit up and help me get us loose."

They clawed their way along St. Germain's shoreline a few meters at a time. Over and over, Ben pushed away, with Clara paddling on the other side, and the river pushed them back into the willows. The repetitive work got his mind churning again.

Ben's worries over Duval's interrupted revelation returned, compounded by his long sleep. He'd never struggled with staying awake for all-night missions before. He grabbed a willow branch and muscled the skiff onward for another five-meter run. "Did you drug me?"

"Did I what?"

"You gave me pills. I fell asleep." He pushed off the next branch, grunting with the effort. "I don't fall asleep on the job. Ever."

"I gave you ibuprofen."

"So you say."

Clara stopped paddling. "You think I'm working against you? Do you think I wanted to smash a policeman's head with a rock and spend the night half-frozen in a tiny boat with a man I hardly know? You are insane."

The boat hit the willows. Ben pushed it off again. "You never answered the question. Did you drug me? Better yet, did you give my position to the cops or Duval? Are you part of this?"

"I can't believe you. I saved your life, and this is my thanks." She dipped her oar in the water and started paddling again. "Think what you want."

One moment the willows seemed an unending barrier. In the next, the skiff sailed into open water. Ben took over the paddling. Wooden docks appeared in the mist to his left. Meudon. They'd made it.

Neither spoke a word as the two climbed out, even when Ben kept Clara from pitching sidelong into the water. The moment she had both feet on the dock, she jerked her elbow free. Ben frowned and retrieved Otto, setting him at her feet. The dachshund yawned and stretched, unfazed by the strangeness of his night.

The first gray hint of morning dusted the eastern horizon over the old-world suburbia of Meudon. Ben hefted his backpack up to his shoulder. "I'll be setting a quick pace. Try to keep up."

Three blocks southeast of the river, on a street lined with multifamily homes, Clara broke the silence. "This town. This is where your imaginary girlfriend lives?"

"Giselle. Yes. Her flat is two blocks west."

Clara's gaze shifted up the street. "Good. I'm only minutes away from a shower."

"Hours, actually."

The look she gave him said she wished she'd brought her bludgeoning rock along.

Ben let out a frustrated grunt. "Giselle won't be at her flat, okay? And I've never set foot in the place. We keep our personal and professional identities well clear of each other. She has another place, one nobody knows about but us."

"How far?"

"Almost five kilometers. The cottage is in Chaville, on the

far side of the Meudon Forest Reserve. But first . . ." He slowed as they approached the next street corner. "A little shopping."

"Not another burner phone." She turned to stand in front of him, scratching Otto's ears. "Remember how well that went last time?"

He sensed from her wry expression that she knew the real reason he'd stopped—the reason he needed to risk exposing his face to security cameras at an all-night pharmacy. She knew. He felt it. But he told her anyway. "We have to deal with your hair."

"You've always hated this color."

"Funny. But this isn't about fashion. It's about disappearing. Pick a new color, and I'll go in and get it for you."

Her lips parted with a reply.

Ben held up a finger. "If you say purple or green, I'm out of here. No pink either."

She dropped her gaze. "Yeah. Okay."

"What's your natural color?"

"Boring."

He didn't have time for this. "Stay here. Keep the dog quiet."

The young clerk at the register kept his eyes buried in a phone. That suited Ben fine, until he saw his own picture in the kid's Twitter feed—a grainy shot of him dragging Clara backward with a gun to her head. The photographer had snapped the shot from high up, probably through the window of a nearby building. The clerk scrolled on.

Had he seen it?

Ben snatched up a basket and picked out a box of dye marked *Autumn Sunrise* in four languages. The wavy locks in the picture looked amber to him, but what did he know? He dropped it in the basket and added a half dozen other items on his way to the counter.

"Bonjour." The clerk kept scrolling his Twitter feed. With the other hand, he ran Ben's items across the scanner and dropped them into a plastic bag. *"Comptant ou carte de crédit?"*

Ben slapped down a fifty-euro note. He had several midsize bills left, thanks in part to the cash he'd taken from Duval. But if he, Giselle, and Clara had to hold out on their own for a couple of days or more before getting Company help, he might have to find someone willing to break a five hundred.

The clerk punched a button to kick open the register drawer and counted out the change. *"Merci."*

Ben headed for the street.

"Wait."

He stopped, watching the rounded mirror above the door. For the first time since he'd walked in, the clerk had looked up from his phone.

"I forgot to scan the bag. They are fifteen cents."

Ben rubbed his eyes to obscure his face as he returned to the counter, playing the part of a man still in need of his morning coffee. Through his fingers, he spied his picture once more on the kid's Twitter feed. Same pic, different post. Below the main text, he saw #savethedachshund.

Great.

He held up the bag for the kid to scan.

"I am sorry." The clerk ran a handheld laser over the barcode. "But my manager—he does not like it when I forget."

Ben set a one-euro coin on the counter. "Keep the change." He walked out.

The forest reserve began one street to the south, after an abrupt end to the city—a twelve-hundred-acre reserve with soccer fields and cricket pitches nestled among its oaks and chestnuts. The most direct route to the cottage involved more than four kilometers of trails, but Ben led Clara an extra five hundred meters out of the way to a runners' club called *Le Sentier*.

They hadn't officially opened for the day, but Ben slipped the manager a hundred—well above the cost of a locker rental— then walked Clara around the long green cinderblock building to the women's locker room. "You mentioned wanting a shower. There's no need to make you wait. Besides, we should change your hair color sooner than later." He gave her the bag from the pharmacy. "I'm fairly certain you know how this works."

She opened the plastic bag and peeked inside. "So do you. Shampoo. Applicator. Gloves. You've done this before."

"The need to change my appearance comes up a lot in my line of work."

Clara lifted out a bag of gummy bears. "And this?"

"You said you were hungry. And . . ." He glanced away, keeping an eye on their six. At least, that's what he told himself. "I, uh . . . I've seen those in your groceries once or twice when we've bumped into each other in the stairwell."

That earned him a smile. "Give me a few minutes, okay?"

"Yeah. Sure." He retreated to a wooden bench across the trail.

A few minutes became twenty, then twenty-five. A couple of customers went in. Ben watched the sky through the bare oak branches with growing unease. Only the most diehard runners hit the forest trails in the dark of a winter's morning. That would change once the sun came up. Hikers. Runners. Too many people who might have seen the social media posts. Why'd the Twitterati have to make such a fuss about the dog? He glanced down at Otto. "You're going to get us all killed, you know."

The dachshund lowered his chin to his paws.

Clara emerged a moment later, and Ben hopped up, more quickly than he'd intended. She'd pulled her hair back into a tousled ponytail, now a light amber brown. She did a slow twirl. "Well?"

She looked different. She looked good. "Uh . . . Good work with the dye."

"Yes. Because 'good work' is what every girl wants to hear about her new hairstyle." Clara kneeled, calling Otto to her side. She scratched his chin. "I will say, you matched my natural color. How did you know?"

"Seemed right for you. That's all." It did seem right, more so than the blue, which he realized now had never let her eyes take center stage. He cleared his throat. "Let's go. We're losing our darkness."

Ben set a quick pace on the trail, gauging how fast he could move without leaving her behind. As they found their rhythm, a cross breeze brought a scent to his nose. Lavender. Ben had bought Clara a small bottle of generic shampoo. No scent. "Where'd the soap come from?"

"I borrowed some body wash from a runner. Nice girl."

He tried not to growl.

She looked up at him. "I didn't tell her anything."

"You didn't have to. There's no way she missed the fact you were dyeing your hair."

"She would have noticed anyway. And I spent the night in a tiny boat on a dirty river with an angry, smelly spy. I needed some pampering. Sue me."

"I don't smell."

Clara raised an eyebrow. "Mm-hmm. So, this woman. Giselle."

Ben's answer came as quick as his steps. "She won't mind."

"Won't mind what?"

It took him a full second to realize Clara had moved past the spent-the-night-together-in-a-skiff topic to a new one. "Nothing. What were you saying?"

"How long have you been seeing each other?"

"A few weeks."

"And this is enough to know you love her?"

The question's abruptness nearly cost him his footing. A runner passed by, giving him time to compose his answer. "A few days ago, Giselle risked getting infected with the plague just to kiss me. We've never said the words, but if that's not love, I don't know what is."

Clara stopped, letting him shoot out ahead.

Ben frowned and beckoned her onward with a tilt of his head. "No, I don't have the plague. I got checked out."

"If you say so."

"I do. The doc gave me a clean bill of health. Now hurry up."

The more trail they covered, the less Ben worried that this lavender-scented girl meant him harm. His earlier suspicions seemed almost comical. He'd been watching her for signs of deception, and seen none. And if Clara had a transmitter to give away his position, she'd had plenty of chances to use it. No cops had come. No Leviathan assassins had appeared on the trail.

Whatever Clara's real story, Ben felt confident he and Giselle could handle her together. Whether at home or in a hotel, Giselle always answered the door armed, and Ben had two guns and his KA-BAR. Clara had a yippy dog.

The forest thinned. Ahead, their trail ended at a T intersection, where it split to wrap around a small lake. Ben pointed. "There, the redbrick cottage on the other side. The one with the dock and the cream-colored Peugeot 308 in the drive."

Caution and training prevented Ben from caving in to his desire to run around the lake. He led Clara off the trail, into the trees. They found a dry patch of dead leaves, colored orange by the rising sun, and he kneeled to unshoulder his pack. He fished a sniper scope from the side pouch and held it to his eye.

Clara hung close, as if by leaning against him she might be able to see through the scope as well. "Is she there?"

"The Peugeot is hers. She bought it last summer. I'm just confirming."

"And she'll be alone?"

"Yes." He didn't see any movement at the perimeter. More than a hundred meters of lakeshore separated her place from the nearest cottages to the northeast and southwest—vacation homes, empty through the winter. Giselle had been prudent in her choice. "She told me she paid cash. Untraceable. The place is clean."

A light flipped on in the kitchen.

Giselle.

The blinds blocked his view, but it had to be her. She'd never been an early riser—hated predawn starts to their operations. He could hear her voice now, pouring herself a cup of coffee. *I hate getting up in the dark. It seems so unnatural, yes?*

"She's there," Ben said, rising to his feet. He couldn't wait any longer. He glanced down to stuff the scope into his bag, and a deafening explosion shattered the morning calm.

21

Ben sprinted down the lakeshore trail, a maddening circular route of nearly a quarter mile. And all the while, the fire burned.

Maybe she had survived. Maybe she had seen the bomb and taken cover before it blew. He'd walked through the cottage with her during some stolen time together before the team left for Morocco. The kitchen had a modern fridge. Free-standing. Or the cast-iron radiator in the mudroom might offer some protection.

The radiator.

"Giselle, get out! Get out!"

The cottage had central heating, fueled by a forty-year-old oil tank in the cellar. The realtor had boasted about the owner refilling the tank without adding a cent to the asking price, enough for two winters—three thousand liters of oil.

The massive secondary explosion knocked him off his feet, stopping him within thirty meters of his goal. Ben rolled onto his side, ears ringing. "No!"

The fire burned with a new intensity. The oil had set the hedges and grass ablaze. He forced himself up again, tried to push closer. By the time he reached the drive, the heat had formed an impenetrable wall.

He wanted to cry out, but his voice had no strength left.

"Ben!" Clara jogged up behind him, shouting over the roar. "There's nothing you can do."

He turned, whipping out the Glock. "You." Instinct. Auto-pilot. Only Ben and Giselle knew about the cottage. No one else. No one except Clara. "You did this."

She backed away, Otto cowering at her ankles. "What? Why would I?"

"You're part of this. You're with Leviathan. The woman in Rome. Did you kill Massir? Were you the assassin who met him at the Pantheon? We both know you brained Duval before he could give me answers."

Her pupils darted left and right, either searching for a handle on the moment or searching for a lie. "I don't know what you are talking about."

"The intercepted call. The cops in the train station. Duval showing up at the cathedral. All of that was you."

"You're insane. Listen to yourself. I heard Duval tell you how he found us. I hit him to stop him from shooting you. Think, Ben. This is the grief talking."

The fire department would be coming soon. The police too. Ben's head throbbed. He pressed what he thought was a knuckle against his temple, then felt the heat and realized it was the barrel of his Glock.

Clara took a step toward him, reaching. He answered with his own advance, putting the gun to her throat. Then he changed his mind and swept up her dog. Ben knew how to settle this. He put the gun to the dachshund's head and growled through his teeth. "The truth. Tell me who you work for, or watch me blow Otto's little head off." If it weren't for his grief, he'd have felt ridiculous, but he needed to know her motives.

"No. Please, Ben." She broke down into sobs. "Listen to me. I am not this person you think I am. Please don't hurt him."

The backpack lay on the trail, a dozen meters or more

away. In his hurry and distress, Ben had left it behind. Clara had brought it for him, but at no time had she gone for either weapon inside—the KA-BAR or the revolver. She didn't have an assassin's instincts.

He lowered the gun to his side and pressed Otto into her arms. "Okay."

She sniffled. "Okay? Okay what?"

"Okay, I believe you. Assassins and spies don't have dogs. They can't be tied down. And your tears tell me Otto is no prop."

"Threatening to shoot him. This was a test?"

He holstered his weapon. "I'm sorry."

Clara took one step closer and slapped him across the face. "You are a monster."

"I know." He wandered over to the Peugeot, running on the same autopilot that had drawn his gun. "The police are coming. We have to keep running."

The Peugeot had survived the blast, minus the passenger side windows and mirror. Ben kicked out a patch of flame on the front right tire and tucked his hand into his jacket sleeve to knock burning debris off the roof and hood. He brushed the shattered glass off the passenger seat and stood clear, pulling the door wide for Clara and her dog. "Get in."

She didn't argue, though he knew she had every reason to walk away.

On the way around the hood to the driver's side, a chunk of black plastic caught Ben's eye, lying on the drive's white gravel. It looked like a corner fragment of a small box, with insulated wire and a piece of silicone chip melted to the interior. Definitely not a piece of the car. He slipped it into his pocket and dropped to a knee to hotwire the ignition under the daggers of Clara's glare.

"I really am sorry," he said, getting behind the wheel. "I had to be sure you were telling the truth."

She let out a huff. "Just drive."

◻ ◻ ◻

Numbness.

Ben couldn't feel pain anymore, not the bruise under his eye from Hagen's fist or the double knot on the back of his head from the crash into the mirror and the strike from Duval's gun. He felt only tingling numbness, like a man phasing out of existence, leaving nothing in the place of his flesh and bone but rage.

The explosion had drawn witnesses who saw the Peugeot leaving the scene. The police would find them, get descriptions. Ben kept to the side roads in a maddening zigzag race for the western border.

"I'm sorry," Clara said thirty minutes into the journey.

"For what."

"For your loss. I'm still angry with you for the accusations—for threatening Otto—but I can see Giselle was both love and dear friend to you. And these people you are fighting. They took her. I'm sorry."

"She knew the risks of our profession. We both did. We walked into the job and the relationship with our eyes open."

Clara turned in her seat, scowling. "What an idiotic thing to say."

Her audacity shook him from his daze. "What do you know about it?"

"You think I haven't heard this phrase before? Hmm? 'He knew the risks.' Is this supposed to bring anyone comfort?"

He knew the risks. The hurt in her voice spoke of someone she loved. *He.* "Your brother."

"I told you Peter took my father's anger for me. He stayed as long as I needed protecting, but when I went off to art school in Bratislava, he took his chance. He joined the army."

"The Slovak Ground Forces?" From what Ben knew about the organization—mostly a shooting club for Soviet-era artillery enthusiasts—the job carried little danger.

"No. The British army. He called ours a joke, and the Brits offered him citizenship for service." Clara hugged Otto tight. "Peter passed an English test at our village church. Seven months later, he finished training as a nurse in their Army Medical Service. Three months after that, he died in a UK hospital. He'd contracted COVID-19 from a patient. A messenger service delivered the letter to our doorstep." She laughed. "A letter. Nothing more. Not the journal he kept. No dog tags. I took the bus home from Bratislava to read it for Father, because his English is terrible. But he must have figured it out. He drank himself into oblivion before I arrived."

Ben remembered thumbing through her book—the sketch of the man passed out at a mechanic's worktable. He had seen it as a study of an old drunk. But Clara had sketched a study in grief.

"'He knew the risks,'" she said, spitting out the words. "Peter's commander wrote that in his letter. 'He was brave. He knew the risks.' How are those any comfort?"

Ben kept quiet, eyes on the road.

"No one asked me about the risks. No one asked Father. And Peter signed up to escape our home, to find a better life, not to become some cog in their machine. Expendable. There is a phrase for it." She rubbed her forehead, as if trying to recall. "I found it on the internet, the percentage of soldiers who will die, written into the general's plan."

"Acceptable loss."

She looked at him, eyes full of tears. "Yes. But it is not acceptable. My brother. Your Giselle. The deaths of those we love are never acceptable."

Clara fell silent, staring out the broken window, and Ben let her declaration stand for them both.

Not acceptable.

He would get answers. And when he had his bearings again, those responsible for Giselle's murder would pay.

Clara wiped her eyes with her sleeve and sniffled. "Giselle

was to be your lifeline. So, now what? Do we run, forever looking over our shoulders?"

"No."

"Then tell me the plan. Where are we going?"

"Luxembourg. I need to see a man about a bullet."

22

No agents patrolled the crossing from France to Luxembourg, and none had for decades. The Schengen Convention had abolished border checks during the EU's first chaotic birth pangs—a blessing to all spies.

An enterprising local had turned the old vehicle inspection area at the former Longlaville checkpoint into a paid parking lot and the guardhouse into a storage shed. Ben glanced through the shed's frosted windows as he drove past. Boxes, bicycles, and a single kayak were stacked inside, a strange mix of utter normalcy. Giselle would have created some story for the kayak or suggest they steal it and ride the river through town. Ben chuckled, but his smile quickly faded.

Clara stretched and adjusted her seat belt. "Where are we?" She had slept since Reims, where Ben had stopped to cover the broken passenger windows with a garbage bag he stole from a dumpster, secured by duct tape from his go-bag.

"This is the border."

"Of Luxembourg?"

"Yes."

"Can we stop for a bite to eat?"

"No." He reached into the back seat, grabbed his backpack,

and dropped it in her lap. "Egg white bars and gummy bears. Don't forget to share with Otto."

She ate, glowering at him and passing the occasional morsel to her dog, while Ben skirted the eastern edge of Luxembourg City. He chose the small highway along the River Syre for the turn north. Any highway made him nervous, but if he didn't reach his goal before sunset, the man he planned to meet might kill him.

"The terrain is rising," Clara said, leaning forward to look out the windshield. "This bullet man of yours, he lives in the mountains?"

"Snipers love a good perch."

"So he's a sniper."

"A good one."

"And you are friends?"

"I thought we were." Ben kept his eyes on the road and the intersections ahead—any pockets where cops might be lying in wait. "Until yesterday, when he tried to blow my head off. His name's William Sensen. He works for my people, not for Leviathan." He shook his head, once again fighting off his own suspicions. "None of this makes any sense."

Ben left the highway and wound his way up a narrow road barely wide enough for the Peugeot. They passed a ruin overlooking a sheer drop. Stone walls. A crumbling tower. Probably some duke's hunting lodge from way back in the day. Americans would have fenced the place off and surrounded it with orange cones. The Luxembourgers had thrown up a hasty metal sign with one sentence in three languages—none of them English. The French line read *Procédez à vos risques et périls*. Proceed at your own peril. Ben nodded and let out a mirthless laugh.

A kilometer past the ruin, he took a gravel road west and continued to climb until it ended in a clearing. "We're here."

"Here?"

"That's what I said."

Clara pointed out through his side of the car. Headstones

and slabs dotted a stepped hillside with the names all worn away and no fence or wall to guard them. "This is a graveyard."

"Sensen lives farther up on the ridgeline, in an old chalet he restored. He calls it *Hochsitz Wipfel*, the Treetop Perch. We met there at the start of a mission once." Ben lifted his pack from her lap and dug out his knife and two spare magazines for his Glock. He pulled out Duval's revolver as well, laying it on the dash. "You know how to use this?"

"Does it matter? If a sniper wants me dead, he'll kill me."

If a sniper wants you dead, kid, he'll kill you. Ben could see Hale's stern face when he'd said those same words years before. How had his schoolmaster's saying wound up on Clara's lips? He kept his hand on the weapon. "What did you say?"

"I said he'll kill me if he wants to. I'll never see him, right? Isn't that the point of a sniper?"

"An old spy I know used to say the same thing."

"Because it's common sense. But I'll take the gun if it makes you feel better." She pushed his hand away from the revolver, picking it up and waggling it at him. "These things are point-and-shoot, right?"

"Cute. Stay in the car."

She saluted. "Whatever you say."

Three paces from the Peugeot, Ben heard a car door slam. He glanced back to see Clara on her way around the hood, following him with Otto on a leash. His head dropped to his chest. "Maybe your English isn't as good as I thought. What happened to staying in the car?"

"I don't like this. Assassins move around a lot, right? How do you know he still lives here?"

"Fresh clippings."

She gave him a quizzical look.

Ben headed for the shadow of the pines, nodding at the rows of slabs and headstones. "Who do you think trims the weeds around these graves?"

23

CHAVILLE, FRANCE

Duval watched the cottage burn, digging a finger under the bandage on his head to get at an itch. The Chaville fire department struggled to manage the blaze, fed by all that oil. He'd arrived at nine o'clock and sent the town's municipal police force out to form roadblocks. Their chief obeyed his every command like a trained poodle. The man knew their place. But the locals wouldn't catch their quarry. Duval didn't want them to.

He needed to catch this one alone.

"I think the bomber is our man Calix from yesterday." Renard returned from gathering witness statements, notebook out, white tape plastered across his face to keep his nose straight. The restriction dulled his speech. "I got a description from a caretaker at the next cottage down. He saw a man, a woman, and a dachshund near the house after the explosion—on the lake side, close to the path."

"I suspected Calix did this the moment we received the call. He's on a rampage. What else?"

The sergeant checked his notes. "Ehh . . . I have a physical description . . . He carried a backpack . . . approached the house

". . . and . . . Ah." He raised his pen like a flag. "A car. He drove off in a Peugeot."

"A cream-colored Peugeot 308."

"Yes. How did you know?"

Duval kicked the remains of a sideview mirror lying on the grass between them. "He left part of it behind." He pulled Renard out of the way of a fireman running between the hoses and the truck. "I'm losing patience, Sergeant. Tell me something I haven't figured out on my own."

"How about this? The witness says the car belonged to the woman who lived here."

"Belonged?" Past tense. "Was she home?"

"The caretaker believes so. I can find out her name from the buyer registry, connect her to Calix."

Duval took some time to process this. Another death. Violent. A justification to shoot Calix on sight—almost. He stared into the dying flames. "I spoke to a witness as well. A jogger. She also saw Calix and the woman near the house, on the lake side, close to the path. But she saw them before the blast, not after." He shifted his gaze to Renard. "She saw Calix using some kind of remote control."

Duval had not met any jogger. He had not debased himself by canvassing for witnesses in years. But her imaginary statement tweaked the narrative to fit his objective.

Renard dutifully recorded every word in his notebook. "Name?"

"Excuse me?"

"Your witness. The jogger." The sergeant held his pen poised at the ready. "I need her name."

"She wished to remain anonymous."

"But, *Capitaine*—"

"She wants to stay out of it, Renard. Is this so much to ask in exchange for her help? Attribute her observations to the caretaker. One witness is all we need in this case."

Chatter interrupted them from the radio on Renard's belt. The sergeant snapped his notebook closed and answered. After a few moments of discussion, he lowered it again. "Chaville's lieutenant says his units are spread thin. He wants us to call in reinforcements from Le Chesnay and Versailles."

"They're not available."

"Sir?"

"You heard me."

"But we have not even checked."

Duval picked up the damaged mirror and held it before his partner's face. "Look what he did to you." He shoved it closer, making sure Renard saw the dirty tape across his nose and the yellowed circles under his eyes in the shattered reflection. "That is Calix's work, or have you forgotten?"

Renard swallowed, shaking his head. "I have not forgotten."

"Then do you want some shoddy municipal police force to catch our man? Or do you want to be the one to bring him in?" He let the mirror fall to the grass. "You and me."

Renard signaled his agreement by relaying Duval's message over the radio. No reinforcements. When finished, he asked a hesitant question. "*Capitaine*, the jogger's statement about Calix and the remote control is important. If the caretaker can't confirm it, won't we need her for the trial?"

Duval turned away again to watch the firefighters battle the blaze. "There's not going to be any trial."

24

A sniper's primary defense is concealment. Stay hidden. Remain a ghost. Be the bogeyman. His second defense is distance. The shooter with the longer reach usually wins. The smart shooters choose to live in places offering plenty of both. What's a sniper when he's at home? In a word—deadly.

Ben left the trail and walked uphill through the tall pines, aware of every dry needle that snapped under the weight of his steps—aware each step might be his last.

À vos risques et périls.

At your own peril.

He knelt, one leg at a time, and stretched his body out to crawl the last five meters to the top of a low ridge. Slowly—ever so slowly—he pushed a couple of rocks aside to improve his view.

A canted valley ran left to right before him, descending and widening to the west to offer a commanding view of Luxembourg's lower hills. To the east, the valley narrowed and climbed until its two ridges met in a level hilltop where a chalet stood, once an old ruin like the castle on the road below. On Ben's last visit, Sensen had described a three-year effort to restore the chalet stone by stone, including its square tower.

The Peugeot's arrival at the graveyard had likely triggered an alarm. By now, Sensen would be lying in his tower, finger on the trigger.

With his gaze, Ben traced an imaginary line up the valley to the chalet. Four hundred meters, the most dangerous quarter mile of his life. He checked the western sky. Almost time.

Keep moving.

He slid his body over the ridge, heading about a third of the way down before turning east and crawling along the down-range side of a fallen log. Running along the ridgetop among the bare trunks of the pines, silhouetted against the sky, would have been suicide.

Splinters of rotting bark showered Ben's neck, sending him into motion before the sound of the gunshot caught up. He rolled right, pressed up to his feet, and ran. "That didn't take long."

He sprinted for a bear-sized boulder, but a second shot split the rock face and steered him the other way. Ben had no choice but to dive headlong into a muddy furrow. He lay there, arms covering his head, waiting for the echoes to quiet.

When he dared to breathe again, Ben noticed an olive drab box lying in the furrow with him, not much bigger than a deck of cards. A camera box? Maybe. A mine? Not Sensen's style. Other than a splatter of mud from Ben's dive, the box looked unmolested by the forest. It hadn't been there long. Inching closer, he saw cursive writing on the top, in black Magic Marker.

Open me.

"You've got to be kidding."

Ever since his phone went haywire in Paris, Ben had been fighting the feeling he'd fallen down a rabbit hole. This confirmed it.

Curiosity bested his caution, and he picked the thing up, willing it not to explode. Inside, he found a wireless earpiece and a note.

Wear me.

Ben wiped his fingers clean on his sleeve and pressed the device into his ear. "Hey there, Willy."

A slug lodged itself into the furrow's edge, inches above Ben's shoulder, followed by the crack of the weapon almost four hundred meters up the valley. "Don't call me Willy." Sensen spoke impeccable English, barely tinted by a German accent. "You know I hate it."

"Yeah, I know. Nice trick with the box."

"Thank you."

"How many did you place?"

"Just the one. You're so predictable."

Another gunshot reminded Ben to keep still. "I placed the box the day I arrived home from Paris. I've been waiting for you ever since. You came up the valley, I drove you into that mud. Easy."

"So, why am I still alive?" Ben pressed his body deeper into the mud, scanning what little he could see of the forest. No escape routes. "You can't expect me to believe Paris was a legitimate miss."

"Not a miss. A message. You're cut off, Calix. Leave. Go home. But first, answer a question. What did you do?"

Cut off. The Company had abandoned him. Ben's vision swam. Until that moment, he'd fought off his suspicions—ignored the signs and clues. He really had fallen down a rabbit hole.

"Calix?"

"I . . . I don't know. I did nothing wrong."

The sniper answered with another shot, close enough to Ben's foot to let him feel it. "Lies bring death, my friend. We all know this truth."

Ben dragged himself deeper into the furrow. He gritted his teeth against the stench of rotting moss and toadstools. "I swear."

"The Company does not put innocents on my list, Ben. Please. Did you sell a secret? Is the pay no longer satisfying?

Or is this some clash of ideals? Confession is good for the soul. Let me be your priest."

"And my executioner."

"If you persist. Tell me your sins, walk away, and live. Remain silent, or approach the house, and die." To emphasize his point, Sensen fired off another round. He could do that all day. Ben imagined he had stacks of his special ammunition up there.

Carefully, Ben checked the pine's lengthening shadows. One more minute. Maybe two. "There's another option. A frame. My mission went south. Massir, the Algerian who gave me the intel that led us there, showed up unannounced."

"Can you produce him for interrogation?"

"I kind of set him on fire."

Crack. A rock exploded. A chunk of it sliced Ben's arm. Behind him, the setting sun shined up the valley, a blinding white winter sun—Ben's only chance at survival. He made his move.

A string of shots missed wide, hitting rock, tree, and mud. Most importantly, they were all low. The sun's glare had stolen Sensen's ability to gauge depth and range. Ben might just have a chance. He shifted his vector with every third footfall, moving from cover to cover, but always advancing. A hundred meters from his goal, the light faded. The sun had outpaced him. Ben fired at the tower window and heard his own ricochets through the earpiece.

"You think you can kill me?"

Ben kept running up the hill. "I'm not here to kill you. I want to talk, find out what's going on. You have to trust me."

"I can't take the risk." The voice came from the rocks and trees to Ben's right, not his earpiece.

Sensen remained invisible until he moved, stepping forward with his rifle aimed at Ben's head. He wore full camouflage with mesh veil beneath his hood—a faceless tactical reaper. "As I said. You are so predictable."

Ben had been sure the shots were coming from the chalet's tower. "How?"

"Remote control, Calix. What century do you think we live in?" Sensen took another step. "Last chance. Confess and walk away."

Ben wheeled a hand upward and caught the long barrel as a bullet traveled through, turning his body at the same time. He heard a window shatter.

He raised the Glock, but Sensen released the rifle and punched his arm to spoil his aim. The German kept punching, hitting him with a double body shot, then drew a larger Glock from his hip. Each man brought his weapon to the other's head, and each caught the other's wrist. They fell and rolled, wrestling on the hillside, firing off rounds to no avail.

"Stop!" Clara appeared from the trees, covering her head and pointing the revolver at the two men. She growled at both of them. "If either one of you hits my dog, I'll kill you. Weapons down!"

Neither man argued. Ben, underneath Sensen, cocked his head and grinned. "I might be predictable. She's not."

25

"Look what you did." Sensen thrust his chin at the chalet's ornately carved oak door. Three bullets had lodged themselves in the wood. "Do you know how long I worked to restore that piece? It is one solid section of Belgian honey oak." He pushed it open and waved Ben inside while Clara covered them both with the revolver.

"Those are your rounds," Ben said, removing his shoes before proceeding into the living room. He remembered Sensen had a thing about that.

"Your assault. Your fault."

"I'll cover the damages."

"How will you pay? From where I'm standing, you're out of a job."

"I'll get it back."

"We'll see."

"Hey!" Clara entered behind them with Otto at her heels. She waved the gun and widened her eyes as if to say *I'm still in charge and don't you forget it*.

The two men shared a look, then both laid their Glocks on a long entry table built from the same oak as the door. Sensen set his rifle in a hall closet and peeled off his top layer of camouflage. "Is she always like this?"

Ben made a *calm down* motion to Clara. "We're good, okay? Nobody's getting shot. Like I said"—he shifted his gaze to Sensen, who still had half his body in the closet—"I'm here to talk."

"And this is why you brought backup?"

"For what it's worth, I told her to stay in the car."

"She didn't listen."

"She never does. But if we want to split hairs, she gave me the advantage. I could have finished you off just now. I chose not to."

"All right." Sensen stepped away from the closet and showed Ben two empty hands. "You spared my life, as I spared yours. For now, we are even." He walked into the kitchen and picked an apple from a wicker basket, taking a bite before continuing. "But I don't buy into your plea of innocence. The Director does not cut a man off without cause."

The Director. Cut off. Those words spoken together drove a spike of ice into Ben's heart. He shook his head. "Our comm network is compromised. Has to be. It's why my phone went crazy just before you shot at me in the alley. It's how Massir and Hagen set us up in Rome. This is all a misdirect by an entity called Leviathan, framing me to break us up from the inside."

The name sent a flicker of recognition across Sensen's features. Clearly he'd heard the rumors about Leviathan too.

The moment passed, and his expression hardened. "Are you so important, Ben? We are all type T personalities with an extra measure of pride, but do you really believe an attempt to bring down the world's most important covert agency begins with you?" He shrugged, holding the apple in a limp hand. "Why not me? Why not Giselle? She's twice as smart as the rest of us."

Another spike of ice. The same numbing emptiness as before.

Ben didn't answer. He couldn't bring her name to his lips, and Sensen didn't know they'd been seeing each other.

Ben and Clara joined Sensen in the kitchen, and Ben kept a watchful eye on their host. They'd left the guns behind in the living area, but he imagined Sensen had hidden one or more firearms in every room. Ben would respect him less if he hadn't.

Sensen lit a fire in a wood-burning stove, and the three sat at a long table of gnarled and polished wood.

Ben knocked on the tabletop. "Belgian honey oak? Like the door and the entry table?"

"All part of a set I bought at auction. Some know-nothing Hollywood actor remodeled his newly purchased castle and discarded its best features." For the first time, he looked Ben up and down. "You look terrible."

"Thanks. I'm trying out a muddy furrow survival grunge thing."

The German cracked a smile and leaned across the tiny space to retrieve a tan bottle from the refrigerator. He offered one to Ben, who waved it off, accepting a clear bottle of Gerolsteiner sparkling water instead. Sensen offered one of each to Clara. "Calix failed to properly introduce us. Call me Sensen. Ben and I used to work together."

"Clara." She chose the sparkling water and used it to point at the dachshund, curled up on the floor beside her. "And this is Otto."

Ben didn't like the way Sensen said *used to*, as if they would never work together again. He finally brought himself to say the words he'd been struggling with since the moment before Clara's entrance. "Giselle's dead."

The smile dropped from Sensen's lips. "I'm sorry. I know you two were close. I could see it in the way she looked at you. And you contend this is part of what's happening to you?"

Contend? Ben didn't argue the semantics. He nodded.

The German did the same and took in a long breath. He

steepled his fingers, a surgeon bringing bad news. "You must realize how this looks to all of us. The mission in Rome went awry. The intel you attained is bad. The enemy agent you blame is dead—burned by your own hand. And the only Company witness who could either exonerate or condemn you is also dead."

Ben pounded the table. "Are you saying I murdered Giselle?"

"I was there," Clara said at the same time, fire in her voice. "Ben's innocent."

Sensen raised his hands. "I'm only bringing the perception to your attention. You were cut off and your Company protections removed. Perhaps your closeness with Giselle exposed her too. Either way, you must try to picture this through the Company's eyes. To them, your sins are apparent. And to me, these calamities can be explained by only one thing—a severance."

A severance. Ben hadn't heard that term in years.

Clara cocked her head. "Ben? What's a severance?"

He didn't like the change in the way she looked at him. "When a spy goes bad, or demonstrates gross incompetence, the Company cuts him off—with extreme prejudice. All protection for covers is removed. All support is gone." He lowered his forehead into his palm. "Enemies can move in and take you at will."

"We call it a severance," Sensen said.

Ben rolled his head to look at Clara. "But it's a myth, a campfire ghost story told at the schoolhouse to scare the new recruits."

The German shook his head. "It is a reality. Your reality. A false mission. A dead team member. Incompetent. Failure. Traitor? How can the Company see you in any other light?"

Ben shook his head, closing his eyes. "They're wrong. I'm clean."

"None of us are clean, my friend. Not one of us is pure."

Clara finished a swallow of her water and stared at him hard. "How so?"

"Consider the graveyard at the edge of my property. Consider the unnamed buried there, rotted, long ago abandoned by even the worms and maggots."

Her bravado seemed to falter at the mention of the graves. Her glass bottle clinked on the table as she set it down. "Wh-what about them?"

"I'm sure each, in life, proclaimed his own purity, as Calix proclaims his now. And upon their deaths, each prayed to God for paradise in the hereafter. Yet each knew in their deepest hearts that they deserved eternal fire." He shifted his gaze to Ben. "This is the nature of man."

"A philosophical opinion," Ben said, waving it away with his Gerolsteiner.

"A fact. Especially in our business. Stop living in denial, Calix. Turn to introspection, and perhaps you'll find your answers."

Introspection. Could this executioner-philosopher be right? Ben had made mistakes in the past. He'd committed acts the rest of the world might see as atrocities. He'd fallen for Massir's gambit. In Rome, he had desecrated a temple, stolen from the homeless, and burned a corpse. In Paris, he'd fought the police. He'd killed a man.

He felt the sniper's eyes weighing on him and raised his own. "You're wrong. This isn't on me. And this isn't on the Company—not entirely. At the source, this is Leviathan."

"Mm." Sensen left the table to stoke his fire, muttering to himself. "Leviathan. A sea monster."

"What do you know of them? Have you heard of an individual called Jupiter?"

"No. But . . . it's odd. A coincidence."

Clara watched them both. "Ben tells me you spies don't believe in coincidences."

"Genau." Sensen stirred his embers with a set of iron tongs. "Just so. And that is the only reason I bring this up. I saw it on my last mission, a month before Paris—a hasty kill in Rotterdam."

"The failed bombing," Ben said.

"Correct." Sensen added a log, positioned it with his tongs, and closed the door. He looked at Clara, as if wary about speaking in front of her, but then wobbled his head, seeming to let it go, and turned to Ben. "Radio traffic from the Rotterdam customs authority alerted the Company to the bomber's presence. A bomb-sniffing dog at the docks had flagged a backpack, but the target escaped."

"A red flag priority," Ben said, filling in the details from what he knew of Company operations. "Protocol requires the watch commander at headquarters to reroute the nearest asset."

"Yes. In this case—me, only one city away, prepping for another job. Cyber ops used cameras across the city to locate the threat and predict his path. I intercepted and neutralized his weapon."

"I saw the news reports," Clara said, looking from one to the other. "They said the bomber accidentally set off his explosives before reaching his target. Only a dozen warehouse workers were injured, but if he'd reached a public square, hundreds might have died."

The German chuckled. "The bomb went off early, yes. But the bomber made no error beyond choosing a predictable path."

Ben followed Sensen with his eyes as the German returned to his chair. "You shot the bomb."

"Cyber ops forecast his route and sent me a location surrounded by warehouses, minimizing the blast effect and loss of life. But a fraction of a second before I took the shot, he turned, and I saw a design on the backpack's top pocket."

"A design," Clara said. "You mean a logo?"

"No . . . *Ein Gekritzel* . . . What do the Americans call it?" Sensen snapped his fingers and pointed at her. "A *doodle*, in silver pen—small but definite. Our would-be bomber fancied himself an artist. He'd drawn a sea monster."

"A leviathan," Ben said.

Sensen pursed his lips. "Probably nothing, hmm? A thread as thin as spider's silk."

"Not a thread. A lifeline. Rotterdam is where Leviathan made their first big mistake—where the whole case breaks." Ben rummaged in his inside coat pocket. "I can fix this. I can find out their plans and prove my innocence."

"My friend—"

"No. Listen. A sea monster must have been on the bomber's mind. There must be a connection. Did you see any part of the device itself?"

"I saw nothing. After the shot, I had to leave. You know the drill. Get far fast. Then get farther faster."

"Please." Ben slapped the fragment he'd found at Giselle's house down on the table. "Look at this. Tell me you recognize it."

Frowning, like a parent humoring a child, Sensen crossed the kitchen and picked up the fragment. A smile formed on his lips. Not an encouraging smile. An *I told you so* smirk. "Yes. I've seen something like this before, but not in Rotterdam."

Sensen left the kitchen, and Ben heard him open the same closet where he'd stashed the sniper rifle. He tensed, but Sensen returned unarmed, carrying a small black case, and popped it open on the table between his guests. He lifted a cloth, revealing two blocks of C4, a remote, and a receiver/detonator.

Sensen held Ben's fragment close to the detonator's lower left corner—a perfect match, right down to the seam in the plastic. "Do you recognize it now? This is a Company demolition package."

Ben stood, knocking over his chair. "No. This can't be right."

"But it is. And these packages are highly controlled. This one is left over from my Amsterdam mission. I've been ordered to hold on to it until my next assignment."

A hole developed in Ben's gut. He nodded. "I had one just like it sent to us for the Morocco gig. For contingencies. Never used it."

"So you still have the package?"

"No."

"Then where did it go?"

"I'm not sure." But he could guess. The evidence told Ben the explosive package he'd signed out for his last mission had been used to blow up the cottage and murder Giselle. But he hadn't seen it in days. "In Rome, on the morning of our last day while we were setting up at the piazza, I gave it to our mission tech to carry back to DC, along with the case we stole." He locked eyes with Sensen. "I gave it to Dylan Morgan."

26

"Dylan can't be involved." The protest sounded hollow the moment it fell from Ben's lips. The fragment matched the detonator in Sensen's case in every detail. Ben let the fragment slip from his fingers. "Unless he turned traitor and joined Leviathan."

Sensen gently removed the fragment from the case and set it in front of Ben. "Open your eyes. There is no great conspiracy of traitors. Leviathan has not infiltrated our ranks. The most likely answer is that you are in denial. Your own guilt is too great for you to comprehend."

Absurdity. Ben kept his focus on Sensen. "I need a meeting with the Director."

"And I would like a pig who whistles."

Ben only stared at him.

"Oh, you were serious?" Sensen laughed. "My friend, you are radioactive—persona non grata. And even if you weren't, foot soldiers like us do not demand meetings with the Director."

"Please. Try to set it up. You have access to lines of communication no longer open to me."

"And be dragged deeper into the mess you've made for yourself? No thank you. I will offer you my guest rooms for the night." He regarded Ben's mud-caked shirt and jacket. "And perhaps some clothes. That is all. Rest. Clean yourself up. But when I wake tomorrow, it will be best if you are gone."

○ ○ ○

The evening may have started with a shootout, but Ben could not complain about Sensen's hospitality. He emerged from the shower to find a button-down shirt and a pair of khaki slacks laid out on the bed. Sensen had him by more than an inch in height, but the two were close enough in size that Ben could get away with wearing his clothes. Clara—not so much. When he checked on her in the room next door, he found her wearing a sweater long enough to be a dress. She sat on the bed between two dinner trays with venison steaks and greens. A third tray, now empty, sat on the floor beside a bowl of water and a contented dachshund.

"Look." Clara tore a page from her sketchbook. "I asked our host to describe the sea monster from the bomber's backpack. He remembered it well."

Ben studied the sea monster drawing. Its three coils wrapped around a globe, and a forked tongue lashed out from between its fangs. Leviathan. Maybe. A poor clue, but his only clue that didn't point straight back to his own agency. He gave her a fleeting smile. "Thanks."

"So where will we go now?" she asked, cutting into her steak. "Rotterdam?"

"*I* will go to Rotterdam. I had some time to think in the shower, let the steam clear my head. You're staying here, where you'll be safe."

Her knife clattered to the plate. "Safe? With the sniper?"

"Sensen has no quarrel with you. I'll work it out—play on his sense of honor and pay him for the favor."

Her lips parted in protest.

Ben held up a hand to stop her. "No arguments. I'm doing

this for my sake as much as yours. I need to stay light and move fast from now on." He took his tray and left.

Sleep came only with the use of a sedative, another boon from Sensen. Ben could safely say he'd paid for it. Several thousand euros covered the pill, the damage to the house from the gun battle, and playing innkeeper to Clara for a week. Ben figured if he hadn't come back for her by then, he'd be dead, and she'd be on her own.

The following morning, he and Clara said their goodbyes at the door to her room.

"Are you sure it's safe for me to stay here?" she asked.

Ben nodded. "Sensen is a good man, or tries to be. But just in case . . ." He gave her the revolver. "Keep it close."

Clara tucked the gun into her waistband and pulled her borrowed sweater down over it. "Come back to me."

"I will."

"You said that before, remember? What if you don't?"

"If I'm not back in a week, ask Sensen to get you a clean passport and a one-way ticket out of Europe, wherever you and Otto want to go." He showed her a roll of bills. "This will cover it, with enough left over to get you started wherever you land."

She glanced down at the money. "A gun. Getaway cash. You're not inspiring confidence with these gifts."

"I have no confidence left."

"I do. This will all come right in the end. You'll see."

Ben saw no trace of exaggeration, no false bravado in those ice-blue eyes. "How can you know?"

She shrugged one shoulder. "I just do. Call it faith."

Faith. That word again. But where had faith taken Ben? On the run. Banished from the Company by the Director. Girlfriend murdered. How much longer could he hold on to faith? How much more could he take?

"I have to take the Peugeot."

Clara gave him a smile. "As if I wanted that piece of junk anyway."

Otto appeared at her ankles, and Ben kneeled to scratch his ears. "You take care of her, you hear me?"

The dachshund's watery gaze spoke of understanding and affirmation. *Don't you worry. I've got this.*

When Ben straightened, Clara wrapped him in a hug and held it for a long time. She let her cheek brush against his. He felt a kiss. In a barely audible whisper, she repeated her former command. "Come back to me."

Downstairs, Sensen sat wide awake and dressed for the day in a large stuffed chair near the door. "I thought I told you to be gone before I woke."

"Maybe you should learn to sleep in."

"This business makes light sleepers of us all. Besides, I wanted one more chance to lay eyes on the strange and tragic creature who came to visit my chalet."

Ben didn't quite catch his meaning. "Tragic, yes. But strange?"

"A man trapped in his delusions, ready to face destruction rather than face the truth of his own failures."

Germans. In Ben's experience, they never minced words. Sensen remained true to his heritage.

"I also wanted to give you this." Sensen handed him a slip of paper. "The address of the pier where the dog flagged the bomber."

"Thanks."

"Don't mention it. And I mean that. Don't mention this to anyone. I've already done you—the severed Company man— too many favors."

Sensen saw him to the door, and Ben paused at the threshold. "While you're feeling generous, I'd like one more favor."

"I told you. I can't get you a meeting with the Director."

"Not the Director. Colonel Hale. Ask him to meet with me—a few minutes, that's all."

Sensen looked as if he might argue, but sighed. "All right. But you know how these things work. He'll choose the time and place, not you. How do I reach you with the rendezvous point?"

Ben hastily wrote a nonexistent email address on the paper Sensen had given him and ripped the piece off, handing it over. "Send it to this address. Use the old schoolhouse code." He turned to go, then glanced back. "By coming here, I've violated my severance. I know you have a duty to report in. What will you do if the Company escalates to a kill order?"

"I'll do my job. And when the bullet enters your skull, you'll know I had no choice."

27

The trek north to the Netherlands took most of the day, including a stop for brunch and some fashion shopping in the military town of Bitburg, Germany, where Americans driving beat-up cars had been a fixture since 1952. He also stopped at a print and copy shop in Liege, Belgium. As before, Ben avoided the highways. He used the utility roads near the North Sea coast to work his way east into the industrial port of Rotterdam. He knew the place well. All the Company men and women did.

Rotterdam has been a smuggler's paradise for centuries, once the largest port in the world, with river access as deep into Europe's interior as Switzerland. Thirty-five kilometers of warehouses, petroleum depots, and megaship piers make it a perfect covert hub, one of Europe's most well-transited entry points for spies, second only to the military airlift center at Spangdahlem.

Ben had passed through Rotterdam no less than eight times in the last four years, once in a shipping container outfitted by Dylan as a tactical command center.

He bristled at the thought of the young tech.

How could Dylan do that to Giselle? Maybe he hadn't. Maybe someone had stolen the demolition package from him.

Unlikely.

From where Ben sat, Dylan looked like the real traitor.

Superstructures towered above the Peugeot's cracked windshield on the port's main road. Containers were stacked like city blocks, filled with textiles and ore, rubber dog toys and clown marionettes—anything and everything imaginable. At some point, one of those containers had brought a Leviathan acolyte to town, and a backpack filled with CRTX, the world's newest and most powerful explosive.

The slip of paper with Sensen's six-letter address brought him to a cargo pier that looked like all the others—containers, cranes, and giant ships. A guardhouse and a ten-foot spiked fence blocked access for all traffic but the big rigs. Ben parked in the dockworker lot as far out of sight as he could manage, in the shadow of some containers stacked on the fence's other side. A be-on-the-lookout alert on a damaged cream Peugeot 308 had likely spread across Western Europe. Before day's end, he'd need to dump it in a river.

He stuffed the paper into his go-bag and took a last look at the PVC badge he'd made at the print and copy shop. Confident it would hold up, he smiled in the mirror. "Agent Tom Porter, Interpol."

The days of fake ID badges made from laminated paper and alligator clips are long gone. White PVC access badges with magnetic strips have become the norm, from government agencies to the corner grocery store. The US military still likes to pretend their badges are special, but anyone can purchase blanks online at eight cents a pop and add a name and face with the right printer.

Alongside the egg white bars and bullets in his go-bag, Ben always kept a stack of PVC blanks. The identity he'd made at the copy shop would last the day, at least—long enough to do some investigating. He pressed his badge against the turnstile reader, then waved it at the guard across the road, careful to cover the logo with his fingers. "A little help? Reader's not working!" He didn't need to speak Dutch. Aussie dominance in the dockworker field had made a corrupted form of English the universal language of industrial piers.

The turnstile buzzed, ending in a pronounced *click*. "Thanks," Ben said, pushing through. He'd run that game a hundred times. No guard had ever challenged him.

"Oi! You! Whaddaya think yer doing!"

Ben had barely made it past the fence. A burly dockworker came hurrying toward him, and Ben answered with a look that said *Who, me?*

The dockworker pointed upward to a four-ton shipping container swinging high above them on the way to the stacks next to the parking lot. "Hard hat." He slapped the top of the one on his head. "Where's yours?"

An Aussie. No surprise, and this one carried himself like a foreman. He had the walk—forward leaning, a touch of swagger. Forklifts had left slick tracks in the previous night's snow. The Aussie rolled over them without the slightest misstep, dropping his voice from a shout to a boisterous bleat as he drew closer. "Your hard hat, mate. Where is it?"

"Agent Tom Porter. Interpol." Ben took control of the encounter, trumping safety with the universal authority of a well-known law enforcement agency. He flashed the badge, then clipped it to his lapel. "Official business. Point me to the temporary crew quarters, please."

The foreman bowed up to him. "I don't care if you're the king of Sweden. You step onto my pier, you wear protection. No exceptions."

Ben liked this guy, but he didn't back down. "I'll get the necessary gear Mr."—he read the man's badge, tensing his jaw—"*Kent*, just as soon as you point me to the temporary crew quarters."

Kent fixed him with a hard stare for a long moment, then tilted his head toward four stories of rusted steel and dirty windows. Nothing but the best for the anonymous cargo sailors keeping the world in motion. "Over there. Talk to old Alard."

He left the man standing there without a thank you.

"Oi!"

Ben paused, gritting his teeth, but he didn't turn.

"What's Interpol want, eh? Is it that bomber again? I thought you cops had given up."

"We never give up, Mr. Kent." He walked on.

The bomber remained unidentified. No identification had been found at the scene. At least, that's what the public reports said, and Ben had no access to the classified versions. But the sketch Clara had drawn from Sensen's description might get him somewhere if the guy had spent any time at all in the crew barracks.

"Mag ik u helpen?" A gray-haired man with a bushy mustache sat in a folding camp chair outside the front door. The stench in there must have been pretty bad for him to prefer sitting out in the freezing cold.

"Alard?"

"Yes."

As Ben's lips parted for his Agent-Tom-Porter spiel, a reflection in the glass doors of the barracks gave him pause.

Alard stood up from his chair. "Sir? May I help you?"

Ben ignored him and turned. A forklift had moved a container stack down the pier, clearing his view of a massive ship. On the bow he saw a white sea serpent with three coils wrapped around a globe. The lettering beneath read Sea Titan Cargo.

Sea Titan. Leviathan.

If the bomber spent any time in the barracks at all before the dog flagged him, he'd have spent hours at most. But he'd have spent days, maybe more than a week, on the ship that brought him in, probably living inside a container, venturing out at night when the only lights were the spots focused on the ship's tower logo. He'd have spent enough time on board for that logo to become so seared in his brain that he absentmindedly doodled it on his backpack.

No coincidences.

"Sir," Alard said, becoming more insistent. "May I help you? You speak English, correct?"

"Correct." Ben wheeled on him, flashing his PVC badge. "Agent Tom Porter, Interpol. I need you to get me on that Sea Titan Cargo freighter. Can you do that?"

"I can introduce you to a deck officer staying in the barracks."

"Good. Let's go." In the corner of his eye, Ben saw the foreman, Kent, watching him. He touched Alard's shoulder. "And before we go to the ship, I'll need to borrow a hard hat. Safety first."

28

With a borrowed hard hat in place, Ben followed a sleepy boatswain—or bos'n, as he called himself—up the Sea Titan freighter's gangplank. A painted name, pale green against the hull's deep blue, identified her as the *Princess of Sheba*.

The creature on the bow held the world in the crushing embrace of its coils, and up close, the dragon eyes seemed to follow Ben. He shuddered and shifted his gaze to the back of his escort's head. "Again, thank you for your time. I'm sorry Alard had to wake you, but a look at your operation will help me wrap my head around the circumstances of this case."

"Don't mention it." The boatswain's response lacked a certain sincerity. He bobbled his broad head back and forth. "To tell the truth, ya might've done me a favor," he said in a South African accent. "Ya violated my rest period near the end o' the cycle. By regs, as soon as we're done here, I can restart the clock fer another six hours o' rack time."

At the gangway's top, an Asian sailor in jeans and a Sea Titan sweatshirt sat slumped in a folding chair. The bos'n kicked a chair leg, and the deckhand snapped to wakefulness. "Mr. Mallory." He jumped to attention, wiping a bit of drool from his chin. "You are awake."

"Which is more than I can say fer you, Mr. Shen. This is Agent Porter from Interpol. I'm helpin' him with an investigation."

The real Interpol had about as much authority as Barney Fife. But the name's mystic power still opened doors. Even better, the Interpol gag took advantage of the human propensity for self-inflation.

I'm helping him with an investigation.

After no more psychological prodding than a fake ID and a confident request, the bos'n had appointed himself Ben's deputy and enforcer.

"An investigation?" Shen asked. "Into the *Princess*?"

Ben held up a hand. "No, no. Nothing like that. I'm taking a second look at the October bombing."

"But Sea Titan had no ships at Rotterdam that day." Shen's gaze shifted to Mallory, seeking confirmation. "I heard two berthed at this pier were both from Jaspen. The police should talk to them."

His information made sense. If the bomber came in on a Sea Titan ship, he'd have been offloaded in a container as cargo, left to sit until the ship moved out again. The smart move, as Ben had learned from his own travels through the port, was to let a truck carry the container off-site, well away from port security. Something must have gone wrong. Maybe the truck didn't come. Maybe the bomber grew impatient. Terrorist organizations ran into unreliable personnel and contractor issues all the time.

Ben kept his smile congenial. "I'm taking over this investigation now that Agent Bolz is in medical retirement. Prostate cancer. Sad story. I'll talk to the Jaspen crews when they come in day after tomorrow. Right now, I'd like to get a feel for how cargo ops are run when a ship like yours comes in."

Usually, a download of unnecessary information worked during a con like this, but Shen reached for his radio. "Having Interpol on board is . . . important. I should call the watch officer—ask him to call the captain."

Not good. Ben had steered Alard toward the bos'n for a reason—a senior deck officer with enough clout to get him on board, but still a bit of a minion, easier to control. Ben didn't need the captain interfering. He'd stonewall Ben either because Leviathan owned him or because no captain wanted cops boarding his ship without corporate approval.

"Brave man," Ben said. "I wish I had guts like yours, waking my captain from his crew rest at a five-star hotel."

Shen paled.

Self-Appointed Deputy Mallory jumped in to help, requiring less prodding than Ben expected. "Ya sayin' I can't handle this, Shen?"

"N-no, Mr. Mallory."

"Ya claimin' ta know the regs better'n me?"

"No. But I—"

"Shut up, man your post, and don't bother the cap'n. I've got this."

Shen answered with a fearful nod. "Y-yes, Mr. Mallory."

He moved to take his seat, but Mallory stole his chair, folding it up with a loud *swack*. "I daresay ya won't be needin' yer chair, since ya jus' volunteered ta stand for the rest o' yer shift." He charged ahead into the underdeck passage with Ben close at his shoulder.

Metallic clangs reverberated through the tunnel in a slow, steady pound—heartbeats in the belly of the beast. They hit Ben's body with palpable force. The loading and unloading of containers never ceased during a mega freighter's time at port. "What are you carrying? If you don't mind me asking."

The bos'n leaned his stolen chair against the white-painted steel wall and shrugged. "Everythin' from frozen fish and microwave dinners in the bulk holds ta forty-foot containers filled with glass marbles, picked up in Shanghai."

"Marbles?"

"Mm-hmm."

"Ever lose any?"

"Ha. Never heard that 'un before. Tell me, Agent Porter. Why're ya really askin' me to show ya the *Princess*? Shen is right. Jaspen had this berth that day. Not us."

The sleep had worn off, letting the bos'n think more clearly and making Ben's job harder. In circumstances like this, Ben had always found a touch of truth worked best. He lowered his voice—a man sharing an important secret with a trusted confidant. "We have new evidence." Ben looked over his shoulder, as if checking to make sure Shen hadn't followed them. "Our bomber had a fixation on Sea Titan Cargo. I need to know why."

Mallory burst into laughter, supporting himself with a hand on the rail of the stairway to the upper container bed. "Well, yeah. I don't wanna insult yer intelligence, Agent Porter, but *ev'ry* sailor has a fixation on Sea Titan." He made an about-face and blew past Ben. "C'mon. Let me show ya somethin'."

29

Ben didn't follow the bos'n at first. The containers towering above—the rhythmic pound of loading and unloading—held him transfixed. What deadly items might be hidden among the glass baubles and frozen fish in that vast Aladdin's Cave? Maybe none. Maybe thousands.

"Ya comin', Agent Porter?"

"Right behind you."

Ben turned to find Mallory only a step away, eyeing him.

"See much action in yer line o' work, Agent?"

"I'm not sure I get your meaning."

Mallory held up his fists, and it took all of Ben's control not to flinch. The bos'n grinned and touched his cheek below his eye, indicating Ben's shiner from the fight with Hagen.

Ben had almost forgotten about it. "Oh that. I wish I could say, 'You should see the other guy,' but this black eye came from a shower door. When the hotel provides you with a no-slip mat, make sure to use it."

"Right. Shower door."

Two decks down, Mallory cranked open a steel hatch and waved Ben through. "Take a look."

Ducking to avoid the bulkhead, Ben stepped into a huge

space, like a dystopian underworld. "Speaking of Aladdin's Cave," he muttered.

"Pardon?"

"Nothing." The two stood on a platform overlooking an Olympic-size pool. Four vertical support beams rose from the water to the ceiling three stories above. The place looked like an upscale health club dropped into a prison yard, with a tennis court, two racquetball courts, and a half basketball court.

"You've no idea o' the challenges o' tennis at sea," Mallory said, clapping him on the back. The bos'n thrust his chin at three stories of rooms at the far end. "Showers, Ping-Pong, billiards. The top floor is the crew bar. The one man universally loved on the *Princess* ain't the cap'n. It's Francisco the bartender."

"Impressive. Truly. But why are you showing me all this?"

Mallory looked at him as if he had asked why it snows in winter. "Don't ya see? Ev'ry cargo hugger-mugger from here ta Singapore wants ta sail for Sea Titan. Bigger ships. Better facilities. Better life. I'm afraid yer bomber's fixation with Sea Titan is a dead end."

A dead end. Sensen had told him the same about the entire Rotterdam angle. Who was Ben to personally bring down Leviathan, anyway? A Company team could sweep through the containers at night with microwave scanners, searching for weapons-grade material or infiltrate Sea Titan to get at the truth. What could a severed spy do?

"You may be right." Ben fought to maintain his smile. He'd take one last long shot, then call it a day, dump the Peugeot, and regroup. "I appreciate the tour. Could I trouble you to show me the bridge while I'm here?" He finished by pressing a psychological button. "You do have access to the bridge, right?"

"'Course I've got access. Whodaya think yer talkin' to?" Mallory directed him out through the hatch again and shoved it closed. "Hope yer in good shape, Mr. Interpol. We've a half kilometer o' passages and stairs ahead with a grand total sixty-meter vertical climb, more than the Leanin' Tower of Pisa."

Lefts. Rights. Stairs. Ladders. Down one story. Up two.

Mallory never wavered in his path, where Ben felt utterly disoriented. If the bos'n worked for Leviathan, playing the fool to set a trap, he had Ben at his mercy.

"How far now?" Ben found the question difficult, his breathing coming harder than expected. He sucked at the air, seeking oxygen, legitimately embarrassed. "Why is this . . . so hard? Feels like . . . a mountaintop."

"Stale air." The bos'n glanced down from the top of a canted ladder. "We rest the diesels in port, meanin' the air pumps gotta shut down. That's why the crew has ta use the dock barracks. It'll be better up here. C'mon."

Ben emerged into fresh, cold air, but Mallory gave him no time to breathe. He went straight across the deck to the first ladder of the ship's upper superstructure, interlocking levels reminiscent of a Jenga tower. Fresh air or not, by the time they reached the flying bridge, he was spent.

At the door to the bridge, the bos'n had a word with the watch officer, but he'd left Ben too far behind to hear. Whatever passed between them, the watch officer didn't give Ben so much as a passing glance when he caught up.

The tour began with the radar tower and emergency equipment. Ben could not have cared less. He left Mallory and headed for a bank of computer screens. "And what are these?"

"Er, that's navcon, our navigation controls. These are the radar screens, fed by yer tower out there. And this'n . . ." He gestured to a map screen filled with moving targets, voice fading. Ben had clearly pushed past the limits of his knowledge.

"Ah." Ben read the acronym on the placard beneath the screen, having no idea what it meant. "The ECLRT." As he spoke, a digital ship passed beneath the active cursor, and a box of data appeared. Location. Stats. Nice. He walked closer.

Mallory followed. "Right. The ECLRT. The long-range tracker." He gave a tentative nod. "You've seen one before?"

"Oh, I'm a bit of a sea tech nut. May I?"

Before Mallory could answer, Ben took control of the mouse. A click on any Sea Titan vessel, highlighted in green, gave him the ship's six-month port history. He moved from one to the next, down the European coastline. "Wow. You have quite a fleet. I assume the *Princess* is the flagship."

"Not quite." Mallory held out a hand to stop the advancing watch officer. "That'd be the *Behemoth*, our largest—currently the largest on earth. She makes runs out o' the main facility in Valencia, on the Spanish Mediterranean."

"The Med, huh?" A quick shift of the mouse set the cursor on the target. The history came up. A tingle passed through Ben's chest. His long shot had paid off. He saw the telltale cities in the history. Tokyo in June. St. Petersburg in September. The *Behemoth* had been docked near the sites of two major bombings within days of each event.

No coincidences.

"She sure gets around."

"True. The *Behemoth* is fast. She makes thirty-six knots on calm seas, twice as fast as the biggest ships coming off the lines only three years ago."

"Mm-hmm." Ben barely processed the man's droning. The *Behemoth* had been nowhere near Rotterdam in October. Doing his best not to be obvious, he shifted the cursor back to the *Princess.*

Rotterdam. Pier 12. October 4–7.

They'd left a day before the failed bombing. Bingo.

This ship. This crew.

Ben turned to look at Mallory.

"What's wrong, Agent Porter?" Mallory sounded cold—no longer the dutiful self-appointed deputy. "Ya look like that shower door jus' knocked the stuffin' outta ya again."

148

"No. I'm—" He stopped. The room's energy had changed.

The map screen and all its revelations had sucked Ben in, degraded his awareness. The watch officer stood at attention. Ben found himself under the hard glare of a black man in a leather *Princess of Sheba* jacket. The title embroidered under the ship's name and the Sea Titan logo read CAPTAIN. The newcomer lifted his chin. "Thanks for the text, Mr. Mallory."

Ben raised an eyebrow at the bos'n.

Mallory grinned. "I sent him a note, after ya woke me while puttin' on ma trousers. I kept Shen from makin' a fuss so we could get ya on board for a proper chat."

The captain crossed his arms. "I checked with port security. No law enforcement agency coordinated a visit today. Why don't you tell me who you are and why you're so interested in my ship?"

30

When caught in the act, spies have a mantra. Deny, drone, counter-accuse. Deny all allegations. Drone on to confuse the enemy. Sow distrust among your captors by tossing out counteraccusations. Spies talk first. Fighting is a last resort.

Ben could feel the Glock's weight at his back. He could hear the weapon calling to him. Most European ports didn't allow crews to carry guns in port, even on board their own vessels. A quick threat of force with the Glock might get him out of this. But with the circumstantial evidence linking the *Behemoth* and the *Princess* to the Leviathan bombings, he doubted this crew followed such laws. These men had him cornered with three-to-one odds, less than optimal for a close-quarters gunfight.

Deny.

"Look, Captain. I'm Agent Tom Porter from Interpol. Just as I said. My HQ coordinated this visit with the port authority. How do you think I got past the gate guard? I'll go talk to the security folks and straighten this out." Ben started for the door.

The watch officer stepped into his path. "Interpol has no agents."

Drone.

"A common misconception." He slid a finger under the badge

clipped to his lapel and lifted it an inch. "See? 'Agent.' Says it right here. The field division is new, created after 9/11. You know. September 11, 2001? The terrorist attacks? Took more than a decade to get the whole thing approved." As he chattered, Ben placed his body between the watch officer and the captain, obstructing their view of each other.

The captain had heard enough. He drew a SIG P2022, the same type Massir had carried in Rome. "I think this man needs to spend a day or two in a shipping container—at least until we put out into deep water. What do you think, Mr. Ruiz?"

The watch officer moved a corner of his jacket aside to show Ben a matching SIG.

Counter-accuse.

"Oh, wow. Guns. Did you know that's illegal here? *Mallory* told me you were packing, but I didn't believe him."

For an instant, both men shifted their glares to the bos'n.

No more talking. Time to fight.

Ben jerked the watch officer into a headlock, using him as a shield and confiscating the SIG from its holster. During the flurry of motion, the captain fired. The watch officer let out a cry, hit in the shoulder. Ben fired back, and the captain clutched his chest. That left only Mallory, who didn't appear to have a weapon. Ben smacked the bleeding watch officer's head against the steel doorframe, shoved him at the bos'n, and ran.

"You're a dead man," Mallory called after him.

Maybe. The bos'n had lured him into a nightmare game of Chutes and Ladders, and Ben had no idea how to escape the board.

The gunshots brought security guards hustling in from both ends of the pier, all wielding MP5s and one holding the leash of a German shepherd.

Ben half slid and half jumped down each ladder. A bullet sparked off the deck in front of him as he reached the superstructure's lowest balcony. Mallory leaned over the railing, two balconies above, lining up another shot. Ben fired off a round to force him back.

The dock security guards yelled at both men in English. "Drop your weapons! Hands up!"

Fat chance.

Alard the innkeeper shouted from the barracks in Dutch. Ben couldn't understand him, but he got the gist. *He's on your side. He's with Interpol.*

The guards moved their aim up and down in confusion.

Two more crewmen appeared on the cargo deck, running beside the stacks—both armed. In seconds, they'd have a clear shot at the lower balcony, and they wouldn't share the dock guards' confusion.

Ben needed to move. If he crawled down the ladder to search the maze of lower decks and passages for a way out, they'd own him. He'd have to stay outside, in the fresh air. The gap between the balcony and the cargo stacks looked to be several meters. Ben pressed his body back against the superstructure for a running start and launched himself from the rail. His chest slammed into the closest container.

Bullets plinked off the steel as Ben scrambled over the edge and regained his feet. Mallory hadn't heeded the dock guards' warnings. One fired a burst to make him listen. "Put the gun down!" Ben kept on sprinting across the containers, leaping from one to the next.

A second burst whizzed past his ear. "You too. Freeze. Drop the gun!"

Yeah, right.

With a reaching leap, Ben caught the yellow clamp of a crane lifting a container from the stack. The guards quit shooting, perhaps unwilling to risk hitting the crane operator. Mallory had no such qualms. He kept shooting, but the container's slow turn gave Ben cover. The operator bailed from his seat, slapping a big red kill switch on his way out.

The crane jolted to a stop, and momentum sent the container into a pendulum swing toward the dock stacks. Ben let go.

The added height helped him cover the distance, but shipping containers don't make for soft landings. Ben's touchdown crumbled into an ungainly roll that ended with his hard hat smacking the steel. He tore it off and chucked it away, grumbling as he scrambled to his feet. "Thanks, Kent."

The German shepherd raced across the dock, but Ben paid it no notice. The containers were three meters tall. No attack dog could jump that high. He kept low to avoid any shots, dropped from container to container until he reached the fence, and vaulted over, tumbling into the parking lot.

Less than a minute later, Ben swerved the Peugeot onto the pier access road. He glanced at the rearview mirror, expecting to see a lone barking dog at the fence. After all, his pursuers weren't real cops.

Instead, he saw the gate rolling open and two security vehicles speeding out behind him.

He let out a disbelieving huff. Impressive.

"Okay, gentlemen." Ben cranked the wheel, fishtailing onto the straightaway that led to the main port road. "Let's keep playing."

31

Concrete.

Snow.

Ice.

Cold winds in a northern port made for slick surfaces. Ben had helped Giselle choose the Peugeot's 308 model for its handling, but she drove with a lead foot, and she'd been tearing around the Paris suburbs in that thing for a year. All four tires had seen better days.

He tried to use the worn treads to his advantage, drifting through the corners while the dock cops played it safe behind him.

Ben had to give them credit for a solid response time. If he had to guess, the embarrassment of letting a bomber escape their net had forced them to sharpen up. But dock cops in Ford Focus hybrids were no match for a trained tactical driver. He'd lose them soon without a problem.

Sirens wailed ahead and to Ben's right. Red and blue lights flashed.

He slapped the wheel. "Seriously?"

Two Dutch police cruisers—VW Golfs—came flying in from the west, side by side, blocking the main port road and Ben's best route of escape. Judging by the rooster tail of white powder, both were sporting snow tires.

The approaching cruisers forced him to continue south over a small bridge. He smashed through a lowering barrier arm and sailed across train tracks into an odd suburban mix of warehouses and brick homes. A reflective street sign read *Welkom in Neiuw Engeland.*

Behind him, dock security peeled off to let the professionals take over. Ben would have to step up his game. He bounced over a roundabout island, corrected for the side skid that followed, and stepped on the gas. The first cruiser slowed to follow the street. His partner jumped the island like Ben and took the lead.

Canals.

Rivers.

Too many bridges—each one, a choke point. If more cops joined the chase, Ben's luck might run out. He needed to escape into the rural area to the southwest where a host of interconnected farm roads meant more options.

A street sign flew by, pointing west. Ben recognized a name from his drive into the port. *Haringvliet*—a long lake formed when the Dutch dammed off a North Sea inlet. That place might offer exactly the escape route he needed. He let the intersection fall behind, waiting for both cops to cross, then hopped the curb into a parking lot serving two warehouses.

He made a wide arcing turn on slick asphalt. Too wide. Ben grimaced a split second before he sideswiped a snow-covered car. White powder showered his windshield, but the impact corrected his trajectory. He flipped on the wipers and punched the gas, downshifting to recover some torque.

The gap between the warehouses had looked plenty wide from the street. A closer look made Ben second-guess, but the cops were too close. He gritted his teeth and committed. The Peugeot shot through the gap. His left side-view mirror—the only one remaining—snapped off with a flash of sparks.

The police cruisers, apparently unwilling to sacrifice their mirrors, skidded sideways to a halt.

Ben spat out the other side into a shallow rear lot and jumped the sidewalk. He hit a westward street at an easy angle for his worn tires. No one followed.

He passed the next cross street. Again, no sign of his pursuers. Only fields and a smattering of houses lay ahead. Another street sign for the Haringvliet lake confirmed he'd found the correct road, and he put the Peugeot into fifth to build his lead. If the cops stayed gone, they'd spare him from the dangerous stunt he'd planned for his escape. But Ben wouldn't bet his life on it.

To spies, phrases like They're gone *or* We're home free *are as bad as black cats and broken mirrors. A rookie who jinxes the mission with an early celebration is likely to get a slap upside the head and a bad reputation.*

Colonel Hale and years of mission experience had taught Ben to fight off such phrases, but like any man fighting pink elephants, he couldn't stop *I did it* from entering his brain.

Lights flashed in his mirror. Both police cruisers cut through the grass from a side road less than a hundred meters behind him.

Ben had never been fond of Europe's rural roads. Deep ruts and stone walls squeezed two lanes into one. His grip tensed on the wheel. One mistake would end this chase.

Twice, Ben had to slow for jinks in the road. Both times the cops and their snow tires cut his lead. No matter. He still had a plan. Maybe.

On the way in from Belgium earlier in the day, he'd driven the full length of the Haringvliet—a lake two kilometers wide and nearly thirty kilometers long. The brackish water of Rotterdam's port remained clear, but the freshwater lake had frozen over. The dams at either end were the only routes across, separated by thirty kilometers of winding shore roads. No cops were foolhardy enough to follow him onto the ice. If Ben could cut across the middle, he'd lose them for sure. A big if. He had to wonder, how thick was the ice?

The Peugeot crested a low hill, and the lake came into view. White. Pure. Dusted with snow. Ben drifted onto the shore road and accelerated southeast, steeling himself for the upcoming stunt.

Well ahead, skiffs lay overturned on the shore, covered with tarps for the winter. A boat ramp. Ben planned to slow fifty meters out and turn to hit it at the correct angle. With too much energy and not enough angle, he'd miss the ramp, jump the bank, and spin helplessly across the ice—assuming he didn't crash right through.

More lights.

Ben's heart sank. Two new cruisers came at him from the opposite direction. They'd boxed him in.

He shoved the pedal to the floor. The tachometer redlined. The engine screamed. He had to reach the ramp before the newcomers cut him off.

The Peugeot won the race, but not with enough margin to slow and change Ben's angle to the boat ramp. At the last second, he shifted into neutral and cranked the wheel hard over.

The tires failed to catch. Ben slid off the ramp and jumped the bank sideways. The rear tires hit the ice first. The Peugeot whirled into a sickening spin.

The car traveled a good distance from the shore before the spinning stopped, far enough for the cold air of the oncoming dusk to quiet the policemen's shouts. Not one risked stepping out onto the ice. Ben found that more worrisome than comforting.

The cops crouched behind their doors, guns pointed through rolled-down windows.

Ben ignored them. The engine had quit. After a few coughs, it started again. He put it into first and tried the gas. The tires whined and kicked up snow, but nothing else. After a few breaths, he tried again, and this time the whine of the tires ended with an ugly *crack*. Ben stopped and killed the engine, as if that made any difference. The ice squeaked.

The vehicular ballet had put him on the Peugeot's lee side, shielded from his law enforcement fans. Small favors. Ben shoved an arm through his backpack strap and opened the door. He slowly shifted his weight onto his leg and climbed out, raising his left hand high. The ice answered his first step with an awful *creak*. *"Nicht schießen!"* *Don't shoot!* He chose German to keep them guessing. No reason to make identifying him later any easier.

One Dutch cop answered in the same language. *"Hände hoch!"*

"Ja, ja." Ben gave him a tired wave. Placing his second foot on the ice sent stark white cracks out in all directions. He resigned his mind and body to a single, terrible fate.

"Hände hoch!"

"Ja, ich habe Sie gehört. Aber schießen mich nicht, schon gut?" He meant that one. *Yeah, I heard you. Just don't shoot me, okay?* As he answered, Ben let the SIG he'd taken from the watch officer hang low, out of sight. He sucked in a deep breath and fired straight down into the lake.

32

The cold threatened to crush Ben.

When the ice gave way, his ankle had been caught in the car's door. He let Giselle's beloved Peugeot drag him down, eyes closed. He saw her. Smiling. A little mischievous. Beautiful. But as his skin lost all feeling, he lost his grip on the vision. Her features faded, replaced by Clara's.

Four or five meters below the ice, the car hit bottom and the door swung out. His eyes popped open. Frigid lake water seared his pupils, without the rapid relief of numbness afforded to his skin. For his eyes, the burning never ceased. Ben had experienced that pain before. Of the varied specialized survival courses in Hale's schoolhouse program, he'd hated Arctic week the most. But he'd gutted it out and learned.

Every frozen lake has a thermocline, with the bottom up to eight critical degrees warmer than the top. Blindly beating at the surface ice is a death sentence. Stay low, where the view is broader and the water warmer. Assess the surface above to find holes or weak points in the ice. If you can overcome the pain of opening your eyes, you might survive.

Ben stayed low and assessed the light and shadow above. Before going down, he'd noticed an island more than halfway across the lake, some hundred fifty meters southeast of his position. He did his best to pick a bearing off the car, prayed he'd chosen the right shadow, and launched himself off the hood.

Was he kicking? He struggled to tell, unable to feel his legs—unable to feel anything but the cold threatening to slice through his eyes and into his brain. Oh, how he wanted to close them. He fought off the temptation. The slightest deviation from his course could mean the difference between life and death.

His target, a border between shadow and light, grew close, taking on detail. He saw river grass, brown and dead. He saw the cracks in the ice, spidering out from the rocks of a shoreline. Some passed over his head, but he didn't fall for their trap. He didn't slow. They were mere changes in the structure of a solid mass, like veins of quartz in granite.

Lungs ready to burst, mind drifting on quartz and marble slabs, Ben dragged himself along the subsurface shoreline, clawing at rocks and grass to reach the other side. He wanted to put plenty of cover between himself and the cops to block both sight and sound. Only when he felt reality slipping from his grasp did he finally stretch out the SIG toward the shore ice and empty the magazine.

It didn't do the job.

He punched the tight grouping of bullet holes. Blood colored the water around his knuckles. He punched again. And again. The ice gave, and Ben dug his knees into the silt and thrust his shoulders up against the break. Air brought a new level of cold to his wet skin. He breathed deep, ignoring the spikes it drove into his lungs.

Lying on the shore, Ben stared up at the evening sky. He wanted to stay there—sleep there.

"Get up."

He spoke the words out loud. Hale had taught him that letting them remain silent in his head siphoned away their power.

"Get up!"

Ben rolled to his knees. The far shore lay four hundred meters from his island, maybe more. Behind him, through the island's grove of evergreens, the red and blue lights still flashed. Within minutes, more cops would arrive. Hopefully they'd start behind him, not in front, and look for a body, not a fugitive.

His fingers stiffened. His limbs shook. Time was short.

At the slow pace of a low crawl, spreading out his body weight, he'd be dead or delusional from hypothermia before he reached the shore. Ben took the ice at a run, on feet he still could not feel.

Three times, he stumbled and fell. The second time, the SIG went sailing across the ice and he had to fetch it, adding several meters to his path. He couldn't leave it out there for the cops to find. The third time he fell, the surface cracked. Water seeped up, and Ben scrambled onward on his belly. He crawled the rest of the way, into the setting sun's last light.

A snow-covered berm separated the shore from a farmer's field. The quiet voices of Ben's arctic instructors warned him to sweep away his footprints as he climbed. As if he could.

"What do you want from me?" he asked out loud. "It's not like I brought a broom."

You making excuses, recruit?

Hale. He'd always been the meanest, the loudest, but always right. For the same reason Ben had chased after the SIG, he needed to cover his tracks now. Pine scrub dotted the shore. He slid down a berm and broke off three small branches, using them to sweep his tracks as he made the ascent again. *Too slow, recruit. You'll never make it now. Why don't we call this training evolution a fail and run you through the lake again? How about that?*

"No, sir. I can finish." Ben dropped down the berm's other side and fell with his back against it, hugging his pack, with an empty gun and pine scrub clutched in a frozen grip.

Colonel Hale stood right in front of him, hands on his hips. *No breaks, recruit.* The colonel leaned in, offering a hand to help him up. *Get that sorry corpse moving!*

Ben let his mentor pull him to his feet. Did the rules permit such help? Would he still pass the training evolution? He didn't care. He just wanted it to end.

A shed rose from the white ahead—shelter from the wind, a heat trap. Life. The instructors were never so kind. They'd have a padlock securing the door. Ben knew how to handle padlocks, assuming he could use his fingers.

He walked backward at an agonizing pace, covering his tracks until, without quite remembering how he'd gotten there, he found himself kneeling before the shed's door. He dug around in his pack. Lock picks were subtle, but not the tool for this job. While other recruits wasted precious time hopelessly fumbling in the cold with rakes and picks, Ben found his compact bolt cutters and ratcheted the teeth down over the lock. Four cranks and the bolt snapped.

Before going inside, he stripped off his coat and rolled his body in the snow.

What are you doing, recruit? Have you lost your mind?

Probably. More than probably. Ben figured his mind was well and truly gone. A minuscule voice deep inside told him hallucinations had set in and set deep. After a few seconds of thrashing about and kicking up powder, he struggled to his feet and beat his chest and legs. Flakes of ice fell away, leaving mostly dry clothes behind. He swept the area with his scrub and ducked inside.

The shed proved a bigger gift than he'd ever imagined the instructors granting. Tarps. Tools. Soil.

Ben tore open five bags of reeking fertilized soil and dumped it on the floor as insulation. The rest he stacked against the door to block as many cracks as possible, supporting his barrier with rakes and shovels.

When he finished, he sat down cross-legged on his heap and pulled a foil bar from his pack—something he'd mistaken for a food ration when the instructors first introduced him to his equipment. He peeled it open to reveal a white chalky stick and planted it in the soil like a baby tree. Now came the hardest and most important part. He had to light it.

The lighter's striker hurt so much, as if ripping the flesh from his frozen thumb. But the flame came fast and unhindered, the beauty of a wind-blocking shed. The white stick caught with a miraculous dark blue glow, promising to burn long, hot, and smokeless.

As a final step, he crushed three hand warmers, starting the chemical reactions, and shoved them under his clothes. He stuck one in each armpit and one down the front of his pants—ignoble, but vital to recovering his core body temperature. The flame stick would do the rest. Or it wouldn't, and he'd be dead by morning.

Don't you fall asleep, recruit.

Why wouldn't the colonel leave him in peace?

Don't you do it. You know what happens when we fall asleep in severe hypothermia.

Ben knew. He remembered the academics. "I don't care, sir. I just don't care."

The colonel vanished. Ben tried and failed to make Giselle appear in his place. He sat back against a bag of soil and covered his face with dirty, frostbitten hands, descending into shaking sobs.

A hand touched his shoulder. He looked up. "Giselle?"

Not Giselle. Clara. Her dog, with his ridiculous, happy-go-lucky grin turned in a circle twice and curled up in the soil between them, head on his paws.

She sat at his side. *I'm here, Ben.*

"Why? Why are you here?"

You know why. I'm here because you want me here. She patted his hand. Ben felt her skin—the softness of her fingers, the warmth. *And I'm not leaving your side.*

He nodded and closed his eyes, ready to let sleep come.

33

"Ben?" Clara jerked upright in bed. Moonlight crept in around the curtains, painting Sensen's guest room in dim gray. No Ben. Only Otto, curled up in a nest he'd made from the bedcover. Why had she called out for Ben? The details of the dream refused to return to her. She shivered. Whatever the dream, it left her feeling cold.

Clara settled down next to her dog. "He's okay, Otto. Ben can take care of himself." The dachshund answered with a bleary *I'm trying to sleep here* frown, and she nodded. "Right. Sorry. Go back to sleep. I will too."

Sleep didn't come. Despite Otto's warmth and the room's mild temperature, Clara couldn't shake the cold from her limbs. She peeled herself out of bed and pushed the covers up around Otto to keep him comfortable. Sensen had banned the dog from all furniture. What he didn't know wouldn't hurt him.

Halfway to the door, Clara paused and laughed at the absurdity of the thought. Her recent life had taught her the foolishness of that old phrase. *What he doesn't know won't hurt him.* In a world of spies and assassins, the exact opposite held true. What Ben didn't know had killed Giselle. What Ben didn't know would soon kill him and perhaps many others.

Clara had thrust herself into Ben's life at the flat, and in response, he'd protected her the way her brother took the brunt of her father's drunken rage. She repaid her brother's sacrifice by letting him join a foreign military, a decision that killed him. Now she'd repaid Ben by letting him run off alone and without answers.

"I should have gone with him," she said, glancing back at Otto as she placed a hand on the door lever.

Did she mean Ben or her brother? Perhaps both.

The thermostat had to be somewhere in the hall. Sensen had an oil heating system like the one that caused the secondary explosions at Giselle's place. The thought shouldn't worry her. It's not like these Leviathan people wanted to blow up the sniper's home too.

Did they?

She definitely should have gone with Ben.

Clara placed each step on the wood floor with caution, careful of creaky boards. If she woke Sensen, his awkward host mode would kick in. He treated her with the strangest brand of honor-bound hospitality, a mix of warm food and cold stares.

An *urgent errand*—Sensen's words—had taken him away for most of the afternoon, and he'd returned with clothes in her size and dog food for Otto. *These are for you.* He'd dropped the bundle on her bed and walked out. As a houseguest, she'd never felt so well looked after and unwelcome at the same time.

A quiet walk to the hall's end, close to the double doors of Sensen's bedroom, revealed no thermostat. Clara frowned. Downstairs, maybe? She reversed course, and the deep rumble of Sensen's voice touched her ears. She backed up a step. Yellow light peeked out through the crack between the doors. Another rumble. He was talking to someone, but who? She stilled her breathing and listened.

"Yes, sir. He came to me."

By *he*, Sensen had to mean Ben.

Cringing at the stupidity of her impulse, Clara pressed an eye to the crack. Through the blur of her eyelash, she saw the sniper at his desk, speaking to someone on a tablet—a *sir*, perhaps the fabled Director. Sensen's body blocked the screen, and he wore a lightweight headset and microphone, preventing her from hearing the other half of the conversation.

"No, sir. I didn't . . . I see. Yes, I let him go. I gave him Rotterdam. I thought it would keep him busy . . . A ship? No, sir, I—"

A long pause. Sensen bowed his head as if cowed by a reprimand.

"He's too close to what, sir? Who is . . . Understood . . . Yes. Zürich . . . I'll pass him the time and coordinates. If he survived Rotterdam, he'll follow through with the rendezvous. Calix is convinced of his own innocence. He won't miss a chance to declare it to a Company man . . . Yes, sir. I'll leave at first light."

Sensen went quiet, listening again, until finally, he let out a sigh. "What about the girl? I can't simply—"

The person in the monitor seemed to cut him off again.

"Yes, sir. I'll take care of it."

Clara fought to keep the pounding of her heartbeat from giving her away.

The girl. Me.

She'd been living under the self-imposed delusion that Sensen was his own man, honor-bound to keep her safe. But she realized now that he had a master—a spymaster. Of all Clara had learned in her short time in this secret world, the most frightening lesson was that spies favored missions and causes over people. Sensen's spymaster didn't know her—didn't care about her. Had she just become a liability?

Sensen set his headset down, rubbed his temples, and swiveled in his chair.

Clara lurched back from the door, praying he hadn't seen

the movement. She hurried back to her room, the thermostat long forgotten.

I'll leave at first light.

She and Otto had a few hours, if that. Sensen might come for her in the night, for all she knew. And then, assuming she'd understood the conversation correctly, he'd go after Ben.

34

I HAVE YOUR BOY

Jupiter watched the small window at the top of his holographic screen, waiting for a response. He'd been checking morning and night for two days, waiting for a response. One would come. His old friend always answered, but always in his own time. The Director had set up the untraceable chat in a remote corner of the electronic ether years ago, when Jupiter disappeared from his old life and name. The Director created the room to bait him, keep tabs on him. Jupiter knew this. But such portals worked in both directions.

A chime sounded from the remote server.

> CALIX SAYS DIFFERENT. HE CLAIMS HE'S STILL
> LOYAL—SAYS HE'S BEEN FRAMED.

> WHAT DO YOU KNOW OF LOYALTY? YOU DEMAND
> IT FROM YOUR SUBJECTS, BUT SHOW NONE. CALIX
> IS LEARNING THAT NOW, PERHAPS MORE THAN
> ANY WHO CAME BEFORE HIM BESIDES ME. HE'LL
> ABANDON YOU. WHEN I'M FINISHED, THEY'LL ALL
> ABANDON YOU.

The cursor blinked, unused for several minutes. Jupiter snorted and shut the server down.

168

□ □ □

Terrance climbed the gently curving staircase from the visitor lot to the main manor of Jupiter Global's executive retreat. Soft blue lighting gave the rose marble steps a lavender hue. He had no fear of approaching his boss in the predawn hours. Jupiter wanted Dr. Kidan's updates on Patient C Prime the moment they became available.

He found his boss on the back lawn, wandering barefoot in his Zoysia grass—not unusual. Terrance knew better than to walk on the grass himself without invitation. He waited for Jupiter to look his way and waved his tablet. "Sir, I have news."

Returning to the porch through the grass with his silver kurta pajamas lit by the moon and stars, Jupiter seemed more deity than man. And why not? It took a demigod to plot so perfectly the journey to this moment.

Jupiter had watched Wuhan and other labs across the globe following the first SARS outbreak and invested heavily in the key industries affecting the outcome. And in 2005, he moved his headquarters and production power to Spain, taking full advantage of an economic future no one else saw. Spain's 2008 collapse emptied cities and flooded the streets with stranded workers. To Jupiter, it brought real estate, prime port positions, and a near-unlimited supply of desperate test subjects. What foresight. What intensity of vision.

"Good morning, Terrance. You have news?"

"It's C Prime, sir. He's on the verge."

Jupiter took a seat at his patio table with his back to Terrance, raising the holographic screen from the glass surface with a gesture. "Give me details."

"The patient evacuated his bladder twice during the night, and the collection system flagged a high white blood cell count. After cross-referencing the result with the evening's round of blood tests, Dr. Kidan believes he'll go symptomatic later this morning."

Jupiter had called up the patient's results on his display. He studied a three-dimensional blood image from an electron microscope. "Time?"

"Eight fifteen local. Give or take ten minutes. Also, there's been a report from Rotterdam. The *Princess*."

"I saw." Jupiter swiped a finger through his display, sliding a text communication and security video from the ship into view. "I read the report an hour ago while working on something else. Our friend Calix has been busy."

"The Dutch police think he's dead."

"Not likely."

Terrance poised a stylus to take notes. "Our reaction?"

"Locate Calix." Jupiter brought up a map of Northern Europe and isolated the section around Rotterdam. "He's desperate to communicate with his master—to defend the honor we've stolen from him. Our people are watching the web for certain markers. Have them focus on traffic in this area." Plucking the map from the hologram, he flicked it over his shoulder through cyberspace to Terrance's tablet. "Once you have him, put Duval on his trail again."

"Consider it done." The stylus paused. Terrance watched his boss over the tablet's edge. "So, may I confirm an appointment for you to meet Dr. Kidan in the observation room?"

Jupiter raised his bare feet from the pavement and let his chair spin to face Terrance. "How confident are we in this result?"

"*Dr. Kidan's* confidence is high." Terrance made sure to emphasize the distinction. If this went wrong, as it had before, he wanted none of the blame. He'd seen what had happened to Dr. Kidan's predecessor.

His boss offered him a reassuring smile, as if reading his thoughts. "Do you trust me, Terrance?"

"Implicitly, sir."

"Then don't fear me. I didn't rescue you from New York three years before the pandemic only to kill you for someone else's mistakes. What did I say when I found you, running hustles in Central Park?"

"A scourge was coming."

"You believed me, didn't you?"

"Yes, sir."

"And your faith bore you out. Do you still believe?"

Terrance nodded.

"Good." Jupiter returned to his display to call up a picture of his parents. The photo matched the one hanging inside the house—a wealthy Greek American and his wife, obviously pregnant, standing in a sea of Hong Kong protestors. Jupiter didn't have to say a word about it. Terrance knew the story.

The street hustles Terrance's crew ran in New York, from shell games to melon drops, were all about creating the illusion of randomness and chaos while exerting perfect control. Terrance's ambition and skill in managing that crew—a form of chaos themselves—caught Jupiter's attention and earned him his position. But Jupiter, driven by the loss of his parents, had learned to manipulate chaos itself.

Jupiter's parents, passionate activists, survived Hong Kong's violent 1967 labor riots, and stayed on for the peaceful marches of 1968. They returned to America late in his mother's pregnancy, only to become two of the first victims of an outbreak that claimed more than a million lives. The marches had been a breeding ground for the Hong Kong flu. Jupiter's mother died in premature childbirth. His father passed hours later.

"Bombs and bullets." Jupiter's gaze remained fixed on the photo. "Policemen with batons. Screaming families. Yet only fifty-one died in total. The chaos became peace, and from that peace—like a butterfly—flew a virus that killed a million."

"Chaos." Terrance spoke the word like a Greek chorus. He knew his lines in this recitation.

"Chaos. The lament of my grandparents. 'No one could have guessed,' they said. 'No one can control it.' So, I vowed to prove them wrong. I watched. I learned. I studied the equations. And when I came of age, I joined the Company, because I thought the man who led us shared my determination to work for the greater good."

"But he didn't."

"No." Jupiter glanced up at him. "I showed him the data. I brought him the map to control, years in advance. We could have prevented the random devastation of the whole COVID-19 affair by creating an outbreak of our own—a controlled burn to stop a wildfire. But the Director turned me away, and we all felt the result." His eyes returned to the photo of his parents. "The same as before."

Terrance turned the tablet, casting the glow of Dr. Kidan's message across Jupiter's face. "You didn't need him. You led us here. You let the wildfire rage and now the world is primed."

"That's right, Terrance. The world is primed. If Dr. Kidan has achieved success, then we stand at the threshold of a new era. Instead of a controlled burn, we'll take complete control of the flames."

35

Ben sipped his coffee in the back corner of Café Giga in Antwerp. The hot liquid stung his lips. The progressive thaw of frost injuries caused pain for hours, sometimes days. Tiny blood vessels in his lips fought to unclot themselves. Nerve endings in his fingers, sliced and split by ice crystals, reconnected with his brain and screamed their displeasure.

He survived the night, but escaping the fields took time, still exposed to the cold. Now, sitting in the warm café with his coffee and a rented laptop, he could assess the damage. He had first-degree frostbite on his fingers, not too bad. But his nose and earlobes had reached the second-degree stage. For the next few days, he could expect constant pain and some visible side effects—temporary, but ugly.

Not good.

No one could deny looks play a part in the espionage game. Try gaining a mark's trust with a pus-filled frost blister growing on the end of your nose. His new look would slow him down more than the pain.

Ben set down the coffee and got to work, creating a single-use account for the email address he'd given Sensen. He tamped down his nerves, hoping against hope that a message awaited him with the details for a meet with Hale.

Today's spies communicate through nanotech with complex encryption algorithms and satellite channels with time-data multiplexing. But when it all goes wrong, there are fallback tricks. A temporary email account works in a pinch. The key is waiting to create the account until after the message you want to hide is sent to the account.

Digital postmen are tenacious. Send a message to an imaginary account, and they'll keep trying to deliver it for days. Neither rain nor sleet nor the infinite black of a nonexistent local-part@ domain will stop them from making their appointed rounds. While bouncing around cyberspace, undelivered, the message is unlikely to get intercepted, and it can't reveal the recipient's physical location. Once you're ready to receive, create the account using a public hotspot, take the message, then delete the account and run.

He finished creating the account. A welcome email from the server populated the inbox, but nothing more. Ben deleted it and waited, fighting off despair as he stared at the empty folder. "Come on . . ."

The laptop beeped. Sensen's email popped in. Relief flooded his chest. He didn't even need to open the message. Using an old Company contingency trick, Sensen had coded the time and coordinates for the meet into the subject line.

Ben jotted down the numbers, deleted the email account, and bolted. He kept his head low as he jogged across the street, wary of the sudden appearance of police cars.

Nobody came.

Why would they? The Company had no reason to come after him now. They could snatch him up at the meeting with Hale—or maybe put a bullet in his brain and be done with it. He didn't care. He needed to see the Director, and Hale might make that happen. Plus, he wanted to pass on the information tying the *Princess* and the *Behemoth* to the Leviathan bombings. The Company analysts needed to take a deep dive into Sea Titan and see what they could dredge up.

Three streets from the café, Ben hopped a tram toward Antwerp Central Station. Hunching over with an arm wrapped around a standing pole, he studied a waterproof map of Europe from his go-bag. Some quick math decoded the string of numbers from the email, giving him the rendezvous time and coordinates. Ben traced a finger down a line of longitude. Zürich. He could refine the rest later. He had eight hours to reach northern Switzerland. With the right train, he could be there in five.

36

A Dutch police diver with the top half of his dry suit hanging from his midsection showed Duval the screen of his camera, thumbing through pictures of a beat-up Peugeot at the bottom of the frozen Haringvliet lake.

"That's it," Duval said, nodding. "That's the one. She's missing a mirror."

The diver chuckled and flipped to the next picture. "She's missing both."

"Even better."

Out on the ice, spotters watched anxiously from the edge of a freshly cut hole. A man surfaced and slapped what looked like an ID badge into one of their hands. They conversed for a moment, and then the spotter relayed the message over his radio.

The man with Duval acknowledged the transmission and frowned. "They still haven't found the body."

A buzz from Duval's phone interrupted them. "Excuse me." He turned away to answer, but the caller had already hung up, somehow leaving a pdf file behind. Interesting. The contents made Duval smile. He clicked off the screen and touched the man's arm. "Keep looking. Our man is down there somewhere."

Renard joined Duval on the way back to their rental car. "I heard you identify the Peugeot. I guess our hunt is over."

"Not in the slightest."

"But you said—"

"I know what I said." Duval looked over his shoulder to be sure the Dutch team was out of earshot. "But I have reason to believe Calix survived. For now, tell me what you learned about the girl—Clara Razny."

"Still considered missing back home. I spoke to the dockworkers and port security here. No one saw her. And the local police tell me she was not in the car when it went down."

Duval considered this for a long moment. "Okay. Contact our liaisons in the Belgian, Dutch, and German police forces. Give them her description. Tell them to watch the morgues."

"You think he killed her?"

"Fits his track record. Besides, she was deadweight."

The sergeant regarded him for a long moment. "Sounds like you'd have done the same."

"In his shoes, Sergeant. I'd have done the same *in his shoes*. If you want to catch a criminal like Calix, you have to think like him."

"I see."

"If you're done questioning my methods, how about showing me your progress on the cottage, eh?"

This snapped Renard from his contemplative stare. He fumbled with a hardened police tablet—the unit's mobile office—and brought up a file. The first page showed a business headshot of a striking blonde. "The owner is Gabrielle Leblanc, thirty-one years old. A corporate security consultant, working mostly from home."

"So Calix knew she'd be inside."

"Possibly. There are two homes. She has a flat in Meudon. The cottage is a recent acquisition. The neighbor's caretaker told me he saw her and Calix there together once before. To him, they seemed a happy couple but . . ."

"But what?"

"The fire brigade found a body inside. Calix killed her. And if not Ms. Leblanc, then someone else." Renard swiped to the next page, a coroner's photo of a blackened corpse. "Female. The height, weight, and age match. But the fire destroyed her fingerprints, and our people found no dental or DNA records."

"It's her," Duval said, taking the tablet. "Who else would it be?" He stared at the charred face until the weight of Renard's discomfort became too great to bear. The man had always been squeamish. Duval flipped on through the file past her car registry, work history, birth certificate. He stopped when he came to a pair of side-by-side images—a candid shot of Leblanc harvested from a social media page and a police body-cam shot of Calix and his hostage at the Paris standoff. "What's this?"

"A hunch. I was looking for similarities between the women he's drawn to. I thought perhaps if I could find a pattern, we might—"

Duval lowered the tablet. "There is no pattern. Calix attacked the victim at his flat with chemicals, then lit the place on fire. He kidnapped Ms. Razny and made her watch while he blew up his girlfriend's cottage. *With the girlfriend still in it*. He is a madman." Duval opened the driver's side door and motioned for Renard to get behind the wheel before heading around the hood to the passenger side. "Get in. We're going."

"Going where? We have nothing to guide us."

"I told you. I have reason to believe Calix survived. I'm tired of following his footprints. And now a reliable source has given me a glimpse of his future—a time and a place. We have the opportunity to get there first." He slapped the roof and dropped into the passenger seat. "Drive fast. We're going to Zürich."

37

Clara waited for Sensen in the chalet's great room. She had no intention of being murdered in her sleep. Otto slept upstairs. When she'd returned from her eavesdropping, he'd given her worried looks, but Clara had settled him down again. And she'd snuck away as quietly as possible. She didn't want him to see what came next.

She nodded off once, maybe twice. Hard to say, sitting up in Sensen's leather chair, waiting for death. She had no illusions of besting a trained assassin, but she had skills—more than Sensen suspected for sure. And perhaps that gave her enough of an edge that she could make him suffer a little before she died at his hand. She only wished she could make his spymaster, Ben's precious Director, suffer too. Not for herself, but for sacrificing Ben despite all his loyalty.

Sensen walked down the steps as the gray-green of early morning lit the room. First light. If nothing else, the man was precise.

He only looked at her for a moment, turning his attention to the hall closet as he descended the last few steps, yet she could feel him keeping tabs on her. "You're up early," he said. "Trouble sleeping?"

"You could say that." Clara became aware of her posture.

179

She had slumped in the chair more than she realized before he came down. She adjusted, trying not to be obvious, hoping he didn't notice her hand sliding into the cushion beside her thigh. "Cold night. Maybe breakfast will warm me up."

"You're on your own, I'm afraid. I need to go out."

"For the day?"

"For several." Sensen drew a carbon-fiber rifle and a briefcase from the closet and laid them both on the credenza between the kitchen and the door. He broke the weapon down into parts that fit into the case's custom foam.

"Going hunting?"

"Correct."

The boldness of his answer shocked her—his actions too, checking the weapon's scope before seating it in the foam. Had he no shame, no need to mask his intentions? She should kill him right now, no matter who he supposedly worked for. Her hand tightened around the revolver's grip. "You're hunting Ben."

Sensen halted his work for a moment, but did not turn. "You should not listen uninvited at your host's door. It is bad manners."

Clara swallowed, but she said nothing. Did he know, or was he fishing?

"I don't blame you. The situation is . . . difficult. And you succumbed to the *Gastdruck*."

"I don't speak German."

He closed the case. "Yes, I know. Perhaps I should have switched to my native tongue when I heard you tromping like a small elephant in my hall." Sensen set the case near the door and reentered the closet, appearing a moment later with a black leather jacket and a matching backpack. "*Gastdruck* is the exhaustive pressure of being a good houseguest. Do you Slovakians have a similar word?"

"No."

"Pity."

What was his game? Bore her first, slit her throat later? The backpack looked well stuffed. She guessed the assassin, like Ben, always kept a go-bag on hand.

"I left ham and butter in the refrigerator. Bread and dog food in the larder. Fish and chicken in the freezer." He shouldered the pack. "I imagine you know how to use an oven, correct?" He lifted the briefcase and opened the front door.

She didn't understand. No knife? No silenced gun? Perhaps he'd poisoned the ham. "You're leaving?"

"We already established that."

"I thought you were going to kill me."

Sensen shook his head without turning to face her. "This is the problem with listening to only one half of a conversation."

"But you're going to kill Ben. I didn't misunderstand that part. What else is the sniper rifle for? This Director you both work for. I heard he was a good man, but he's a monster."

"The Director only wants a safer world. And he'll do what's necessary to achieve that goal." Sensen walked out. "I'll see you when I return."

"Wait!" She bolted up from the chair, gun leveled.

The German let out a sigh. *"Dieses Mädchen."* He lowered his head, growling at the flagstones. *"Sie geht mir auf den Keks."*

Her finger tightened on the trigger. "I told you. I don't speak German."

"I said, you're getting on my nerves."

"I can't let you kill my friend."

"You understand nothing." He dropped his case and had a handgun out and pointed at her head before it hit the flagstones.

Clara froze. She should have shot him in the back when she had the chance. Now? Could he dodge bullets? Could she?

Sensen echoed the voice in her head. "If you pull that trigger, Clara, you will die." His eyes flashed down for a nanosecond, then returned to hers. "You cross this threshold and leave my protection? You die, because I will not be responsible for you. That is your reality. Your best and safest move is inaction. Enjoy my house. Get rest." He frowned, gesturing upward with his chin. "Your dog is happily asleep upstairs, correct?"

What did Otto have to do with this? Clara nodded.

Sensen kept his gun steady while bending at the knees to recover his briefcase. "Then perhaps you should leave him be."

"You're saying I should let sleeping dogs lie."

"I'm saying you need to stay out of my way." Sensen lowered his gun and walked off, letting the door fall closed.

Clara tracked him through the front window with the revolver's front sight, begging herself to pull the trigger and unable to do it, until he disappeared into the detached garage. Moments later he sped away on a classic black motorcycle.

She stood there, pointing her gun at an empty drive for another thirty seconds, or perhaps five minutes. She didn't know. And then she ran upstairs and woke up the dog.

38

JUPITER GLOBAL INDUSTRIAL COMPLEX

The squeaking drove Terrance mad. Watching through successive hallway security cameras, he tried for more than a minute to identify which of the two stainless steel breakfast trolleys had the bad wheel. The second—had to be. Both were pushed by nurses in full biohazard protective gear. He checked the time in the screen's upper left corner and keyed the microphone hanging at his shoulder. "Hurry up, ladies. You know how he hates delays."

The first nurse kept her head low and quickened her steps. The second, who Terrance decided must have the squeaky wheel, shot an *I'm going as fast as I can* scowl at the camera.

Terrance gave a tiny shake of his head, huffing to himself. "Death wish."

The words elicited a cough from Dr. Kidan, standing beside him, though the sound might have doubled as a whimper.

He offered the Pakistani microbiologist a reassuring smile. "Not you, Doctor. Keep your answers brief and to the point, and you'll be fine."

"But my predecessor—"

"Made mistakes. Don't repeat them."

A bead of sweat broke out on the biologist's forehead.

Good. Terrance liked maintaining Jupiter's reputation as a man with a low tolerance for incompetence. It kept things running smoothly. He keyed the mic and made sure to let his own impatience shine through. "Where are my trolleys?"

Long windows set into the observation room wall gave the appearance of two-way mirrors looking into side-by-side apartments. An illusion. The windows were LCD screens, showing feeds from tiny cameras in the patient facility across the compound. The two apartments currently in view were in the incinerator section.

A floor-to-ceiling panel slid open in the kitchenette section of each apartment, revealing the trolleys.

"Thank you. About time."

Both patients rolled out of bed when the trolleys appeared—a learned response. They'd been taught by experience that if they didn't move quickly enough, the panel would close and not open again until the next meal. Patient E Prime crossed his rooms with rapid steps and wheeled his trolley out. Patient C Prime moved slower. Understandable, given his place in the experiment. They wore matching tank tops and shorts, and with each having committed to daily showers and shaves, they looked quite different from the men Terrance had recruited at the Valencia soup kitchen.

A red box flashed on his tablet, and he nodded to Kidan. "He's here."

Jupiter entered from a door at the far end. The microbiologist took a step, as if to meet him halfway, but Terrance caught him with a backhand to the chest. "Don't."

"How are our friends this morning?" Jupiter paced along the false windows, watching the subjects lift the silver domes off their platters.

Terrance lowered his tablet. "E Prime is in high spirits. C Prime is beginning to feel some effects. Not long now."

"I see he's still spry enough to take advantage of the food."

All the subjects in the program had signed on to a closed nutritional test hosted by one of Jupiter Global's many subsidiaries. The supposed test involved rich foods made healthy by imaginary nutritional magic. The patients never questioned the literature.

That morning, C Prime chose the Belgian waffles with Chantilly cream and bacon. E Prime, a bulky man, chose the vegan omelet. Who knew?

Whether waffles or soy, none of the subjects savored their meals. Without fail—and without suspicion—they tore into every bite.

Jupiter fixed his gaze on the microbiologist. "Your assessment, Dr. Kidan?"

"Healthy—" The doctor's voice caught in his throat. He coughed, and after a hard look from Terrance, he started again. "The patients are healthy enough to represent a normal human reaction. C Prime's tests, however, show that his health is about to change.

"So you are ready to proceed?"

"Yes, sir."

Jupiter waited.

Terrance smacked the biologist on the arm. "So *proceed*."

The doctor lifted a miniature tablet from his lab coat pocket and walked to the first false window. "Dr. Xue's efforts achieved only a quarter of your stated objectives—bubonic to pneumonic crossover, full aerosolization, an increased period of asymptomatic virulence, and sudden symptom onset. She solved the sudden symptom onset issue only, inadvertently creating a bubonic assassination weapon, which your people so ably applied in Rome."

"I am aware of the objectives. And I am aware of Xue's failure."

"Yes. Of course." Dr. Kidan opened an app with patient stats next to a column of colored buttons. "I only highlight this to show you how far we've come since her . . . departure." He let out a shaky breath. "Right. Here we go." He pressed the top button.

A green circle appeared on the observation window into E Prime's room, drawing attention to a ceiling vent. With no more than a whisper, nano-droplets blew in, digitally colored pink so the observers could watch the dispersal pattern. The subject never looked up from his meal, even as the pink cloud surrounded him, drawn in through his mouth and nostrils.

Dr. Kidan referenced his stats. "Male. Early forties. Potential liver issues but otherwise healthy. The bacteria's Rome variant, known as PB1, could only be applied by injection. We just introduced nano-fine water vapor containing PB2, the new variant. As you can see, we've solved the aerosolization problem."

In the apartment, the subject dabbed his lips and sat back in his chair, letting out a light burp of satisfaction. He showed no signs of distress.

Dr. Kidan gestured at his patient like a man gesturing at a new type of car. "Notice the high bacterial load taken in. Yet E Prime is entirely unaware of his infection, and will remain so for a minimum of ten days, likely more."

Jupiter's expression darkened. "I'll have to take your word for it."

Dr. Kidan answered with a nervous laugh. "No, sir. No, you won't. Please, let's leave this patient to his post-breakfast ablutions and have a look at C Prime."

The three moved to the next LCD window and watched the man eating his Belgian waffles.

"I'm still waiting," Jupiter said.

Terrance checked a running clock in the corner of the display. Dr. Kidan had promised a result within ten minutes of 8:15. The clock read 8:23. He could feel heat developing in the air around his boss.

Jupiter let out a sigh that might have been a growl.

"There!" Dr. Kidan's fingers flashed over his tablet, and the LCD window zoomed in on the patient. C Prime scrunched up his face and scratched his left shoulder. A black boil seemed to appear before their eyes. Dr. Kidan pumped a fist. "Yes!"

When the other two looked at him, he straightened and coughed. "I mean . . . Good. We've achieved the expected result."

Dr. Kidan zoomed the display out again and they watched C Prime stumble to the door. He mashed down on a large red button above the light switch. Nothing happened. He slapped it again and again.

"The button does call a nurse," Dr. Kidan said. "Unfortunately, there's nothing we or anyone else can do for him now."

The black boils now covered C Prime's arms, neck, and face. He stopped slapping the button and sank to his knees, gasping for breath.

Jupiter turned to the microbiologist. "What about contagion levels?"

"Oh, he's contagious, via the pneumonic transfer. Despite being asymptomatic, C Prime has been contaminating his quarters for sixteen days." Dr. Kidan tapped his tablet, and the LCD window took on an orange hue. Tiny pink circles were everywhere in the room—on the furniture, the breakfast trolley, floating in the air. "You're looking at a large volume of live PB2, each little bacterium searching for a new host. We can't even risk recovering the body for an autopsy."

The patient lay propped against the door, eyes open, unmoving. Dr. Kidan pressed the last button on his tablet screen, and the room burst into flame. He grinned. "PB2 achieved all your objectives, Mr. Jupiter. And we've produced a large volume."

"You've mastered the pace of this disease. Well done. But tell me, can you do the same with the less contagious variant—PB1?"

The microbiologist cast him a questioning look, as if wondering why anyone would want to do such a thing, but nodded. "Yes. We can manipulate the bacteria to select a range of timelines for symptom onset."

"Good. I may have a use for that." Jupiter pressed a hand against the false window, looking utterly absorbed by the smoke and flame. "You've created a masterpiece, Dr. Kidan. I asked for a nation killer, and you delivered."

39

Duval watched his partner climb from their rented Renault in Zürich and tried to decide if he looked better or worse without the bandages. Calix's pistol whipping had left Renard with a twisted beak and a face of mottled yellow and purple. Duval had not fared much better. Deep breaths and coughing amplified the pain of his broken ribs, and his head still hurt at night, thanks to the braining he'd taken from the Razny woman.

He pulled himself up from the passenger seat and frowned across the roof at his partner. "You look like a creature from a zombie movie."

"I don't find that funny, *Capitaine*."

"Don't growl at me, *Sergeant*. I didn't smash your nose."

"No. Calix did." Renard touched his face and flinched.

Duval chuckled, plucking the nerve. "Don't worry. This time he won't have a gun to club you with."

They left the rental in a public parking lot between the three facilities that shared the Zürichberg's wooded hilltop—the zoo, the university sports complex, and the towering headquarters building of FIFA, the International Football Federation. Whoever lured Calix to this place had chosen well. The zoo's perimeter walls forced him to a single point of entry and exit, and the random bag and wand checks at the gate made bringing a gun inside too risky—for a criminal, at least.

When the young security guard eyed the bulge in Duval's jacket, he flashed his badge. The kid backed off.

"How do you know he'll be here?" Renard asked.

"I told you. I have contacts in several intelligence agencies. This tip comes from a source high up in an international agency."

"What agency?"

"None of your concern. Let your captain have his secrets."

"Okay, but why doesn't this secret agency pick him up?"

Duval steered his partner right at a fork in the path, following a sign that read TROPICAL RAINFOREST in four languages. "Because he is ours, eh? Yours and mine." He swatted the sergeant's arm with the back of his hand. "What's wrong? Are you afraid of him?"

"No." Renard let out a dissatisfied grunt. "Certainly not."

Shaming the sergeant seemed to work. He quit prodding Duval and put his energy into the path's steep grade, wheezing audibly through his crushed nasal passages.

The lush trees and foliage, so out of place in the wintry alpine city, parted, and the two walked out into a small square with tables and food carts. Parents sipped lattes and caramel macchiatos while children played on a rubber-padded playground. At the far end, a glass dome rose four stories to become the highest point in the zoo—Zürich's Masoala Indoor Rainforest. The American's coordinates had fallen like crosshairs on the structure's peak.

Renard made for the coffee cart.

Duval caught his elbow and yanked him toward the square's edge. "Calix knows us by sight. You want to spook him?" He chose an alcove partially blocked by trees and sat Renard down on a bench. "We stay hidden and keep watch."

"You're sure he'll be here?"

"What did I tell you, eh?"

"Yeah, yeah. Your source."

He'd pulled Renard out of sight just in time. A man in a brown leather jacket emerged from the tree-covered path and quickstepped toward the dome, head low, shoulders hunched. A hoodie, pulled low over a stocking cap, hid his face, but Duval knew him by his gait—he hoped. He thrust a chin in the newcomer's direction. "There. You see? Calix."

Renard moved to stand.

Duval laid a heavy hand on his shoulder to keep him seated. "Easy, boy. Where's he going to run? Give it a minute, and we'll move closer. We can pick him up on his way out." He watched, grinning when Calix used the motion of opening the dome's door to check over his shoulder. His face looked worn and abused, much like Renard's, yet still recognizable.

Renard bucked under the weight of his hand. The sight of Calix appeared to have awoken the sergeant's rage.

Duval nodded. "Yes, my friend. That's the anger and focus I've been waiting for. You don't need any coffee now, eh?"

"You're right. I don't want your source to get him first. That pleasure is ours. I want to see the look of shock in his eyes as I pound my fist into his face."

"And I'll make sure you do. You deserve the first punch." Duval held a straight face as he made the promise, but Calix would be dead before Renard got close enough. "Come on, it's safe now. Let's take the bench by the playground." As they walked, Duval's hand brushed the bulge in his jacket, the one that had sparked the security guard's interest. He'd bought a new Springfield .45—excellent range and stopping power. The American wanted him to capture Calix, but Duval could justify a killing in a confrontation gone wrong. Bad things happen in the field.

○ ○ ○

Sensen's black motorcycle left the autobahn at the outskirts of Zürich. Clara watched him wind around the exit loop, heading east along the city's north side. He looked up as he gunned it beneath the overpass. Had he seen her?

She'd found the keys to Sensen's compact pickup hanging on a cupboard door in the kitchen and thrown whatever she might need into the cab—some clothes, the bread and ham, Otto's dog food. Nothing went into the pickup's bed. There were red stains, possibly rust. Clara thought it best not to take the chance.

She broke a dozen laws while speeding south in search of the motorcycle, and at least a dozen more after she picked him up on the A4 between Saarbrücken and Strasbourg.

If Sensen saw her, he gave no indication. No erratic driving. No sudden turns. He zipped past the fields and suburbs like a man out for a fast-but-leisurely Sunday drive. Clara held back, trying to keep two hundred meters between them, until the assassin's route turned south into the city, forcing her to close the gap.

Where was he going?

She'd overheard *Zürich* during the late-night conversation, but she'd gained no specifics. "We have to think like an assassin," she said to Otto, who lay beside her in the truck's cab.

The dachshund raised his head, as if to look for the motorcycle over the dash, then set his chin on his paws and let out a huff.

"No?" She had to agree. Sensen hadn't chosen the meeting place. The higher-ups had picked it for him. "So you're saying we need to think like a spymaster."

She had no idea how to do that. She'd only just learned to think like a spy.

Each turn brought the anxiety of losing sight of her target. And each straightaway brought the relief of picking him up again, until the inevitable happened. The motorcycle passed through a crosswalk. Before Clara reached the same spot, an elderly woman stepped off the curb.

Clara stomped on the brake pedal, dumping poor Otto onto the floor. Her protective instinct brought her eyes inside the cab. When she looked up again, the motorcycle had vanished.

The old lady paused right in front of her to give her a stern look. Clara ignored it and pulled around her, one tire bumping up onto the sidewalk, listening to angry shouts fading behind.

A hundred meters past the crosswalk, she saw a roundabout. Three roads peeled off from the circle, none running straight ahead and all hidden from view by apartment buildings.

She'd lost him.

Panic followed her through two spins around the circle, squinting up the streets to no avail, until she gathered her wits and focused on the signs. Two bore the names of Zürich subdivisions. Nothing useful. The third sign, pointing south, read ZOO, with the silhouettes of an elephant and a giraffe.

The zoo. Secure gate. No guns.

Otto seemed to decide he'd live longer if he stayed on the floor. Clara glanced down to give him a nod and took the zoo exit. She punched the gas. *I think like a spymaster.*

40

A blast of heat washed through Ben the moment he opened the door to the zoo's rainforest dome. The temperature inside might not have been higher than twenty-one or twenty-two degrees Celsius, a midsummer day in Paris, but compared to the freezing alpine winter of Zürich, it felt like he'd stepped into the Amazon.

Forced air and hanging strips of black vinyl protected the captive ecosystem from the outside environment. Ben pushed through these into a lush forest of bamboo, ebony, and persimmon. The geodesic ceiling rose to a peak more than thirty meters above, and some of the trees were so tall, they threatened to pierce it with their upper boughs.

"Mr. Roy?" A young man of Indian descent, wearing the royal blue polo and gray khakis of a Zürich Zoo guide, called to him from a wooded walkway guarded by a composite chain. "Mr. Jacob Roy?"

Ben swallowed the shock of hearing his old cover name and offered a pleasant smile. "That's me."

"This way please." The guide unclipped the chain and gestured up the walkway, but he seemed to struggle to hold Ben's eye. His gaze darted everywhere but Ben's face. A tell. The inability to look someone in the eye could mean a number of things—deceit, irritation, fear. What was his problem?

194

Your face, you idiot.

Ben remembered his battered and frostbitten features. He removed a wad of tissue he'd picked up on the train from his back pocket and dabbed his nose. The pressure hurt, and it left spots of pus on the white paper.

Great.

The guide was no spy. He just didn't enjoy looking straight into the eyes of ugly.

Ben solved the young man's where-do-I-look problem by nodding for him to lead on, and the two headed for a steep spiral stair enclosed within a wire-net shell. Relief colored the guide's voice. "Your party is waiting in the north tower."

"My party?" Ben had resigned himself to the strong possibility he'd walked into a trap, but if the Company still wanted to put him down, he'd rather Hale do it alone. "How many are in this party?"

The guide glanced over his shoulder as they rounded the spiral stair's first turn, catching himself before his eyes reached Ben's. "A figure of speech. There is only one. Your friend, yes?"

"More like an old coach."

"Ah. A coach. Good." The guide stretched a hand toward the FIFA headquarters building, visible through the dome's upper panels. "Football?"

"Hunting."

"Oh." The man didn't make another peep for the rest of the climb.

At the top, he drew an umbrella from a mesh pail and used it to point at the other tower, two stories higher and joined to the first by a rope-and-plank bridge that dipped into the forest canopy. "Over there. Your coach is on the upper platform." He offered Ben the umbrella.

Ben waved it away and shielded his eyes against the sun shining through the glass. "I don't see him."

His escort had already started down the stairs.

195

"Hey," Ben called after him. "Why would I need an umbrella anyway?"

"The rain."

Rain? "But we're inside."

The guide didn't answer.

Ben tested his weight on the bridge's first plank. It seemed sturdy enough. As he crossed, he passed a blue-green chameleon walking the rope railing with slow, rocking steps. A fruit bat hung upside down from an overhanging tree branch and hissed at Ben. He frowned back. "You too, huh?"

The steep angle of the sightline between the bridge and the upper platform prevented Ben from scoping it out. Hale probably planned it that way, leaving him no choice but to trust his former schoolmaster or walk away. *Give your enemy no options.* Isn't that what Hale had taught him? He sighed and started up the stairs spiraling around the tree at the platform's center.

"Couldn't stay away, could you, kid?" Hale stood from a wooden bench as Ben reached the platform.

"I need answers."

"I have some. But maybe not the answers you're looking for."

Ben thought he sensed concern from the old tyrant. More than concern. Affection. Hale made two long strides and wrapped him in a hug. "You look like death. It hurts me to see you like this."

Hale had seen Ben suffer before. A lot. In all those cases, in the broad scope of schoolhouse training, there'd been a safety net—well out of Ben's sight, but present. Hale's response to his appearance now told him with absolute clarity that all safety nets were gone.

The schoolmaster released him and gestured at the bench, sheltered by a wooden awning. "Have a seat, kid. Let's talk."

41

Clara's foot tapped an erratic beat on the yellow-painted asphalt at the ticket booths. Who in their right mind went to the zoo in winter? The answer was an American family of eight, and they were hogging the only open window. The father wanted to haggle the price of every extra attraction the zoo offered.

"The special white lion exhibit—how much is that again?"

His wife, rolling a double stroller back and forth to rock her twins, offered Clara an apologetic shrug.

Clara answered with a curt smile. Her foot never stopped tapping.

The security guard singled her out for a random check. Of course—because why stop the small army rolling a miniature troop carrier through the gate and carrying enough supplies to last until spring? He found nothing. She'd left the SIG in the truck with Otto. Getting detained by zoo guards and arrested by the *polizei* wouldn't do her or Ben any good.

The army, with its stroller troop carrier, marched south from the hub inside the gate. Clara chose east, if only to escape the whining and bickering. She needed to concentrate.

Find Ben.

She doubted Sensen could get a sniper rifle past the gate,

even a zoo gate. A rifle is a rifle. But now that she had a confined area to search, she didn't need to track down Sensen or bash him over the head with a potted plant—the only viable weapons in sight. If she found Ben, she could get him safely out of there.

"Ben?" Clara shouted up the path.

A young couple, barely out of their teens, watched her with worried looks. The girl caught her elbow. *"Hast du dein Kind verloren?"*

Clara didn't speak German.

The young man held his hand waist high. *"Dein Kind."*

They thought she'd lost a child. What was she supposed to say? No, I lost my spy.

"Uh . . . Yes. *Mein* . . . *kind.* Ben. He's always wandering off and getting into trouble." She waved away their worried looks. "No problem. I'll find him." She reinforced the declaration with a nod.

The girl nodded back, adding an unconvinced smile. Her husband pulled her onward, mumbling to her in German.

Maybe she shouldn't shout Ben's name—for many reasons. She hurried on.

"Where are you?"

Why were all zoos laid out like a maze on a child's cereal box? Clara began to think she'd have to search every path and every building. She came to a broad plaza-slash-junction with camels, paired together in little thatch-roofed hothouses all around the space. A camel spa. She half expected to see them wearing towels and lounging on teak benches. Ten camels in all. No Ben.

She plopped down on a circular bench to think. Some spy she'd turned out to be. The nearest camel stopped roving his tiny space and stared at her. Clara stared back. "Do you think Ben expected a sniper to interrupt his meeting?" The camel absently chewed something she hadn't seen him pick up. "You're right." She slapped the bench. "Ben let his opponents choose the meeting point. How desperate is that?"

The camel wandered off. Clara looked to her right to see a little boy gazing at her, mouth slightly open. His mother pulled him away.

The Company chose the location, one meant to favor their sniper. And with security checking bags at the entrance, a sniper would need to shoot from beyond the zoo walls.

Clara's eyes drifted uphill to a glass geodesic dome rising from the trees. Turning her head, she saw the FIFA headquarters building, the highest structure on the Zürichberg hilltop. The rooftop offered a clear view of the dome—a clear shot for a sniper. A sign on the junction's north side pointed the way, identifying the place as the Masoala Indoor Rainforest.

Clara left the bench at a run.

42

Ben watched a bright red macaw wheel past the platform to land atop a mushroom-shaped baobab tree, the enclosure's centerpiece. Beyond the treetops and the glass panels, snow-covered slopes rose from Lake Geneva to a dozen or more rocky peaks. "Quite the sanctuary you found."

"You wanna talk about the scenery or business?" Hale sat heavily beside him, resting his hands on the worn knees of his jeans and glaring out at the mountains. "I cut a trip to Venice short for this." He lolled his head over to fix his glare on Ben. "I'm retired, kid. Remember? I left the game a week before you graduated from the schoolhouse. We had a party and everything."

No matter what security measures the zoo had in place, Ben knew a Glock was hiding under Hale's gray canvas jacket. He grabbed for it.

The colonel trapped his wrist in an iron grip before his fingers got halfway to the target.

"Your reflexes are pretty sharp for an old retired guy." Ben gave him a thin smile. "You and I have seen each other plenty since then. We both know Company agents never leave the game."

Hale released him, pushing his arm away. "They do when they're told to leave."

"You mean me, right? Are you confirming this is a severance, a campfire horror story come to life?"

"I'm not the Director's buddy, kid. He doesn't tell me anything. But from where I'm sitting, this can't be anything else." Hale let out a breath and eased himself back next to Ben. "I received a briefing on my way here. I know about Rome, Brussels, Paris. I know about Leviathan and the man you call Massir. And Sensen told me you paid him a visit at his place in Luxembourg." He chuckled. "You should take it as a compliment that he let you live."

"He won't do it again."

"So I've been told."

Ben could swear Hale made a slight tilt of his head—a minuscule movement, perhaps a shift of his gaze. Disturbing, but the need for answers kept him locked in his seat. "Tell me this. Did the Company analyze the case contents? Rome might have been a setup, but Dylan told me the case contents were genuine—the chemical foundations for CRTX explosives."

"I might say Dylan knows his business, if I were privy to such information. Where are you going with this?"

"If the chemicals are real, we should still be able to backtrack the order, follow the money."

Hale crossed his arms. "*We* does not include *you* anymore. Nor me, officially. But I have it on good authority the money trail led to a dead end. Those chemicals appeared from nowhere—a rabbit out of a hat."

"Impossible. That only works if . . ." Ben fell silent, trying to let his thoughts catch up with his conclusions.

The flat line of Hale's mouth threatened to turn upward into a teacher's grin. "Go on."

"Leviathan is synthesizing the compounds for CRTX in-house. But if they can do that, they can make tons of the stuff. We're talking the explosive power of a nuke."

"I wouldn't worry. They'd still need a big rig to move a bomb that size. And frankly, CRTX shouldn't concern you." Hale shifted on the bench, stretching out an arm to touch Ben's shoulder. "C4 is more your speed—the kind found in a standard Company demolition package."

"So you know about Giselle?"

"Word travels fast when a team lead kills one of his people."

"I *didn't* kill her." Of all the sins Ben's friends forced him to deny committing, Giselle's murder hurt him the most. But with Hale, he swallowed his anger. He needed to keep this civil. "Talk to Dylan."

Hale drew his arm back and snorted. "You're saying Dylan—little Dylan who doesn't carry a gun and can barely talk to a woman like Giselle without stammering—turned into a cold-blooded killer and blew up her house."

"Cottage."

"Whatever. Let's talk about that, and feel free to stop me when I run out of actual-no-kidding facts." Hale counted each statement on his fingers. "You start a relationship with a team-mate, a gross violation of Company rules. Your girlfriend buys a safe house off the books. You check out a demolition package, which goes missing. And not long after, the safe house blows up with said girlfriend inside." He lowered his hand. "What's the Director supposed to think?"

"He should give me a chance to tell my side of the story. I passed my demolition package to Dylan in Rome." Ben showed him the detonator fragment. "And I found this at the scene. Either Dylan wanted to frame me, or the Company took her out with a similar package as part of my severance." Ben tucked the fragment away. "Prove me wrong."

"Not my job. I'm not the Company's PR man. And the Director's not the one on trial here."

On trial. Ben should have laughed. He never saw a trial—never had the chance to stand in his own defense. The trial ended days ago, relegating him to the world's longest and most painful execution. He needed a stay in view of an appeal. "Ask the Director to meet me, let me plead my case."

"I'm not a messenger boy either." Hale folded his arms and crossed one leg over the other, a false relaxed posture that Ben knew would put his right hand closer to his gun. "Look, kid. There are two reasons for a severance, and two reasons only. Either you turned traitor or botched something huge. You tell me which case this is."

"I'm no traitor."

"Okay. Say I believe you—"

"*Say* you believe me?"

Hale held up a hand. "Stick with me, kid. If you're no traitor, then you must be an epic failure. In that case, think of this as getting fired. All you need to do is list your failures. I'll document them as your intermediary, and everything'll be fine." He pulled an imaginary slip of paper from his inside pocket and offered it to Ben. "Here's your pink slip. Sad. Sure. But not the end of the world. Try starting over. New city. New job. You've always had quick hands. I bet you could flip burgers with the best of 'em."

"Pink slip? The Director sent a sniper to shoot at me. He froze accounts." Ben pointed with both hands at his frostbitten face. "Look at me. We inflict this kind of punishment on petty dictators and drug lords—the truly wicked. I'm one of the good guys."

"You *were* one of the good guys. So you say. But now, good or bad, you're out. Take the severance and walk."

Rain came pouring down in torrents. Ben looked up through half-closed eyelids to see streams of water shooting from sprayers near the dome's peak. Rapid droplets pelted his face, unchecked by the wood pergola above the bench.

He heard the pop of an umbrella—felt the handle pressed into his hand. Hale tilted it into place to protect them both. "It rains on the just and the unjust, kid. And that's no joke. I want to believe you're not a traitor. But either way, you made some big mistakes. Unforgivable mistakes."

"No." Ben rubbed the rain from his eyes. It smelled of steel instead of clouds—unreal. None of this was real. He shook his head and repeated the denial with more force to make himself heard over the fake storm. "No. I made mistakes. We all do. But I don't deserve this."

Hale laughed. "Then why is it happening?" He pressed himself up to leave, stepping out from under the umbrella's protection, as if an operative of his caliber didn't need it. He snapped his wet fingers in Ben's face—as good as spitting. "Wake up, kid. It's over."

Ben stood and grabbed his arm. "We're not done."

The colonel spun, landing a blow to Ben's solar plexus with the heel of his palm, hard enough to drop him back against the bench. "I said it's over."

"But . . ." Ben wheezed, fighting to recapture his breath. "Leviathan . . . I have . . . new intel."

Hale cocked his head. "What intel?"

Ben never got the chance to answer. They were interrupted by a cry from the rainforest. Not a macaw or a monkey cry, but a human voice—a woman's voice, shouting a clear name. "Ben!"

43

Ben fought through his shortness of breath to regain his feet. He joined the colonel at the platform's oak railing. Below, Clara ran up the path, amber hair matted to her head and shoulders by the downpour. Her head turned frantically left and right. "Ben! Where are you?"

Three men converged on her position. The young zoo guide in the blue shirt hurried in from a side path carrying two umbrellas, perhaps thinking this woman had freaked out after wandering into a man-made storm. Two others burst through the hanging vinyl strips at the entrance.

Ben recognized Duval and his partner. He cupped a hand to his mouth. "Clara. Watch out!"

She looked up, shielding her eyes against the rain. "You watch out. Sensen is here!"

As if he hadn't seen that coming. Part of him had expected to die the moment he and Hale sat on the bench. "I know!" Ben pointed. "He's on the FIFA rooftop!"

Hale rolled his head over to look at him. "Really, kid?"

Duval and his partner kept coming, but the guide with the umbrellas got in their way. The three collided. Clara ran into the bushes—safe, if only for a moment.

The French cops both had guns. Ben had left his in the go-bag, in the woods outside the gate. He needed a weapon.

Ben and Hale stared each other down. The colonel pressed

his lips together, pushing out the salt-and-pepper gristle on his chin. "Don't be stupid, kid. Sensen's here to protect me, not kill you. Don't give him a reason."

They both made their moves. The colonel went for the Glock. Ben chose to use the weapon already in his hands. He thrust his open umbrella into Hale's chest, stabbing him with the dull point and trapping his hand with the taut black fabric. The umbrella also obscured Hale's view, and Ben took full advantage. Still pushing, he kicked a heel into the inside of Hale's knee.

The colonel wouldn't go down that easy. But Ben didn't want him to go down. He needed a shield. With Hale off-balance, Ben steered him to the platform's east rail, cutting off Sensen's sightline from the FIFA.

Hale fought back. He threw wild punches with his free arm. Ben blocked them all and kept him pinned against the rail. Within seconds, he had a hand inside the colonel's jacket. He threw a final vengeful punch through the umbrella fabric into Hale's solar plexus, and backed away, leveling the Glock. He crouched low, still wary of Sensen.

The grimace on his mentor's face gave Ben a measure of satisfaction.

Both men blinked and squinted in the rain. Hale wheezed. "You said . . . you had intel."

"Sea Titan Cargo. Valencia, Spain. *Behemoth*. Jupiter. Take a look." Ben grabbed the rail and vaulted over.

A shot split the rain-soaked air. Birds and bats launched themselves from every tree. Ben caught the rope of the plank bridge under his armpits, body swinging, desperately holding on to the Glock. He dropped again. Branches whipped at his face. Another shot rang out. This time, glass shattered above. Ben landed with a painful splat in mud and rotting leaves.

"Calix!" Duval and his friend blocked the path to the exit, weapons up. Duval fired.

A broad leaf split to his right, and Ben rolled deeper into

the dubious green cover. He felt a tug at his elbow. He swung a left, but pulled the punch when he saw Clara lying next to him in the dirt.

Rain dripped down her face. "You're in danger."

"*I'm* in danger? You're the one in danger. I left you and that dumb dog in Luxembourg for a reason. Tell me Sensen didn't order you to stay put."

"Of course he did, at gunpoint. Come on. We need to go."

She jumped to her feet, and Ben followed. He pushed her into a crouching run as a trio of bullets sliced the foliage around them. "Why didn't you listen to him? You never listen. You never stay put."

"But Sensen came to kill you. This is a trap."

"My whole life is a trap."

A plan formed. With all the bullets flying, Ben didn't have time to hunt for the zookeeper access points hidden in the dome's concrete foundation, and he didn't want to. For once, he needed Duval. He grabbed Clara's hand. "Run!"

They sprinted straight down the path toward the exit, with Ben firing the Glock the whole way. Ten rounds for two opponents might sound like good odds. They weren't. Ben wished Hale had brought a bigger gun with a bigger magazine.

The zookeeper buried his head, and the French cops split, diving into the bushes. Ben kept shooting to keep them pinned, leaving a trail of cordite and sulfur hanging in the air behind him until the Glock answered his pulls with sickening, empty *clicks*. He chucked the weapon into a fishpond and pushed Clara ahead through the vinyl.

She went for the double doors, but he steered her back into the entryway's corner and pressed a finger to his lips.

Clara shot him a glare for all the manhandling.

He mouthed, *I'm sorry.*

They waited.

Hot air pounded them from a stack of heaters—a flowing

barrier to keep all the tropical creatures safe from the alpine cold. In the time compression caused by the adrenaline flowing through his system, it occurred to Ben that his presence had rendered the barrier useless. At least one glass panel had been destroyed in the gunfight, possibly by Sensen. How many birds and bats were now hurtling free into the frigid mountain air?

Duval came through the vinyl first, focused on the exit. Ben let him pass and threw a head-level elbow at the form coming through next. *Crack.* Duval's partner screamed.

Ben let the partner fall, gasping and groaning, and wheeled a fist at Duval. The French cop spun, predictably, and caught the back of Ben's knuckles with his face. A tug-of-war for the gun might send a stray bullet into Clara. Instead, Ben dropped his left fist hard onto Duval's wrist, and the weapon fell. Ben kicked it away, out of sight beneath the heaters.

A knife came out. Duval was no slouch.

Before Ben could react, Clara moved in and grabbed the Frenchman's arm. She gave it a twist worthy of the schoolhouse defense course and jammed the knife against the doorframe, knocking it from his hand. Nice. Ben let her do her thing and drummed the guy's temple with three rapid rights. He saw Duval's knees buckling.

"Enough," he said, nodding for Clara to back off. He spun Duval around and locked an arm through both elbows. He needed a shield.

The vinyl rustled. The partner. Too bad. From their limited contact, Ben kind of liked the guy, but he couldn't afford to let him follow. He kicked backward and heard another scream. He motioned to Clara. "Stay behind me."

"Why?"

"Sniper."

"Oh. Right."

The first bullet came flying the instant Ben pushed Duval through the doors.

44

Sensen's first round clipped Duval's ear and missed Ben by an inch. Amid the Frenchman's cries, he heard the ricochet—metal on pavement. It hadn't hit Clara. "You okay?" He refused to believe the German would intentionally shoot Clara, but a stray round might clip her.

"I'm fine." Clara laid a hand on his shoulder and offset her torso a little to the right. A good position, and he loved her calm. Instinct? Or had someone taught her to communicate through body signals in the heat of battle? Either way, they could do this. "We're getting out of here."

"I know. I trust you."

"You must be the only one." He kept sidestepping toward the tree-covered path. The second round passed clean through Duval's left bicep. As it turned out, dirty French cops made poor shields against tungsten bullets. But if Sensen didn't mind shooting him, why not center his shots for a better chance at Ben?

Bulletproof vest.

Duval was wearing protection. A standard vest couldn't stop tungsten rounds from entering Duval's body, but it would slow them, preventing them from exiting Duval's back and tagging Ben. "Stay low," he said to Clara. Two strides later, they reached the path.

Ben hugged the foliage, keeping clear of Sensen's view. He

pushed Duval up against a lamppost. "Leave me alone. Understand?"

Duval sneered at him. "You're a dead man."

"Not by your hand. You're out of your league." Ben smashed the back of his head against the post and let him drop, senseless.

"Halt!"

Three security guards raced up the path, batons out and ready. Clara moved off to the side. "Don't hurt them, Ben."

He shot her a look that said *You're asking a lot.*

The guards slowed. Clara shrugged. "They're only doing their jobs."

"Hände hoch. Die Polizei kommt."

Ben frowned at the guy and forced him into English, just for the distraction. "I don't understand you, buddy."

"Hands up. The police are coming."

"Which means I'm short on time. You three should run away now."

They didn't listen.

The guards advanced, and Ben laid out the first two with three rapid punches each. The third guy raised a can of pepper spray. Ben smacked the crook of the guard's elbow with the second guy's baton—which he had confiscated—and turned the arm to point the can back toward its owner. The can went off. The young man fell to his rear, clutching his face.

Ben took Clara's hand and the two continued their run down the path. On the way, she smacked his arm. "I told you not to hurt them."

"If they want to do security work, they need to learn how to take a punch."

"Not funny."

"Do you hear me laughing?"

"The first guard"—Clara pressed her lips together—"the one you punched in the throat. He said they called the police."

"Correct." Ben slowed to a stop at the camel junction, still keeping an eye on his position relative to the FIFA building. "With all this gunfire, I'm betting the entire Zürich police force will be waiting outside the entrance."

"So . . ." She squeezed his hand—a signal of urgency, not affection.

"So, we can't escape using the front gate." Ben thrust his chin at a south-pointing sign that read REPTILE HOUSE, AQUARIUM, CHILDREN'S ZOO in three languages. "We need to find some cows."

Hale chose the zoo to keep Ben contained, creating something known as a forced funnel. But Ben knew as well as his mentor did that forced funnels were illusions. A good field operative could always find another way out.

"Cows?" Clara said. Puffs of white drifted behind them as they ran—labored breaths in cold air.

"I know, right? European petting zoos always have cows. Goats, I get. Ponies? Sure. But cows? Cows are for burgers and milkshakes, not petting or riding."

"That's not what I meant. I'm asking you why we need them now."

The wail of sirens rolled up the hill from the city below. It had become their song. "Big animal. Big access point where we can escape." He pointed at a sign. "I'll let you pick. Elephants, lions, or cows?"

"Fine. I get it. Cows it is."

"Thank you."

A scene had developed at the petting zoo. What Ben initially took to be a crowd seemed to be a single family with a ton of kids locked in a surreal battle with five zoo guides.

There were kids everywhere—noisy, squealing kids. Each carried a bag of feed and hurled fistfuls at the sheep and goats while their father shouted and gesticulated at the pack of guides. One, a girl in her twenties, spoke rapidly into a radio, eyes on the edge of panic.

Chaos.

Ben and Clara's arrival didn't help.

Radio-girl ditched the argument with Super-dad and pushed out a palm to stop the two newcomers. She seemed to think Ben and Clara were guests fleeing the gunshots. That impression didn't last. She took a long look at Ben and the baton he'd stolen from the guards and backed away, calling to the others.

Ben shook his head. So much for hiding his exit point.

The keepers and the family parted like waves to reveal a pen of furry alpine milk cows at the section's rear. Ben and Clara hopped the fence, stopping when they found a toddler who'd apparently crawled through wires to join the herd.

Clara passed the girl over the fence to her mother. She gave the woman a stern look. "He needs to pay for a babysitter, okay? You need a break. Tell him tonight."

Ben gave her a quizzical look. "Do you know these people?"

"Long story."

"Later, then."

The sirens were loud now. New voices spoke in solid tones on the keepers' radios. The professionals had taken over, and they'd soon close any windows of escape.

Doors painted to match the barn setting at the back of the pen opened into a wide concrete feeding station instead of an exit. Ben let go of Clara's hand and raced to the back, relieved to find a gate to the left. He flipped the latch and shoved it open. "This way."

He passed between a line of stalls and a set of offices. Unlit passages led off in both directions. The whir of machinery blocked out all other sound. Ben kept to the main hall, navigating a long curve before pounding up a metal ramp to a garage-style door. He grabbed a control hanging by a thick orange cord and powered the door up. "Loading dock," he said, breathing hard and looking back. "I told you we'd—"

The hallway behind him was empty.

Clara was gone.

45

Duval woke up handcuffed to a hospital bed. A sling constrained his other arm, strapped to his body with nylon and Velcro. An attempt to move it sent a shock of pain through his body.

Oh, yes. Calix had shot him from behind.

But how could he? Calix had run out of bullets during his charge for the exit—tossed his gun away. Perhaps he had backup.

A fog of medication obscured his memories. Duval grasped at the images. Calix used him as a shield. Yes. So, the shooter and Calix were enemies, not allies. Maybe the American had sent someone else. It fit. The man had always been clear about Duval's expendability.

"You could have told me," he muttered in French. "I'd have dropped to give your man a clear shot."

The curtain next to his bed flew back. Renard lay on a matching bed. He looked angry. Hard to say. A new bandage covered half his face. New yellow bruising spread from underneath it, all the way to his temples. He spoke in a muffled voice, slow, as if each word hurt. "You are awake."

"Obviously." Duval jerked at his handcuff. He noted both Renard's wrists were free. "What is the meaning of this?"

"We should have taken our time—made a plan, flanked him. You said we would take him together when he came outside. You promised me the first punch. But you chased that woman into the dome. And the moment you saw him, you opened fire." Renard paused to suck in a breath through his mouth. "You idiot."

"How dare you speak to me in that manner. I'll have you fired." The sergeant tried to snort and winced. He moaned.

Duval rattled his handcuff again. "Renard, I order you to tell me what is going on. Why am I chained to this bed?"

"You are not a man who knows how to make friends. Did I ever tell you this, *Capitaine*? I have known for quite some time. The paramedics, for instance. You thrashed about and called them names. In your flailing, you hit one in the face. This is when the needle went in. You've been sedated ever since."

"And the thrashing of an abused man is an excuse to handcuff him to the bed?"

"No. The handcuffs are the work of Major Graf, another of your would-be friends. He did not take kindly to our running an operation on Swiss soil without coordination." The fraction of Renard's features that Duval could see darkened. "You told me headquarters had sanctioned this. You told me we were cleared to operate in Zürich. You lied."

Duval let his head fall back on his pillow. "We didn't have time."

"We had the long drive from Rotterdam."

The door to their shared room opened, and a grizzled police major walked in, followed by a lieutenant. The younger officer carried a file brimming with notes and forms. The major's name tag read GRAF. So this was the man responsible for chaining Duval, a fellow lawman and the hero of the zoo confrontation, to the bedrail.

Graf spoke French, acting as if this were a courtesy rather than a snobbish insult, implying Duval did not speak German. "Recovering, are we, Captain?"

"Slowly." He raised his cuffed hand as far as he could. "I'd recover better without these chains."

"Do you promise not to attack the nurses as you attacked your paramedics?"

Duval laughed.

The major waited, raising a bushy black eyebrow. This Swiss blowhard really expected him to say it.

"Yes. I promise."

"Good." Graf gave the lieutenant a nod, and the young officer stepped around him to unlock the cuffs. On the way, he passed the file to his boss. Graf opened it and frowned. "I have a lot of information here—all that I need, in fact. The zoo staff all provided statements. Your sergeant has also been most helpful."

"Has he?" Duval, rubbing his wrist, shot a glare at Renard, who looked away.

"Oh, yes. By all accounts, you fired first—using a weapon you had no authorization or right to carry in my country. I'll give you one chance to tell me why I shouldn't lock you in a cell and throw away the key."

Duval told him of Calix's exploits in Paris. He told him about the bleached and burned body at the flat, the cottage explosion, the dead ship captain, and the wounded watch officer in Rotterdam. "And he had a hostage."

"You mean the woman you chased into the dome." Graf referenced the file. "My witnesses tell me she did not look like a hostage at all."

"I believe she is . . . confused. Stockholm syndrome."

"Thin. And your reasoning for ignoring the proper authorization channels?"

"We had a lead. We had to move fast."

"Ah. Yes. A lead. Excellent. I will follow up for you." Graf lifted several pages of handwritten notes, turning to a blank section, and readied a pen. "What is the source of this lead?"

"Anonymous."

The pages fell into place again with a pronounced *flap*. "What a shame."

After a long silence, Graf sat on the edge of Duval's mattress, clicking his tongue, and set the open file on the table beside the bed. A photo paper clipped to the corner showed a dachshund seated on some sergeant's lap, gnawing a bone like an office pet.

Duval recognized him from Paris. "That dog is evidence."

"That dog is no longer your concern." Graf closed the file. "Nor is anything related to this case."

"You can't do that. This is *my* case."

"No, Captain Duval. It's mine. You are going home as soon as you are well enough to travel." Graf leaned close, supporting his weight with a palm laid directly on Duval's gunshot wound. "Never return to Switzerland. I don't care if you are chasing the next Bin Laden." He squeezed, eliciting a grunt. "Never. You understand?"

Duval answered through clenched teeth. "Yes."

"Good." Graf took his file and left with his lieutenant in tow.

The cuffs were gone. His wounds were dressed. Duval had work to do. He eased himself from the bed. "Get up, Renard. We're leaving."

The sergeant didn't move. "No. The doctors want to keep me under observation. I will stay for two days. The chief sent me an open-ended ticket home."

"Open-ended, eh?" Duval snapped his fingers and held out a hand. "Give me the tablet. I want to see them."

"I said, he sent *me* a ticket. Not you. The chief says you can fend for yourself." Renard yanked the curtain closed. "You're fired."

46

Ben hunched down in his seat on the train to Montpellier, using the window's reflection to watch the car's television. The international manhunt had hit full swing. If he made it to the station, he'd have to give up public transportation for a while.

The news reports flashed his face across the screen four or five times an hour. They had a pair of videos and one good photo—his fake Interpol badge. The Dutch had pulled it from the lake bottom. Thankfully, he'd made the photo pre-frostbite, so his nose looked significantly different.

The videos included a webcam from the rainforest that caught his gun-blazing charge and a shaky police bodycam shot from his Paris standoff. The news report on the television froze the image at the juiciest moment. There was Ben, holding a gun to Clara's head.

Ben searched. Oh, how he'd searched. But he never found her.

He haunted the hilltop forest surrounding the zoo far longer than wisdom allowed. After recovering his backpack from the hollow where he'd stashed it, he walked the perimeter, always moving—watching the cops and onlookers for Clara.

The medevac chopper flew in for Duval and his unfortunate

partner. Paramedics wheeled injured guards out the front gates to a pair of waiting ambulances. The SWAT bus rushed onto the scene, late to the party as usual. The beat cops cordoned off sections of the parking lot for reasons Ben could not fathom, and lined up a crowd of witnesses.

None of the witnesses were Clara.

The medics didn't have her. The cops didn't have her.

When the K-9 units arrived, Ben knew he'd lingered too long. He pounded a fist into a tree and ran down the hill to the outlying train station at Dübendorf.

The frozen video behind the reporter took over the train's TV screen and zoomed in on Ben. They wanted the viewers to see as much of his face as possible, but all Ben saw was the gun he held to her head.

Why hadn't he brushed past her in the hallway outside his flat? That day, Ben had convinced himself he needed to prevent Clara from being caught in the explosion, but she would never have continued to the flat once he passed her by. So why did he do it? Had Ben dragged Clara along because—in the first moments of his life's collapse—part of him wanted her near?

And now she'd been taken. But by who?

Leviathan owned Duval. Ben had no doubt. If Duval knew to find him in Zürich, so did they. He'd been too worried about the sniper, the schoolmaster, and the dirty cop—the obvious threats. But the most dangerous enemy is the one you don't see coming.

The news program moved on to the French political primaries, and Ben let his head rest against the window. His reflection faded, leaving only some nameless valley flying by outside. No villages. No lights. Only the deep, empty dark that lies between the setting sun and the rising moon. He closed his eyes, noting no difference, and let himself fall into the void.

The station announcement woke him. *Arrive maintenant. Gare de Montpellier Sud.* Ben shook enough blackness away to join the slow march of red-eye travelers shuffling up the aisle to change trains. Most still had hours left on their journeys. Ben did too. His ticket told him to find Platform 7 and catch the 2:15 to Barcelona. He made his way to the exit instead.

With Ben's face all over the news, continuing on the rails ceased to be an option. The girl who'd sold him his ticket might recognize the pictures at any time and call the police. He had to find an alternate mode of travel, and he knew just who to ask for a ride.

Four years in the spy game had taught Ben that money talks, and it talks loudest at the waterfront's smelliest and goriest piers. Even better, guys with hands drenched in blood and guts rarely mix with screens. One of Hale's crustier schoolhouse instructors had taught Ben that.

A field operative needs to know where to find safe passage when the press blows his cover. And there's only one guaranteed place. After generations of screen addiction, when humankind finally succumbs to phone-in-hand disease and walks with heads permanently bowed, one segment of society will still comfortably and constantly watch the horizon. Fishermen. You'll find them on a hundred boats, beaches, and docks—eyes on the water or their lines, but never on a phone.

The predawn crowd at the Sète fish market did not disappoint. The fish, gutted and tossed on stacks of ice, were hake, if Ben remembered correctly from his last trip to a Mediterranean quay. Hake only came out at night, and the night trawling life's forever-darkness attracted many scruple-free crews.

Ben's cuts and bruises—his blistered nose and cheeks—fit in well here. And he didn't see a single screen. These men had no time to look at tweets or listen to news reports about a zoo gunfight that left no bodies behind. He waited for a skipper to wander away from the pack and followed him out to a boat gently rocking at the quay, not the smallest trawler on the line but far from the biggest.

The skipper stopped a pace short of the water. "If you're planning to mug me," he said in French, "at least wait until I've collected my due from the market chief. I'd hate for you to waste your time."

"I wouldn't dare." Ben held back, giving the man some social distance. "I imagine you're pretty quick with that rusty fillet knife you're hiding. I like to keep my throat unventilated."

The skipper hopped into his boat, glancing back with a grizzled smile. "Not as quick as I used to be. You want something, boy? A job? My crew's full."

"I need a ride."

"Where?"

"Valencia."

"Two days' roundtrip for my crew and me. And the fish avoid the Spanish coast this time of year." With a heavy grunt, the man hauled a crate of netting from his boat and climbed out onto the dock to pick it up. "No sale."

"I'll make it worth your while."

The man stood there, waiting for Ben to get out of his way.

Ben didn't move. "We leave now and steam at your best speed to Valencia. No trawling. No crew. I'll pay you the cost of two nights' catch, twice what you'd get if you fished east for the night you'll miss. You'll make a good profit. We both know you'll pick up a slack crew in Valencia and trawl all the way home."

Most people need money. And those who don't need money want it anyway. Whatever this man's story, Ben had his attention. He could see the numbers crunching behind the fisherman's eyes—calculations to decide how much to inflate the price.

"Three nights' catch, and I want half up front. My boat takes two men to run. You'll work when you're told. Understand?"

"Done." Ben offered him a roll of cash.

The skipper took it and shoved the crate into Ben's arms.

The reek of the sea bottom filled his nostrils. "Welcome to the crew of the *Lazy Ostrich*. I'm Basile. And your name?"

"I'll answer to hey-you and crewman."

"Fine by me."

Eight hours had passed since Zürich. For eight hours, Clara had slipped farther and farther away. And for eight hours, the world had slipped closer and closer to Leviathan's next attack.

47

The Swiss doctor's condescension made Duval sick. Who was she to tell him what his body could or could not handle?

She jogged backward down the hallway in front of him. "Please, Mr. Duval. Return to your bed. A bullet passed *through* your bicep, nicking your artery. The repairs I made will not hold if you refuse to rest."

"It is *Capitaine* Duval." He brushed her aside with his good arm, plucked a paper bag full of meds from her hands, and hurried on. "You've done enough. If the repair ruptures, I'll seek further medical attention. I've got a job to do."

"What job?" she called after him. "Renard told me you'd been fired."

Duval silently waved her away, then slapped the exit bar and walked out into the cold Swiss night.

A cab waited for him. He'd called ahead—made a point about getting a driver who spoke French. "Where to?" the man asked in English as Duval dropped into the back seat.

He sighed. Typical. "The Econotel, Zürich Nord."

With no cooperation from Graf or his own headquarters, Duval had few clues to rely on in guessing Calix's next move. He needed to call Rotterdam and interview witnesses, find out what Calix wanted with the cargo ship. Time to get back to basics.

His phone rang. He held it to his ear. *"Oui?"*

No voice. Only static.

"Quoi! Allô!"

Nothing.

Duval lowered the phone and checked the screen. Another pdf file waited for him, like the one in Rotterdam. He clicked it to open, and let out a disbelieving laugh when he read the message. Incredible. His strange American benefactor could work magic.

Duval banged on the Plexiglas barrier. *"J'ai changé mes plans."*

The driver shook his head. "English, German, or Italian. No French."

Imbecile. "I said I changed my plans. No hotel. Take me to the airport."

o o o

Jupiter wiggled his toes in the Zoysia grass, enjoying the moonrise. Soft by nature, the Asian creeper became softest on cool nights when moisture from the soil inflated the blades— like a million tiny pillows for his feet.

Walking beyond the intersecting circles of the patio lights, he found one of his many special creatures. Curled up at the base of a blue wisteria, the scaly pangolin looked exactly like the coiled water dragons on the Ming dynasty medallions hanging on Jupiter's wall. He made a clicking sound to wake it and watched the little mammal scurry away across the lawn.

The pangolins, protected by their reptilian plate armor, were the perfect neighbors for his blue tigers. And their meat was delicious—the reason they'd been hunted to near extinction. Like the tigers, Jupiter rescued the pangolins, and he managed their population on his reserve, enjoying the fruit of his labors while ensuring both species' survival. Perfect control.

"Sir."

Jupiter sighed and turned. "Yes, Terrance?" His assistant stood at the patio's edge.

"There are news reports you should see. Word has come from Zürich that your—"

Jupiter coughed.

"—our French recruit has failed . . . again . . . and in quite spectacular form."

Terrance had drive and more raw intelligence than most of Jupiter's people, but he still failed to grasp his master's full vision. He failed to see all the paths about to merge. "Don't panic, Terrance. All is well. Duval's accomplishments—or lack thereof—are exactly as I hoped." He strode to the patio, stepping once again into the light. "Like Hagen, I sent Duval to harry Calix and help him see how far his hero, the Director, had pushed him out into the cold. Giving them both a do-not-kill order ensured Calix's survival. Now we'll provide Calix with more competent help and shift into our final phase."

"So, you want me to call the woman?"

Jupiter nodded.

"But the target has gone dark again. What coordinates should I give?"

"Why, here of course."

"I don't get it."

The statement frustrated Jupiter. He closed his eyes for a moment, letting the image of the little dragon-like pangolin curled beneath the blue wisteria center him. When he opened them again, he gave Terrance a patient smile. "We set up our own bomber to fail in Rotterdam, leaving him stranded at the docks. The clues left behind brought Calix to Massir, and later to the *Princess*, where he learned of the *Behemoth* and Sea Titan's connection to Leviathan. We even showed him where the *Behemoth* docks. So . . . now that you understand the path I laid out for him . . . where would you expect our friend Calix will turn up next?"

Terrance opened his mouth to reply, but the light on his face faltered and he closed it again.

"Here!" Jupiter stomped a heel into his precious grass. "Calix will come *here*." Had he not just said that very thing? He clenched his fists to soak up the oncoming rage and released it back into the air by opening his fingers. *Wisteria. Pangolins.* "Calix will want to infiltrate our facility to gather intelligence and destroy our new weapon. He's coming *here*. Make your call. Tell our asset to get in place and be ready to engage. And then send your final note to Duval."

"Yes, sir." The assistant backed away, turning to go.

"Wait." Jupiter raised a finger. "Where are we in our production efforts?"

In this, at least, Terrance showed self-assurance. "I checked with Dr. Kidan before coming to see you. The CRTX layer is set, and the seed tanks are in place. The rest are being loaded now. Given the rapid self-replication rate of PB2, the bacteria will propagate through the water vapor in all ten thousand tanktainers by the time the *Behemoth* reaches her target."

"And you've delivered the captain's final orders?"

"I'll do so tonight."

"Good." Jupiter lifted his chin, indicating they were done. He wanted to return to his moonlight. "Go and make your calls. I want my prize before the final phase begins."

48

Basile's rusty fillet knife kept Ben awake for the entire journey. Nothing screams *Slit my throat and rob me* louder than handing over a big wad of cash.

The fisherman gave him few opportunities to rest anyway. Mop, brush, wrench, funnel—he made sure Ben's hands were always occupied. Shrewd. But the time spent detailing the boat confirmed Ben's suspicions about the man. He'd chosen his captain well. He found six hidden compartments with cover panels all but invisible to the untrained eye. And he doubted he found them all. Ben had picked a smuggler.

"You know," he said, laying his mop aside, "I don't think making me swab the deck is getting us to Valencia any faster."

"Yet here we are." Basile thrust his gray-whiskered chin at a row of lights to the southwest, outshining the sunset's red glow. He turned the wheel a few degrees. "I'll drop you at the marina."

"Not the marina." Ben walked forward to the pilot house and pointed south, where the lights turned from the warm yellows and oranges of resorts and restaurants to a cold, industrial white. "Take me to the cargo docks. I'm in a hurry."

"The cargo docks are too high for my *Ostrich*."

"They must have berths for tugs and runabouts." Ben opened his go-bag and retrieved the second half of his payment. He laid it on the dash between the radar and the fish finder. "Get me as close as you can to the big ships."

A mile out from the docks, Basile cut the engines and inclined his head northwest.

Ben looked to see a cutter slicing through the chop, moving fast on intercept heading. The orange paint visible in its deck lights left no doubt. He groaned. "Spanish Coast Guard."

"Yes. And going somewhere in a hurry. Hopefully not here." Basile swept the money off the dash and shoved it deep in his pocket. When his hand appeared again, it held the knife—a move Ben did not know how to interpret. A threat to him? To the coast guard? Or maybe Basile simply needed to feel the knife's cool handle in his palm when he felt stressed.

The trawler slowed to a drift, and both men watched to see if the cutter adjusted course. In the failing light of dusk, Ben couldn't tell. For the first time since they'd met, Basile spoke English. "Did you see the news reports last night? Strange happenings in Zürich and Paris."

Ben froze. He'd been too confident in his instructor's theory about fishermen and screens. He'd tucked his Glock in his waistband hours ago, concealing it with his coat. But could he draw faster than Basile could slash with the knife?

Basile kept his gaze on the cutter. "They say a madman is on the loose. He took a hostage, doused a man with chemicals and set him on fire, blew up his woman's cottage."

"You don't say." Ben hadn't heard any mention of the cottage on the train.

"Mm." The skipper let out one of those deep *c'est la vie* grunts only old Frenchmen could make. "With the woman inside." He turned to give Ben a hard look. "It is bad, my friend. Very bad. I wonder if the Spanish Coast Guard is looking for this man, and how much they might pay for his capture."

The cutter continued on its heading, on a course to pass them by. Basile could change that with a burst of throttle or a touch of his emergency beacon switch.

Ben shifted his weight to prepare for a showdown. "I don't believe everything I see in the news. There are always two sides to a story. These days, the media services report only one. I believe this man they call a monster is fighting for his life, and maybe a cause—a good one."

Basile squinted one eye at Ben. "What cause?"

How much should he reveal? "The attacks. Munich. St. Petersburg. Tokyo. Another attack is coming—possibly a disease like the plague. I expect the man in the news is trying to stop it."

The admission did seem to help. Basile's hard look turned fearful. "The plague?" He waggled a finger over his own nose and cheeks and thrust his chin at Ben. "Like your blisters?"

"No." Ben let out a halfhearted laugh. "These blisters are from frostbite. I recently spent some time at the bottom of a frozen lake."

The coast guard cutter passed between the *Ostrich* and the shore, speeding on its way to some urgent call that had nothing to do with Ben—so he hoped.

Basile pushed up the throttle again and corrected their heading. He laid the knife on the dash. "The news program I saw made no mention of a frozen lake."

"And I never said I was the madman in the report."

"Mm." Basile made another of his distinctly French grunts and seemed to focus on managing the boat. After a time, as the shore lights grew brighter, he spoke again. "You paid me a lot, my friend—enough to give me a few days off. But I'm going to ask for something more."

"Like what?"

"I saw inside your bag earlier. The SIG Sauer 2022."

"You want it?"

"Mm. And don't tell me you need it. I know about the Glock hidden in your waistband. A very different gun. Makes me think the SIG is a recent acquisition, and that the previous owner is no longer a concern."

Ben didn't correct him. And why shouldn't he do Basile this favor? He pulled the weapon out. "It needs a cleaning. Like me, it spent some time on the lakebed. Also, you'll need ammunition. The magazine is empty."

"Not a problem. Ammunition I can get. Guns are more difficult." Basile hefted his knife for a moment, then dropped it in his pocket and took the SIG. He racked back the slide and looked down the chamber. "Yes. This will do."

Basile tossed the weapon onto a folded fishing net and glanced around, breathing in the air. "I would not call this warm, but it's warmer than Montpellier, for sure. I might stay a night or two. I hear the Hotel Sol is nice. Since I'll be around—and if you *were* a madman trying to stop the next attack—would there be anything an old fisherman can do to help?"

Ben hadn't expected such an offer. He grinned and clapped him on the arm. "Enjoy Valencia's beaches, and forget about the madman. I think that's best for all concerned."

49

Duval swallowed painkillers straight from the bottle on his way through Valencia's small airport. The morphine had worn off fifteen minutes into his cab ride.

A black sedan waited for him at the curb. The driver leaned against the hood, holding a tablet with his name in bright white letters. A woman—attractive. Nice touch. Perhaps he should quit mourning his failed police career and work for his American friend full-time.

The woman said nothing when she opened the door for him and remained silent as they left the airport boundary. The highway shifted from four lanes to two, then one. Streetlamps and office buildings gave way to houses, then dark fields.

Duval coughed. *"Où allons-nous?"*

Still nothing from the woman. Perhaps, like the cabbie, she didn't speak French. He tried English. "Where are we going?"

No answer.

He felt a modicum of relief when a town appeared ahead—a little barrio, older than the community surrounding the airport. The sedan weaved its way through a maze of streets built originally for horses, amid houses of ancient brown brick and peeling plaster. But the barrio also passed.

Again the driver took them into the dark.

Towns and barrios came and went. Fields. Suburbs. The woman behind the wheel traded pavement for cobblestone, then gravel, then pavement again. Wherever they were headed, this could not be the fastest route. Duval stomped the floorboard, gritting his teeth against the pain that shot through his arm. "I insist you tell me where we are going."

Still no answer.

At length, the sedan eased to a stop. The driver stepped out, walked around the hood, and opened Duval's door.

"Here?" He poked his head from the car and squinted at the dark. No streetlamps. No houses. Only trees.

The driver gestured at a worn path in the grass.

"There are only the two of us. Where is my contact? Where is the agent who will help me take down Calix?"

"I *am* your contact, *Capitaine Duval*. Get out of the car. I want to show you something."

She spoke French. Melodious French. Relieved, he climbed out, pausing to pop another pill before following her up the trail. The woman moved with easy grace on the rough terrain. Duval did not. He stumbled over a root and bumped his bad arm against a pine. It took all his self-control to bury the pained yelp demanding to escape his lungs. He didn't want to embarrass himself. What if this beauty became his new partner? A smile crossed his lips at the thought. So much for Kenard.

The trees parted a short distance from a cliff overlooking a sprawling industrial complex. Billowing exhaust, silver blue against a sea of mercury high-intensity lights, poured from several factory buildings stretching out like spokes from a central wheel of steel and glass. Warehouses lay between the spokes, and trucks and carts ran through the alleys in steady streams despite the late hour. A central ring-shaped structure had to be the company headquarters, but not—Duval surmised—the place he should expect to find the CEO.

The woman caught him looking past the complex to a house on the small mountain above. More than a house. A modernistic, gleaming white castle. "Yes," she said. "That is his enclave. His Olympus."

"The American."

"His name is Jupiter. And he's quite pleased with all you've done."

Duval tore his gaze from the castle to meet the woman's eyes. "Pleased? I have failed time and again. Look at me. A mess. I was meant to capture Calix, not absorb bullets for him."

"You were meant to drive him." Once again, she turned her gaze to the complex. Her body followed. The toes of her elegant mid-calf boots flirted with the edge of the cliff.

Duval took the meaning of her body language. "Here? This whole time, he wanted me pushing Calix toward this place? Why not simply say so?"

"Sometimes the act of shepherding a man is physical. Sometimes it is psychological. Jupiter told you all you needed to hear to get the job done. And as I said. He is pleased with your work."

"I'm glad." Duval dropped his gaze to the rocks at the cliff base far below. "I . . . uh . . . could use a new position, so to speak. My pursuit of Calix cost me my job."

The woman nodded, signaling she already knew this. "I wouldn't worry about it."

A good sign. Duval breathed a little easier. He liked Spain. Warm winters. Cheap housing. Better beaches than France. Things were looking up. "So, what's our next move. When do we grab Calix?"

"He's on his way. But you shouldn't worry about that either." She turned to face him again, now holding a gun. Duval hadn't seen her reach for it.

What was she playing at? He laughed—nervous. "I see. A joke for the new guy. Very funny."

But she didn't laugh, or even smile. The woman walked around him, putting herself between Duval and the path.

He backed up, heels at the cliff's edge. "I don't understand. What is this?"

"Why, Mr. Duval, this is the end." She put the barrel to his head and fired.

50

Ben ran and hopped over the giant blocks of stone piled against the seaside walls of the Port of Valencia's channel barriers. A paved access road topped each barrier, but he needed to stay clear of the light during his approach to the main piers. He saw too many eyes up there.

From what he could tell, Sea Titan dominated the port. The big shipping corporation owned half the piers, and five looked custom built, all secured by one big perimeter fence. The sign above the primary gate read SEA TITAN MAIN—as in the tallest mast on a ship or the Spanish Main. The killer running this place had a decent sense of humor.

Most cargo docks were shared. Gaining extra time and space over the competition took serious political maneuvering. Ben had to wonder how many truckloads of cash it took for Sea Titan to convince Valencia to let them have their own private section—an ideal arrangement for a large-scale criminal enterprise.

The sheer number of craft with the Sea Titan serpent emblazoned on their hulls might have seemed daunting in a search for a specific vessel, but Ben had no trouble finding his target. The *Behemoth*, the largest container ship on earth, rested proudly against the seaward side of Sea Titan Main's giant outer pier.

He crawled up the stone blocks to the spot where the container stacks sat closest to the chain-link fence and settled in to watch the guards make their rounds.

No wires ran along the fence. Not surprising. Sensors and electrification required too much maintenance so close to salt water. He dug a set of wire cutters out of his pack.

Two security guards patrolled the stacks. No dogs. Good. And the guards kept mostly to the landward side, watching the road running down the pier's center between the cranes and a six-story office building. While clipping the links, Ben counted the seconds between his sightings of each guard. A rhythm emerged. He picked his moment and pushed through.

What he saw as he crept to the edge of the stacks made his heart sink.

Everything Ben had learned so far left him convinced Leviathan had developed a weaponized version of the plague and planned to use the *Behemoth* to deliver that weapon to its target—most likely the United States. He needed to get on board, not just to prove his theory, but to gain hard evidence he could pass to authorities. But Ben saw no viable path onto the *Behemoth*.

Sea Titan ran a tight ship, so to speak.

A security man checked IDs and faces at the gangplank's foot. Another stood watch above him at the ship's rail. In his current state, and after the stunt he'd tried to pull in Rotterdam, he'd never get past them. The cranes were no help either, loading tanks set in rectangular steel frames the size of shipping containers. The open frames offered Ben no place to stow away without being seen. He considered hanging on to the outside of one, but only for a moment. Each of the six active cranes had two spotters with high-powered flashlights. He'd never make it from the dock to the ship without being seen.

Climbing the mooring lines, scaling the hull from the seaward side—none of it looked remotely possible, thanks to the vessel's sheer size. If Ben had special equipment and a Company team, maybe he could make a reasonable covert assault. But he had no equipment, and his team had abandoned him.

The pier's administrative offices looked more accessible, especially with the day staff gone for the night.

Armed guards and a ten-foot fence topped with concertina wire look scary, but a smart field operative always prefers a remote, guarded compound over a downtown corporate headquarters. Single-building facilities use compressed security—lobby guards, cameras, and motion sensors, all within a confined space. Compounds with a long perimeter fence are forced to spread their security thin, and once you're inside, the structures and offices rarely have defenses beyond keypad locks or swipe cards.

Ben hoped Sea Titan Main followed the usual security pattern.

Two men argued in the corner office on the top floor, backlit by bright fluorescents. Ben's best bet for finding incriminating evidence or a way onto the ship lay in there, but he'd need management to clear out first. He looked around for options.

A forklift sat idle and unused only fifteen meters away.

He bobbled his head. It might work.

One guard strolled out of sight at the far end of the stacks. The other walked past Ben's hiding spot, so close he could've reached out and tapped his shoulder. He didn't. Ben let the man walk on several more paces, then made a silent run for his target.

The diesel engine cranking up blended nicely with the other sounds of industry on the pier. But an instant later, a metallic crash sounded behind Ben—way behind, from the heavy equipment lot. The guard turned to look, gaze settling on Ben. Ben held his breath, trying not to show it, and moved his hidden hand to his Glock. With the other, he gave the man a curt wave. The guard answered with a nod and moved off to check out the other noise.

Ben let out his breath. Some clumsy dockworker had almost gotten him caught.

Shaking his head, he released the brake and drove down an alley between containers. A sharp turn brought his forks under the bottom container in a stack of five. He shoved the lift control lever to the maximum height marker and flipped the override toggle. The image of row after row of container stacks tipping and falling like dominoes flashed in his head, but Ben knew the little forklift had nowhere near the capacity for such mayhem. Its pump motors whined to protest the impossible task of lifting the containers. Ben bailed from the cab, leaving it running. He could already smell the hydraulic fluid heating up.

A conga line of big rigs blocked the road between the cranes and the main office, ready to drive away with incoming cargo from the pier's other berth. The gate guards had stalled the fleet, checking the lead driver's paperwork. Ben ran straight across the yard and grabbed the rear bumper of the last truck in line, sliding underneath.

He lay on his back, listening. No footsteps. No cries of alarm. No one had seen him. Ben rolled over and low-crawled forward, willing his lungs to keep working despite the exhaust fumes.

Closer to the administrative building, he rolled out the other side and hopped up, dusting himself off. The glass door at the entrance swung open on his first pull, unlocked. And, as predicted, no guards watched the lobby. Most of the building looked dark. The staff had gone home for the day. Ben took the stairs to the sixth floor.

The corner office stood open, with loud voices coming from inside. Ben pressed his body against the wall next to the stairwell exit with one finger holding the door open and listened.

"Three hours," a young man said—a New Yorker by the sound of it. "I want her moving in three hours. This shipment is Mr. Jupiter's highest priority. I already told him we were on schedule."

An older voice with a Spanish accent fired back. "That is your mistake. Not mine. We are loading as fast as possible.

And the team you sent aboard to connect the tanktainers with hoses is slowing us down. What are the hoses for, anyway?"

Ben heard an exasperated sigh. "We've been over this. The hoses are part of a pressure system to prevent nitrogen leakage during the voyage."

"I've never heard of such a thing."

"Because you're a dockmaster—not an engineer. How Sea Titan transports our goods is not your concern." The New Yorker pounded on something. "Your job is to *get it moving*."

"Fire!"

The cry, echoed by others, came from outside the building.

A young man in a slick suit and a middle-aged Spaniard in dungarees ran to the elevators. The New Yorker grumbled and groused, repeatedly punching the button. Seconds later, the two were on their way downstairs.

Ben slipped into the office. Through the big corner window, he saw smoke rising from the container alley where he'd left the forklift—an orange glow too. Nice.

A moment later, the management kid and the dockmaster ran into view and joined the others heading for the fire. They'd be busy for at least several minutes. Ben's gaze drifted to the *Behemoth*. From the elevated perch of the office, he could see the activity on the cargo deck. Teams of men and women moved and climbed among the thousands of tanks in container frames—*tanktainers*, the dockmaster had called them. The teams joined the top center of each tank to the bottom of the one above it with a short black hose. Longer hoses chained to the deck connected each stack. From what Ben saw, the hoses made the entire load one interconnected unit.

"The bioweapon," he said under his breath. "But where's your protective gear?" The hose teams wore work gloves, nothing more. Did they know what they were handling? Or did they think those tanks were full of compressed nitrogen, as the tank markings said?

The dockmaster and his very good friend were at the fire, and the pier's response team seemed to have it under control. Ben had to move faster. He checked the computer. Locked, with no time to play password roulette. He scanned the desk. A thick manila envelope with a Sea Titan logo lay beside the keyboard, secured with an old-school string-and-button seal and marked BEHEMOTH PASSAGE PLAN. Ben unraveled the seal and slid out a thick pack of papers. The cover page listed the destination as a Sea Titan dry dock facility near Cartagena, not far down the coast.

"Who loads up with cargo for a trip to the dry dock?"

Weird—or incredibly suspicious.

Ben sat in the dockmaster's chair and thumbed through the pages. The charts mapped the short journey to the dry dock facility, backing up the cover page's claims. But behind those were weather charts for the whole Atlantic. Why would the captain need Atlantic weather forecasts if he never planned to leave the Mediterranean? There were also notarized registration and licensing papers for a Jaspen cargo vessel called the *Clementine*.

Voices. Ben heard the New Yorker bawling out the dockmaster, getting louder. They were on their way back—at the road by the sound of it.

He tried to push the papers into the envelope again, but they stuck out a half inch, blocked by something inside, maybe a folded corner or a paper-clip. He tried tapping, blowing, shaking—nothing worked. Ben couldn't abandon the envelope on the desk with documents sticking out, a dead giveaway that he'd been there. He pulled the whole stack out and turned the envelope upside down.

A thumb drive dropped out and clattered on the desktop.

"Huh."

He stuffed the drive in his back pocket and hurriedly shoved the papers into the envelope, retying the string seal. A quick check at the window gave no sign of the two men. They must already be in the building. He turned toward the desk but stopped when movement caught his eye. What Ben saw sent a bolt of electricity through his chest.

Two men in coveralls dragged a woman through the parking lot—a woman with amber hair.

51

Keep your emotions in check.

How many times had Hale spoken those words during Ben's time at the schoolhouse? Spoken, whispered, shouted, screamed. *Keep your emotions in check, recruit.* Hale beat that drum in the field every time Ben showed a hint of frustration with a teammate, and in his interrogation resistance training the instant a bead of sweat mixed with a tear.

No matter how much pain you're in, or if an enemy interrogator just emptied a full magazine into your best friend. A good operative waits until the mission is done to lick his wounds. Wipe the blood off your face tomorrow. Mourn later. Emotions have no place in the field. Emotions cause mistakes.

With Hale's voice fresh in his ear from their Zürich meeting, Ben heard it again.

Keep your emotions in check.

The swell in his chest at the sight of her with those men—the urge to shout her name through the window—almost overwhelmed him. So many emotions. Hale's voice shoved them all back into their box and shut the lid.

Instead of shouting, he returned the envelope to the desk, careful to match the angle to the way he'd found it, and moved to the hall. The elevator dinged. With the New York kid's angry voice growing louder, Ben slipped into the stairwell and eased the door closed behind him.

Descending the stairs without jumping whole landings at a time took all of Ben's self-control. Making a racket—getting caught—wouldn't help her. And he knew without a doubt who he'd seen. Amber hair. A sweatshirt and jeans like those she'd worn in Zürich.

"Clara." The name escaped his lips as he checked the yard from the building exit. "You're alive."

The men had dragged her toward the parking lot's rear. Ben used a rolling truck as cover to conceal him from the guards and crane spotters on the other side of the road and jogged along the edge, Glock held low. Where had they gone?

There. Brake lights from a blue Sea Titan cargo van. Before the driver could shift into reverse, Ben raced up to his door and threw it open, pressing the Glock to his cheek. "Shut it down."

Whether the man spoke English or not, he got the drift and turned the key.

"Out." Ben backed up to give him room and motioned to the man in the passenger seat, shorter and younger than the other. "You too. Hands where I can see them. Move around the hood."

He maneuvered both men until their backs were against the van's side, out of view of the dockworkers and guards across the road. "Where's the girl?"

The driver didn't answer. Neither did his buddy, but the shorter man's darting eyes told Ben what he needed to know. "In the back, huh? For your sake, I hope she's healthy."

A bundle of zip cuffs peeked out from the right breast pocket of the driver's coveralls. Ben tapped the same spot on his own chest and pointed to the cuffs with two fingers. "Cuff each other." He waited for them to do as they were told, then whirled a finger in the air. "Now turn around."

He couldn't have them following him or crying out, and

bashing their heads against the van might make too much noise. Ben reached into his go-bag and dug the cattle prod baton Hagen had used against him at the flat. He jammed it into each man's spine, and they both fell, convulsing, and then went still. He regarded the weapon with new appreciation. "I've been lugging you around since Paris. 'Bout time you made yourself useful."

With one more set of zip cuffs, Ben bound one man to the other, then removed their boots and made gags from their shoelaces and sweaty socks. He waved a hand in front of his nose as he stood to assess his work. "Wow, that stinks."

He'd kept his emotions in check, done his job, been thorough, accounted for the threats. Now he hoped his patience would pay off. Maybe they'd shoved her in the back of the van alive. Maybe not.

He readied his Glock and pulled open both doors. "Clar—"

The face staring back at him shocked him into a long silence. Finally, he cocked his head. "Giselle?"

52

Giselle sat with her back against the front wall of the van's cargo bay in a sweatshirt and jeans, hands and feet bound with zip cuffs, sneakers lying on the floor beside her. "Ben? You're alive."

He laughed—a quiet, almost giddy laugh. "That's rich coming from you."

"How so?"

Were they really having this conversation? "Because you're the one who's supposed to be dead. The cottage blew up."

One side of her mouth curled into the smirk he used to adore so much. "So did your flat."

She had a decent point, but then Ben shook the Glock. "No, no. My face was all over the news."

"As if I've had time to watch TV. And you must admit, you no longer look like yourself—to put it mildly. Perhaps try to look a little more happy than mad, yes?"

"Sorry, I . . ." He let his voice fade. What could he say? How much had he wished for this in the hours after he watched the cottage burn? He should feel elation at Giselle's survival, not disappointment that he hadn't found Clara. "How did you get out? I saw the light come on in the kitchen before the explosion."

"Think, Ben. I use automated lights to deter intrusions in my absence. You know this. I was never there. But let's talk the cottage later. Mission first. We *are* in a Sea Titan parking lot, after all." Giselle inched forward and rolled up to her knees, holding out her wrists. "Do you mind?"

"Right. Mission first." Ben recovered his go-bag and found the wire cutters.

When he tried to clip the flexicuffs, she dodged the cutters and draped her arms over his head to pull him close. "Well, mission second, yes?" she said, and kissed him.

The kiss banished all disbelief. Ben knew her lips. He remembered the warmth of her breath and the scent of her skin. She'd come back to him. Why wasn't he walking on air inside?

He returned the kiss with passion, then pulled back. He needed to regain control of the situation and control of himself. *Keep your emotions in check*. He pushed her arms up to duck out of her embrace and snipped the cuffs at her wrists and ankles. "No. It's like you said. Mission first."

While Giselle kept watch, Ben dragged the two thugs to the van's rear and dumped them into the back. As quietly as possible, he closed the doors. "We need to get out of here and regroup."

"Wrong."

Same Giselle. Always contrary. Always battling for dominance. He used to love that about her. He checked the magazine on his Glock and handed her Hagen's electric baton. "What do you mean, wrong?"

"I mean we can't leave—not yet." She smacked him in the arm with the weapon and walked away, heading for the cover of the pier's heavy equipment yard. "This way. Leviathan has a bioweapon."

"*I* know they have a bioweapon," he said, chasing after her. "That's why I'm here. How do *you* know they have a bioweapon?"

"Remember Rome? The enemy agent who died? What do

245

you think I've been investigating since the Company blew up my house?" She reached a row of tracked, mobile cranes and slowed to let him catch up. They walked down the line together, crouching and watching the activity at the ship. "This is a severance, Ben, for both of us. If we can help the Company stop Leviathan, perhaps the Director will forgive us for whatever he thinks we've done and let us back in, yes?"

"Yes," he said softly. "Exactly what I was thinking." Then he said it again with more confidence. "*Exactly.* So let's make it happen. Here's what I'm thinking. The *Behemoth* was a launch point for the Tokyo and Munich attacks. And tonight, those tanks they're loading are all connected like one big bioweapon." He tilted his head, scratching his ear. "There's just one problem—"

"The workers aren't wearing protection," Giselle said, finishing his thought. "Odd for evil minions loading a plague ship, yes? You are meant to think this is a boatload of nitrogen, just as the tank markings say."

He nodded. "It's the obvious conclusion. And I'm struggling to find evidence to the contrary."

She winked. "Forget your misgivings, *mon chéri*. The tanks *are* a weapon."

"How do you know?"

"You investigated from the Leviathan angle, starting with their last known attack in Rotterdam. *I* started with our Rome clue—the plague. I looked for experts and found a Chinese microbiologist who vanished this summer and a Pakistani named Kidan who recently walked away from a dream job at Oxford. I tracked them both to Valencia. The first one, Dr. Xue, is dead."

"What about the other one?"

Giselle grabbed Ben's chin with two fingers and directed his gaze to the *Behemoth*'s gangplank. "Here he comes now."

53

Kidan had parked his brand-new Jag in a second employee lot near the heavy equipment. Ben and Giselle waited for him in the shadows between a pair of high-capacity forklifts that made the one Ben had caught on fire look like a Tonka toy.

"That's Kidan's car," she said, nodding at the Jag only a few meters away. "I stowed away in an equipment truck that followed him, under a pile of hoses." She showed him a tear in the knee of her jeans. "I tripped getting out and knocked a crate of chains and fasteners off the truck bed. That's how those thugs captured me."

Ben remembered the crash he heard while stealing the forklift. He let out a bemused huff. "You almost got me captured too."

"Sorry."

"Don't mention it. But how do you know about the tanks?"

"I breached Kidan's lab at a massive industrial compound owned by Jupiter Global Industries, not far outside Valencia."

"Jupiter." Ben said the name as he would speak the name of an unwanted ghost.

"Yes. The name with which your Algerian friend taunted you in Rome. Jupiter Global owns Sea Titan, although the trail of shell companies is hard to follow." With her eyes, Giselle followed Kidan as he strolled across the yard, heading their way.

"In his lab, I saw a mockup of the tanktainer design—a scale test. The tanks are filled with water vapor. Seed canisters push the bacteria into the first tanks, and it . . . infects the whole system, replicating on its own."

Ben watched her. Same Giselle. Laser focus. Like old times. "Why didn't you contact me?"

She kept her gaze on Kidan. "Focus, Ben. Remember what Hale used to say about emotions?"

"Yeah. I remember. What about the lab? You got inside. Did you get a look at his computer?"

She gave him a silent *duh* roll of her eyes. "I couldn't crack the password." Kidan had reached the parking lot's edge, a few steps from his Jag. She gestured at the scientist, lowering her voice to a whisper. "That's why I need him, yes? Come on."

They ambushed Kidan at the vehicle.

Giselle hit him with just enough shock from Hagen's cattle prod to put him down but not out, and the two dragged him back into the shadows between the heavy forklifts.

The left half of Kidan's body woke up before the right. With a disturbing partial crabwalk, he scrambled back against an oversize tire. "Don't shoot. I'm only a scientist."

Only a scientist. Ben let out a sour huff and touched the man's nose with the barrel of his Glock. "You scream. You die. The guards might come running, but it won't matter for you, because your brains will be splattered all over this tire. Got it?"

Kidan nodded.

Ben nodded too. "And for the record, you're not a scientist. You're a death merchant with an advanced degree. Now"—he gestured at Giselle with his gun—"she's got some questions. I suggest you answer them."

Together they lifted him to his feet, grabbing the lapels of Kidan's lab coat with one hand each. Giselle thrust her chin at the ship. "Tell me what kind of disease you and the other minions are loading onto the *Behemoth*."

"I don't know what you're talking about."

She snapped her fingers and held out a hand to Ben.

He slapped the Glock into her open palm. They'd played this game before.

Giselle, a perfect actress on her favorite stage, rested the barrel against his temple at an almost casual angle, luring him in with a relaxed smile. Then the electric baton appeared from nowhere, an inch from his eyeball. A single arc sparked between the prongs.

Kidan went rigid.

Ben paced behind his teammate, slipping into an old rhythm. "You failed to answer her question. She hates that. So here's the deal. Answer the next question or lose an eye. And before you choose, please understand we know more than we're letting on. Lie to us, and my associate will use her cattle prod."

Giselle didn't have to repeat her question.

"We engineered a new bacterium. W-weaponized plague. Multiple forms."

"Multiple forms?" Ben stopped pacing and squinted at him. "How so?"

Kidan hesitated.

The prongs crackled.

"They serve d-d-different purposes. The one on the ship is highly contagious. The other kills a single victim and dies before it can spread."

A single victim. Rome. The contagious version worried Ben far more. What was Leviathan planning to unleash? Hadn't the world suffered enough? "Show us. Take us to your lab and bring up the data. I want proof. And . . . formulas."

Giselle shot him a look that said *Formulas? Really?*

Ben walked out of Kidan's sightline and shrugged. He had no idea what microbiologists called them, but the bio-death-merchant career field had to include something like formulas.

The good doctor seemed to take his meaning. "I can't."

The prongs crackled again, lighting up his face.

"B-because he confiscated them. He took my data, my samples. Jupiter took it all."

Ben had to shush the man because his voice had gone up too many octaves. Maybe Giselle was a little too good at her job.

"Jupiter," she said. "He's your boss, yes?"

"Yes." Kidan tried and failed to push the back of his head through the forklift's steel frame, unable to escape the cattle prod. "He took everything. I swear."

I swear.

A little fear makes lies obvious. The idea that fear tactics including the threat of bodily harm have no place in an interrogation is a twenty-first-century invention, ignoring centuries of practical experience. A good field interrogator knows that, yes, fear brings lies, but it also makes those lies stand out, enabling the interrogator to get at the truth. An individual locked in fight-or-flight mode loses guile and reverts to childish tactics like I swear *and other pointless oaths.*

Kidan's *I swear,* told Ben the words preceding it were a lie. *He took everything.* Not true. The scientist–slash–death merchant, unwilling to let his master take complete control of his valuable creation, had held something back—maybe a lot.

"Everything." Ben clicked his tongue. "Too bad. In that case, we're done here." He walked behind Giselle and let his fingers graze the small of her back. The same old routine. "This place is too hot. We need to go. Don't leave any evidence behind."

The prongs crackled again, moving closer.

"All right. All right. Don't hurt me. I . . . I kept copies."

Ben put his face close enough to Kidan's to let the man smell his breath. He used one finger to tilt the baton up and away. "Where?"

54

"Can we talk about the hair?" Ben lifted his gaze to the Jag's rearview mirror, meeting Giselle's eyes.

"Now?"

"Yes, now. It's bugging me."

"Let's get off the property first, yes?"

Kidan drove, with Ben beside him holding the prod and Giselle behind him depressing the seatback fabric with the Glock. The two had assured the scientist that despite what he might have seen in the movies, the bullet would happily pass through the cloth and aluminum to sever his spine, so he'd better keep his mouth shut at the gate.

He did. The fence rolled back, and the guard waved them through.

"Good," Ben said, patting Kidan on the arm. "Now. Take us home. I can't wait to see what kind of luxury selling out mankind will buy."

The scientist claimed he kept copies of everything on his laptop at home, a fifteen-minute drive from the port. The management kid with the New York accent had mentioned the *Behemoth* shipping out in three hours. That gave Ben and Giselle time to get the data, but not enough time to convince the local authorities to stop the ship, especially with Ben's current reputation. They'd have to find a way on board and do this themselves. They could do it—together. Ben had been fighting this battle alone. A well-trained teammate made all the difference.

He waited until the complex's blue glow faded from the mirror before pressing Giselle again. "The hair, Giselle. Why amber?" It bugged him. A spy on the run often changed hair color, but she'd chosen a color so close to the one he'd picked for Clara.

Giselle tossed her disheveled locks back and forth like a bad shampoo commercial, toying with him again. "What's wrong? I thought you'd like it."

"Why would I like it?"

"Morocco, silly. In the souk?" She widened her eyes and nodded at Kidan, indicating she couldn't be more specific in front of an enemy. "At the start of the job, you said, 'Watch the lady with the amber hair. She's too pretty to be out here on her own.' *Too pretty*, you said." Giselle pushed out a lip. "I was jealous."

Too pretty. Ben remembered those words. Maybe that experience had influenced his choice of hair color for Clara too. He nodded. "I guess that covers it."

"Covers what?"

"Nothing."

Kidan coughed. "I can park and get out if you two want to talk."

Ben raised the cattle prod.

The scientist pushed his body against his door to keep clear. "Or I can drive, if you're in a hurry. Do you want me to speed? Run red lights? Perhaps you want some music. I have satellite. Two hundred channels."

Ben resisted the urge to jab the prongs into his liver. "Follow the rules of the road. Other than that, shut up and drive. Got it?"

"Yes, yes. Okay."

The scientist looked sufficiently cowed, and he didn't seem

252

to be driving them into danger. A warehouse district south of the port had given way to an empty coastal forest, but Ben saw luxury beach villas ahead. He glanced at Giselle in the mirror again. "What about your cottage?"

"I told you. Part of the severance." Her expression darkened, and she took on an exaggerated suburban couple tone. "Do you really want to keep discussing our private business in front of your new friend?"

"Fine. We'll talk later."

"You bet we will. I must hear about this mysterious woman with the blue hair, yes?"

Now he felt like Kidan—a man under interrogation. "Yes. Of course."

After five minutes of awkward silence, Kidan pulled into the garage of a two-story condo overlooking Pobles del Sud Beach, south of Valencia proper. Giselle kept the Glock glued to his ribs until they reached his home office on the second floor.

Moonlight glittered on the black water of an infinity pool outside on the balcony, and beyond the pool, Ben could see the port, with the *Behemoth* brightly lit, still at its berth. "Nice place for a man who's *only a scientist*," he said, clamping a hand down on Kidan's shoulder. He steered the scientist to the desk. "We're here. Now show us what you've got or I give this nice lady the cattle prod again and we go back to square one."

"Yes." Kidan shook his head, smiling. "No problem. I have the drive here in my top drawer, as promised."

Ben watched the scientist work his way around the desk. The smile seemed forced. The *as promised* sounded rehearsed. Ben lowered his gaze to Kidan's fingers, opening the drawer, quivering with anticipation. Was Kidan dumb enough to pull a gun?

The scientist raised his eyes, watching them both, and dipped his hand into the drawer.

"Giselle! Hold fire!" Ben lunged, putting his body between her and the threat.

55

Ben stabbed the crux of the scientist's arm with the cattle prod. Kidan yelped and convulsed, smashing his flailing wrist through a glass double-helix sculpture. He dropped into his chair and clutched the arm. Red stains spotted his lab coat.

"Don't move," Ben said, threatening him with the cattle prod. He opened the drawer all the way. No gun. A remote with a single red button lay in an organizer among the papers and pens. He inclined his head, motioning for Giselle to look.

She seethed. "A silent alarm. *Toi idiot.* You tried to call the cops?"

Kidan growled back at her. "Private security. A man in my position cannot be too careful."

"I guess paranoia and death merchant go hand in hand." Ben kneeled to yank the wires from the button. As he worked, he felt Giselle's glare boring into him.

"And you," she said. "You should have kept out of the way. I might have shot you through the back, jumping between us like that."

"We need him."

"For now." Her lips flattened, and she shifted the menace of her gaze to Kidan.

254

The scientist swallowed.

Ben opened the laptop in front of him. "Show me the data, Dr. Kidan."

"But my arm, it—"

"Data first. Medical attention later. I'll make it easy and do all the typing and clicking for you. Give me the password."

Kidan complied. He'd saved everything.

For all his failings as a man, Kidan's record-keeping deserved high marks. His notes rivaled those of the most meticulous researchers on the planet. Ben scrolled through page after page of data. Most of it made no sense—not to him. He wished Tess was there to translate. Now that he and Giselle had the data, they'd make sure she got the chance.

A few phrases stood out. *Asymptomatic contagion phase. Predicted infection rate.* And he kept seeing the same R_0 symbol over and over again, followed by increasingly large numbers.

"What is R zero?"

"We pronounce it R naught," Kidan said. "R_0 is a measure of a disease's potential using the number of people each host infects. It combines the duration of pre-symptom contagiousness with the ease of transmission. For instance, the virus causing the measles has an R_0 of eighteen, meaning one host will infect eighteen others before being quarantined."

"And this R_0 figure increases in cities, right?" Ben shot a glance at Giselle, remembering the pandemic and the impact it had on the world's larger cities, especially New York.

Kidan nodded. "Climate and population compression are most important. A disease in London has far more potential than the same disease in the Gobi Desert. In urban areas, our modeling for PB2 shows incredible promise."

Potential. Promise. A parental pride showed through the strain in Kidan's features caused by his wound.

"A high R_0 is bad. Got it." Ben scanned the pages. Each progressive cycle of Kidan's experiments boosted the figures until the R_0 reached into the hundreds. A hundred hosts could each infect another hundred before showing symptoms. Each of those could infect a hundred more, and so on.

The exponential math boggled Ben's mind. "We should kill you right now." He sensed Giselle's finger tightening on the trigger again and raised a hand. "Hang on. Figure of speech."

"If you say so."

"I do." Ben scrolled on. The file included diagrams—CAD-style drawings of the bacteria plus the layout of the ship-turned-weapon. One showed the stacks of forty-foot-long tanktainers on the cargo deck with a sketch of the tanks and hose system in the margin. "It looks like one big bioweapon. How does it work? What's inside the tanks?"

Kidan clamped a hand over the growing bloodstains on his sleeve, and Ben saw glossy red on his fingers. The glass had cut deep. The scientist stared down at his wound as he answered. "The bacteria propagate during transit, populating the water vapor in the tanks. When the cranes lift the tanktainers from the ship upon arrival, the hoses break away and snap a valve into place, beginning a measured aerosol release—invisible."

"An aerosol weapon," Ben said. "And wherever the tank travels by rail or truck—"

"The bacteria spreads." Kidan looked up at him with a defiant grin. "To every corner of the target nation."

Ben returned his gaze to the laptop and the cut-out diagrams. "What about the liquid filling those bulk holds? If the disease is in the tanktainers on the deck, what's down below?"

"That's not a liquid. It's . . ." Kidan paused, then shook his head and set his pallid features. "No. I'll answer no more questions until you treat my arm."

Kidan raised his arm to show his captors, and a thick red drop fell onto the desk. The blood had soaked his sleeve to capacity. Ben didn't need him passing out. Not now. He had more questions. "Yeah. All right. You have a first aid kit?"

"In the bathroom." The scientist directed him with his gaze.

"Fine. I'll be right back." He tapped the desk with the cattle prod and placed it in Giselle's free hand. "If he moves, zap him. Don't shoot him. We need this guy to get a jump on a cure if this thing gets out."

He caught her eye with a warning look, and she answered with an exaggerated nod. "Zap. Don't shoot. I've got it, okay?"

"Okay." Ben walked down the short hall and rummaged through the bathroom cabinets for the first aid kit. He'd just found it when he heard a double *crack* from the Glock.

56

Ben snatched up the first aid kit and ran down the hall. "Giselle?"

She held the Glock at a low angle, finger still on the trigger. Kidan was slumped over the desk, face lying in the shattered glass from his sculpture, blood spreading out beneath his chest.

Giselle cast a vacant glance at the first aid kit in Ben's hand and let out a quiet huff. "I doubt that will help him now."

"I don't see a gun, Giselle. What happened to 'Zap, don't shoot'?"

She answered in a quiet monotone. "I tried to scroll through the computer file—only for a moment. But when I took my eyes away, he grabbed the broken sculpture and tried to stab me. You understand, yes?"

The base of the DNA sculpture, with its two broken helix strands ending in wicked tips, lay on the floor beneath Kidan's limp hand. "We needed him, Giselle. What if this thing gets out?"

"The file mentions an antidote." She walked to the computer and reached over the dead man as if he wasn't there. "I saw it before he went for the sculpture. Leviathan has the cure."

"Good luck getting it from them." Ben rested a shoulder

against the curtain, eyeing the neighboring balcony. He saw no lights, but the owners could still be at home, and Giselle's gunshots left nothing to the imagination. The cops might be on their way. He snapped the laptop closed and tucked it under an arm. "This data should be enough to get the Company's attention. But that'll take time we don't have. For now, we need to stop the *Behemoth*."

Giselle grimaced, eyes canted down at the computer. "Gross."

He followed her gaze. Blood dripped from the laptop's corner—the blood of a man who liked to play around with infectious diseases. "Good point." He grimaced, wiping the blood off on the motionless scientist's back, and strode past her with a shrug. "Best I can do. Let's go."

She didn't move, didn't even turn—just stared out the balcony doors.

"Giselle. Come on."

"Look at her, Ben. Do you see her? Resting now. Feeding. But soon she'll be ready to leave her den and become the monster Leviathan created her to be."

"Yeah. Sure." Ben watched her. He didn't like her tone—admiration instead of horror. "But we don't want the monster loose, right? We need to get this data to the Company without showing the enemy our hand."

"Why?" She turned, nodding at the computer. "Why give it to him?"

"Him? You mean the Director? Why wouldn't we?"

Giselle stepped close, within inches of a kiss. The Glock and the cattle prod hung at her sides. "Look at what he's done to you, Ben. Your face. Your life. You are homeless, nationless, a hunted man." She reached up with the hand holding the Glock and traced a knuckle from his temple to his chin. "No safe havens. No place to lay this beautiful head. Why do you persist in serving him? Why are you so desperate to please the man who asks for everything and leaves you nothing?"

Did he have to justify himself, even to her? "Stopping Leviathan is our duty. We took oaths. The severance doesn't change them. It's all a mistake or a trick. Once he knows, he'll fix it. You'll see."

She closed her eyes, shoulders tensing, and when she opened them again, her shout knocked him back a step. "Wake up!" The rest came through clenched teeth. "He doesn't care about you. To him we are nothing—cogs." She backed away from him, spreading the Glock and baton wide. "Our homes are gone. Our lives? Gone. How long should we suffer these indignities? Do you think Leviathan would treat us this way?"

"Leviathan?" How could she go there? Even after all they'd suffered, how could she compare the enemy to the Director? "I don't understand. You're not making sense."

"Ben, what if we didn't hand this bioweapon data over to anyone, hmm? What if Jupiter sees a larger picture? Perhaps a controlled release of the plague is . . . healthy for the world—an ordered and effective version of the chaos we've already experienced. We had a chance at a global reset, yes? But we blew it."

Now she was talking crazy—straight-up crazy. "You're scaring me."

"Oh, don't be scared." Her demeanor shifted. In an instant, her defiance gave way to the pleading of a playful sweetheart. "And"—she smiled, tilting her head—"don't be mad, *mon rêve*. My dream. I did this for us."

The blood drained from Ben's face. He felt the same vanishing of tissue and bone he'd felt when he watched the cottage explode. "Giselle, what did you do?"

She lowered a shoulder in her sultry way, sauntering toward him one slow step at a time. "I saw the writing on the wall long before Rome. I saw the brilliance of Jupiter's Tokyo attack, the control wrapped in chaos. I put out a quiet feeler, and he found me, embraced me."

"Jupiter. You're working with him? What you're saying is treason."

"Treason is in the eye of the beholder, yes? He wanted you. So did I. Our pursuit of you is of mutual benefit."

Idling engines. Car doors shutting. Ben heard voices—either cops called by the neighbors or Kidan's private security. Giselle needed help. Ben could save her, but not here. Not now. They had to leave. He reached for her.

"Don't!" The Glock came up as fast as the bullets could fly from its chamber.

Ben froze, then slowly raised both hands to shoulder height, shamed by the fact she'd outpaced him with his own gun. "I'm sorry. Relax, okay?"

"I am relaxed. You are the one who needs to relax." Another smile. Another lowered shoulder and a sultry step. She didn't seem to care about the voices outside. Who were they? "You must listen. You must hear me out."

"I'm listening. I always listen to you, right?"

"Because you love me. Yes. I said the words. We've loved each other from our first assignment together. You know it. And love prompted me to act on your behalf. You are too good—too skilled—to be the Director's lackey. You must see this." Another smile. Another step.

In this madness, would she come close enough for Ben to take the gun? Could he outmatch her reflexes? He forced his shoulders to relax. "And with Leviathan?"

"Think of this as a brilliant young lawyer might, jumping from a firm where his talents are not rewarded to one which would value him greatly." The Glock came close to Ben's striking range, then paused. Giselle knew his abilities well. "*Mon rêve— mamour*—you belong with Leviathan. You belong with me."

No. Whatever happened, he didn't belong with Giselle— not anymore. "Clara." The name escaped his lips on instinct. "What did you and Jupiter do with Clara?"

"The blue-haired woman?" She scrunched her nose, as if she'd been suddenly hit with a foul smell. "We did nothing with her."

"Don't lie to me. I know Leviathan sent Duval to Zürich. She disappeared after he attacked us. And I know you chose that hair color because you'd been watching us. You wanted me to think you were her when I saw you at Jupiter Global."

She shrugged. "Am I your love? Is she? I had to ask in my way. And you answered with the disappointment on your face."

"I care about Clara."

Her eyes flashed. "You should care about us, yes? You and me." Giselle flicked a dismissive hand. "It is behind us now. I forgive you. She no longer matters."

"She does matter. The people in Tokyo, Munich, and St. Petersburg matter. The lives Leviathan took and the families they destroyed with those bombs matter."

"Sacrifices in the name of control. Preparations for a mass culling of the pride. The pandemic taught us the failure of chaos. In the face of crisis, too many pursued their own ends, leading to a global meltdown. We could not band together, even to face the worst crisis of our collective lives."

"And how will releasing another disease help?"

"Aren't you listening?" She sighed, tilting the Glock. "Culling the pride. Control over chaos. If Leviathan controls the antidote, Leviathan controls the outcome. Jupiter Global's pharmaceutical subsidiaries will team up and miraculously provide the cure. Governments will bow and scrape, desperate to give them whatever Jupiter desires."

Insanity. Both she and Jupiter were out of their minds. But in Ben's experience, crazy people made big mistakes. The *Behemoth* could be their biggest. "It's a giant, slow-moving cargo ship. I'll call in the cavalry. A Company team will interdict the ship. Your whole plan is a waste."

"Ben, Ben. The Company won't listen to you. And even if

they would, don't you think Jupiter has accounted for such contingencies? Remember the material in the bulk cargo holds you asked Kidan about?"

He closed his eyes for a moment, letting out a breath. "CRTX. The ship is a floating bomb." He saw the diagram in his head. "There must be tons of it in there. Thousands of tons."

"Ten thousand tons, to be exact—with the explosive power of a sixty-kiloton nuclear bomb. If the Company attempts to board or sink the vessel, Jupiter's people will detonate the weapon, sending thousands of steel canisters filled with plague flying a kilometer or more from the blast center. Kidan's creation is resistant to seawater, Ben. It might wash up on any shore."

"But Jupiter doesn't want just any shore, does he?" Ben recalled the weather charts for the Atlantic he saw in the *Behemoth*'s passage plan. "He's going after the United States."

"Yes, *mamour*. The United States will fall. The Director will suffer for his crimes against us. And you can be there to watch. Go to Jupiter. He's been waiting for you so long, but he wants you to come willingly. No strings. Just as you are."

Someone pounded on the door. Ben shot forward and grabbed for Giselle's wrist. The Glock went off, but missed wide. He pulled her close, held her tight, looking down into her eyes. He had her. The success—the ease—of the maneuver surprised him, until he felt the cattle prod jammed into his belly.

The shock sucked away all muscle control. Ben dropped to his knees. But Giselle pulled the prod away before he lost all consciousness.

She frowned at him with the look of a scolding, disappointed wife. "Renounce him, Ben. Can't you see? This is for your own good. The United States—the Company—they don't deserve your loyalty. Curse your precious Director and let Jupiter make you a prince among Leviathan's operatives. Rub your victory in the Director's traitorous face."

Ben fought for control of his lips. His reply came out as a grunt.

Giselle kneeled to grip him by the collar. "What, *mamour*?"

How had their relationship gone so wrong? Ben wanted to say so much. He wanted to declare his loyalty to his country, his agency, to her. She needed help, not a bullet. But he could only manage one word. "No."

"Too bad. If you won't see reason, then I suppose you should go ahead and die."

She hit him again with the crackling prongs.

57

Ben's eyes popped open, and he gasped for breath. He tried to sit up. Failed. Tried again. Barely made it. An object fell from his chest to the floor with a *thump*, but he didn't have the energy to look. Heat seared his stomach. A soreness like he'd never felt wracked his body.

Giselle.

Traitor.

He'd been tased before. All the Company's agents went through the experience at least twice in the schoolhouse—more if they made a fuss. But this hurt more, or maybe not all the hurt came from the physical wound.

A fog clouded Ben's vision and took longer to clear than expected. The bright light of a rising sun pouring into the room didn't help. How long had he been out? He rolled to his knees and crawled to a gray mass he thought was the desk, waited for the vertigo to stop, and pulled himself to his feet. A greasy wetness clung to his fingers. Ben squinted at his hand. Black? No. Dark red. Blood.

Blurry shapes took form. The desk. The broken DNA sculpture. Kidan's body. Ben grimaced and wiped his fingers on the scientist's lab coat. "Sorry," he said to the dead man. "That's twice. I know." The fresh stains looked so much brighter than the dried blood where he'd wiped off the laptop.

The laptop.

He looked around. Gone. What else had she taken? He checked his waistband and his front pockets. Giselle had made off with the evidence, but also his Glock, his wallet, and Kidan's keys. She'd taken the Jag, where Ben had left his go-bag with his protein bars and cash. He punched the balcony doorframe. "Oh, we are so broken up."

What about the voices he'd heard?

Outside, the rising sun glistened off the pristine infinity pool beneath an empty, picture-perfect balcony, so different from the mess inside. Ben drew closer and shielded his eyes against the sunlight. As best he could tell, the neighbor's balcony was empty too. Giselle or Jupiter must have called off any cops or security.

The more time passed, the more clarity Ben gained, until he noticed something off with the desk. Giselle, despite her earlier protest about the laptop, had dipped a finger in Kidan's blood and scrawled on the desk.

While pulling himself from the floor, Ben had smeared the first letter, but he could still make out a *C*. "Call me," he said, reading the bloody message, then shook his head. "That's messed up." Why and how would she think he'd even try?

Then it dawned on him—the thing that had fallen from his chest when he sat up.

A compact satellite phone lay on Kidan's floor—black against the white shag carpet.

The pain in Ben's abdomen returned when he bent to pick it up, bringing with it a soreness in his limbs and a slight vertigo. Giselle's confiscated cattle prod had done a number on him. Holding the phone in his palm, he flipped up a short, thick antenna and pressed the power button to bring it out of sleep mode. The screen came to life with a waiting message in glowing blue letters.

> My love,
> You must be angry with me.
> I must apologize for the little prick,
> but one day you will thank me.

Ben touched his abs and winced. "Little prick? Is that what you call it." He scrolled on.

> Jupiter is a patient man.
> He is still willing to meet.
> Go to him. He is your cure.

Ben closed the message and found a single speed-dial number saved on the home page. Instead of her name, Giselle had assigned the contact to *Mamour*, the French shorthand for *My love*. He shifted his gaze to the bloody *Call me* scrawled on the desk and snorted. "Yeah, right."

Ben had to regroup. He could deal with Giselle's insanity later—or never. Right now, the priority was stopping Leviathan's attack. He drew in a breath. "The *Behemoth*. Three hours."

Three hours had passed long ago.

The rising sun no longer blocked out the Mediterranean beyond the beach. Ben opened the balcony door and scanned the many piers at Valencia's port. The *Behemoth* had left.

"Okay," Ben said, holding his aching gut and trying to reassure himself. "Not good, but not the end of the world." A cargo ship like the *Behemoth* took days to cross the Atlantic, and with the marine tracking apps available online, any civilian could find it. The US Navy should have no problem hunting it down.

He nodded. He'd find an internet café and send a message home, a worthy risk. If only Giselle had left him some proof.

The thought brought his time in the dock office to mind. The sealed envelope. The thumb drive.

Ben's hand went to his back pocket, and he smiled. He'd never told Giselle about the drive, and when she cleaned him out, she'd missed it.

As he drew the thumb drive out, wondering what might be on it, he saw a spot of dried blood on his forearm. Splatter from picking up the laptop? He scratched it off, and found a needle mark underneath. The blood was his, not Kidan's.

I must apologize for the little prick . . . Go to him. He is your cure.

"No . . . She wouldn't."

All that pain in his stomach—he'd assumed it came from shock burns. Ben pulled up his shirt to get a look at his abdomen. The two burns were there, raised marks left by the prongs. But not far away, closer to his navel, he saw a gray blotch with three lines spidering outward.

Giselle had injected him with the plague.

58

Ben walked the beach behind Kidan's place, shoes tied together and slung over his shoulder, sat phone held loose, ready to fall from his fingers.

The gentle wash of water over sand filled his whole body, but it couldn't drown out the rush of his thoughts.

The idea of the disease—the sheer weight of it—felt different this time. In Rome and the hours after, Ben suffered the worry and stress of unanswered questions. Had Massir infected him? Was he a walking dead man?

This time he knew. He'd seen the effects firsthand. The infection was spreading, attacking from within, and no amount of violent action could stop it.

The certainty hit him in alternating waves of horror and peace.

A rocky point with a low bluff separated the resorts and residences from the industrial piers. Ben plodded toward it without purpose, leaving absentminded footprints to be quickly washed away by the surf. For the hundredth time, he glanced down at the phone.

Call me. Written in blood.

He selected the *Mamour* speed dial and pressed send.

"Ben. You called. I am so proud."

So many angry words hovered at his lips—accusations, re-bukes. "Why, Giselle?"

"You know why. I did this because I love you. I did this be-cause you are stubborn like a mule, and you need a little push to get you moving on the proper road."

"You said 'I love you' last night for the first time, and this morning you're making career decisions for me? One of us is more invested in this relationship than the other—that's all I'm say-ing." He frowned at the incoming waves. "How long do I have?"

"Days. Decades. The choice is yours, and so is your position at Leviathan, if you'll only accept it. Jupiter is your cure."

That phrase again. *He is your cure.* "You mean he has the antidote?"

"*Naturellement.* I told you he is a master of control, yes? He is not so foolish as to release a disease without first creating the cure. And he will give you this cure if you go to him humbly and ask."

"Not a chance."

"Oh, Ben—"

"I'll die before I turn traitor, before I sacrifice my soul for my own gain."

The line went silent for a time, followed by a wavering sigh. "It hurts me to hear you say such things."

"Good."

"I did this for us, not me."

"Keep telling yourself that." *Of all the pushy girlfriends.* He stopped his plodding and looked out at the sea. Several boat-ers had made an early start to the day, taking advantage of the calmer morning waters. A green and white sail passed slow across his view. On the rocky point, a pair of kids cast lines into the waves, oblivious to the danger so close at hand. "Tell me this. Am I contagious? Should I wade into the Mediterranean with a stone around my neck and end it now?"

"No, *mon rêve.* You are not contagious—as long as you prom-

ise not to bleed on anyone. I injected you with a special version
Jupiter had Dr. Kidan make just for you."

"I thought your boss wanted me to come to him willingly,
without coercion."

She made a regretful clicking sound with her tongue. "True.
But he will overlook the nuance for you, his greatest prize. Go
to him now. Be healed and be forgiven."

Ben hung up the phone and hauled back his arm to chuck
it into the sea.

He paused, unable to complete the throw.

How long do I have?

Days. Decades. The choice is yours.

Giselle had told him he had days, not hours. Not mere minutes
like poor Massir in Rome. Maybe death had him in its grip, but
Ben still had time to stop the *Behemoth*. And he knew someone
who might have the skills to extend his window of opportunity.

Leviathan would be monitoring the sat phone. Ben didn't
doubt it for one instant. He took the risk anyway, opening the
text feature and entering a memorized number. He wrote the
data bursts to the operator in Company short code.

911//REQ AMBROS

Urgent medical aid needed. Requesting code name Ambrosia.
He only trusted one person to help. Tess.

An immediate reply came back.

ID?

The operator wanted his identification number. Not a chance.
Ben repeated the message, adding a please.

911//AMBROS//PLS

"Just put her on the line," he said out loud, pressing the send
key.

He waited. The blue glow behind the sat phone's screen went dark. The surf rolled over his feet, getting higher with each cycle. No reply came back. Why had he expected any different? He laughed to himself and set off again toward the point.

Three steps later, the phone buzzed in his hand.

> AMBROS HERE//GO

Tess. Wonderful, amazing Tess. Ben's thumbs flew over the keys.

> BC HERE//REQ RV//REG 1//HZD4

Ben Calix requesting rendezvous in Region 1, the United States. Medical Hazard Level 4. He used his initials for clarity. Code names and ID numbers no longer mattered for him. Leviathan knew he had the phone. As to the medical hazard, the level 4 designation included possible contagions. Ben couldn't trust Giselle's assurances. He didn't want Tess walking into this blind. He told her the risks. She'd choose to help or not. Either way, he wouldn't blame her.

The screen didn't stay empty for long.

> APPRVD//DT?//FAC#?

Approved. What date and time? Which facility?

Ben pulled his thumbs back and gritted his teeth. Tess expected him to respond with a facility number that translated to a location known only to Company agents—agents like Giselle. Whatever number he typed, Giselle and Leviathan would see, turning Tess's mission of mercy into a trap. He racked his brain, searching for a solution, then allowed himself a thin smile. Tess would finally get that dinner he'd promised so long ago.

> 36H//CE DREAM

Thirty-six hours. At the place we dreamed about when we were stuck in that dank hole in Chechnya. At least, Ben hoped she'd get all that from his improvised code. He held his breath, until the answer came through.

CUS

See you soon.

He powered off the device and tossed it sidearm, far into the water.

59

A second dark blotch appeared on Ben's abdomen before he reached the Hotel Sol.

The walk from the point at Pobles del Sud to El Cabanyal Beach north of the port facility had taken him forty-five minutes and left his muscles aching as if he'd run a 10K. The increased soreness worried him. Lifting his shirt to check, he'd found the second mark, joined to the first by one of the black vein-like extensions.

Ben wondered if Giselle's estimate of days might be optimistic.

He straightened his clothes and body, looking as healthy as a man with crusted frostbite blisters on his face and carrying the plague could look, and walked past the hotel doorman with the confident stride of a paying guest.

The desk clerk posed a larger challenge. Ben needed to convince her to call down a recent acquaintance to whom he'd never given his name—an acquaintance he hoped could solve his next big challenge.

Tess had come through, as always. Now, with little money, no weapon, and no passport, Ben had to find passage to the United States, and fast. He waited his turn at the check-in desk, ignoring worried glances from a young couple seated in the lobby and surrounded by far too much luggage. He pitied the taxi driver coming to take them to the airport.

"*Buenos días, señor. Puedo servirte?*"

Ben blinked. His turn had come. The clerk had acknowledged him. Where was his brain? "Pardon?"

"Ah. You are American." The young woman gave him a condescending smile. "I asked if I might help you."

"Yes. Thank you. I arranged to meet a new friend here for breakfast. I think he overslept. Will you ring him for me?"

"Yes, of course. The name?"

"Basile."

"Basile what, sir? I'll need a surname."

How could he be so foolish? He'd never gotten Basile's last name.

"Sir? The surname?" Her smile morphed from condescension to suspicion. "I will need it so I can check our registry."

"I'm so sorry. I've forgotten. Like I said, he's a new friend. But I owe him breakfast, and I'd hate to welch on this debt. It's bad form and bad luck." He shrugged. "How many Basiles can you possibly have staying here at this moment?"

The clerk gave him a flat look.

Ben slid a fifty-euro note across the desk, the last one in his pocket. "Please. It's important."

She accepted the note and shifted her gaze to her computer screen, expressing her exasperation with a steady, heavy tapping of the keyboard's down arrow. After several seconds of this, she frowned, eyes still on the screen. "As it turns out, there are two. Basile de la Fontaine and Basile Palomer."

This time, he didn't hesitate. Ben snapped his fingers and pointed at her. "Palomer. That's it. Well done. Tell him Hey-you is here to see him."

Another flat look.

"Trust me. He'll understand. Just make the call."

He'd taken a gamble, but the odds were heavily in his favor. *Palomer*—French for "pigeon keeper." A last name like that meant birds and bird terms were an inescapable part of Basile's life, hence *The Lazy Ostrich*. Besides, Ben doubted he'd find a single De La Fontaine running a fishing trawler anywhere on the planet.

The girl spoke Spanish on the phone, and the Basile on the other end seemed to understand. Had Ben's Basile given any indication he spoke Spanish? He began to question his choice.

She looked at him sideways, nodding, frowning, said something sharp, and set the phone in its cradle.

Ben raised his eyebrows.

The clerk pressed her lips together. "Señor Palomer remembers a *Hey-you*—I think. He did not sound very sure. Nevertheless, he'll be right down."

Outside, an irritated cabbie argued with the young couple from the lobby, probably attempting to explain the significant difference between the volume of his trunk and the collective volume of their luggage. Ben claimed the couch where they'd been sitting and watched the elevators.

Moments later, the doors of the center elevator opened to reveal a man who looked nothing like the skipper Ben remembered. From his loafers and white slacks to his straw fedora, the clean-shaven Basile waltzing through the lobby might never have dropped a net in his life, except for the flash of black on his belt. Ben saw it only for a nanosecond when the breeze of his stride parted the man's linen sport coat—a scaling knife in a black sheath.

Ben stood, and would've laughed if not for the growing ache in his bones. "I hate to be trite," he said in French. "But you clean up nice. You look fifteen years younger than you did on your boat."

Basile removed his fedora and bowed. "I'll take that as a compliment, which is the manner I believe you intended. The

Spanish beaches have been kind to me." As he replaced the hat, concern creased his brow. "But I see they have not been as kind to you. Are you okay, my friend?"

Ben let the gravity in his expression answer the question. "We need to talk, Basile." He glanced around the lobby, noting the number of ears that might perk up with alarm at whispered words like *plague* and *attack*. "Let's go for a walk."

Few beachgoers disturbed the sands of Playa del Cabanyal. The early hour and December's cooler weather afforded Ben that advantage. A fisherman tugged at his line. A pair of women jogged together, insulated from each other by their earbuds and whatever music or podcasts played on their phones. No one else.

Ben waited for the joggers to pass, then drew a breath to make his case to Basile. The act of expanding his lungs doubled him over in pain.

Basile bent beside him, laying a hand on his back. "You really aren't okay, are you?"

"Don't touch me."

The fisherman jerked his hand away. "My apologies. But I am no threat to—"

"It's not that." Ben straightened, groaning. "Please keep a little distance, for your own safety."

"A social distance, you mean?"

Ben set off again without answering the nervous joke. He set a slower pace than before.

Basile followed, walking beside him, but staying more than an arm's length away. He let out a low whistle. "So we are no longer talking in hypotheticals, as we did on the *Ostrich*. The madman found the plague."

"Correct. My enemies injected me with a weaponized version." Ben could see the growing fear in Basile's eyes. "Try to relax, the version I carry is not contagious unless I bleed on you. And you can call me Ben now. My time in this world is short. I no longer see the point of anonymity."

"All right, Ben. What can an old fisherman do to help?"

"I need to get to the United States."

Basile laughed—a hearty laugh that wiped away the somber tone of Ben's declaration. "My friend, my friend, you overestimate the capabilities of my boat."

Ben pressed his lips together. "I'm not talking about sea travel. I need to get out of here by air. Tonight."

The fisherman remained silent for several paces, then released one of his deeply French grunts. "Mm. What makes you think I can help you with air transport? I am no travel agent."

"I saw the panels on the *Ostrich*."

"Panels? What panels?"

Ben would've felt insulted if he hadn't detected a hint of playfulness in the question. "You're a smuggler, Basile. The beach life suits you because you know it well. You didn't buy that fedora in a shop yesterday. I noticed the inside rim when you bowed at the hotel. The band is dented from the hook where it hangs, most likely in that closet on the bridge of your boat."

"Okay. Perhaps I am, but smuggling is an expensive affair." Basile looked him up and down. "And I no longer see your bag of money. Can you still afford such help?"

"Give me your knife."

The fisherman's eyes narrowed.

"I'll give it back. I promise."

Slowly, Basile removed the fillet knife from its sheath and placed it in Ben's waiting hand, watching him carefully. "You keep it. You know, in case you *are* contagious."

"Thanks." Ben removed his belt and turned it over to run the blade down a long track of crisscrossing threads. They snapped as he bent the leather, revealing a shallow pocket with pink bank notes inside. He withdrew four 500-euro bills, folded together. "Is this enough?"

"So, you're a smuggler too," Basile said, reaching for the bills. "You have any more?"

Ben pulled the money back. "Not enough to spend foolishly. This will have to do, and I'm hoping another five hundred will buy back the SIG I gave you."

"What happened to that nice little Glock?"

"My girlfriend stole it."

"Meh." The smuggler bobbled his head. "It happens. With the dying-friend discount, I think I can return the gun, clean and with a full magazine, *and* make your travel arrangements for twenty-five hundred." He rubbed his fingers together. "But I'll need the cash up front."

"Done." Ben placed the bills in his palm.

Basile tucked them away, then seemed to consider what had just transpired and rubbed his hand on his pants. "Are you sure you're not contagious?"

"Yes. Now—" Pain shot through Ben's abdomen. He grunted, forcing himself to stay upright, and drew a breath to start again. "Tell me how this works."

Basile shrugged. "I don't know. But I have a friend in the air cargo business in Marseilles. She'll have the necessary connections here. But I can tell you, if we pull this off and get you on a plane, it's going to smell bad. Very bad."

60

Goats are mean. Ben had no idea the gregarious farm animals could turn into such vindictive tormentors, but then, he'd never been trapped with the bearded terrors in an eight-foot-by-ten-foot air-cargo livestock pen before.

And they stank.

Basile had not lied about the smell. If anything, he'd understated the problem. But the stench was a key piece of the smuggling puzzle, shielding Ben from discovery.

The wall of musk had hit Ben like a force field ten feet away from the pen. Basile's contact explained that the stench mostly belonged to the billy, the only adult male in the shipment, who had an excellent track record of hiding contraband. The EU and US inspectors checked a sampling of the cargo pens during loading and unloading for every flight, but they always avoided the male's pen, thanks to the smell. The same billy had made more than a dozen journeys back and forth across the Atlantic.

The pen's top half was mostly chicken wire, so Ben had to bury himself under a pile of straw during loading and unloading at each transfer of a two-stop flight. Unfortunately, the vindictive goats peed on the same straw with impressive regularity. Worse, the male refused to let him sleep. Every time

Ben managed to nod off, the billy rammed him in the arm, leg, head—whatever he left exposed. The goat seemed to blame him for each bump and burble of turbulence.

When the jet bounced on the final landing, the billy lowered its horns and threatened to charge him again.

"Stay in your corner," Ben said, flashing Basile's knife. "I promised your owner I wouldn't gut you, but you can only push a man so far."

The billy snorted.

Of everything Ben had suffered, burying himself in urine-soaked straw to sneak through the lengthy US customs process ranked among the worst. By the time he sat up, gasping for air, the pens were on a flatbed trailer, accelerating up a highway on-ramp at the eastern extent of Dulles International Airport. A cold wind bit at his cheeks. Empty trees and piles of brown slush flew by on a wintry afternoon. Virginia's Route 50, outside Washington, DC, looked the same as always. He leaned his head against the chicken wire, holding the knife out behind him to keep the billy from attacking again, and let out a rueful chuckle. "Welcome back, Ben."

The trucker topped off his tanks near Fairfax, at the I-66 interchange, and Ben bailed when the guy went inside for a snack. Even with the pen far behind him, he couldn't escape the smell. He sniffed his jacket and grimaced, shooting a glance at the truck stop. He had some US cash. The air cargo smuggler had graciously changed out his last euros for dollars—after a hefty conversion fee. His rendezvous with Tess wasn't for three hours. Plenty of time for a shower.

○ ○ ○

On a day that seemed like a thousand years ago, a Red Cross chopper had dropped Ben off five klicks outside the Chechen village of Vedeno for his first mission for the Company—a solo job. It went south fast.

Posing as a South African buyer, he met with an arms dealer who claimed to have the market cornered on one-kiloton suitcase bombs. As it happened, Company intelligence said a similar weapon had gone missing from a classified Spetsnaz outpost near Grozny two weeks earlier.

They met in the garage of the town's only mechanic—Ben, the Chechen dealer, and a third man who arrived two minutes late. Ben lifted his chin as the extra man sauntered in. "Who's this?"

"Didn't I tell you? This is not a simple buy." The Chechen slapped a black hardened suitcase down on the garage table, bouncing the ratchets and wrenches. "It's an auction. Who wants to start the bidding?"

The newcomer and Ben sized each other up. Ben cocked his head. "Spetsnaz, right?"

The Russian's lips spread into a thin smile. He nodded. "And you are CIA."

"Close enough."

They both turned to face the dealer.

Ben grabbed the case and ran.

One bullet grazed his side on the way out of the garage. Another lodged itself in his arm. But the real damage came from the grenade. The Chechen didn't have much of an arm, so the toss came up short. An old Lada parked in the gravel parking lot and the Russian, who'd raced after Ben, took the brunt of the blast. Still, four small fragments penetrated Ben's leg and back. He used the cloud of dust for cover, evaded the dealer, and called for armed medical support.

Not too many top-notch surgeons hung around the North Caucasus in those days—even fewer with the clearance to patch up a wayward agent carrying a suitcase nuke. The Company sent in a three-year field ops veteran who'd allegedly been shipped off to Nowheresville Dagestan for losing an earring inside a senior agent's abdominal cavity.

Just rumors. Probably.

Ben found the medic—Tess—at the rendezvous site, a converted shack north of Grozny. In his rush, and thanks to the lowered mental capacity that comes with severe blood loss, he failed to check the suitcase for a GPS tracker.

Tess found the tracker moments after she arrived, checking the case before checking her patient's wounds. She ripped it out, but disconnecting the tracker killed the power source. The last bread crumb it transmitted would lead the dealer straight to the covert medical suite. She chucked the device at a woozy Ben in frustration. "Way to go, rookie. Your dealer will be here any minute. Except this time, he'll bring friends. We've gotta move."

As night fell, the two piled blood bags, drugs, and instruments onto a gurney and pushed it fifty meters into the trees. The dealer and two thugs showed up minutes later.

Ben lay chest down on the gurney, following their movements through the scope of an M4 while Tess cut away his clothes. "So, you come here often?" he said, keeping his voice at a whisper.

"Cute," she whispered back. "Like men haven't been hitting on me since the moment I touched down in these worthless mountains." Without the slightest warning, Tess cut into him with a scalpel and began digging the first bit of shrapnel from his upper thigh. "I'm so sick of this place. The handsy law enforcement. The obsession with knives. The lurid looks and catcalls from *every man everywhere*"—Ben felt a chunk of iron yanked from his body—"including outside the mosques. But you know what I hate most about this place?"

Ben let out a grunt, feeling her slice into his back to go after the next piece. He kept his eye pinned to the scope. The arms dealer located the disconnected tracker and held it up. The men shouted at one another, shaking their heads. "I don't know. The grenades?"

"The food. That's what." Tess rooted around in the wound with surgical pliers. "If I never see a slice of goat meat again, it'll be too soon."

The dealer shoved one of his friends, a little larger than himself. The guy shoved him back.

Tess held her train of thought. "Man, I could go for a burger right now."

With killers so close, Ben should've hushed her, but he fell victim to the irresistible pull of her Georgia accent and kept the conversation going. "I'll see your burger and raise you some crinkle fries. You went through the schoolhouse, right?"

"Yeah." She got to work on the next chunk, digging in with the scalpel. "So?"

"So, remember that place all the students used to go in Mt. Vernon, the one with applewood bacon burgers and the frozen custard? If we get out of this alive, I'll take you there. I promise."

The third piece of shrapnel left his body. Ben had almost grown addicted to the sudden rise and fall of pain when she pulled them out. He heard Tess's sweet southern laugh. "You're thinking of the Shake Shack off Highway 1. I love their burgers. It's a date. Roll onto your side. I need to get at that bullet."

□ □ □

The Shake Shack. Highway 1. Ben kept an eye on the restaurant from across the parking lot at the Sunshine Motel, wearing the blue Bill's Squirrel Stop sweatshirt and ill-fitting jeans he'd purchased at the station.

He'd paid cash for the room. The clerk hadn't argued, and she hadn't asked for a name, giving Ben the impression she made similar transactions all the time. He stood at the window to peek through the curtain. Would Tess remember their conversation from so many years ago, in the heat of a secret battle? He touched the scar the Chechen's bullet had left in his arm. If only he'd come to see her for lead and iron poisoning this time, instead of the horror he faced now.

61

A black Honda Accord pulled into the lot. The woman behind the wheel climbed out and stretched her arms. Tess had dressed the part for a fast-food lunch date, wearing a faded green jacket and Levis. Ben pressed a cheap truck-stop flashlight laser-pointer key chain against the window and dropped the red spot on the Honda's hood. A glance his way and an almost imperceptible nod told him she saw it and had traced the source to his second-floor room. He closed the curtain and retreated to the bed.

Ten minutes later, he heard a knock.

"It's open."

The door swung inward, leaving the diminutive medic silhouetted in the frame, dwarfed by the oversize duffel bag slung over her shoulder. She lifted the strap over her head and let the duffel fall with a heavy *thump* on the threadbare carpet. "When I said, 'It's a date,' Calix, I meant a meal, not a motel room."

He shrugged. "Don't read into it. Although, we both know I move pretty fast—four years from asking a girl out to taking her out. Glad you remembered."

"Oh, I remembered." Tess reached outside the doorframe and lifted a Shake Shack bag and a drink carrier into view. "Even the applewood bacon."

While Tess donned protective gear in the bathroom, Ben gave her a rundown, including the *Behemoth*, the files he saw at Kidan's place, and Giselle's return from the grave to declare her loyalty to the enemy and stab him with a new strain of the bacteria. Then he dove into the food she'd brought him. He'd pictured the burger as some kind of momentary heaven, but the bacteria robbed him of that too. His taste buds failed him. The burger might as well have been warm, soppy ash.

"You smell like goat," Tess called from the bathroom. "You know how I feel about goat."

"Sorry. I crossed the pond using an alternative transport solution—deeply alternative. I showered, though."

"Didn't take." She reappeared wearing white polypropylene from head to toe, along with a mask and googles. "No biggie. The mask helps. Welcome to dating in the post-pandemic age."

"Yeah. Right." Ben answered the joke with a sad smile.

"Too soon? I thought we were flirting, but if you're still upset about Giselle, I—"

"Strangely enough, it's not her. I encountered someone else along the way. I lost her too. I think I . . ." He trailed off. "Never mind. Forget it."

Tess sat down on the bed beside him. "Wow. Someone else. You do move fast, Calix."

"Can't help it." He circled a finger over his exhausted features—the sunken, bloodshot eyes, and the frostbitten nose. "Women throw themselves at a face like this."

She took samples of his breath and blood and slid the receptacles into a compact analyzer linked to her tablet. "I heard about your severance," she said, waiting for the machine to do its work. "For what it's worth, I'm sorry."

Ben sensed an unspoken caveat. "But . . ."

"But nothing."

"Spit it out, Tess."

"Okay. We can go there if you want." She walked away from

the bed and turned, looking stern behind the mask and goggles. "You have to admit. The circumstances are odd. Severances don't come every day, Calix. And they don't come undeserved."

Tess too? How did all his colleagues find it so easy to see him as a traitor?

Before he could defend himself, she went on. "Take Giselle, for instance—your secret against-policy girlfriend-turned-traitor. How could you not know about her treason? Reason suggests you did, and either joined in or turned a blind eye."

"Either way, I deserve what I got, right?" He looked down at his hands, beginning to believe they were as dirty as she claimed.

"Calix . . . Like I said. I'm sorry."

The tablet beeped. Tess checked the screen, then removed the mask and goggles. "At least Giselle told the truth about one thing. You're not contagious, as long as you don't bleed on anyone."

"Silver linings."

"It is a silver lining. And here's another one." Tess shed the upper half of her polypropylene overalls as she spoke, tying them around her waist below her T-shirt. "This bacterium isn't too far removed from the one you encountered in Rome. I had an inkling, so I came prepared. I brought meds."

A hope Ben spent the last thirty-six hours suppressing rose to the surface. "You can help me beat this thing?"

"I can help you fight the battle. I can't help you win."

"Meaning?"

She showed him the tablet. A computer-generated bacterium rotated on the screen. "See this? That's your bug. Mean and nasty. Normally we fight plague with antibiotics, but a weaponized bug resists them. Only the specific cocktail of engineered antibiotics, enzyme inhibitors, and stimulants created by the same folks who created this ugly bug can stop it."

"The antidote."

She nodded. "Think of it as a key to the bacterium's lock. Unique and intricate—able to work all the tumblers. With a month of study, a team of microbiologists might pick the lock, but—"

"By then, I'll be dead."

"Yeah." She removed a CO_2 injector from her kit and wiggled it in the air. "I can give you this, my own cocktail, to slow down the replication and treat a few symptoms. Take a breath. Here it comes." She jammed the injector into his thigh.

The hiss and cold of forced air.

The prick of a needle stabbing through his jeans.

Ben felt every milliliter of medicine entering his bloodstream. Would it help?

As if reading the question in his thoughts, Tess pursed her lips, handing him a packet of five similar injectors. "At best, these'll buy you two extra days. Take one in the morning and one at night." She handed him another, larger injector. "I brought this too."

He turned it over in his hand. A clear window enabled him to see the red fluid inside. "What is it?"

"We call it a *kick*. Think of it as adrenaline on steroids combined with the ultimate painkiller. The effects are impressive, but there are . . . Let's call them drawbacks. The Company hasn't fielded it for safety reasons. In your case, those reasons don't matter."

Tess explained how the kick worked, and Ben slipped it into his pocket with the other injectors. He stared at the curtain separating him from shops and streets outside, filled with unsuspecting Americans who'd already suffered through one terrifying pandemic. "What about them? What if Leviathan's weapon gets out?"

"The R_0 you told me about doesn't leave much room for optimism. Natural plague victims need to start receiving treatment within a day or two of infection. Strong symptoms give them plenty of warning. But the weaponized critter you described doesn't show itself for sixteen days, and kills fast once it does. If your info is good, any antidote we create will be useless."

"*If* my info is good?"

Tess shrugged. "Severance, Calix. The Director made the judgment declaring you're not trustworthy. Don't blame me."

He let it go. "Okay, let's assume I'm not a traitor or an incompetent and I'm giving you solid intelligence about the coming attack. What's the prognosis?"

"Total devastation. And I mean total." She glanced at her screen and the rotating bacterium. "All mammals are affected by Yersinia pestis, the original bubonic plague bacteria. Controlling it in the human population will be hard enough. In the animal population, it will wipe out entire food supplies—truly reshape America."

Reshape America. Control from chaos. "Then help me contain it. Help me stop this attack. Go to the Director. Or better yet, take me to him."

"No way. I wouldn't take a severed spy to the Director, even if I could. I'll send in your blood. I'll make a report on this bug. It's the best I can do."

That wouldn't be enough. He snapped his fingers. "I lifted a thumb drive from Sea Titan's offices." He handed it over. "I found that in an envelope addressed to the *Behemoth*'s captain. Can you check it?"

"Maybe." She connected the drive to her tablet, glancing at him sideways. "This better not give me a virus."

"Funny."

Tess huffed and shook her head. "Empty."

"What?" Ben sat forward and looked at the screen. Sure enough, the drive contained no files.

"Stop wasting my time." Tess yanked the drive and chucked it into his lap. "And don't you dare start in on the *Behemoth*, this fabled ship with a nuke's worth of CRTX and ten thousand

289

tanks of plague. I ran a search for her after I took your samples."
She swiped the screen to show him a marine cargo tracking
site. "She's in dry dock—never left Spain. An empty drive. An
imaginary plague ship. You have no proof to back your story.
All you have are words."

He couldn't believe Tess would turn on him like this. "I have
a deadly disease. You saw the results."

"Your disease is bad, but it's a far cry from the monster you
described from Kidan's files. All your illness tells me is that
you had direct contact with the same enemy you encountered
in Rome."

"But Giselle—"

"Had you cornered—unconscious—so you say. And you want
me to believe she let you come running home with knowledge
of Leviathan's whole plan?" Tess dropped the tablet into her
bag. "Look at this from my view. As far as I know, Giselle is
dead, and you're trying to use me to feed the Company more
bad intelligence."

"Tess, please . . ."

"I *want* to believe you." Tess softened her voice, reaching
to touch his cheek, but pulled back, setting the hand in her
lap. "You know I do. But I can't take the risk. And by the way,
changing your story to make Giselle the villain isn't helping.
The last I heard, you were blaming Dylan for your troubles.
Poor little guy. The Company recalled him from an assignment,
put him through an investigation." She raised an eyebrow. "But
Dylan came through the investigation clean. No severance."

"Wait." Ben had looked down to rub the spot where she
injected the cocktail. It had started to burn. He looked up.
"You're telling me Dylan is stateside?"

Her softness vanished. "Whatever you're thinking, don't."

"I need to see him. I know he's not happy with me right now,
but he can help with my situation."

"I doubt he can help. And I *know* he won't want to. And to

say Dylan's 'not happy' is a gross understatement." She pressed her lips together. "Have you ever heard the term *shootin' mad*?"

His attempt to answer became a fit of coughs. Ben's symptoms were worsening. He swallowed against the sandpaper in his throat. "I'm dying, Tess. And Dylan's a grade-A geek who hates guns. How bad can he hurt me?"

62

The pepper spray hurt. It hurt a lot, given Ben's condition. So did everything else Dylan threw at him.

Ben had spent a full day of his precious time preparing for the encounter, but he started with the direct approach out of respect for his former colleague. He rang the bell at Dylan's front gate. Big mistake.

Shady Oak, Virginia, boasted acreage lots, Potomac views, and distinguished residents from Washington DC's elite political and diplomatic circles. How Dylan nabbed a house there was beyond Ben's comprehension. During a recent mission, the young Welshman had bragged about an online auction and creative bidding strategies, but Ben had zoned the rest out as geek chatter.

Ben showed up looking presentable in a fresh polo and jacket he'd picked up at the local Walmart. More than a day had passed since he met with Tess, and he'd kept busy preparing for this encounter. He needed Dylan—more than he planned to let on.

When Ben rang the bell, the geek appeared on a video monitor wearing a Game Gear headset. "Go away. I'm busy."

"It's Ben."

"Yes, Grandpa. I can see you. Here in the twenty-first century, we have this thing called live two-way video."

The Welsh accent only exacerbated Dylan's sarcasm. Ben bit back an angry reply. "Dylan, I don't feel well, and I'm short on time. A bioweapon is headed our way. How about you skip the okay-boomer jabs and open the gate?"

"What part of 'go away' don't you understand, traitor?"

Traitor. Of all the things Ben imagined he'd be called in the spy game, traitor had not been among them—especially not by a member of his own team. "Dylan. I said open the—"

A stream of pepper spray hit him in the face.

By the time Ben could see again, blinking against his tears, the screen had gone dark. "Fine. You wanna play? You're on."

Tess's cocktail of antibiotics and symptom-fighting meds had given Ben a smidgeon of relief from the bacteria, not enough to feel like himself, but enough to go a few rounds with the likes of Dylan. And he'd bought some extra goodies for the occasion, all stuffed into a new backpack. Ben also had the *kick* Tess gave him, but she'd warned him not to use it unless he had no other choice.

After wiping his eyes and face with his shirt, Ben ran along the property's redbrick wall, searching for a good entry point. He found an oak with overhanging branches and nodded. "You'll do."

How many times in his career had Ben dropped over an eight-foot fence or wall? Never once had he so much as twisted an ankle. This time faux grass gave way on impact and he fell another six feet into a square, carbon fiber pit. The extra distance, combined with the disease and the weight of his backpack, drove him into the floor—an undignified heap of arms and legs.

Laughter. Dylan's voice—undercut by a whining hum. "Oh how the mighty Saber has fallen."

Ben zeroed in on the source. A drone about the size of a

volleyball zipped into view to hover beneath the oak tree's overhanging branches.

"You chose the most obvious route over the wall, Grandpa. Try not to be so predictable."

The drone's camera twitched and zoomed to watch Ben haul himself from the pit.

Ben dusted himself off and looked up with a growl. "Is that all you've got?"

It wasn't.

Ben took one step into the yard and a sprinkler head popped up. A burst of high-intensity light seared his brain—an instant migraine. Ben shielded his eyes and stumbled sideways, only to catch a blurred glimpse of a larger head rising from the grass. A drum with a wide gun barrel attached to each side swiveled to track him.

"Dylan, don't you—"

The device opened fire.

Ben hoisted his backpack up as a shield, knocked back by the rapid pelting of hard rubber slugs. A ripple of four caught his kneecap. "Aagh!"

"Oh, I'm sorry. Did that hurt?" The camera drone haunted him, following wherever Ben went but staying just out of reach.

Still blocking the rubber projectiles, he retreated to the cover of a tree trunk deeper in the yard. He waited until a whirring noise told him the drum had run out of ammo, then dealt with the drone. He stepped into the open and swung his backpack at his tormentor.

The drone shot upward, but it clipped a branch, slowing it down. Ben let the backpack go at the apex of its swing and hit his target. The drone fell to the grass, one rotor spinning, the other broken. He hobbled over and picked it up to glare into the camera. "Remember. You did this. Not me." Ben walked to the brick wall and smashed the drone to bits.

He still had to deal with the flashing sprinkler head. By

covering his eyes with his coat, Ben reduced the light to a faded blink and walked close enough to find it with his foot. He stomped it into the grass.

Head pounding, knee aching, eyes burning, Ben marched up to Dylan's porch steps. "I'm coming in one way or another. Open up or get clear." He dug through the contents of his bag, drawing out a steel square, six inches on a side, with holes in each corner.

A panel next to the door slid down, exposing a large round disk. Ben instantly felt heat and nausea developing in his chest. He sighed and jammed his KA-BAR straight into the device. A spark flashed. The heat and nausea went away.

A speaker next to the door crackled. "Harsh, Ben. Truly harsh. Do you have any idea how much an acoustic incapacitator costs?"

"Then you shouldn't have turned it on." Ben returned to his work.

A camera lens in the porch ceiling turned, zooming in. "Now what?" Dylan said. "What've you got there?"

"I went shopping."

"Shopping for wha—" The kid paused as Ben drew out a plastic grocery bag. "Wait. You didn't go to Walmart."

"Yep. Walmart. It didn't have to be this way."

"Okay. I can see you're angry. We both are. And maybe we both said and did things we regret. But that's no reason—"

"I'm not bluffing, Dylan."

A laugh—nervous and uncertain. "My door is double-reinforced steel. You'll never get through."

"I guess we'll find out. I don't know if I ever told you, but I scored high in field chemistry at the schoolhouse."

Walmart. Low prices on everything an isolated field operative or a homegrown terrorist could possibly need. The idea that you can buy cold packs, geriatric laxatives, fuel additives, and powdered sugar all in the same place—without a photo ID or a federal explosives license—is ludicrous, bordering on criminal.

The only piece of the old recipe missing from the store shelves was iron oxide—more of preference than a necessity. Ben had filed all he needed off the bumper of a rusty Ford in the motel parking lot.

Ben carefully lifted a ball of pinkish-gray putty from the Walmart bag and mashed it against the door next to the knob. To this, he added a model rocket ignitor and attached a roll of wire. He covered the putty with the steel plate and used a miniature drill to drive metal screws into three of the corners.

"Stop that. Desist!" Another drone swept in to harass him, buzzing his head.

Without a word, Ben snatched it from the air and held it fast. He drilled the fourth screw through one of the drone's skids, securing it to the plate's last corner. The rotors spun with wild abandon, but the craft could not escape.

"Here's the thing," Ben said, packing up. "Nonlethals don't stop a determined home invader. They just make him mad. Final warning, Dylan. Get clear. I'll give you ten seconds." He walked away, trailing the wire behind him.

Dylan's six-foot pit provided convenient cover. Ben lowered himself inside and covered his ears. "Three, two, one . . ." He touched the wire's alligator clip to a pair of nine-volt batteries duct-taped together.

The blast shook the last leaves of winter from Dylan's trees. Dry and brown, they fell all around Ben. He groaned and pushed himself to his feet to survey the damage, watching the curling wisps of smoke clear away.

Nothing remained of Dylan's door but smoldering masonry and torn steel. A stone fell from the transom above and landed with a sad *plunk* on the pile of debris.

"Warned ya," Ben said under his breath, and drew his SIG.

63

Two more drones appeared as Ben approached the rubble. He shot them down, picked up the closest, and hobbled on through the haze. He found Dylan cowering behind a bank of flat-screen computer monitors at the corner of his open-plan living and dining room. The moment the kid's face rose into view, Ben hurled the drone's remains at him, forcing him to duck. "Fly too close to the sun, did we, Icarus?"

"Making you the sun, right? Just the sort of narcissism I'd expect from a traitor."

That word again. *Traitor.* He growled and leveled his SIG. "Get out here. I need your help."

Dylan took his time. "You know," he said, finally dropping into a rolling chair. He took a long look at the remains of his door before spinning to face the computers. "You could've put a little less shock in your shock and awe."

"Sorry." Ben pulled up a chair beside him and winced as he touched the swelling at his kneecap. He kept the SIG pointed at Dylan. "It's not an exact science."

Dylan stared at him open-mouthed. "No, Grandpa. Chemistry *is* an exact science. It's the very definition of an exact science. Google *exact science*, and you'll find chemistry is right at the top of the list."

"Yeah, well, I could never get my ratios right in the field. And your Walmart only had C&H sugar. It's not the same as the old Tate & Lyle stuff. Besides—" He grabbed a fistful of Dylan's collar and pulled him close so he could see the red marks around Ben's eyes left by the pepper spray. "You had it coming."

"Real nice." The geek pulled his chin back, trying to turn away from Ben's breath. "Way to social distance. I talked to Tess. She says you're not like . . . corona-contagious, but that doesn't make it okay to go around breathing on people."

The kid had guts—or a big ego. When faced with a gun-wielding, plague-carrying psycho who'd just blown up the front door, most people would be inclined to keep their criticisms to themselves. Not Dylan. Probably a side effect of always seeing *high-value asset* next to his name on Company documents.

Ben stared him down for another heartbeat, then let him go, nearly pushing him from his chair. He thrust his chin at the monitors. "First things first. The neighbors are sure to have reported that explosion and the gunshots. Bring up Fairfax County PD's system and call off any vehicles heading this way."

"That's illegal."

"Everything you do is illegal. Besides, I know you have their dispatch system on the hacker version of speed dial. You bragged about it during that op in Budapest, remember? Get it done. You don't want the local constabulary crawling through your house any more than I do."

The Fairfax police dispatch system showed two cars speeding toward Shady Oak. With a flurry of keystrokes, Dylan sent them both a false alarm/return to station order. "Happy?"

Ben's attempt at an answer became a fit of coughs. He grimaced at the pain and fought to regain his voice. "Do I look happy?"

"That's your own fault. You shouldn't have turned—"

"If you say *traitor*, I will use the remainder of my homemade explosives and blow us both into next week."

"I was going to say turned . . . against the Company. Not that such semantics make any difference."

Ben lifted a spare cold pack from his bag and nursed his smarting knee. "I didn't turn against anyone. The severance was a mistake."

"The Director doesn't make mistakes. You're guilty."

"Of what?"

"I don't know. Stuff. You did the stuff. You tell me, Grandpa."

"Stop calling me that." Ben tapped the central monitor with a fingertip. "Okay. I need you to find a missing boat."

"Boat? What boat?"

"Don't play dumb. You talked to Tess. A cargo megaship called the *Behemoth*, registered to Sea Titan Cargo, is heading this way. It left Spain the day before yesterday carrying thousands of tank-tainers filled with aerosolized plague. Now it's gone dark."

"Okay, I *might* have looked into your boat." Dylan held up air quotes as he said the word. "And I *might* have found it. I'll show you, but first, we need to establish boundaries."

Really? Boundaries? The gall of this kid, after kneecapping Ben in his yard of horrors. "We're kind of past boundary issues, aren't we?"

"You want my help or not."

"Fine."

"Good." Dylan pushed Ben's chair, rolling him an arm's length away. "I'm allowing your diseased self to violate the two-llama distance rule, but only so you can see my screens. You get no closer than this. And you don't breathe on me, my keyboard, or any of the mice and trackballs. Got it?"

Ben flattened his lips.

"I'll take that as a yes. And finally"—he glanced back at the rubble and the dead drone lying on his faux wood floor—"don't . . . touch . . . anything."

Dylan scrubbed his wrist pad and keys with a Clorox wipe, then brought up a satellite map depicting the world's shipping traffic. "There. All done. See?"

"See what?"

The kid shook his head, grumbling to himself. "It's like trying to show my mother how to use Alexa." He tapped a key, zooming in on the Spanish coast and panned the display to a long structure, a few miles south of Valencia. "I've tapped into the ONR's classified—"

"ONR?"

"The Office of Naval Research. I tapped into their classified tracking system. The public site Tess showed you compiles data from ship transponders across the globe. But the Navy uses"—Dylan rocked his head back and forth—"*other* methods to track ships. Even so, their program agrees. The *Behemoth* is not on the water." He moved the cursor over the long structure. White text appeared on the screen.

BEHEMOTH

DRY-DOCK

SEA TITAN STN 1

UFN

"She's in dry dock for repairs, Ben. The *Behemoth* left Valencia almost three days ago and parked at Sea Titan's largest maintenance station two hours later. UFN means until further notice."

"I know what it means." Ben wanted to punch the screen for its lies, or maybe Dylan for his pedantic tone. The ONR's program couldn't be right. He lifted his chin. "There's no sign of her at the dock."

"It's a covered facility."

"Sure, but look." Ben traced a strip of empty concrete visible beside the covered dry dock with his pinky, careful not to touch the screen lest he break Dylan's rules. "No people. If Sea Titan's biggest ship is there, where are all the workers?"

"Thin."

"I know what I saw, and you don't load a ship with cargo if she's headed for dry dock."

Dylan threw his hands in the air, spinning his chair away from the screen. "You're hopeless."

"No arguments there. Humor me and keep looking."

"All right." The geek spun himself back to the keyboard. "As a matter of fact, I did. I knew you'd keep harping after I showed you the truth. Take a look." He scrolled the map to a cluster of ships leaving the Strait of Gibraltar. A packet of text followed each vessel. "These are cargo haulers, easy to find because they're running with their transponders on, as required by law. Your missing plague ship might"—he raised a finger—"*might* falsely report shutting down in dry dock and then hide from the online tracking apps by running with her transponder off. Smugglers do it all the time."

"So how do we find her?"

"We use this very program. I told you, the ONR uses alternative tracking methods. Real-time satellite imagery matching, electromagnetic shadow hunting—highly classified stuff. For instance, check out this smuggler." Dylan zeroed in on a small vessel, highlighted by a red triangle. The packet of text following the boat began with its name—*Lazy Ostrich*.

Ben huffed. "I know that guy."

"Then you should probably tell him he's not as sneaky as he thinks. Your friend is running dark, without a transponder. The ONR is still able to see and identify him and record his movements. Not that they care. His operation is too small. He's no threat to the United States."

Ben took note. If he lived long enough, he'd have to send a word of warning to Basile.

"Now," Dylan said, zooming out to the whole Atlantic. Thousands of ships tracked across the display. "The ONR system tracks and identifies and flags false reports. If the *Behemoth* skirted the dry dock and headed into the Atlantic, I'd be able to find it with a simple search." To demonstrate, he typed the name into the program's search bar, omitting dry-dock results, and hit enter.

"Nothing," Ben said, frowning at the red *Zero hits* result.

"Face it, Ben. There's no plague ship. Either you've turned traitor and you're trying to feed us bad intel again, or you've been played—and played hard. Admit defeat and give yourself some peace before you kick off into the great beyond."

Ignoring Dylan's boundaries, Ben pushed him aside and tried the search himself.

"Hey!"

The ONR system spat out the same result. Ben rolled his chair away again, shaking his head. "It can't be. Jupiter must've hacked the Navy's classified server to digitally hide the ship. There's no other explanation."

"Spoken like a true crazy man," Dylan said, cleaning his keyboard with another wipe.

The insult of the action got to Ben more than Dylan's harsh words. His grip tightened on the SIG. "Your self-assurance is getting on my nerves, kid. Things aren't always so clear cut. For instance, not too long ago, I thought *you* were the traitor. The remote detonator I found at the cottage made me think you'd murdered Giselle."

The geek, oblivious, kept scrubbing his equipment. "Yeah. Don't remind me. And thanks for passing that little theory to Hale. Even with intelligence coming from a discredited source like you, the Company still had to follow up. Try to wrap your brain around the humiliation of having all your clearances suspended—called back to the States in the middle of an assignment." Dylan crumpled up his wipe and let out a caustic laugh. "You did that to me. But the investigation cleared me. You, my former friend, were given a *severance*—a final judgment."

"So you're not interested in my side?"

"I don't need to be. That's what a judgment means, Ben. No more questions. No more quibbling. The investigation and trial are over, leaving nothing but the binary. A one or a zero. Either you're innocent or you're guilty." Dylan, seeming to forget his fear of Ben or his disease, rolled close enough to poke him in the chest. "And you've been found guilty."

64

"Are we done?" Dylan thrust a hand toward his obliterated foyer. "Because I have a contractor to call, and you've run out of arguments."

"No I haven't."

The geek narrowed his eyes.

Ben set the thumb drive he'd taken from the dockmaster's office on the desk next to the keyboard.

"What's this?"

"Evidence. Maybe." Ben told him where the drive had come from. When Dylan balked, claiming it might have a virus, Ben shook his head. "No virus. Tess already opened it once."

"And? What'd you find?"

"Nothing. It's empty."

The kid rolled his eyes.

Ben held up a hand. "*But* if it contains hidden files, I'll bet you can find them. In the worst case, you prove it's really empty and ridicule me some more."

Dylan wiped the drive down and held it between his fingers, turning it back and forth. "No. In the worst case, I trigger a virus Tess didn't find and the thing floods my system, wiping out the electricity for the entire eastern seaboard."

"Why would a virus in your system wipe out the electricity for the eastern seaboard?"

The geek looked at him sideways. "No reason. Forget I said that." He set to work at his keyboard. "Hang on, I'll need to partition off a safe space on my system to check your drive."

While he typed, Dylan chattered on. "You know. Accusing me of killing Giselle was bad enough. But when you insist on your innocence in the face of this severance, the accusation you're making is far worse."

Ben didn't follow. Maybe the disease had dulled his mind. "Explain."

"Your declaration of innocence is a declaration that the Director is dealing falsely with you his agent. You're calling him faithless, thus proving yourself to be the same."

Faith. That word again. "I am not faithless."

"Really?" Dylan blew on the drive's connector and plugged it into his machine. "Let me put this into geek speak for you."

"Because that'll help."

"It will. I promise." A window appeared on the left monitor—green computer code on a black screen. "I'm running a program to dig through the formatting data on your drive and look for hidden files. I'm mining for raw data. Ones and zeros, when you get down to the heart of things."

"Binary," Ben said.

"Correct. In geek terms, a thing is either a one or a zero. Either it is, or it isn't. Our boss, the Director, is either the good guy we all follow, or he isn't. We work on faith that he is." Another window came up, symbols instead of code. Dylan squinted at the screen, as if he hadn't expected to find it, but he finished his argument. "By declaring your severance unjust, you're accusing the boss of being a bad guy, a zero. If that's not being faithless, I don't know what is."

Ben opened his mouth to argue.

Dylan held up a hand to stop him. "Hang on. I found something." He tapped the enter key. A whole series of files came up—lists of numbers and three-dimensional drawings of docks and piers. "Whoa. What do we have here?"

They both leaned in. "I think those are coordinates," Ben said.

Dylan clicked through the files. "And these look like 3D radar and sonar returns. I think I know what this is, and it's definitely not a virus."

A roll of a trackball moved the files over to Dylan's main screen. He dumped them all into a program he grabbed from the ONR site and waited. A time bar counted down. A single window opened. A digital ship sailed through a three-dimensional harbor, viewed from the waterline, with every obstacle above and below the surface visible.

Dylan rotated the image to a top-down view. The ship followed a red line through the water, heading for a pier. "This is navigational data for docking a large vessel."

"Like an autopilot?"

"More like an auto–harbor pilot. GPS isn't enough to safely dock a ship. But having the radar and sonar profile for the entire harbor gives a ship with the right propulsion system nanometer precision. Cargo companies use it to avoid paying for a human harbor pilot. They can just come in on their own. It's totally legal at a lot of ports."

"So, you've gotta ask yourself why," Ben said. "Why did Sea Titan hide this totally legal data on the thumb drive?"

Dylan didn't answer.

Ben nodded at the screen. "What harbor is this?"

"How should I know? There are no names."

"You have the coordinates in front of you."

"Oh. Right." Dylan fed the last coordinate into the ONR's tracking program, and the map jumped to a cargo pier in Baltimore harbor labeled SEAGIRT MARINE TERMINAL.

"Houston, we have a target." Ben fell back in his chair. His body ached, as if prodding the genius had sapped the same amount of energy as running a marathon. "Okay. I'm assuming the ONR tracker can show us the schedule for Seagirt Terminal. Show me the bookings for the next couple of days."

"Whatever you say, boss." Dylan tapped a few more keys, speaking in a voice that said *I'm humoring you, boomer.* "But if the *Behemoth* is in dry dock or even pretending to be in dry dock, it won't show up."

"No. It won't." Ben sat forward again, watching Dylan scroll through the list. "Stop. There."

The cursor hovered over a slot allocated to a Jaspen ship. The *Clementine.* "That's why the registration papers for another ship were in the envelope."

"What are you talking about?"

"Run your ONR tracking program on the *Clementine.* The *Behemoth* is coming in under a different name."

Dylan typed *Clementine* into the search bar. "Like they're planning to repaint the ship enroute?"

"I wouldn't put it past them."

As before, the search came up empty, showing only the ship's scheduled arrival in Baltimore for a slot before sunrise on the day after next. The ONR tracker showed no trace of the *Clementine* on the water. If Jaspen Cargo even owned a ship named *Clementine,* Leviathan had wiped her digital signature from the face of the earth.

Dylan ran the search three times. "This has to be a glitch."

"What happened to all your certainty, kid?" Ben laughed, coughing and groaning as he did. "You've got a missing ship. Either the *Clementine* scheduled to arrive at Seagirt Terminal exists, or it doesn't. A one or a zero. But you can't say which. How do you like your binary theory now?"

65

The Haitian cab driver who picked Ben up outside the 7-Eleven a half mile south of Shady Oak didn't seem to mind his hunched stance or sickly complexion. Maybe he picked up strung-out addicts at that corner all the time. He worked in the DC area, after all.

Cabbies use cameras and share info with other drivers—occasionally with the cops. Long walks and public transportation are the safest plan for a fugitive spy in the cold, but Ben no longer had the energy. His aches had doubled since his arrival at Dylan's place. His muscles had lost half their strength. He'd have the cabbie drive him to a strip mall a couple of blocks from the motel.

"Take me to the pharmacy off Lukens Lane in Mount Vernon." He kept his hood up as he dropped into the back seat. Dylan had pointed out new plague blotches on Ben's arms and neck, and he wanted to keep the marks covered. The hood helped with his chills too. Mostly. Ben shivered.

The cabbie eyed him in the mirror. "You know we got drugstores dis side o' Fairfax, fren. No need ta go so fah. I show you."

Ben waved a handful of cash. "No." He could barely get the

308

words out. "This one is special. My prescription is waiting. Please."

The look the guy gave him said *I should be taking you to a hospital*, but he put the cab into gear without another word.

Watching to make sure the guy kept his eyes on the road, Ben pressed his evening injection against his thigh. He barely felt the prick or the medicine's cold rush. Each injection of Tess's cocktail made less difference than the last—little better than placebos. He only had one left. Not great. He needed to survive another day and a half.

The Baltimore port schedule put the *Clementine*—aka the *Behemoth*—in her berth at ten minutes after five, two mornings away. Dylan promised to send everything they'd learned to the Company, but he made no guarantees. He could pass the intelligence, but he couldn't make them act.

He'd also done Ben one more favor.

The failure of Dylan's binary theory created doubt—something the kid didn't experience often. Playing on the uncertainty, Ben convinced him to send a message requesting a meeting with the Director. As with the intelligence, the kid made no guarantees, but he agreed to make the request on Ben's behalf.

"Give it at least a day," he'd said. "Thirty hours or more. This will take time to pass up the chain, and the boss might be anywhere in the world. He'll need travel time."

Thirty hours. Cutting it close.

If the Director believed Ben's tale, they'd have only a small window of time left before the plague ship's arrival. A Company team needed to stop the *Behemoth* in the harbor before it reached the berth without setting off the bomb. If Leviathan saw them coming, they'd detonate the nuke's-worth of CRTX in the hold, destroying half the city and unleashing the bacteria. If the ship reached the berth, the first tanktainer the cranes lifted from the deck would also unleash the bacteria, initiating a slow release of aerosol plague.

If the Director didn't believe his story, Ben would have the same tiny window to stop all of that himself. Impossible.

Resting his head back against the seat, he stared up through the rear window and rehearsed his story. The details grew more obscure with every passing minute. Focus came harder and harder. The empty branches passing overhead warped at the window's edges, twisting and spinning him into delirium.

He saw Paris. His flat. Clara on the stairs. Groceries in one arm, dog in the other. The first of many similar encounters.

He'd first noticed her ice-blue eyes, partially hidden by random strands of blue hair. Maybe that's why it bothered him so much. The blue hair stole well-deserved attention away from her eyes. Maybe. Her lips were moving, asking him a question. Ben strained to listen over the grinds and rattles of the taxi's engine.

"We should get coffee some time—get to know each other. Good neighbors learn about each other's lives. It helps see beyond our own tiny worlds."

She couldn't know about his life. No one outside the Company could know. "Sure, but I'm in a rush. Maybe some other time."

Maybe some other time. Next week. When I come back from my trip. How many times had he put her off when she'd asked for nothing more than an hour and a cup of coffee? What he wouldn't do to have that hour now. Ben had thrown himself into an unsanctioned relationship with a teammate instead.

But Giselle had been persuasive. Alluring.

He saw her walking with him in the forest near Chaville. They laughed and shared stories. Dylan's unending complaints. Hale's parochial schoolhouse wisdom. He could be himself with her. Giselle had made him feel safe.

Liar. Traitor.

Giselle sold him out. Clara ran into a sniper's field of fire to save him.

A speed bump bounced his head off the vinyl. The taxi. The pharmacy. Ben didn't want the cabbie pulling up to the building. He had to control what the cameras saw. He dropped his cash over the seat. "Stop here. This'll do."

Ben stumbled out of the taxi into the parking lot. He trudged toward the store, tripping over a speed bump, caught himself, and walked on, fighting through a fit of coughs to keep his face low and shielded from the cameras.

When the coughing fit ended, he still heard the cab's rattling idle. The guy hadn't driven away. Ben glanced back.

The Haitian lifted his chin. "You stay safe, fren. Get 'ealthy. Okay? You need another ride, you call. Ask for Rayan. I come."

Ben gave him a grateful nod. He doubted he'd live long enough for a next time.

He waited under the pharmacy awning, in the security camera's blind spot, until the cabbie drove out of sight, then limped over to the sidewalk for the two-block hike to the motel.

A police cruiser rolled up to the intersection ahead. The cop looked his way. He flashed his lights.

Ben made an abrupt turn and hurried at a hopping gate across the parking lot of a small grocery. His knee cried out for mercy. Dylan's nonlethal rounds must have cracked something.

No coincidences. The kind Haitian cabdriver had called the cops, maybe to help a man he saw as an addict get clean, or maybe he supplemented his income by feeding them intel on the DC drug scene.

Got caught in a cab, huh? In your condition? Hale haunted him, grumbling in his ear. *You know better, kid. Sloppy. Real sloppy.*

"I was tired," Ben said, ducking into a service alley between the grocery and the pharmacy. He suppressed the pain in his knee and the aches in his body and picked up his pace. "I cut a corner."

And we know how well that goes.

"I'm almost dead. What do you want from me?"

311

A *whoop-whoop* sounded from the grocery lot—one cycle of the siren. The cop was playing this cool.

Contingencies are key, right, kid? A good spy always has an escape route.

Ben nodded to the voice at his shoulder. "I got that part right. I have a way out." A patch of woods with a creek running through it separated the pharmacy strip mall from Highway 1 and Ben's motel. The creek, part of the area's drainage, ran for miles. He could hide there for a while. He just had to get over the six-foot fence behind the grocery.

The dumpster helped. Ben climbed up and took the fence with a single up-and-over heave. He favored his bad knee on the landing, and wound up turning his ankle on the other leg.

Perfect. He limped into the woods. At least there were no new sirens.

No sirens doesn't mean no police. Cops are sneaky. Spot one cruiser and expect three more. Look left, kid, toward the street.

Ben caught a glimpse of white and blue through the trees. A police cruiser ghosted along the road next to the woods. Slow. Searching. Why did Hale always have to be right?

His hand grazed the injector in his pocket—Tess's kick. She'd said the burst of energy could last up to five minutes. After that, depending on the progression of his disease, he might never move again. He pulled his hand away. Not yet.

A steady slope brought him down to the creek. Ice clung to the larger rocks, but most of the drainage ran free. Ben steered clear of the water, keeping to the trees along the bank as long as possible, then splashed through a moss-covered culvert beneath a cross street. The cold sliced into his shins.

South of the culvert, the creek cut a deepening path to the Potomac. When Ben tried to climb the steep bank, he fell in the mud. A well-placed stone found his damaged knee. He slid down into the water, holding it, stifling an angry cry. "Aagh!"

Are you crying now? Go ahead. Get caught. Give up.

"No. I need to see the Director. I need to finish this."

You sure? Look up. There they are.

Ben spotted another cruiser on the road above. He retreated into the culvert and sat down in the cold wet and the muck to wait out the cops.

Hours later, he stumbled through his motel room door, kicked it closed behind him, and collapsed on the bed, grabbing a bottle of ibuprofen off the nightstand. He swallowed four pills and let the open bottle roll onto the comforter behind him. The voice in his head—Hale's voice—ordered him to peel off his soaked clothes and nurse his knee and ankle. Ben laughed at the voice and closed his eyes.

He didn't open them again until morning.

Not morning. The light slipping in through the crack in the curtain was all wrong. He'd slept until the afternoon—almost evening.

"Gotta move. Things to do." Ben had to say it out loud to convince himself.

Sitting up proved too difficult. He rolled off the edge of the bed instead, leaving a muddy depression behind. The ankle held, a little sore, but the moment he tried to put weight on his other leg, he gasped. The swelling on his knee looked like someone had stuffed a tennis ball under his jeans. A wrap might help stabilize the joint. He tossed down more ibuprofen and looked around. "Where'd I put the duct tape?"

Ben found the tape on the bathroom sink, but in the brighter light, he noticed the grime in his fingernails and the mud caked on his hoodie and jeans. Disease or not, he didn't want to see the Director that way.

"Better shower first."

Ben pulled the hoodie and T-shirt over his head in a single gingerly move, and the shriveled, spotted thing staring back at him from the mirror sucked away whatever heat remained in his blood.

313

66

Día de Muertos. The creature in the mirror reminded Ben of a Day of the Dead costume. Dark veins crept up his neck and the right side of his face to blacken the skin at the corner of his mouth and beneath his eye. The blotches on his chest and right arm had swollen into bulging knots. The oldest, on his abdomen, had broken the skin and crusted over with pus.

Ben grabbed the toilet's rim and retched.

Both mind and body wanted to expel this dark spirit. A half-digested egg white protein bar splashed down, surrounded by yellow bile and red swirls of blood.

Blood. The same decay he saw on the outside had eaten into the lining of his stomach. Had it set to work on his organs too? He needed to be careful. His blood contained deadly pathogens. Ben poured bleach into the bowl.

Stumbling into the bedroom, he ripped open his backpack and fished around inside. "Come on. Where are you?" He turned the bag upside down and shook it. Tools, first aid supplies, and homemade explosives wrapped in cellophane spilled out. With one more shake, Tess's cocktail injector dropped onto the carpet, the last one. Ben sat back on his haunches, and rammed it into his bare arm.

314

He felt the medicine go in, but nothing else—no relief. The monster inside had grown too daunting and too armored for Tess's pea-shooter weapon. He still had the kick injector in his pocket. He banished the thought of using it from of his mind. Twenty-four hours, give or take. He only had to survive one more day.

The shower helped. At the very least, the steam hid the ugly creature in the mirror. Without the dark details, Ben could see a semblance of the spy still in there—still pressing on. He dressed in a T-shirt and shorts, slammed down another four ibuprofen, and let his eyes close once more, unsure if they'd ever open again.

Hey, wake up.

Ben groaned.

Clara. Smiling. Blue hair falling to one side as she rolled onto her shoulder under the boat tarp and readied a playful finger to flick his nose. *I said wake up, silly.*

"I'm . . . I'm awake. Why did you let me sleep?"

I didn't let you do anything. You are the one in charge, remember? Now get up and get us moving.

Ben's eyes snapped open. The empty room broke his heart. Night had fallen.

Passing in and out of consciousness wouldn't do. He considered the kick.

"This will wake you up," Tess had told him when she explained how it worked. "You'll feel like a new man—aware and capable. But the crash will come soon and come hard. It's one of the drawbacks. The kick is the ultimate gateway drug. Instant addiction, and nothing will ever satisfy the need. You'll want it the rest of your life. For you, that won't be long. If you take this in the latter stage of your disease, the crash alone might kill you."

Maybe he should start with some coffee.

He made a pot, drank two cups, and poured a third before checking the clock by the bed.

Ten o'clock. Time to go.

He'd set the meeting for eleven p.m., long after closing time at Arlington National Cemetery. Ben took the Metro from Vienna/Fairfax Station, and the smattering of passengers traveling at that late hour parted wherever he walked. At the first stop, Dunn Loring, a young woman boarded with a sleeping baby. She hugged the child to her chest and hurried past Ben to the back of the car. He didn't blame her.

At West Falls Church, a small crowd of students got on, groups and pairs returning to Marymount University from Fairfax's restaurants and bars. Most had the same reaction as the woman with the baby. But one girl lingered despite the urgings of a friend. Small. Korean, if Ben could guess by the urgent whispers of the girl tugging at her elbow.

The one who'd lingered responded to her friend in an even tone and gently pulled her arm free. She carried a cane but never let it touch the car floor as she crossed the aisle and took the seat next to Ben—on his right, not his good side. No hood could hide the blotches there.

He turned his face away lest he frighten her and make her regret her choice, masking the move by pretending to sip from his paper coffee cup.

The doors closed. The car moved on in silence, and another stop went by. More students boarded, murmuring to each other and avoiding Ben to join the growing crowd at the car's rear. After a while, curiosity got the better of him. "You're not scared?" he asked his seatmate in a rasp. He hardly recognized his own voice.

"My friend says I should be. But she worries too much. Most people do." The girl didn't turn her head when she spoke. Her gaze remained level, unfixed.

Ben risked a closer look.

"Yes. It's true. You're sitting next to a blind woman. So now, are *you* scared?"

316

He laughed, descending into a coughing fit, and buried his head in his arm. "I'm sorry."

"No problem. I've already had the virus."

"Different disease."

"Drug addiction? This is what my friend Seo-yun assumed."

"No." Ben shook his head, as if she could see him in their reflections in the car window. "I didn't do this to myself."

"Thus, the opposite must be true, or so your tone implies. This was done to you. An injustice."

He faced her directly. She couldn't see his Day of the Dead mask anyway. "You sound like a philosophy major. At Rice, I used to hate talking to the philosophy majors."

"Psychology."

"Even better. Are you charging me for this talk?"

"Not tonight. The first hour is free."

Ben managed a smile. He liked this young woman. In a different time, he might have tried to recruit her for the Company.

She didn't let up. The girl planted her cane on the floor and rested her small arms on the head. "Back to you . . ."

"Ben."

"Thank you. And I'm Ha-eun. Please, Ben, tell me more about this injustice you suffered."

He opened his mouth, then shut it again. Ben's woes, substantial as they were, faded in the serene face of a blind girl. "How did you lose your sight?"

"A birth defect. I've never known a sunset except for the coolness in the air when the light is gone. I've never seen the leaves change in fall. Those things are abstract to me."

"And isn't that an . . . an injustice, as you say? Don't you deserve better?"

"What, truly, do any of us deserve?" She laid three fingers on his knee.

A simple touch, a gesture to emphasize her words, but Ben

had not imagined anyone ever touching him again. Not even Tess had been willing to touch him.

"I battled anger for many years," Ha-eun said. "I raged against the injustice of my life, until finally my mother begged me to stop. I will tell you what she told me. Stop asking what you deserve, Ben. Try asking, 'What is my purpose?'"

Ben waited, but she didn't continue. And despite the danger, death, and nation-ending threat that should have dominated his thoughts, he found himself pushing her to go on for fear they might reach her stop before she gave him the answer. "So, what is your purpose, Ha-eun?"

"I don't know yet. But I keep busy by seeking that purpose each day. For instance, tonight I think my purpose is to sit beside a wronged man on a train."

A robotic voice announced their arrival at Ballston-MU Station, and the car slowed to a stop. Ha-eun pushed herself up with the cane and felt for Ben's hood. Tentatively, he guided her hand, and she peeled the hood back to rest her delicate fingers in his hair.

"Be well, Ben," she said, then joined her friends and left.

67

No thief or spy ever broke into Arlington National Cemetery. There'd never been a need. The walls were too low. Ben tossed his paper cup at a street receptacle and stepped over an eighteen-inch stone barrier, then wandered southwest into the graves. He knew the place well. He'd buried two friends there, men whose military service was a matter of public record. Their Company service—not so much.

He passed the fourteen-foot Greek obelisk memorializing Howard Taft and passed JFK's giant circle. Neither of his friends' graves was near these monuments. The foot soldiers of America were lost in the great ordered sea of white stones farther south. Ben altered his course to join them.

The wide swath of grass and graves where Ben stopped to wait offered plenty of visibility, and the patches of dogwoods and magnolias provided enough cover to keep the Director's security detail happy. Ben didn't concern himself with the cemetery's roving guards. If one appeared from the trees to challenge him, he'd know the Director hadn't come, and there'd be little point in going on with his journey. None did. The only guard in sight marched in slow, even time before the Tomb of the Unknown Soldier a hundred fifty meters away.

The moon had reached its peak, giving the gravestones their own luminescence. Ben scanned the rows. The night, the stones, the tomb sentinel reaching the limit of his post—all stood still.

"Calix!" The voice rolled from the dogwoods like thunder. The Director followed, still shouting. "Who do you think you are?"

Men and women in dark suits and overcoats emerged from the trees to the north, south, and east—seven that Ben could see, all carrying Swiss APC9 submachine guns and not shy about letting them show. They formed a circle around him.

Ben felt the weight of the SIG in his waistband holster, but he kept his hands well clear, out in the open despite the biting cold. He'd hate to get riddled with lead before speaking his piece.

The Director turned up the collar of his gray wool coat, breath fogging as he spoke. "Son, when I ask you a question, you answer. Who do you think you are, summoning me in the middle of night?"

"Sir, there's—"

"Speak up!"

Ben coughed, fighting to recover at least a portion of his voice. "There's . . . there's been a mistake. My severance. It's . . ." He faltered again, and the Director's glare threatened to shove every rasping word back into his mouth, but he had to get it out. "It's wrong, sir."

"I see. Well, why didn't you say so before?" The Director paced the circle of his detail, matching cadence with the sentinel at the tomb. As he passed Ben's shoulder, he barked, "Stand up straight and face me like a man. Or have you forgotten all your training?"

Ben turned.

So did the Director. "You're leveling quite an accusation, son."

"No, sir. I didn't mean to—"

"Oh, yes." The Director pressed his lips together, cocking his head. "I think you did. The words you used were clear. Mistake. Wrong. You've questioned my actions, not just to my face but to several of my subordinates. So, now I'm here. Let's hash this out." He shoved his hands into his coat pockets, weighing it down about his shoulders, and thrust his chin at Ben. "Think of me as a walking suggestion box. No consequences. File your complaint."

No consequences? That didn't sound right. But what else could the Director do to him?

"I . . ." The words refused to come. All that time—begging Sensen, Hale, Tess, and Dylan to get him this meeting—and now the disease eating Ben's body and clouding his mind robbed him of his last words.

"Clock's ticking, son." The Director tapped a wrist with no watch. "Spit it out."

"Unjust."

"Couldn't hear you. Louder, please."

Ben raised his eyes to meet his boss's hard glare. "I said, it's unjust, sir. This whole thing is unjust." He gained speed and clarity as the argument he'd been preparing for days fell into place. "The severance, hounding me when all I'm trying to do is serve the Company, my country—it's wrong. Massir tricked me, and Rome went bad, I know, but not bad enough to merit a severance. I'm a good spy, sir. Why are you doing this to me? I deserve an answer."

"Mm." The Director gave him a sage nod. "Good speech. But you've got some flaws in your logic. Let me ask something. Are you on the Company's oversight committee?"

"No."

"No . . ."

"No, *sir*. I am not. The Company has no oversight."

The Director returned his hands to his pockets and started pacing again. "No oversight. Sustained for decades. An unprecedented achievement in the history of America's intelligence forces. Impressive. And is that your achievement? You aren't oversight, but you're determining this severance's justness or unjustness, so you must have founded this Company, right?"

Ben kept silent.

"I'll take that as a no."

A man in the security detail suppressed a snicker, doing a poor job of it. The Director, still pacing, smacked him in the chest with the back of his hand. "Stow it, Mardel." He came to a stop with the spotlight from the Tomb of the Unknown Soldier splitting the mist behind him. He thrust a thumb over his shoulder. "Can you hear them?"

"Sir?"

"The whines and complaints. All those warriors, dumped into holes on muddy battlefields, burned into oblivion, ashes scattered to the four winds. Anonymous. Forgotten." The Director put a hand to his ear. "Listen. Can't you hear their cries? 'Unjust! Unfair!'"

"No, sir."

"No. No you can't. They gave it all. Good soldiers, every one." The Director looked back, as if seeing them—as if he'd recognize the Unknowns by their faces and the name tags on their uniforms. He returned his attention to Ben. "And what are you, son?"

Ben knew the answer his boss wanted. Hale had asked him the same question a thousand times at the schoolhouse. "I am a soldier, sir."

"Correct. Like the Unknowns, although many of them were drafted." He raised a finger. "Here's a significant difference. You volunteered." The Director drew in the air with an imaginary pen. "You signed your life over to me, so I could create something new. And for my part, I housed you. I fed you. I trained you." He stopped face-to-face with Ben and leaned to within an inch of Ben's diseased, puss-oozing, blackened nose. "I *made* you, son. And I will unmake you at my pleasure."

Ben swallowed.

The Director huffed and walked around him, catching him hard with a shoulder and stopping a half step past his ear. "Now that we've settled the pecking order. Do you have anything else to say?"

A soldier. A cog. Just as Giselle said. That was all Ben had ever been to this man. Ben let out a quiet laugh. "Okay." He dropped the sir. "What about the *Behemoth*?"

"You mean the cargo ship resting comfortably in the shade of a Spanish dry dock?"

"She's not in dry dock. I'm telling you, the *Behemoth* is coming to Baltimore—the biggest bioweapon the world has ever seen, enough to make the last pandemic look like a mild flu season."

"Or," the Director said, keeping his voice low, "a ship called the *Clementine* is coming to Baltimore, carrying tanktainers full of ammonia, pesticides, and cheap wine. Think, Calix. You've now become the king of red herring intelligence. You fell for Massir's lie about a sale of CRTX chemicals, getting your team ambushed in Rome. And the case you sent us after that debacle ate up our HUMINT and analytical resources while we tried to determine if anything about it could lead us to Leviathan."

"I know, but—"

"And here you go again. Leviathan fed you the perfect story about a plague ship booby-trapped with a nuke's-worth of CRTX." The Director walked on toward the circle's edge. "They want us to expose our water assault tactics, then burn thousands of man-hours inspecting every tanktainer on board and tracking any cargo that slips past us. Meanwhile Jupiter detonates a dirty bomb in Miami or sets the Houston refineries ablaze." He shook his head. "I'm not going to let that happen. I'm done with you, Calix. Thanks for wasting my night."

The detail parted, allowing the Director to walk through.

Ben drew his gun. "No!"

With a rippling clatter, six APC9s came to shoulder height. The Director raised a hand. The detail held their fire.

"You can't leave," Ben said, keeping the SIG level, fighting back the blur in his eyes and mind. "I won't let you leave without giving me an answer. I signed my life away. Fine. And now it's gone. But at least tell me why. Why me? Why the severance? It can't be all about Rome. Tell me, sir. You owe me that much."

The Director kept walking. "I don't owe you a thing." He snapped his fingers, and the detail followed him toward the dogwoods.

"I deserve better! Do you hear me?" Ben held the Director in his sights until he disappeared, then fell to his knees among the graves and cried.

68

"Ben." A soft hand touched his face. "Are you still with me?"

He kept his eyes closed. No more hallucinations. He didn't want to hear Hale anymore. He didn't want to see Clara again. Why wouldn't the disease just take him and leave his body here with the other dead cogs?

But this hallucination looped an arm under his elbow and hauled him to his feet. "You're not dead, *mamour*. I can see your breath, yes? Get up."

"Giselle?" Ben's voice had grown so weak, he doubted she'd hear the question.

"Correct, *mon rêve*. My dream. I'm here. I will always be here."

Reluctant, he gave up on death and opened his eyes. She stood before him, strong, blonde once again, and Photoshop perfect, as if they had walked out of Rome together the day before.

"How did you find me?"

She showed Ben a picture of himself on her phone, resting his head back in a taxi. "Your cabdriver called the police. He gave them your picture."

"Rayan. Nice guy. Not his fault. He thought he was doing me a favor."

Giselle swiped to another image of Ben, this time from a Metro station security camera.

His illness had made him incautious. "So why haven't the cops snatched me up? You can't tell me they didn't track me to my motel after I hid out in the woods or figure out I left the Metro at the cemetery."

"Don't you see? You are under Jupiter's protection. He still has hope for you." Giselle lifted his arm over her shoulder and helped him walk between the graves. "Remember the police and SWAT teams in Paris, Rotterdam, Zürich? The Director cast you out into the cold. Now, Jupiter has wrapped you in his warm embrace."

"The Director. He met me here. You must have seen him." Ben lolled his head over to meet her eye. "You could have taken him out. Isn't that what your Jupiter wants?"

She laughed, leaning her temple against his forehead. "I am no superwoman. The Director casts a wide protective shield of operatives and surveillance wherever he walks—so inaccessible. But not Jupiter. You may come to him freely."

A coughing fit caused him to stumble, and Ben let Giselle lift him up again. They had reached the outer wall. "That's why you're here. You want me to go to him, trade my loyalty for my life."

"For your dignity, *mamour*."

"There's no dignity in being Jupiter's trophy."

"There is dignity in being valued. And if not for dignity, do it for justice, Ben. Aren't you ready for justice?"

They crested a low hill. A black sedan idled on a road at the bottom. The rear passenger door stood open. Ben stopped at the hillcrest.

Giselle didn't push him, not physically. She let her head rest against his and whispered into his ear. "You've suffered enough. It's time, Ben—time to see Jupiter. Aren't you ready to end this?"

He nodded. "Yeah. I'm ready for the end."

○ ○ ○

Consciousness darted away from him like a fox hunted in the woods, always in reach but never in hand. The hum of the tires and Giselle's familiar perfume tumbled together in a white noise of sound and scent. Blurred highway signs flew by. The sedan rolled to a stop.

"We're here, *mamour*."

"Where?"

"Wait and see."

She helped him rise from his seat into the dim echoing gray of a parking garage and once again draped his arm over her shoulder to help him walk. "Come. The elevators are over here."

The driver stayed with the car. Clearly Ben was no threat to these people.

The elevator smelled like vinegar, a sign of fresh caulk between the brushed steel panels. "New building?" he asked in a quiet rasp, wondering how much longer he'd have a voice at all.

"Yes. Brand new." Giselle passed a finger over the touchless control. "This skyscraper is not open yet. One of Jupiter's child corporations started the project three years ago, a measure of his foresight." She glanced up at the rolling floor numbers, rocketing through thirty. "He built the tallest structure in Norfolk."

Norfolk. A burst of cortisol, the body's fear hormone, heightened Ben's awareness. He stared at Giselle. "We're in Norfolk?"

"Oops. I wanted to surprise you when we reached the roof, but the cat is now out of the bag, yes?" Giselle shrugged, raising her hands palms up. "Oh well. But isn't it wonderful? We'll be able to see *Behemoth* from here."

Norfolk. Not Baltimore.

Ben had expected skepticism from the Director, but he also expected the Company to follow up on his reports as a matter of risk management—maybe even call in a team to check things out. But he'd pointed them to Baltimore. The papers in the envelope—the thumb drive—all fake, and Ben bought it, just like Massir and the case. He really had become the king of red herrings.

He'd given the Company bad intel. Again. No one was coming to stop the ship.

Ben's failure could not be more complete.

69

The elevator doors opened to a rooftop garden with topiaries and deep green grass. Curved glass pillars, glowing blue, lit the space and bounded a winding stone path. Giselle walked Ben down a set of steps to the first stone and backed away, allowing a pair of grunts packing MP7s to move in and check him out.

One patted him down. The other stood between Ben and the garden, hands clasped behind his back. "Arms out to the sides, Calix. You wearing a wire? Locator?"

"Maybe you haven't heard. I'm no longer in the Director's good graces."

The grunt snorted. "We'll check anyway, if you don't mind."

The handsy one lifted the SIG from under Ben's sweatshirt and held it up with a thumb and forefinger like a dirty sock. "Gun." He handed the weapon off to Giselle and kept working until he came to the slight bulge of the injector in Ben's right front pocket. Tess's *kick*. He dug the cylinder out and wiggled it before Ben's eyes. "What's this?"

"Antibiotics." He wished they'd get it over with. His arms burned from holding them outstretched, muscles worn to exhaustion.

"Doesn't look like any pill bottle I ever saw."

Giselle intervened. "He's telling the truth. He used the sat phone we gave him to call in a medic. That's a Company CO_2 injector."

"Whatever." The man finished his checks by running a wand over Ben's front and back. "He's clean."

The grunt blocking Ben's path nodded to his friend and stepped aside.

Ben let his arms fall, grateful for the relief. "What about my meds?"

Mr. Handsy slapped the cylinder into his chest. "Fat lot of good they'll do ya."

Ben clutched the injector in his fist and let Giselle walk him into the garden.

A man with dark hair and a Mediterranean tan rose from a patio table near the path's end. He spread his arms, and his black Mandarin-collar suit shimmered in the light from the pillars. "Ben Calix, as I live and breathe. What a joy it is to finally see your face." He tilted his head and pulled the other chair from the table, making room. "It's not as pretty a face as it might have been if you'd come to see me when Hagen so politely asked, but that can be remedied. Come. Sit."

Giselle lowered Ben into the chair and helped him lean his elbows on the tabletop's mosaic tiles. Ben recognized a fourth member of their rooftop party standing a ways off and looking out at Norfolk over the aluminum railing—the angry New Yorker who'd bawled out the dockmaster, and probably the one who'd planted the envelope and thumb drive for Ben to find. Jupiter had executed an impressive chess strategy, and seeing the young man gave Ben the feeling of looking into his playbook. "You brought a friend. May I meet him?"

"Not now. Terrance is sulking because I didn't invite him to the grown-ups' table. But the truth is, I only brought him to the garden to prove a point." Jupiter opened his palm, and

Giselle gave him Ben's stolen SIG. With barely a look to aim, he swung the weapon out and fired.

Terrance collapsed, bleeding from a hole in his temple, utter shock in his open eyes.

Jupiter waved a hand at the two grunts. "Get him off the grass."

Ben let out a deflated breath, watching the guards drag Terrance to the elevator. "Why?"

"Zoysia grass," Jupiter said. "Highly impressionable, like a memory foam mattress. We can't leave him there too long."

"I meant why did you kill him?"

Giselle giggled. "He knows what you meant, *mon rêve*."

"I killed him as a show of faith," Jupiter said, handing her the gun.

"Faith?" That word again. The young man had put his faith in his boss as Ben had put his faith in the Director. Was one side any different from the other?

Jupiter wiped his hands on a napkin and set it aside. "Terrance held a high position in my organization. With that shot, I created a vacancy. I want you to fill it."

"You're right. You're showing a lot of faith in my motivations. But what if I didn't come here for a cure and a job? What if I came to stop this attack and kill you before your disease finishes me off?"

Jupiter gasped in mock surprise. "Did you see my shocked face. Want to see it again?" He repeated the gesture, then flattened his features. "I saw the strain in your body while my men checked you for weapons. You can barely lift your arms, let alone fight." He laughed. "Kill me? For what, some kind of perimortem catharsis? I'm not the one who wronged you. Quite the opposite. I'm offering the life the Director stole from you, and so much more."

A slight nod brought Giselle over to pull Jupiter's chair out for him. He walked to the rail. "I expect the *Behemoth* at any moment—the *Clementine*, as her hull paint shows now. And yes, we booked her reservation here, not Baltimore. A digital shell game." He pointed at Norfolk's long harbor. "There. Can you see her?"

Ben squinted, trying to focus through the blur in his eyes. Lights drifted on the horizon, a city skyline on the move. "I see her. Floating death."

"Life, Ben. Not death. New life. Perfect control born of controlled chaos. Order created by a structured and well-planned apocalypse." Still gazing out at the ship, Jupiter held up a pistol grip with a trigger and toggle switch for Ben to see. He flicked the switch up, and an LED on top flashed from green to red.

Ben stiffened. That thing had only one possible purpose.

Jupiter flicked the toggle down again. The light went green. "We gave the captain a manual detonation switch on the bridge, of course, but now that the ship is in range, I have full control."

"You wouldn't." Ben put all the strength he could muster behind his voice. "If Giselle told me the truth in Spain, the volume CRTX you packed into *Behemoth* carries the explosive power of a sixty-kiloton nuke. We're in the blast radius."

"On the edge, actually. We might feel a hot wind and suffer a few broken windows on the lower floors, but nothing more. CRTX creates no ionizing radiation. The rest of downtown, however . . ." He flicked the switch up and down, over and over like a bad pen-clicking habit. Red, green. Red, green. A game. "I'm tempted, Ben. Half of Norfolk and Portsmouth will need new office space, including that hospital over there. And we're standing at the top of a brand-new building. I'd make a fortune." He stopped flicking, ending with the toggle up and the LED red—armed. His finger caressed the trigger.

"But that isn't what you want, is it?" Ben hurried the statement, causing a fit of coughs. He held out a finger to stop Jupiter from taking any action before he managed to speak again. "A bomb even as big as this one and laced with plague is no apocalypse."

"No," Jupiter said, voice thick with disappointment. "This world has become too accustomed to death. A sixty-kiloton bomb and one or two cities filled with plague are not enough to overwhelm the system. Distributing the *Behemoth*'s tanks to recycle yards and storage lots across the nation is more elegant, and will allow the disease to strike with far, far more terror. No one will know the source. Invisible. Unstoppable." He turned and gestured with the remote at Ben. "You see? We think alike, you and I. Visionary. You could go far with Leviathan."

Another nod from Jupiter brought Giselle to Ben's side. She lifted him from his chair and walked him out onto the grass.

"I appreciate that you came to me," Jupiter said, "even though you took some prodding. The gesture means a lot. But we have a long way to go in the trust department. If you deliver, you'll advance fast. If not—" He shot a glance at the bloodstain on the grass. "Show me your loyalty now and start this relationship off right." Jupiter showed Ben a second device, an injector like Tess's but with white, cloudy fluid showing through its window. "I am your cure, as I am the cure to all that ails this world. Come, Ben. Receive your first reward."

Ben felt Giselle's warm whisper on his ear. "Go. You can take these last steps on your own. Kneel like a knight of old. He likes that. Then you will be healed and we can be together." She ducked out from under his arm and eased him onward.

Ben's every wheezing breath came shallower than the last. The city lights and the harbor merged into a muddled yellow-orange haze. He took one shaking step toward Jupiter, then another. The third step cost him the last strength in his legs and dropped him to his bad knee.

"Closer. And down on both knees, if you can," Jupiter said, looking down at him. "It's an older tradition, but important to me. It is a sign both to me and to my enemy of where your allegiance lies. Trust me. This act alone will show him the folly of treating good operatives like you and me as fodder for his designs. This act will hurt him, as I know we both want to do."

"Yes. I'll do it." Ben bowed his head and shoulders, using the movement to hide the movements of his hand. He held Tess's kick tightly in his palm, where it had been since the pat-down at the elevators. A touch of a button extended a three-inch needle from the injector and primed the CO_2 charge.

The remote trigger, still armed, had become a red blur in Jupiter's right hand, and the delicate antidote injector barely a shadow in his left. A promise of death and the hope of delaying disaster in one hand. A promise of the life Ben deserved in the other.

Ben fixated on the shadow. *The life he deserved. Justice.* He'd suffered so much injustice and answered it with so much rage. His ears rang with his own rasping voice shouting at the Director hours before. *I deserve better!*

The Director hadn't answered—not then, and not now. Instead, Ben saw the Korean girl from the train. He felt her gentle fingers touching the swollen knee that now throbbed beneath him. *Stop asking what you deserve, Ben. Try asking, What is my purpose?*

What is my purpose?

Ben put his full weight on the bad knee, gutting through the pain to bring his leg into a better position beneath him, then plunged the kick's needle through his own sternum, straight into his heart.

70

For the first time in days a full breath of oxygen filled Ben's lungs, accompanied by the scorching sting of a needle stabbed into his heart. His falling blood pressure surged. Adrenaline and painkillers coursed through his system. His mind and vision cleared beyond any level he'd ever experienced. He sprang forward, going for Jupiter's detonator.

Jupiter backed into the rail. "Shoot him!" His finger clamped down on the trigger, but Ben had him by the wrist, and he had a thumb over the toggle. As the trigger closed, Ben flipped the switch and swept Jupiter's legs out from under him.

The LED went green.

Gunfire cracked.

The two fell sideways together.

Ben held his breath until their shoulders hit the grass. He felt something snap under his hip, heard the crunch of breaking glass. The antidote. So, that was that. In minutes, he'd be dead.

At least he'd been spared the sight of thousands dying in the explosion.

During the fall, he'd noted four rapid shots from Giselle and the guards. One slug fragged off the railing, slicing his cheek. But with the kick numbing the pain, he didn't care.

The shock of hitting the ground had loosened Jupiter's hold on the remote. Ben wrenched it from his hand and rolled, using his would-be boss as cover.

Jupiter writhed in his grasp. "Let . . . go."

Ben didn't bother answering. Out on the channel, the *Behemoth* continued maneuvering for its berth. He'd bought the world some time, but not much. If he could survive long enough to call in the Company—alert them to the *Behemoth*'s location—maybe they'd stop the cranes before they pulled the first tank clear and activated the aerosol release.

Unlikely.

With senses heightened by the kick, Ben became aware of men and women in black armor appearing over the garden walls. The elevator doors opened to reveal more grunts in suits. Jupiter had more guards. Of course. Men like him had whole armies at their disposal. Ben's desperate play had been hopeless from the start.

Another burst of gunfire erupted across the garden. Ben hunkered down as best he could behind Jupiter and raised the remote to smash it against the concrete base of a railing post.

"Don't!"

He froze. Ben knew that voice.

I don't owe you a thing.

Cautiously, he lifted his head. "Sir?"

The Director walked through the topiaries, ignoring the path and tromping down the Zoysia grass, with an armored escort and dead grunts in suits lying all around. An agent at his shoulder turned and fired. Another body fell.

What was happening?

The Director reached Ben and plucked the remote from his fingers. "Smashing it might trigger the bomb, son. That's remote device 101." He passed the device to a waiting agent who locked it in a padded case. "I thought Hale taught you better."

"Yes, sir . . . He did."

Was this a dream, or was Ben dead? He replayed the last burst of gunfire. A bullet must've found his head. Yes. Shot through the skull before the disease could get him. Weird.

Three agents fought to pry an angry, bellowing Jupiter from Ben's one-armed hold.

"Let him go," the Director said. "We've got him now."

Ben nodded absently and relaxed. As they stood Jupiter up, he saw blood staining the white shirt under that ridiculous Mandarin jacket—a stomach wound. Looked bad. An agent shoved an injector into Jupiter's neck and the screaming stopped. Jupiter went limp.

Ben felt limp too. His legs refused to respond to his commands until the Director bent down and helped him to his feet. His bones ached. His cheek burned. He touched it. Blood. The bullet fragment wound. Not a dream.

I'm not dead. Not yet.

Across the lawn, an agent sat at the table with the Chinese mosaic tiles. Another kneeled beside her, treating an arm wound. She smiled at Ben from under her helmet, giving him a nod.

Ice-blue eyes. So familiar. If only he could remember why.

His thoughts failed him. With the kick fading, the fog of the disease crept back in. The blue eyes drifted away from him, and Ben followed their lead until his gaze settled on a blonde woman. He knew this one, even by the back of her head. Giselle lay facedown in the grass. No one tended to her. They all seemed busy with other things.

The Director had Ben's whole weight now, holding him up. Ben's muscles had nothing left. His heartbeat slowed. The kick was gone.

Not yet. He had things to say.

"I'm sorry."

"I know, son. I know."

"The *Behemoth*. There's a manual switch for the bomb."

"Don't worry. We've been watching—listening." The Director peeled something from Ben's sleeve and held it close enough for his failing vision to bring it into focus. "Remember this? An echo, like the one you used in Rome. Passive. Undetectable. I planted it on you when I shoulder-bumped you at the cemetery." He grinned. "I like to kick it old school."

"You followed me."

"Every step of the way. By sacrificing you, we drew Jupiter into the open. We've got him, Ben. And with the intelligence we extract, we'll take down Leviathan and all the organizations tied to their operations."

A low hum sounded from above, so much stronger than Ben's fading pulse. A FLUTR medevac craft. The Company needed to get their wounded prisoner to a hospital before he died. Ben saw the dark shape against a darker sky—four ducted rotors, swiveling into position for a soft and stealthy landing. He smiled. "I've never been this close to one. For Jupiter?"

"No, son. Jupiter can take the next flight. I called this one in for you. Before you go, please understand that I'm proud of you—so very proud."

They were the last words Ben heard.

71

Ben woke to the irritating nip of a finger flicking his nose.

"Hey, wake up."

A hand lingered over his face, backlit by white fluorescents, ready to flick him again.

He made a groggy swat at the target and didn't get anywhere close. "Clara, you really have to stop that."

She'd been there like an angel at his side since he first woke on the gurney with an IV bag of cloudy white fluid pouring into his veins, rolling across the hospital roof. He'd tilted his head back to see the FLUTR craft lifting off, already banking away. A real FLUTR medevac—like the ones the Company reserved for the brass and top-tier agents.

In the hours—maybe days—since, morphine drips and doctors with ventilators had pushed Ben in and out of consciousness. Clara still hadn't explained where she'd been or why. He didn't care. Not too much, anyway. She was with him, whether he deserved her or not.

"I'm going to sit you up a bit. The doctors said it would help your breathing. Can you support your weight?"

"Some. I think." Ben pressed his hands into the mattress, surprised to feel his muscles working so well. "Yeah. I'm good. Let's do it."

With an electric whir, the bed tilted, and Ben scooted back into a comfortable position.

Clara adjusted his pillows, supporting his neck, and when she eased his head back again, he turned toward her, crinkling a fresh bandage on his cheek. "Amber."

She narrowed her eyes. "Clara."

"I mean your hair color. You didn't go back to blue."

"Blue was the Director's choice, not mine. Your psych profile suggested it would mess with your head. Something about upstaging my eyes."

Ice-blue eyes.

The morphine muddled Ben's mind, but not as much as the disease had. He remembered ice-blue eyes under blue bangs in a French stairwell. Ice-blue eyes above a dachshund, unwelcome in Sensen's kitchen. Ice-blue eyes under a black helmet on a garden rooftop.

Her arm.

Through the sheer sleeve of Clara's dress shirt, Ben saw a bandage. "You were there. You're—"

"A Company girl? Good job, Ben Calix. Took you long enough." She still had her Slovakian accent, though not quite as strong. "Yes, I was there, with you the whole time."

"But on the roof, you took a bullet for me."

"A scratch. And I put myself in the line of fire for all the agents on the rooftop, not just you. I did it for them. For the Director. I had my doubts about him for a time, but not anymore."

Ben fought to recapture images from that night, but he could still only see flashes. When he used Jupiter as a shield, Giselle had tried to flank him, not noticing the armored agents coming over the walls. She'd been seconds from putting a round in Ben's brain. "So, who shot Giselle?"

Clara poked at Ben's pillow. "Read the report if you want to know. You have the clearance now."

"What clearance? I don't understand."

"Don't try. Rest. You still have a long way to go."

He slept on and off, but every time he woke, he found her there. Was it duty or something else? Clara brought him food and explained his treatments far better than the doctors with all their medical jargon, even though English was their first language and her second. Kidan's antidote had been the key, just as Tess had predicted. And Jupiter had stocked the building in Norfolk with gallons of it, likely anticipating the need to inoculate his people after releasing the bacteria.

"What about your background," Ben asked the next day, propped up again and holding a cup of orange Jell-O. "Your dad. Your brother. Was any of it true?"

"All of it. I'm not your average recruit. I didn't go to the schoolhouse. For this operation, the Company needed someone Jupiter's spies couldn't possibly identify. Hale recruited me in Bratislava. No one else knew." Clara dipped a spoon into his cup, stealing a bite. "He trained me—the retired spy working off the books—while I continued my art studies. For a few months, I had . . ." Her gaze drifted to the window, as if searching for the right word.

"A kind father."

She sniffed and laughed. "And the world's meanest uncle all rolled into one. I'm a little mad at him. He kept me in the dark on many of the mission's details, too many if you ask me. But I suppose that's the nature of our work."

He finished the Jell-O and let her take the cup to set it aside. "And your orders?"

"To keep you safe. Get you out of Paris. Notre Dame was Hale's idea. He created the hole in the security, not the workers. I knew all that, but once we reached Meudon, I didn't know what would happen next. I'd done my job. The rest was up to you."

"What about Sensen?"

"Terrifying." She smacked Ben's chest. It hurt. "You dragged me to the home of an assassin I knew nothing about." She hit him again.

"Hey!" He shielded the spot with a jumble of arms and tubes. "Go easy."

"You never did. You left me in his graveyard, and then his home. And when he left, I thought for sure he'd gone to kill you. I felt responsible."

"So you followed. You tried to save me."

She pursed her lips. "Don't start crying or anything. I'd have done the same for anyone else. But Sensen went to Zürich to protect you, not kill you. And by following him, I crossed a line. Hale pulled me out. My part was done."

"Not entirely. You showed up at the endgame. You begged to be part of the rooftop assault, didn't you?"

She laughed. "Don't flatter yourself."

Ben saw a hint of red in her cheeks. A revelation on its own. He pressed for more. "Come on. Give me details—the play-by-play from the moment you stepped onto the roof. It's only fair, considering what I've suffered."

She bent close to his ear and lowered her voice to a whisper. "I told you. Read the report."

For someone who'd never gone through the schoolhouse and who'd worked only one field op, Clara had a knack for keeping secrets. Whenever he tried to steer her toward Jupiter and Leviathan, she deftly redirected the conversation. But he got the sense the Director had things under control, and Ben had come to realize he didn't need all the answers.

The disease had ravaged his body. Muscle damage. Nerve damage. Ulcers in his stomach and lesions on his organs. The doctors didn't clear him to leave for another two weeks, and even then, he had months of rehabilitation work ahead.

Clara came the morning of his release too. While she helped Ben pull a hospital gift shop sweatshirt over his head, an extra doctor showed up, adding to the four already there. The new-comer wore no lab coat and held a dachshund in her arms.

"Tess," Ben said.

"Otto!" Clara abandoned her patient and scooped the dog from Tess's arms. She rubbed her forehead against Otto's, earn-ing a low groan from the dog—something between satisfaction and annoyance.

Tess brushed brown hairs off the front of her dress with perfectly manicured fingers. "Sorry it took so long. The Swiss claimed they still needed him for evidence. When I pulled him from the cargo kennel, I found a Ziploc taped to the back filled with unit patches, photos, and one Swiss National Police Service Medal."

Clara didn't seem to hear her, speaking a kind of baby Slo-vakian to the dog. Ben watched her, mulling over the reaction. "So, I guess Otto was yours before Hale recruited you."

She shook her head and set him on the floor. "Not at all. Otto arrived on my doorstep the day after I moved into your building—with a big red bow on his back and a state-of-the-art GPS tracker in his collar."

"The collar." Ben slapped his forehead. "That's how the French police found us in the park. The Company pulled the GPS track from Otto's collar and made an anonymous call to the cops."

Clara made kissy faces at the dachshund. "Yes they did. Didn't they, Otto?"

The head Company doctor watched all of this with no amuse-ment on his features. He removed his glasses and walked out. "I think we're done here."

A car waited in the parking lot to take Ben to his new DC apartment. Clara said her goodbyes next to the sedan's open door, including a surprise kiss on the cheek, but left without giving him her number.

Tess lingered, waiting for her to go.

"You have something you need to say?" he asked.

"I have something you need to hear." She pressed a paper sack of pill bottles into his hands. "You'll be taking these for months. But when they're gone . . ."

"I know. The kick. If what you said is true, I'm an addict now." He shrugged one shoulder. "I don't feel like an addict."

"Some wounds you picked up out there won't ever leave you." She swallowed hard, twisting her features and fighting to smooth them out again. Tess had never been one to show emotion. "The kick was one of those wounds, Ben—maybe the worst of them. And I'm the one who gave it to you. I'm sorry."

"Did you know? About the reason for the severance, I mean."

"At our meeting in Brussels? No. But Hale briefed me before I came to you in Mount Vernon."

"So the kick was the Director's choice, not yours."

She shrugged one shoulder, as if that was poor consolation. The kick had saved Ben's life, enabled him to complete the mission he hadn't known he'd been assigned. He should be thanking her, not accepting an apology. "Tess, I think you're—"

"Listen." She wrapped her hands around his, holding the bag of meds together. "You use these exactly as prescribed. And when they're gone, you take things day by day. When you feel the withdrawal coming—and you will—you call me. Wherever I am. Whatever I'm doing. I'll be at your doorstep in hours."

"To bring more drugs?"

She let out a short, sad laugh and released him, turning to go. "No, you idiot. To keep you alive."

He watched her go, smile fading. How bad could it be?

Once she'd disappeared into the hospital garage, Ben lowered himself onto the sedan's pleather seat and shut the door. "Where to?" he said with a laugh. He motioned between the driver and himself with both hands. "You see what I did there? Swapped . . . roles . . ."

344

The driver rolled up the tinted barrier and cranked the engine.

Out on the highway, Ben noticed they were headed west, deeper into the DC metroplex. The apartment Clara had told him about was supposed to be east, across Chesapeake Bay. He tapped on the glass. "Hey, driver. Where are you taking me?"

The barrier rolled down. The Director glanced in the rearview mirror to meet Ben's gaze. "Haven't you learned anything?"

"Boss?"

"Let's stop by the office. I've got things to show you. Do you mind?"

Ben shook his head.

"Good answer."

He made Ben wait ten minutes or more before he spoke again. "I'm moving you up, Ben. We just had to get through that little hiccup."

"So you could catch Jupiter?"

The Director raised an eyebrow.

Ben shrank into his seat. "I mean, if you want to tell me. If not, that's good too."

"Yes. To catch Jupiter. And I'm glad I can finally tell you. All this started after the attack in Tokyo. We needed a fall guy, one we thought could endure the worst. Hale put your name up for the job. After that, we put out the whispers that we had big plans for Ben Calix—that *I* had big plans for you. In doing so, we made you a prize Jupiter couldn't resist—not with our history together."

"He was a Company man."

"Once. A long time ago. One of my best. But arrogant." The Director shifted his eyes to the road, signaling for a lane change. "It's almost painful for me to say, but I know him better than he knows himself. I hung you out like bait on a hook. He gulped you down, thinking he'd arranged the whole meal, and we reeled him in. It's that simple."

Bait on a hook. Ben noticed the Director never apologized. At least he'd told Ben his purpose. This time.

"So now what?"

"We check out your new corner office. As it turns out, I really do have big plans for you. A supervisory role. More responsibility. Bigger picture. Start thinking about who you want on your new team. Any names come to mind?"

Ben had a few—one in particular.

"If you say Clara, I'll reach back there and smack you. You know what happened last time you started a relationship with a teammate."

Ben nodded, bouncing his head for emphasis. "Right. But what *about* Clara. She's—"

"Special?"

"You could say that. If she can't be part of my new team, what will she do? Will we work together at all?"

The Director turned down a ramp toward an underground parking garage, and the tinted barrier started rolling up again. "I guess we'll have to wait and see."

Author Note

I am not a spy.

Early in my Air Force student pilot days, an intelligence officer sat us down in a secure room and told us we were all spies because combat pilots fill out intelligence reports after every mission, reporting anything observed during flights over enemy territory. At the time, I considered the term *spy* in that context a stretch, and I still do. But little did I know in that moment how far beyond the flight deck my career and God would take me. I'm not a spy, but I've worked with a few and learned a lot.

In this story, for some fun, I wanted to give you a look behind the curtain at the reasons Ben does what he does or knows what he knows. Some of what I wrote is pure fiction fun, like Ben's cleaning system. Some is extrapolation through research and old friends. And some is founded upon experiences, training, and conversations in a long career. "Pick up the trash" is my favorite among the latter, based on hockey, just as I said, offered by a man very much like Hale.

My other favorite is the frozen lake scene. As a former combat survival instructor, I feel this one is something more people should know. Yes, most lakes have a temperature inversion that can make a difference. More importantly, having the presence of mind to pause and find your escape route will likely mean the difference between life and death. Once you're out, get a fire going, because hypothermia is sure to follow—although, to critique Ben, lighting a fire in a shed full of fertilizer was a less than optimum solution.

A COVID-19 disclaimer: The traditional publishing timeline from manuscript to bookshelf is a long one. *The Paris Betrayal* was 85 percent complete before COVID-19 struck. Imagine having an almost-completed manuscript about the threat of a global pandemic when you're suddenly struck with an actual global pandemic.

Ben Calix is based upon the biblical Job, who experienced great physical suffering through a disease covering his whole body, so I didn't feel I could drop the bioweapon portion of the megabomb/bioweapon combo I had developed. But I did my utmost to make changes that would prevent the story from hitting anyone too close to home. In this process, DiAnn Mills, Lynette Eason, and Edie Melson all offered excellent advice, and I am grateful. DiAnn Mills, as a mentor and teacher, also deserves a great deal of thanks as an ear and voice during the project as a whole.

Finally, a word about Job.

In preparation for the writing of this story, Dr. Gary Huckabay created a detailed analysis of the book of Job and all its characters—no easy task. Then he advised me throughout the writing process. Upon the foundation of his analysis, I built the characters of the Director, Ben, Giselle, Tess, Sensen, Hale, Dylan, and Jupiter. On this, I also built the story's implied theological conclusions regarding God's sovereignty. I cannot adequately express my gratitude to Dr. Huckabay for his hard work and insight.

For more on Ben and Job, including a comparative Bible study and book club resource, visit my website at www.jamesr hannibal.com.

James R. Hannibal is no stranger to secrets and adventure. A former stealth pilot from Houston, Texas, he has been shot at, locked up with surface-to-air missiles, and chased down a winding German road by an armed terrorist. He is a two-time Silver Falchion Award winner for his Section 13 mysteries for kids and a Thriller Award nominee for his Nick Baron covert ops series for adults. James is a rare multisense synesthete, meaning all of his senses intersect. He sees and feels sounds, and smells and hears flashes of light. If he tells you the chocolate cake you offered smells blue and sticky, take it as a compliment.

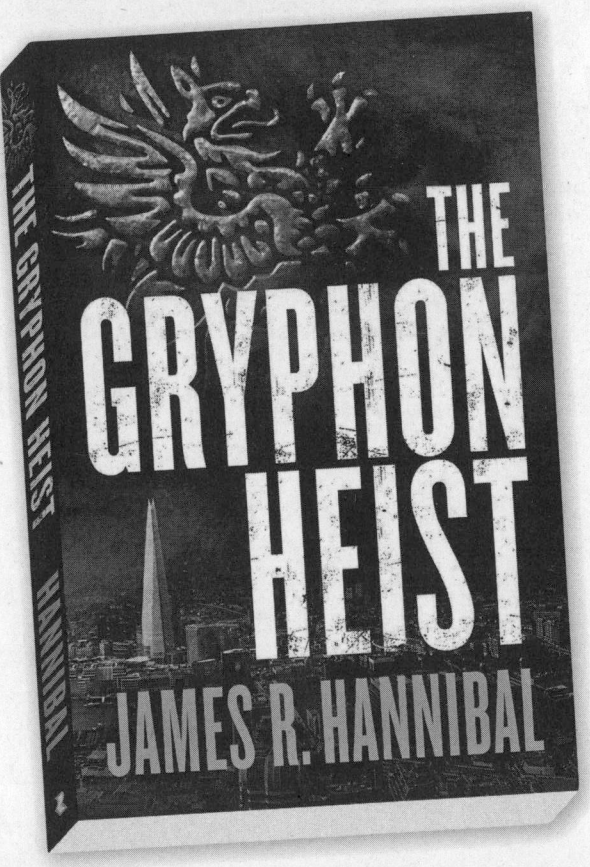